Also b

A
GOOD
Wolf
IS HARD TO
FIND

TERRY
SPEAR

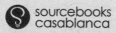
sourcebooks
casablanca

Published by Sourcebooks Casablanca, an imprint of Sourcebooks
P.O. Box 4410, Naperville, Illinois 60567-4410
(630) 961-3900
sourcebooks.com

Cataloging-in-Publication data is on file with the Library of Congress.

Printed and bound in the United States of America.
OPM 10 9 8 7 6 5 4 3 2 1

To Cathy Porter who says my books are her "happy place," which makes me so happy! And to your beloved brother, Michael R. Donnan, who will always be loved and remembered for taking care of baby sister after their mom had passed when they were young. Making memories with family is so important. Thank you for sharing your story of your loving brother with me.

Chapter 1

IT WAS STILL LIGHT OUT WHEN ROXIE WOLFF slipped booties on her Saint Bernard, Rosco, to protect his feet from the cold on an early evening walk in the deep snow. It was starting to snow lightly, though it was supposed to come down heavily tonight, which was great for the Silver Town Ski Resort. With her quadruplet siblings—sister, Kayla, and brothers, Landon and Blake—Roxie was co-owner of the Wolff Timberline Ski Lodge at the resort.

Rosco was much better at *not* running off to chase after squirrels and bunnies than when he was a pup, but they still often walked the avalanche rescue dog on a leash. Then she heard something running nearby in the woods. She glanced in that direction. Her gray-wolf hearing was much more enhanced than a human's as she tried to discern what she'd heard. Rosco was also listening, his ears perked, his nose tilted up, sniffing the air. She glanced at the bare oak branches covered in a fresh coating of white snow. The Douglas firs also wore blankets of white. All the fresh powder had been perfect for the ski season this year.

"What did you hear?" she whispered to Rosco.

He looked up at her and wagged his tail. She smiled. She knew he'd heard what she'd heard, whatever it had been. She was frozen with indecision. Her curiosity as a wolf shifter made her want to check it out. Black bears should be hibernating, unless something woke one up by disturbing its den, and then it was better to avoid the bear. Wolves other than the shifter kind lived out here too, and she didn't want to run into a wild wolf pack. They could attack a dog. Maybe even her. They were territorial, though this was the Silver wolf pack's territory, and pack members let other wolves know it was theirs all the time. Cougars also ran out here, so she wasn't sure just what the animal had been. Maybe deer. Elk even.

Whatever it had been, she didn't see a whisper of movement of any kind of critter and didn't hear anything but the wind blowing through the trees, knocking clumps of snow off that promptly fell to the piled-up snow around the trees.

"It was probably nothing," Roxie said, trying to reassure herself as much as she was trying to do the same for Rosco. "Go do your thing."

Then she saw what she thought was a ghost in the screen of snow. A red-bearded ghost. A man dressed all in white.

Rosco pulled at her to go in a different direction, stealing her attention. He'd finally found a place to relieve himself, thankfully, and she looked back to observe the man in white further, but he was gone. She glanced around, trying to see anyone, but whoever it had been had left.

"Come on, Rosco. Let's go home." She and Rosco headed back to her house. She was still looking over her shoulder, watching for any sign of movement, looking for the man in white, but she didn't see him. The night was getting darker, but with her wolf vision, she could still see as well as if it were daytime. Snowflakes landed on her hat, her coat, her eyelashes, and Rosco's fur.

Rosco kept looking over his shoulder too, as concerned as Roxie that something was out there that they should check into or watch to protect their backs. Though he hadn't pulled at his leash to go check it out. Why hadn't he seen the red-bearded guy? He would have woofed, at least, to tell her a stranger was there.

If someone, a hiker, had been in trouble, Rosco would have picked up on that and immediately alerted her. Maybe he had sensed the man, even if he hadn't seen him. There might have been a wild animal of some sort out there too. It wouldn't have been one of Silver Town's wolf shifters, or he or she would have greeted them. Of course, visitors to the resort who wanted to shift and run might not know she was a wolf shifter and would keep quiet.

As soon as she arrived at her home, Roxie

stomped the snow from her boots and pulled Rosco's booties off before they entered the house. Princess Buttercup, their golden tabby rescue cat, came to greet them, winding around Roxie's legs first and then Rosco's. Sometimes Roxie put Buttercup in a pet carrier and took her with them on walks, but the cat had seemed happy at home, and Roxie had wanted to go and come back quickly because of the impending snowstorm.

She got a call on her phone while she locked the door and Rosco nosed Buttercup back. It was her brother Blake who lived in the home next door. She knew just what he was calling about. "Already done."

"I thought I was supposed to walk Rosco tonight."

"You have enough on your plate with taking care of three-month-old twins and trying to get them down for the night. Unless"—she smiled and pulled off her gloves—"you wanted a break and planned to leave the babies with Nicole to handle on her own."

He laughed. "Nah. I just didn't want you to think you had to do all the dog walking now that we're taking care of the twins."

"I know the two of you aren't getting enough sleep. So it's fine with me. Besides, Kayla and Nate are taking Rosco for more walks now too." She thought of mentioning what she'd believed she'd heard in the woods, but there wasn't any sense in alarming anybody about anything. Particularly since she didn't know what had been out there and she didn't want her brother worried. "I'll talk to you later. Have a good night's sleep if you can get it."

"Night, Roxie. See you at the lodge in the morning."

"Yeah, see you. Oh, and give the babies a good-night kiss from me."

"Will do."

She sighed, missing the way things had been, living with all her siblings. She reconsidered whether she should tell Blake about the mystery man, but she didn't want him trying to track the man down in the snow when the guy hadn't acted dangerous or anything.

She thought she'd be fine having the whole house to herself—until Kayla moved out to be with Nate in their new home on the property on the other side of Blake and Nicole's home. She really missed their time together.

Special Agent Dylan Powers with the U.S. Fish & Wildlife Service was searching the woods near Silver Town, Colorado, for four men he'd been tracking through the week for illegal hunting. Like him, the thirty-year-old men—Jim Johnson, a criminal attorney, Xander Stone, an orthodontist, Eddie Jones, a western-clothes chain store owner, and Fennel Keaton, a professor of English at a community college—were from Denver, and none had wives or kids. As a gray wolf having an enhanced sense of smell, hearing, and night vision, Dylan felt he was endowed with superpowers that made this job just the right one for him.

Dylan had been trying to catch the four men ever since the season for hunting with rifles had ended. They were well known to him. All of them came from wealthy families in Denver, and they all felt they were above the law, able to buy their way out of practically any misconduct, which they'd proven any number of times on illegal hunting trips.

Snow was falling steadily in the mountainous, wooded region, and Dylan knew no matter how long he wanted to keep this up, if the visibility dropped to zero, he would have to hunker down in his tent until it let up. If he got too cold, he would just strip off his clothes and turn into his wolf. His fur coat would keep him warm, and if he remained in his tent, snuggled in his sleeping bag, that would keep the wind off him. But he wanted to catch these men before the snow got too bad.

Dylan wasn't stalking the men and waiting for them to hunt, even though he knew their hunting licenses had been suspended for two years. But they'd made this easy for him. They always went on their hunting trips this time of year. They loved to kill wolves, and Dylan had already turned them in for injuring a wolf he had managed to save. A real wolf wearing a tracking collar, not a gray wolf shifter like him. Dylan had arrested them, and then what had happened? They had been released on a $5,000 bond for each of them. They could have each gotten a $100,000 fine, loss of their hunting licenses for a lifetime, and a year in jail for the wolves they had killed earlier, but they were found innocent of the charges, even though Dylan had caught them in the act. Then a judge caught them hunting on his own property, made a citizen's arrest, and turned them over to the authorities, and they were charged with killing an elk. That time, the charges stuck, and they lost their licenses for two years.

So now what were they doing? Hunting on property near Silver Town.

He saw snowshoe tracks leading off in another direction and quickly turned to observe a red-headed, bearded man in the mist of snow, dressed in mostly white—a snowsuit, white snow boots, a white knit hat, and his backpack a white-gray-beige blend of camouflage for winter so that he blended in with the snow—except for his red beard and long, curly red hair covered in snowflakes and icicles. He was standing among the trees, peering at Dylan for a moment. He wasn't carrying a rifle, or Dylan would have stopped him and questioned him. He wasn't carrying a bow or quiver of arrows, like he could have been if he was bowhunting.

He looked like a mountain man—like Dylan had been forced to be when he was a teen—except that this guy's clothes were new, not worn out and dirty like someone who lived in the woods for months or years on end. Dylan suspected the man was sizing him up, trying to determine why he was out here alone, just like Dylan was trying to figure out the redheaded guy. The man was downwind of him, so Dylan couldn't determine if he was anxious to be seen or not.

Then the redheaded man took off at a medium pace away from Dylan, as if he had places to go, things to do, and Dylan wasn't a worry to him. Dylan watched him, feeling uneasy about the man. He wasn't sure what was bothering him about the man, but his wolf senses made the hair on the back of his neck stand up.

Dylan heard a shot fired from a rifle—maybe ten miles away—and headed in that direction, certain that the men he was after were hunting illegally once again. Why else would someone be out here shooting with a rifle? Unless it was another hunter shooting out of season. About fifteen minutes later, another shot was fired some distance from the first. It was unlikely they would wound their prey and race after it to shoot it again. They were all great shots. Had they found something else to kill?

Soon Dylan reached an area where they had killed an elk and left it behind in the snow. What the hell? It was bad enough that they were killing animals illegally, but to not even pack it out?

He smelled the scents they'd left behind— Jim's, Xander's, Eddie's, and Fennel's. He saw their deep footprints in the snow, though the snow was coming down in blankets of white now. The snowfall would soon fill up the tracks.

He glimpsed the sight of a wolf running into the woods off in the distance. A young wolf. A shifter? If the wolf was a shifter, he would be the age of a teen. Dylan just hoped the men he was hunting didn't try to kill the wolf.

Dylan was continuing to search for the men when he realized from the scents and footprints he followed that there were only three hunters now. Had they split up? Eddie was no longer with them.

The wind was blowing so hard, he was afraid that everyone would be lost. Maybe that was why Eddie was no longer with the other three. Maybe they'd lost him. Maybe this time, the men would find themselves in a worse situation than just illegally hunting. Dylan could only hope they'd learn from their mistakes and change their ways.

He finally found tracks going in different directions and frowned. What the hell? The men had split up again, two of them going one way and the third traveling in the opposite direction. They had to be crazy to do so in this weather. All four men should have stuck together.

He started to follow one of them: Jim, the lawyer, because he was always the one in charge of the others, and he was alone and could get himself into real trouble, Dylan was thinking. After about a half hour, Dylan realized Jim was heading to the ski lodge where Dylan had parked his pickup truck. Wouldn't someone notice that Jim was carrying a hunting rifle? If anyone saw him, they could have him detained for questioning, figuring that he would have been out in the woods shooting wildlife out of season. Dylan just hoped he could prove that these four men had killed the elk, or at least one of them had.

He saw the lights of the ski lodge ahead, no tracks, but he kept getting whiffs of Jim's scent. Dylan swore Jim figured he could get away with anything because he knew the law and could manipulate it. Having friends in influential positions—judges, lawyers, the police chief—helped. His scent led Dylan to the ski lodge's outdoor swimming pool, which surprised Dylan. Sure, to get out of this weather, Dylan could understand that. But why hadn't the other men stayed with him?

The patio must have been heated. The snow was melting and there were no discernable footprints. Just as Dylan glanced at the swimming pool, he saw the reflection of a man wearing a gray parka with the hood up to help hide his face, a gray knit cap, and ski goggles coming up behind him, rifle butt raised, ready to strike him. As Dylan turned to fend off his attacker, Jim hit him hard in the side of the head with a resounding thud. White lights flashed before Dylan's eyes as he found himself falling, warm water enveloping him, and then...only blackness.

———

Roxie was feeling a little down about being on her own now. Most nights, she kept the family's Saint Bernard and their cat to keep her company because she wasn't used to being alone.

But Valentine's Day was coming, and she wasn't seriously dating anyone. She felt like a lost cause when it came to finding a mate. Sure, there were a lot of bachelor males in Silver Town, Colorado, a wolf-run town, and she liked them, but settling down with one of them forever and ever? Nah.

She glanced out the window and saw the snow still steadily falling. She sighed. She could mope about being by herself at home, or she could take a swim at the lodge and at least get some laps in. She always felt better when she did. She went upstairs to her bedroom and changed into her swimsuit, then pulled her sweats on over them. She slipped on socks, boots, gloves, a parka, and a knit hat.

Then she grabbed a pool bag and added a bottle of water, a beach towel, a plastic bag for her wet bathing suit, and a pair of panties to it. She left her home to walk to the lodge close by. They had an indoor-outdoor pool that was great to swim in no matter the time of year.

The pool was closed at ten in the evening, but because she was one of the lodge's owners, she could swim in it anytime she wanted when she wasn't working. She reached the lodge's doors and went inside, waved at the new night manager, Eliza Fraser, and then headed inside the pool area to swim.

After setting her bag on a chaise lounge, Roxie began removing her gloves, parka, boots, socks, and sweats. She stretched and went down the stairs into the pool. Then she began to swim her first lap. She considered just swimming to the divider to the outside part of the pool but decided to dive under and swim the whole distance to get a little more exercise. She dove under and surfaced, but before she started swimming again, she saw a male body, fully clothed and wearing a backpack, sinking to the bottom of the pool facedown. She gasped.

Chapter 2

HER HEART RACING, ROXIE SWAM TO THE MAN sinking to the bottom of the swimming pool as if her life depended on it, when it was *his* that truly did. When she finally reached him, she struggled to lift him to the surface of the water. Thank God for the buoyancy in water so that he and all his gear felt lighter than they would out of water. She reached the surface and rolled him over so his face was out of the water.

As soon as she flipped him over, she saw he wasn't breathing. Her heart nearly stopped with concern. His eyes were closed, his lips blue, surrounded by a dark-brown beard. He was fully dressed in a blue parka, pants, hiking boots, and a black knit hat, making him seem even heavier as she swam him toward the outdoor pool stairs as fast as she could. But she also saw a trail of blood he was leaving in the water. Her thoughts were flying as she considered her next moves. Why was he bleeding? She was afraid now that he was dead from a gunshot wound and hadn't just fallen in the pool and drowned. Yet with her sensitive hearing and that of any other wolves at the lodge, wouldn't someone have heard a gun-shot fired?

She finally reached the stairs but couldn't move him up them until she removed his backpack. Every second ticking by felt like hours as she struggled to unfasten the pack. The clasps finally released, and she frantically pulled at the straps.

She yanked off the backpack and climbed out, slipping on the wet pavement. A heater warmed the patio so that ice and snow wouldn't accumulate, but the pavement was still slick. She reached down and tried to pull the man out of the pool. He was deadweight.

"Help! Call 911! Help!" With everyone's enhanced wolf hearing, someone should be able to hear her, she hoped.

Having heard her panicked cries, Rosco escaped through the wolf door at the house and ran straight for her, sure-footed on the patio, his large feet spreading, enabling him to grip the pavement better. As a mountain rescue dog, he had saved several people buried during avalanches and was trained to go to someone in distress. He immediately grabbed the man's hood and began pulling him too. Rosco was a godsend.

They finally tugged the man up the stairs the rest of the way. With the injured man lying flat on his back on the patio, Roxie cleared his air passageway and began to give him mouth-to-mouth resuscitation. She did chest compressions in between ventilating him and shouted for anyone to hear her.

Then he coughed up some water and she prayed he would be okay, but she worried about where the blood in the water had come from. At least he was breathing, his heart pumping well.

Now Rosco would provide a living blanket for the man until she could get help, though she didn't want to leave the man alone for anything. Her adrenaline was rushing through her veins, but the longer she was out of the warm water, soaking wet in the freezing weather in her bathing suit, the more she was going to be susceptible to hypothermia, the same as the man.

"Rosco, come here. Lie down with him. Warm him." Once the dog had settled next to the man to help warm him, she raced to the door that led into the lobby and shouted at the manager, "Call 911! A man was drowning in the pool. I revived him. He needs urgent medical attention."

Eliza immediately grabbed the phone. "You need your clothes. Why don't you stay on the line with the dispatcher, and I'll go out to him."

"I've got this." Roxie felt the man was her responsibility since he'd nearly died on her and her family's property. She raced into the pool room and grabbed her sweats and pulled them on. She slipped on her socks and boots and yanked on her knit hat. She grabbed her parka and beach towel and then dashed back out of the swimming-pool room, through the lobby, and outside to where the man was lying on his back, shivering. Once she reached him, she placed her parka on top of him, while Rosco's head and front legs rested on his chest. She pulled off the man's knit hat and wrapped his head in the towel like a turban to keep him warmer and saw blood on his hat. She would have used her knit hat on him, but her hair had gotten it wet. She hadn't thought of that when she'd put it on her own head. But the towel might stop the bleeding better anyway.

She didn't recognize the man, though he smelled like a gray-wolf shifter. She was glad for that. Wolf shifters overcame injuries twice as fast as humans did. She just hoped his injuries weren't too grave. At least he was breathing, and the color was return-ing to his lips. She got down and pressed her body against his, trying to warm him and herself too. He was about six one, too big for her to move him into the lodge.

Then it seemed like everyone was coming to the man's aid at once. The ambulance arrived, EMTs, Sheriff Peter Jorgenson, Deputy Sheriff CJ Silver, her brother Blake, and brother-in-law Nate Grayson, who both lived in homes next to hers. Her other brother, Landon, lived farther away at the home next to his wife Gabrielle's Silver Town

Animal Clinic so he wouldn't know that all this was going on tonight—yet.

"Hell, Roxie," Blake said. "You'll catch your death. Go inside." He gave her his own parka to wear since hers was still warming the man.

Nate retrieved the man's camping pack from the swimming pool stairs.

"I'm not budging from here until I know he's going to make it, Blake." She knew her brother would feel the same way about the guy if he had been swimming and had saved his life.

Nate shook his head at her.

"Hey, Nate, tell me you wouldn't do the same if our roles were reversed," she said, annoyed.

Nate gave her a cocky little smile. She loved her brother-in-law who was just as protective of her as if he had been her brother from birth.

The injured man's eyes fluttered open, blue eyes, the color of the aquamarine sea, and for a moment, he caught her gaze and held on.

The EMTs made sure his vital signs were stable; then they carried him to the ambulance on a stretcher and drove him to the clinic where Dr. Kurt Summerfield was already waiting for him.

Her rescue mission done, Roxie hurried inside the lodge to get warmed up. Peter, CJ, and her family joined her inside to speak with her. Rosco trotted along behind them. Eliza had already made a cup of hot cocoa for Roxie to drink to warm her up, which she appreciated. She thanked Eliza for it and took a sip.

"So what happened?" Peter asked Roxie, readying his pen and notepad. The sheriff would be questioning the victim at the clinic once he had recovered enough and was able to speak.

"I was just swimming my first lap in the pool when I dove under the divider to the outside pool and saw the man sinking in the water."

"Facedown," Peter said.

"Yes. I took him to the stairs, dragged him out, and saw he was unconscious. He had no vital signs. I was able to revive him, and you know the rest."

"So you didn't see what had happened?" CJ asked.

"No. He was already in the pool when I found him."

"You didn't catch a glimpse of anyone leaving the scene?" Peter took more notes.

"No. I mean, someone could have been nearby, hurrying away, but I was too busy trying to turn the man over and get him to the stairs to save his life. I just didn't think of anything else."

"Okay, thanks, Roxie." Peter turned to CJ. "I want you to check the security videos."

"I'm right on it," CJ said.

"I'll get them for you," Eliza said.

"If you don't need to question Roxie any longer, she has to get warmed up," Blake said, rubbing her arm, ever protective of her.

Roxie was wearing Blake's coat, but she was still chilled, her hair wet, her clothes damp from pulling them over her wet bathing suit.

"Yeah, that was a great rescue, by the way," Peter told her.

"Thanks. My army training helped." She'd had basic first aid training, though everyone in the pack who was old enough regularly took lifesaving classes in case any of their people or visitors to the area were injured. She was just glad she'd managed to get the man out of the pool on her own and get help for him. She hoped he'd be all right.

"Let's get you home," Blake said.

She quickly finished her cocoa and handed the empty mug to Eliza. "Thanks again."

"Sure thing."

"I believe I've had enough of a swim for the night." Even though it was just half a lap.

Blake and Nate escorted Roxie and Rosco home. They were glad Rosco wouldn't leave the house through the wolf door now unless he realized it was an emergency—like if he heard someone yelling for help or in distress. He had even saved an avalanche victim once when they had forgotten to lock the wolf door and he'd heard the man crying out. Since then, they always left it unlocked when he was home.

"What do you think happened?" Nate asked.

"Maybe he was drunk, disoriented, and fell in?" Blake said.

"I didn't smell any liquor on his breath," Roxie said.

"Uh, right. Neither did I," Blake said.

She definitely would have smelled alcohol on the victim if he'd been drinking since she had resuscitated him.

"Are you going to be okay?" Nate asked her as they stopped inside her house.

"Yeah. Sure. I need to get out of this wet bathing suit." She pulled off Blake's jacket and gave it to her brother. "Thanks. Sorry it's a little bit damp."

"Hey, you needed to get warm. Your hair's still wet. You need to drink something hot again," Blake said.

"Oh, shoot. I forgot my pool bag on one of the chaise lounges," she said.

"I'll secure it," Nate said. "Let us know if you need anything else."

"Nicole wanted to see to you," Blake said.

"But she's home with the twins and doesn't need the stress." Roxie appreciated that her sister-in-law had been anxious about her.

"And Kayla wanted to come right away too, but we didn't know what the danger was," Nate said.

"She doesn't need to come. I'll be fine. I'm off to take a hot shower. Thanks, Blake and Nate. I'll talk to you tomorrow."

"Night," they both said to her.

Roxie locked the door after they both left. She

was glad at least her sister and one brother lived in the two houses next door, along with their mates, whom she also adored, so that they could help each other out whenever they needed it.

She headed up to her bedroom, Rosco settling down with Buttercup in his bed. Roxie stripped out of her boots, damp socks, sweatpants, and wet bathing suit. Then she slipped into the hot shower to take the chill off. While she was washing up, she kept thinking about the man with the beautiful blue eyes and wondering where he had been wounded, how he had fallen into the pool, and who he was.

Until she knew the answers to her questions, she wouldn't be able to sleep. She left the shower and dried off, ran a hair dryer over her hair, then dressed and drove into town to the clinic. Since everything in Silver Town was wolf-run, they didn't have the same rules about only family visiting patients who were staying at the clinic. She was desperate to see the injured man, to learn what she could about him, to see if he was going to make it.

When she arrived at the Silver Town Medical Clinic, the office manager, Carmela Hoffman, was on duty. "Hey, Roxie. Thank you for saving that man," she said. News traveled fast around there.

"He was bleeding. How was he hurt?"

"He was hit on the side of the head."

"Next to the swimming pool?" Roxie thought he might have hit his head when he fell into the pool.

"CJ is getting the security tapes from Eliza to see if it happened at the lodge or if he was dragged from somewhere else. But the injured man is a tall guy, so I can't imagine he would have been carried from somewhere else and then dumped there. Peter said it was more likely that he was attacked at the pool and then left to drown, if the blow to his head hadn't been enough."

"Oh God, that's awful. He didn't tell Peter anything yet?"

"The victim has a mild concussion. He can't remember what happened to him. Tom is pulling guard duty to make sure he's protected in the event this was a case of attempted murder."

"Oh, sure. Good idea. The man's name?"

"Dylan Powers. He's a special agent with the U.S. Fish & Wildlife Service. His driver's license and badge were on him."

"Oh, a special agent." That made Roxie think he was on a job and someone he was after had done this to him. "Can I see him?"

"He's asleep. If you'd like, you can sit with him. He's in Room 3."

"All right. Thanks." Roxie really wanted to ask him what had happened. But she also wanted to let him know who she was and that she was there for him since he didn't have any family or friends here that she knew of.

She walked down the hall to where Tom Silver

was sitting at the door on guard duty. He was Darien Silver's triplet brother and third in command of the pack. Darien and his mate, Lelandi, were their pack leaders. "He's asleep."

"That's what Carmela said. I still would like to sit with him for a while."

"You're welcome to."

"Thanks." She knocked on the door to the room where Dylan was staying. She hoped he wouldn't mind that she had come to sit with him. He didn't respond, so she opened the door and peered in. He was sound asleep. At least his cheeks and lips were a normal color—no longer gray skin and blue lips. She was glad for that.

She went inside, closed the door, and sat down on one of the comfortable blue visitors' chairs, ready to get some answers from him once he woke.

———

Dylan's head felt like it was splitting in two. He reached up to touch it and found it was wrapped in a bandage. How did he get here? What had happened? He could smell the antiseptics and something else. A female wolf and he recognized her scent. He realized he smelled of chlorine and... dog? He turned to look in the direction of the window, and there she was—a pretty woman with shoulder-length silky dark hair, sound asleep in the chair near the bed. He raised his brow. He vaguely remembered seeing her worried brown eyes when she was standing over him and while others came to help him. He was in a hospital room.

Then it all came flooding back to him. Tracking Jim Johnson, losing his tracks, seeing Jim's reflection and his own in the pool before Jim struck him on the side of the head with the butt of his rifle. Dylan didn't remember anything after that, except when he had looked into the woman's beautiful, caring eyes.

Had she been part of a security detail at the ski lodge? Hopefully, they had caught the bastard striking him on video. Maybe Dylan could get him on more than just killing an elk this time. Jim wouldn't get away with it. Attempted murder? Dylan didn't think Jim could explain that away easily this time. Dylan sure hoped he could nail him. With any luck, he hoped the law enforcement personnel here had caught the bastard already.

Chapter 3

DYLAN NEEDED SOMETHING FOR THE AWFUL headache he was experiencing and thought about pushing the nurse's call button, but he looked at the woman sleeping in the chair and sighed. He didn't want to wake her. He rubbed his head, surprised Jim would go to such extremes to prevent him from charging him with the illegal killing of an elk. As a *lupus garou*, Dylan knew his injury would heal in half the time that it would take humans to heal. But that didn't lessen the pain he was feeling right now.

He studied the woman again. She was curled up on the chair wearing a pretty pale-blue angora sweater that looked so soft and huggable, formfitting jeans, and fluffy blue socks. Fur-topped snow boots were sitting next to her chair, and a blue parka was lying on top of another. She wasn't wearing a law enforcement badge or a gun, so he wasn't sure what she was doing there.

A nurse came in to check on him, and he was surprised to smell that she was a gray wolf too. "Good, you're awake," she said. "I'm Charlotte Grey."

"I need to see the sheriff." Dylan didn't remember talking to him yet about what had happened, but they needed to catch Jim and his cohorts pronto. He glanced at the woman sitting in the chair.

"That's Roxie Wolff, part owner of the ski lodge. She saved your life."

Dylan looked back at her. She was so petite that he couldn't imagine her being able to pull him out of the pool, but he was damn glad she had saved him.

"She had to resuscitate you. What were you doing in the pool? I mean, the doctor said you were struck on the side of the head, but they checked your ID, and you weren't registered as a guest at the ski lodge. Were you just there to go day skiing? Do you have any idea why or who the man was who struck you? Oh, let me call the sheriff for you." Charlotte pulled out her phone and said, "Hey, Peter. It's me, Charlotte. I was checking on Dylan Powers. He has come to and was asking to see you." She paused. "Okay, good. I'll tell him you're on your way." She slipped her phone into her pocket. "The sheriff is on his way."

"Okay, thanks. Why is...she here?" Dylan asked, motioning to Roxie.

Charlotte smiled. "I'm sure she wanted to know what had happened to you and why. Just as we all do."

He guessed that he hadn't told anyone what had happened. "Can...can you get me something for my headache?"

"Yeah, sure. Sorry. I should have asked you how you were feeling first thing. Your vital signs are all fine. I'll be right back with some pain medication." Charlotte left the room.

Roxie stirred and suddenly sat up straight and stared at Dylan. "You're awake."

He smiled at her. "I think I owe you my life."

She frowned at him. "Who nearly killed you?"

"Jim Johnson, a hunter I was tracking and planning to arrest for illegally killing an elk."

He heard footfalls coming down the hallway, and then a sheriff and the nurse came into the room. The sheriff was a gray wolf too, to Dylan's amazement.

"I'm Peter Jorgenson, the sheriff of Silver Town. You can call me Peter."

The nurse gave Dylan some over-the-counter pain medication. "If you need something stronger, let me know," she said, then left the room.

Peter said, "If you're feeling up to it, can you tell us what happened?"

Dylan was puzzled. "You're wolves."

"Uh, yeah." Peter smiled. "All of Silver Town is wolf-run. So tell me about the man who hit you."

"Wolf-run." Dylan couldn't believe it. "I'm a special agent for the U.S. Fish & Wildlife Service."

"Yes, we found your driver's license and your badge indicating you work for the FWS. We knew you had suffered a blow to the head. Doc said you were lucky you didn't end up with a skull fracture and only have a mild concussion. With our faster wolf healing abilities, you should be good in no time. We also found your gun and discovered you have a license to carry it. I have it locked up at the gun safe at the sheriff's department for now, but I'll have it returned to you as soon as you're released from the clinic. You were awake for a few minutes in your clinic room when I came to see you earlier, but you were disoriented. You didn't tell us what had happened to you prior to passing out on us and Dr. Summerfield shooing me out of the room. So now what's the story? Do you remember anything?" the sheriff asked.

"I was tracking four men who were hunting illegally. They're armed with rifles, including the one who tried to crack my skull. That's Jim Johnson." Dylan gave the sheriff the men's names and occupations. "Eddie drives an SUV that I found parked at the lodge, which means they could be staying there when they're not out hunting. Eddie's Colorado license plate is EJWEST, a personalized one so it's easy to recognize."

"They were hunting out here?" Peter shook his head and texted someone. "Thanks, Dylan. We'll put out an all-points bulletin on the SUV. When Jim registered for parking at the lodge, he gave someone else's vehicle's make and model and license plate number, so this gets us right on track."

Man, Jim had thought of everything.

"Yeah. The four hunters have suspended hunting licenses. They separated, either on purpose or they lost each other in the snowstorm." Dylan glanced at the window and realized the snow was still coming down.

"So the one hunter followed you to the lodge?" the sheriff prompted.

"No, I was tracking him to the ski lodge, but the next thing I knew, I was the prey. I saw his reflection in the swimming pool right before he struck me."

Peter rubbed his bearded chin. "We smelled his scent but couldn't locate him. He's human."

"Right, they all are. I've caught these guys before so they know me."

"But to go to such lengths to kill you? I mean, hell, that's taking it to the extreme, don't you think? They don't get much time or many fines for hunting illegally, as far as I've seen, unless they've done it in our territory, on our property. Then we give the max allowable by law," Peter said. "For attempted murder, that's a whole other story."

"Yeah, I agree. They'd killed an elk, but I had also seen a young wolf. A teen wolf if he was a shifter. They've killed wolves before, so I was worried they might hunt him down next."

"Hell." Peter yanked out his phone and called someone. "Hey, we've got a problem. Four hunters are illegally hunting in our territory, one of them who nearly killed Dylan, and possibly a teen wolf shifter is on his own in the woods. Check and see if any of our teens are missing. As soon as the weather clears, we're on our way to apprehend these guys. All right." He glanced at Dylan. "Yeah, he's a special agent tracking these men. I'm not sure he'll be able to go with us. I'm sure Dr. Summerfield will say no."

"I'm headed back out as soon as the snowstorm lets up," Dylan said.

"Okay, yeah, he's going with us if Doc says it's all right. I'll talk to you later." Then Peter slipped the phone in his pocket. "All right. So in the morning, or when this storm lets up, we'll begin a manhunt."

Roxie pushed her hair back. "What about the security video on the outside pool? It should have caught the man striking you."

"Yeah, we checked, but we couldn't get a good look at his face. Just the description of what he was wearing. But we can track his scent," Peter said. "I asked your brother to look into room reservations for the four men."

Dylan said, "The hunter who hit me was Jim Johnson, the alpha human leader of the pack, so to speak. He's a criminal defense attorney. The others just follow him. I'm sure that they also wanted to illegally hunt, but Jim is truly the one who is in charge when they go hunting."

Roxie got a call then. "Yeah, Landon?" For a

couple of minutes, she didn't say anything, and then she looked at Dylan. "Jim Johnson. Yeah, that's him. Did he return to the room?" She let out her breath. "Okay, yeah, I'm with the victim and the sheriff at the clinic. I'll let them know." She got off the phone and said, "Jim Johnson had a room at the lodge. So did Fennel. Maybe that's why Jim returned there. But when my brother Blake and Deputy Trevor Osgood checked on both of them, the rooms had already been cleared out. There was no luggage or anything else at all."

"Jim must have run to the room and packed everything in the car right away after he attempted to kill me. Were there any other recent scents?" Dylan asked.

"Just Jim's, the same scent near where you were hit at the swimming pool," Roxie said.

"Thanks so much for saving me, by the way." Dylan gave her a lopsided smile. His head hurt too much to give anything else that resembled a more normal smile.

"You're welcome. Imagine my surprise to see you facedown in the pool while I was swimming." She shuddered.

The sheriff got a call back and answered it. "None? Okay, thanks." When he ended the call, he shook his head. "Luckily, we have no missing teens."

"Okay, so I guess what I saw was just a wild wolf." Dylan had been worried that a teen wolf shifter could be out in the blizzard while the hunters were still out there and could be hunting him down.

The sheriff cleared his throat. "Most likely it's a lone wild wolf out on his own. When we go out, you can show us where you saw it. We'll try to track him down and see if we can find him to make sure it is just a wild wolf and not a shifter. So tell me all about the men you were tracking."

Dylan explained more about the four men, where they were located in Denver, and prior illegal hunting incidents.

The sheriff shook his head. "You'd think their occupations would suffer because of their arrests."

"Yeah, money takes care of everything," Dylan said.

"Well, we're going to get out of your hair and let you rest," Peter said. "You look like you're about ready to go back to sleep."

Dylan was tired. The pain medicine had seemed to kick in. He glanced at Roxie, wondering if she was going to leave too.

She rose from the chair. "I'll go home, now that I know you're okay and know what this is all about."

"I'm taking you home because of the heavy snowstorm," Peter said. The snow had picked up since Roxie had driven to the clinic. "Or you can stay with me and Meghan for the night."

"I have to take care of Rosco and Buttercup."

"Your brother can get them." Peter seemed to be

taking his role of friend and sheriff to heart, making sure she didn't get herself into trouble.

"All right. I don't want you to risk driving me home. I'll stay with you and Meghan."

"Have you ever been here before?" the sheriff asked Dylan.

"No, actually, I haven't."

"Well, since the town is wolf-run, we take illegal hunting seriously. We don't want anyone like these men here on the loose who might end up killing one of our own kind. You've got all of us to help you with this case. Because they killed the elk and Jim tried to murder you in our territory, they're under our jurisdiction. We get results."

"But the men always get off on criminal charges based on illegal hunting." Dylan hated that they did, though he liked that Silver Town was wolf-run, and having wolves at his back sure appealed. Like him, their enhanced senses would help them track down the hunters.

"Not this time." Peter spoke with assurance.

"Good." Dylan was glad for that, but he wouldn't believe it until he actually saw them sentenced for their crimes and getting stiff penalties.

Then the sheriff and Roxie left Dylan alone, and he sighed. He wanted to go out and look for the men right now while they were stuck some place in the snowstorm. Dylan finally closed his eyes. But all he could envision was being out in the snowstorm, seeing the wolf running, the dead elk, the man in the hooded parka's reflection in the pool, the warm water as it enveloped him, and Roxie's pretty brown eyes staring back at him. Her lips had been moving but he couldn't hear her words.

———

"Oh, Roxie, I can't imagine what you had to go through." Sheriff Peter's mate, Meghan, was helping Roxie add a couple of blankets to the guest-room bed for her.

"I'm just so glad I was able to revive him. Thanks so much for taking me in like this." Meghan and Peter had a lovely home, but Roxie really preferred being in her own home for the night.

"Think nothing of it. It's too dangerous to drive home in this, and though Peter would take you to your place—"

"It's too dangerous for him also. I worry about the teen wolf Dylan saw." Roxie couldn't quit thinking of him. What if he was one of their kind? Or what if he wasn't? He would still need to have protection.

"Dylan had been injured." Meghan sounded like she thought he might not have remembered the situation clearly about that. She gave Roxie a warm sleep T-shirt to wear for the night.

"Yes, but he seemed clearheaded about that. Tired,

but he seemed to know what he saw. I'm just worried that even though the wolf might not have been missing from anyone's home here, what if he truly is a *lupus garou* and was camping or hiking or something? Maybe he was staying at one of the cabins even."

Peter joined them and said, "We're checking at the campsites too. So far, no one has reported a wolf family at one of the campsites that have a missing teen."

Roxie sighed. "Okay." She decided she would also go on the search tomorrow for the wolf and the hunters. "Thanks for everything."

"If you need anything, just let us know." Then Meghan and Peter headed for bed.

Roxie pulled off all her clothes but her panties, slipped on the soft T-shirt featuring a sleeping wolf, and climbed into bed. She called Blake as she pulled her covers over her. "Hey, I'm staying with Meghan and Peter overnight because of the snowstorm."

"What are you doing over there?" Blake sounded concerned.

"I just went to see Dylan, the man I rescued from the pool." She told her brother what she'd learned about Dylan. "The weather's so bad, Peter offered for me to stay here. But that means I need you to take care of Rosco and Buttercup tonight."

"I'm on it."

"Thanks. Are you going out with the search party tomorrow?" she asked.

"No. We need to stay at the lodge in case any of those men return there."

"Oh." She hadn't thought of that. When they said the one man had packed their bags in the vehicle, she figured they hadn't stuck around and wouldn't be coming back. "I want to take Rosco on the search for the hunters and the teen wolf. Can you handle any issues we have without me for the time being?"

Blake was silent for a moment.

"Okay, listen, I'm doing this."

"Yeah, it's fine. You know I just worry about you, right? I'd go, but that's fine. I'm glad Dylan is doing well."

"Me too. I'm going to sleep, Blake. We have a busy day tomorrow."

"We do. We are all proud of you. Good night, Roxie."

"Thanks, and night, Blake." She set her phone on the bedside table and closed her eyes, but all she could think about was diving under the divider in the pool and seeing a fully clothed, backpack-wearing male body sinking to the bottom of the water. And giving him mouth-to-mouth resuscitation, praying she could revive him.

Chapter 4

IN THE MIDDLE OF THE NIGHT, DYLAN WOKE, SAT up in bed, wondered where he was, and realized *again* that he was at the clinic in Silver Town. He ran his hands through his hair and settled back against the pillow. He hoped he would be able to get out of here shortly so he could head out on the search for the hunters. Though he suspected by now Jim had picked up his friends and the elk and hightailed out of there, if the sheriff and his men hadn't already arrested them.

He closed his eyes, thinking it would never be daytime, but before he knew it, Dr. Summerfield was looking at his chart, the nurse on duty was checking Dylan's vital signs, and Sheriff Peter Jorgenson was getting ready to send out search parties. He was standing at the foot of the bed with his hands on his hips, eager for the doctor's verdict.

Hell, Dylan felt fine and sat up in bed, but then he got dizzy and fought cursing out loud. Dr. Summerfield raised a brow and Dylan suspected then he'd voiced the curse for everyone to hear, despite his best intentions.

"How are you feeling?" Dr. Summerfield asked. "Your vital signs look good."

"I'm ready to search for the guys I was after before the one got the best of me," Dylan said.

"You appear to still be having a headache. We'll give you something for it, and I believe Peter wants to talk to you," the doctor said.

"I do too," a man said, coming into the room and looking like he was in charge. "I'm Darien Silver. My mate, Lelandi, and I run the pack here. Well, the whole town actually. My brother Jake, my second-in-command, and my brother Tom, my third-in-command, will be searching with you. One of them will be with you at all times in case you have any residual effects from the injuries you suffered."

Dylan really had thought he'd do this on his own—with search parties, sure, but not...*with* them. From the firmness of Darien's voice, Dylan knew the plan was nonnegotiable. "Yeah, sure." He understood why the pack leaders set the rules. They wanted to make sure that no one was hurt unnecessarily while under their charge.

He suspected Darien was already steamed over Dylan nearly being killed at the lodge swimming pool. Since no one was budging, Dylan didn't wait for anyone to leave. He climbed out of bed, grabbed his boxer briefs out of a storage closet for the patient's belongings, and pulled them on under his gown. His clothes smelled like they'd been washed, no chlorine smell.

"I'll wait for you in the waiting area." The sheriff left the room.

Another man joined them. He looked similar to Darien, with dark hair, dark eyes, and the same tall stature. "This is my brother Jake. I'm serious about Jake and Tom sticking with you," Darien said.

Dylan pulled off his gown and slipped on his pants. He assumed that Darien wasn't as worried that he might collapse from his injuries as he was worried that the attacker who attempted to kill Dylan would try to finish the job. Especially if Jim knew Dylan had recognized him when he struck the special agent at the pool.

Darien said, "I'll leave you in good hands. Welcome to Silver Town." Then he left.

"If you have any dizziness or feel otherwise poorly, get in touch with my nurses or me," Dr. Summerfield advised, and then he left.

The nurse finished her paperwork and followed him out.

Jake said, "Sorry for such a poor welcome to the town."

"It has nothing to do with your town and all to do with the men I'm after. So think nothing of it." Dylan slipped his sweater over his head, then sat down on the chair to pull on his socks and boots.

"Well, your savior, Roxie Wolff, is coming with us too. She's bringing her family's avalanche rescue dog, Rosco. He actually lay down with you to keep you warm while she went to get help."

"Oh, I guess that's why I smelled of dog and chlorine too. I figure Jim was gone by the time Roxie found me in the pool." When Dylan had gained consciousness poolside, he had worried that Jim could have still been there, and she could have been a victim too.

"Apparently she was swimming in the pool indoors when Jim attacked you. When she swam into the outside pool, she saw you sinking facedown and rescued you," Jake said.

Dylan frowned. He realized she had to have been freezing when she dragged him out of the pool. He kept rethinking the whole situation over and over again, trying to recall the spotty details of what had happened.

"She kept you warm too."

"She was wearing a wet bathing suit at the time?" He had thought she was wearing sweats when he saw her. But everything had been a bit hazy while his head had been splitting in two.

"Yeah, when she pulled you out. But she returned for her sweats, grabbed her jacket, and covered you up with it. You don't remember any of this?" Jake looked worried that maybe they shouldn't take him on the search for the hunters.

"Vaguely." But Dylan was going no matter what. As soon as he was dressed and ready to go, Jake gave him his gun, and he and Tom drove Dylan to the lodge. Several search parties had already gathered, and then Dylan showed them the way. Everyone could smell the way that Jim had gone initially to the lodge. Dylan smelled a fainter scent of the other three men, most likely when they'd left the lodge and gone out hunting. But they hadn't returned this way.

He didn't see any sign of anyone's tracks in the snow. Plenty of snow had fallen since then to fill in all the tracks.

Then he saw Roxie standing with the Saint Bernard and a group of men. With dark hair and dark-brown eyes, Roxie was striking, wearing a bright-blue jacket, black pants, and blue snow boots, and looking ready to get to work. Since she'd saved his life, he thought it only right that he buy her lunch or dinner at a local restaurant. Then again, she could be mated, and her mate might not like that. Well, then he'd buy them both a meal. He wasn't going to give up on thanking her in some way for saving his life when she could have suffered from the cold like he had and hadn't even been wearing as many clothes as him.

She saw him then, her eyes widening, and she frowned. He was hoping for a smile of recognition, that she was glad to see him even. Maybe she didn't believe he should be out on the hunt for the men after what he'd gone through.

He walked straight through the gathered groups to see her. She petted Rosco, arching a brow as she watched Dylan approach.

"I thought the doctor would give you bed rest for longer. Certainly not allow you to go on the search like this," she said.

"Other than a mild headache, I'm fine. I know the men's scents. I need to show everyone the way," Dylan said.

"I'm sure we can find the humans' scents. Wherever the one who nearly killed you at the swimming pool had been, the others' scents should be close by. Right?" she asked.

"Uh, yeah." But that didn't mean Dylan was going to relegate his work to the good citizens of Silver Town. "I'll take you to where they killed the elk first."

Then he led the pack. Jake and Tom Silver were nearby, watching out for him, but Dylan was sticking close to Roxie and her dog, watching out for her.

They walked for about four miles and found the scent of the elk the men had killed, but it was buried under snow now. So Jim and his hunter friends hadn't removed the evidence like Dylan thought they would. But maybe they had returned for it and couldn't find it. A couple of the men dug the frozen elk out of the snow, documented the kill, and collected a spent casing. "We'll send the elk to a big cat rescue reserve," Jake said, while Dylan headed toward the area where he'd smelled the men before they split up. Jake and Tom were nearby, searching the area too.

About one hundred and fifty yards from there, Dylan smelled the distinctive odor of death, though it was not all that potent yet because of the freezing weather. By the serious looks on their faces, the others had smelled it too. Dylan frowned. It wasn't an animal but a human's scent. He was smelling that only the four men had been right in this vicinity. This wasn't good.

"A dead body is located near here," Tom said and radioed it to the other searchers to let them know they had even more trouble than they'd bargained for.

The first thing Dylan thought of was that one of Jim's companions had succumbed to hypothermia. He could understand if they'd left him behind to find help. Then again, no one had called for help. Though maybe they hadn't had any cell phone reception. But…Jim had been in this vicinity too. He would have known his friend, if that was who this was, had been suffering. If that was the reason he had returned to the lodge, he should have told them at once that his friends were missing, one near death or dead. Not tried to kill Dylan. *No.* Something was off about this whole business.

Several people began digging around in the

snow, and Rosco was helping them, like he would for an avalanche victim. Dylan wanted to keep searching for the other men, but he had to know who they'd find buried in the snow here.

That was when a man said, "I found the body."

"That's Michael Hoffman," Jake said. "He's retired army special forces. You met his wife, Carmela, the clinic's office manager."

"Oh, sure." Dylan shook Michael's hand.

Then Michael, Tom, and Jake pulled the body free of the snow and discovered the man had been shot dead, straight through the head.

Dylan just gaped at him. "That's Eddie Jones, one of the men I've been after. He owns a western-store chain and he's a longtime friend of Fennel, Xander, and Jim." What the hell had happened? Dylan had heard two shots fired, one that must have taken down the elk and the other fired a short time after that some distance from there. When Dylan had found the dead elk, he thought they'd just gone after more prey and were shooting something else, not killing one of their own. Unless someone else had accidentally shot Eddie. Their scent trail had led away from the elk and Eddie, so he'd followed that.

Eddie had been hastily buried with branches. Add to that the recent snowfall and they wouldn't have found him for a good long while—if they hadn't had their enhanced sense of smell. The scene appeared to have been a deliberate cover-up.

"He doesn't have any ID on him," Jake said, searching through the dead man's pockets.

"Do you think one of the other men shot him?" Tom asked.

"Unless someone else was in the woods, I do. I don't smell any other scents right here, just the four men," Dylan said. "From the trauma to the head, it appears Eddie had to have been shot at close range. It's unlikely that the shooter wouldn't have recognized that he was shooting a man and not an elk or deer. I heard two shots fired. I thought they'd killed two animals, not the elk and one of their own friends."

Jake got on his phone. "Dr. Featherston, we've got a human body out here. I'll have someone bring you here to check it out. Okay, thanks. I'm calling Trevor after this." Jake said to Dylan, "Dr. Featherston is our medical examiner. He'll do an autopsy. Trevor Osgood is another one of our deputy sheriffs. He'll bring him out here to see to the body."

"Good," Dylan said.

Jake was on his phone again then. "Hey, Trevor, we need you to pick up Dr. Featherston and bring him out to the crime scene." He gave him the particulars and the location of the body.

Tom got a radio call from the sheriff and said, "Yeah, we have a dead man by the name of Eddie Jones. He was shot in the head. We're not sure if it was accidental, but it looks like a homicide. Jake just got ahold of the ME and he's coming out here with Trevor."

"I've got to keep looking for the other three men," Dylan said, not being able to do anything about the dead man. "I keep thinking Jim got Eddie's SUV and then picked his friends up, and they took off from wherever they'd been. I wouldn't have thought Jim would go so far as to add murder to his criminal activities." He thought Roxie would stay there with the dog, but she walked right beside him, ready to continue looking for the other men.

Dylan took a deep breath of the chilly air before he turned to Roxie. "Are you mated?" He knew when Roxie's eyes widened, he'd asked the question in the wrong way. "I mean, I want to buy you dinner or lunch, whatever works, to thank you for what you did for me, and your mate too."

Jake and Tom were nearby. They glanced at him and smiled.

"My mate," she said, sounding amused, "didn't save you."

Dylan sighed, figuring she'd have one.

"If I had a mate."

He brightened at once. Not that he was going to be dating her when they lived so far apart, but at least he'd have her all to himself if they shared a meal.

"So yeah, I would like that. Of course, my

brothers might not want me dining out with you if you are still a target."

"Uh, yeah." He hadn't thought of it that way.

"But I'm not worried. The whole town of wolves will be watching over us, so we'll be fine." She smiled at him.

"Yeah, these guys don't stand a chance. Everyone who is out here today will smell their scents. The hunters won't realize we know who was actually out there based on their scents." That was one good thing for him as a wolf. And, of course, their night vision.

"They thought you saw them commit the murder!" Roxie exclaimed.

Dylan considered that notion for a moment. "Yeah, that could be the reason Jim tried to murder me. I had been out there, and Jim must have realized I was tracking him back to the lodge. I was still so far behind him that I didn't have a visual of him. I was just following his scent and tracks."

"That makes this situation even more sinister."

"Yeah, but hell, I didn't see what had happened at all with regard to Eddie's death." Dylan wished he had or that he'd even been there to stop it. He wouldn't have hesitated to shoot Jim in the shoulder to stop him from killing Eddie if he'd been there to see it. "Do you smell a wolf's scent in this area?"

"I do and there's a tent over there," Roxie said, suddenly spying a small, one-person white tent blending in with the snow and surrounded by snow-covered fir trees. "It's not that far from the crime scene."

"Yeah. It's so hidden back there and covered by snow that I almost missed it." Dylan was thinking that she had an eagle eye.

Rosco ran to the tent and walked inside as Dylan, Roxie, Jake, and Tom were trying to get to the tent in the powdery snow.

"There are no recent tracks. There's no sign of anyone in the tent, but the smell of a wolf is all around it. I don't recognize the wolf's scent," Jake said.

"Hell, I bet that's the teen wolf I saw. I wasn't sure if he was a wild wolf or a shifter," Dylan said. "But I smell that the three men have been here." He rubbed his head, a headache returning. "Jim, Xander, and Fennel's scents are here. They came across the tent and then—"

"It looks like the three men were together for a while, and then one went to the lodge to get the vehicle while the other two went after the occupant of the tent, maybe worried the person who owned the tent had witnessed the shooting of the hunter," Roxie said.

"Maybe that's why they split up. But still, in this snowstorm, they could all have been in trouble. The wolf teen would most likely have been the only one to manage in the snowstorm." Dylan was glad for that at least.

Jake and Tom were searching inside the tent now, and Tom said, "I found an ID—a Colorado Driver Instruction Permit. It shows a blond-haired, sixteen-year-old boy named Luke Milhouse from Denver, Colorado."

Tom brought the instruction permit out to show them and then took a picture of the teen and shared it with the rest of the Silver Town wolf pack in case anyone saw him. He could be in the worst sort of danger if he'd witnessed the killing and the hunters were searching for him, planning to tie up loose ends. What was he doing out on his own anyway, without any other wolves to watch out for him?

Now they were on the search for the boy while others in the search party took pictures of the tent and campsite and checked to see if it could also be a crime scene. If Luke had witnessed the murder, they needed to put him in protective custody. They needed to know why he was out here on his own. They needed to learn if he saw what had happened. Or what he had heard, if he hadn't seen it.

Someone called Jake and he relayed to Dylan and the others with him, "Michael found another male scent and tracks near where Eddie was shot. He was downwind of us and took off in another direction."

"Could he have been the shooter?" Dylan asked.

"Possibly. If Eddie had turned around and the unknown man shot him," Jake said.

"I want to check it out," Dylan said, and the four of them, plus Rosco, headed in the direction where Michael had found the other tracks. When they reached the location, Dylan shook his head, recognizing the scent. "He's a trapper. I've never caught up to him to arrest him, but he sets out illegal traps and I've located some of those. So I know his scent. But…" Dylan took another whiff of the scents in the area. "Another wolf has been in the area. Do you recognize his scent? What if he's a shifter and saw the killing too?"

"It's no one I know. I would think if a wolf was out here and he was a shifter, he'd let us know about it. Okay, so what do you want to do? Try and track the trapper down? Or the hunters?" Jake asked.

Hell, Dylan wanted to go after all of them! The teen wolf included. "The hunters because they're headed in the wolf's direction, and I want to save the young wolf if we can." Dylan figured the trapper hadn't shot Eddie. One of Eddie's friends probably had.

"Okay, Michael, you and the others try and locate the trapper, but watch your step in case he has left some lethal traps around," Jake said.

Dylan and Roxie continued on as before, watching for any sign of Xander and Fennel. Dylan really didn't believe that Jim would be out here, and he suspected the other two men were also gone. But he was looking for wolf tracks too.

More people arrived to help with the search, and Dylan was surprised to see so many wolf shifters coming out to assist.

Roxie said, "An unknown wolf teen is missing. And we have a murderer or murderers on the loose. If we were just searching for a missing juvenile, some of the searchers would be in their wolf coats. But while armed human hunters could possibly be out there, that's a different story."

Dylan totally understood that. "The hunters have been charged with killing wolves too, though they managed to get the charges dropped. These men wouldn't hesitate to kill a wolf. Since the boy is running as a wolf, that concerns me." But as a wolf, the boy could run farther, faster, stay warmer, and hide better in the surrounding terrain.

If he didn't want to be found, the hunters wouldn't be able find him. At least Dylan hoped. He wondered again why the kid would be out here on his own. The kid reminded him of himself at that age, losing his parents and then not wanting to be raised by human foster parents. He'd lived like a mountain man of sixteen for a couple of years, protecting wolves from illegal hunting even in his youth. Which was why, after he had collected his inheritance when he turned eighteen, he went to college, earned a bachelor's degree in biology with a minor in criminology, and joined the FWS.

They'd been out there searching for any sign of the men or the teen for two hours when a snowmobile pulling a sleigh showed up with hot cocoa for everyone. "Hey, I'm Roxie's brother, Landon," the driver said to Dylan. "I missed all the drama last night. I live in the country with my wife, Gabrielle, at our home next to the veterinary clinic. She's the vet. You must be Dylan."

Everyone was coming over to get some hot drinks.

"I am. Good to meet you," Dylan said, shaking Landon's outstretched hand. He gave him an update on what they'd discovered.

"That's not good. We're going to have a new crew come out to take over so that those of you who have been out for a while can go in and get warmed up," Landon said.

Dylan didn't want to go in, but the longer he'd been out here, the more his head began to hurt.

"We're going in," Roxie suddenly said very seriously.

He thought Roxie meant that she and Rosco were going in. He wasn't surprised. Landon had brought the dog some food and water, but the Saint Bernard was probably tired.

Landon frowned at her, looking a little puzzled.

"Dylan can't be out here any longer. Not after having lost consciousness in the pool only last night." She put her used paper cup in a trash bag on the sleigh.

Landon looked at Dylan as if he was trying to judge whether he'd go along with it. Dylan didn't want to leave the search. Roxie appeared to know he was going to disagree with her and quickly said, "Besides, he's taking me to lunch for saving his life."

Landon chuckled.

"He offered. I'm not making him do this," Roxie said defensively to her brother.

Dylan smiled. "No, it was all my idea."

"Take care of him, Roxie," Landon said.

"Yeah, I sure will. Come on, let's go, Dylan." Roxie took hold of Dylan's arm as if she was afraid he wasn't going to go along with the plan if she didn't force him to.

But he wouldn't mind taking something for his headache, and he wanted to have lunch with her. "What about the rooms Jim and the others were staying in?"

Overhearing their conversation, Jake and Tom hurried to finish their cups of cocoa and ran after them. "We checked their rooms over thoroughly. Jim must have packed everyone's bags and taken off after he hit you," Tom said. "We didn't find anything left behind."

"You don't have to go with us," Dylan said, assuming they'd want to keep on with the search.

"Are you kidding?" Jake said. "Darien told us to watch your back while you're out in the wilderness with these guys on the lam, and we're doing it. Once you're at the lodge, we'll head back out."

Dylan had never been part of a pack, so he wasn't used to how much they worked together. But he really liked how they did that and got things done.

When they finally reached the lodge, he remembered that Roxie was a co-owner of it, so he really needed to take her somewhere else where *he* could pay for her meal. "Hey, can I take you to a restaurant where I can get you a meal that I'm paying for?"

She chuckled. "We're here now and you need to rest. You can have dinner at my place tonight if you aren't busy or aren't leaving town already."

Rosco ambled into the lobby to his giant, faux-fur dog bed next to the two-sided fireplace, which fit in nicely with the decor of the ski lodge. With the fire's flames flickering and crackling, the bed was nice and warm and toasty. Rosco curled up and went to sleep. The lodge had been decorated in hearts, flowers, and fairy lights—very festive and homey.

Dylan smiled.

"What? You're not into sweethearts and such?" she asked, sounding amused.

"With no sweetheart to give anything to, not really. By the way, I just wanted you to know that after we found Eddie's body, I decided I'm sticking around. I want to make sure the teen is found safely too."

"Can you do that with your other work commitments?"

"Yep. Since these guys killed the elk and were illegally hunting, they're still wanted by the FWS and under my purview."

"All right." She led him into the Howling Wolff Bar and Grill. "Do you want to stay at the lodge? You can't sleep at the clinic tonight unless you get injured on the job again or off it."

"Yeah, sure." He and she took a booth that over-looked the pool. "I love this place."

"I guess you've never stayed here before. I hadn't recognized your scent, though I might have missed seeing you."

"No, I've never been to Silver Town. I didn't know it was wolf-run. Denver isn't like that. The wolves there are on their own. There are no orga-nized packs. This is pretty neat, actually."

"It is. My brothers, my sister, and I were so glad to sell our ski lodge in Vermont to open the ski lodge here where the whole place is wolf-run. We love it. If you're around still by Valentine's Day, you can come to the big bash we're having here."

"I'll see if I can make it. I normally don't go to parties."

"Lone wolf. I get it."

He smiled. He didn't think of himself as a lone wolf. He just wasn't in a pack.

"So since you're from Denver, you might know

Nicole Grayson. She ran Mile High Investigations as a private investigator there. She and her brother, Nate, run the Silver Town Investigative Services here now. Nate was out on the search today, but you might not have met him. Do you know them?" Roxie asked.

"Uh, he came with another man about the time the emergency crews arrived at the swimming pool, right? I didn't know him, but I think you said his name, Nate, if he's the same one."

"Yeah, it sure was. He's my brother-in-law, married to my sister, Kayla."

A female server brought them menus. "Hi, I'm Minx."

"Dylan Powers." He reached out to shake her hand.

"Oh, the dead guy in the pool," Minx said, sounding shaken, then shook his hand.

He laughed. "Revived." But he was taking some pain medication as soon as he got his drink.

"Oh, Dylan, maybe we should have sat somewhere else, like at one of the booths that has a view of the mountains." Roxie sounded apologetic that she hadn't thought of it before that.

"No, this is fine. I'm warm and dry this time, and I'm going to have a fantastic meal with a lovely lady."

"Okay, if you're sure."

"I am."

"I'll be right back with some water and take your orders." Minx hurried off.

"As to Nicole Grayson, yeah. I know her. Congrats to Nate on mating your sister. I heard he was in the army, and their parents had a stationery store," Dylan said to Roxie.

"Right. He was an Army Ranger. So he got out of the army and joined Nicole in her PI business. Nicole married my brother Blake."

Dylan chuckled. "So you keep it all in the family."

She laughed. "Sort of. I was mentioning them because Nicole had been a PI in Denver and I thought you might know her, both of you being wolves and all."

Minx came and set glasses of water on the table and then Dylan took his medicine. Of course, Roxie was watching him, and he knew she figured she'd been right in making him return to the lodge.

Minx had her order pad out so Dylan asked for a pulled pork sandwich and fries. Roxie ordered macaroni and cheese and a salad. She asked for Earl Grey tea, and he was having a soda.

"Be right back with your drinks," Minx said.

A few minutes later, Minx brought them their tea and a soda, then left them alone again.

"Anyway, so I wondered if you had, um, dated Nicole at some point or another." Roxie took a sip of her water.

He wanted to laugh, but he knew she was being serious, maybe worried he might upset things between her brother and Nicole if he had dated her. Dylan shook his head. "No. I actually ran into her on a case I was working." Dylan took a swig of his soda. "Nicole saw me while I was conducting surveillance on a man smuggling exotic and endangered birds. I was surprised that Nicole caught me at it."

Roxie smiled.

"I caught him red-handed with some of the birds, there was a shootout, and I arrested him. Nicole was sure glad that I was a wolf and one of the good guys. From then on, if Nicole discovered anything in her line of work that could help me with mine, she'd tip me off. And vice versa."

"It sounds like your work can be pretty dangerous."

"Sure thing. There's a lot of money to be made in the business, and way too many of the crooks get away with it."

"Like the hunters you are after."

"Yeah. Just like them."

Chapter 5

ROXIE REALLY DIDN'T WANT TO HEAR THAT Dylan had been seeing Nicole when they lived in Denver. Especially since she really liked him. She sighed. "I'm glad you hadn't dated Nicole."

"Nope. It was strictly a business matter. No drinks or dinners out, no movie nights, no kissing, nothing." Dylan smiled at Roxie, assuaging her worry that he ever liked Nicole in a boyfriend-girlfriend way.

"Good. I don't know how Blake would take it if he knew you were Nicole's old boyfriend."

"He doesn't have to worry. It was strictly business between us. Besides, it sounds like the two of them were meant for each other, and that's all that matters."

"Absolutely. So do you have any siblings? Any other family in Denver or elsewhere?" Roxie asked.

"No. I was an only child, which was the same for my parents. That was one of the things that attracted them to each other. But then they died."

"Oh, I'm so sorry." Roxie and her siblings had moved on after their parents had died, though they been really close to them. That was part of the reason she and her siblings had left Vermont to move to Silver Town. The whole family had worked together running the ski lodge there, and they had wanted a fresh start.

"There's no need to be sorry. My dad and mom loved to fly, and he and Mom got caught up in a bad storm and crashed. I miss them, but I know they were doing what they loved most of all in the world at the very end."

"You were lucky you weren't with them at the time."

"Yeah, my dad was a good pilot, but he loved to take risks. Mom loved it too, but I—I just couldn't do it anymore. I'd get airsick every time. So I wouldn't go with them."

"Oh, no."

"Yeah. So of course I felt guilty that I hadn't gone with them. Maybe I could have done something to keep them from dying like that, but when my dad took control of the plane, he was in charge. I couldn't have talked him out of flying so recklessly for anything."

"I understand. How old were you?"

"I was sixteen at the time and without any other family to take me in."

"Oh, no. I was thinking you were already an adult and on your own." She couldn't imagine him being on his own like that at such a young age and fending for himself.

"I grew up really fast, believe me." But then he changed the subject. "So you have your two brothers, a sister, their spouses and...?"

"My sisters-in-law, Nicole and Gabrielle, each have three-month-old twins with their husbands Blake and Landon. Nelda and Gary Grayson, parents of Nicole and my sister Kayla's husband, Nate, opened a brand-new stationery and gift shop here and have adopted us as their family since our parents are gone too." Roxie couldn't wait for the babies to start walking and talking. Even now, she loved to see them smile and grasp at her fingers.

"That's wonderful. Twins, eh? I'm really glad for them."

"They're so happy to have them." Roxie was too.

"I bet."

"I'll tell Jake you're staying here with us at the lodge." Roxie texted Jake, and he texted back that he was glad about it. She knew Dylan had been hurting. He'd winced several times while they were on the search for the hunters and then while looking for the teen wolf and had rubbed his head a couple of times too. Then he appeared so eager to take the medicine with his water that she figured he had been hiding how much he'd really been in pain.

She pulled her phone out while they were waiting on their meals and checked the lodge's room reservations. "Okay, we have a couple of rooms available for five days that have views of the

mountains. Which would you like me to book and for how long?"

"I..." He smiled and took the phone from her to check out the rooms, brushing his hand over hers, and he pointed at the first room. "This one."

"Okay. For how long?" She hoped he was staying for a while.

"Five days. If I get this wrapped up, I can cancel early."

"All right. It's done." She set her phone down on the table.

"I'll settle up after lunch."

"We've got this."

"I do have an expense account."

"I know, but after what happened to you on our property, we're taking care of the bill."

"All right. Thanks so much."

Then their meals were delivered, and Dylan took a bite of his sandwich. "Hmm."

"Good, huh? We pride ourselves on having really great food. The same with the other restaurants in town." Maybe she and he could try out one of the other restaurants if he was here long enough.

"Yeah, this is great. I know where I'm coming when I want a pulled-pork sandwich from now on."

She smiled. "Thanks. Do you have extra clothes with you to wear for the next few days?"

"In a bag in my pickup truck parked here at the ski lodge. I parked here when I found Eddie's SUV in the lot, then followed their scent into the woods. When I'm trying to hunt these guys, I always take a week's worth of clothing so I'm prepared. It saves me having to buy clothes in a hurry."

"Do you want me to get your bag for you after we eat so you can go lie down in your room?"

"I don't have to wait for a later check-in time?" He sounded surprised.

She smiled. "Nope. Your room is ready. That's one of the perks of being a co-owner of the lodge."

"Oh, well, thanks. I can grab my bag though."

After they ate lunch, Dylan looked like he was really feeling worn out. Roxie walked with him out to his double-cab black pickup truck. She hadn't planned to, but he really didn't look well. He grabbed his bag and thanked her again for the meal and the room, but she wasn't letting him out of her sight until he was settled in his room. She wouldn't forgive herself if he suddenly collapsed someplace before he was able to lie down on his bed.

They went back inside to the check-in counter, and he got his key card. After that, she showed him where his room was on the second floor.

She exchanged phone numbers with him. "If you feel poorly at all, call me, the doctor, or 911. Don't tough it out."

"I will call for help if I need it. I just didn't sleep well last night because the nurse kept disturbing me, making sure I was all right when I just wanted to sleep."

"She was making sure you didn't take a turn for the worse."

"Right. Are you going back out on the search with Rosco?"

"Without you? No. When you're feeling perfectly fine, I will. That'll give Rosco time to recuperate too."

"Okay, thanks."

Roxie left Dylan to sleep and was about to head down the hall when she saw Deputy Sheriff Trevor Osgood carrying a chair in her direction. "Have you got guard duty?" she asked.

"You bet. Jake sent me. Is Dylan getting some bed rest?"

"He is. He should never have been on the search with us earlier today." She really thought he should have been at the clinic longer, but then she figured the doctor had to know best.

"I know how he feels though. It's his job and he wants to get it done right."

"You guys are all the same," Roxie said.

"Don't tell me you wouldn't feel the same way."

Yeah, she would, but she wasn't going to tell Trevor that. "Take good care of him."

"I will."

Then Roxie went downstairs and got the master key to check out the hunters' rooms. She knew the sheriff and his deputies were thorough, but for her own peace of mind, she wanted to check the rooms out, smell their scents, and make sure nothing was left behind before the rooms were released to new guests.

"Are you going to check over the hunters' rooms?" Kayla asked, coming in to work on some promotional stuff for the summer.

"Yes."

"Everyone's been up there already."

"You too?"

Kayla smiled at her. "Of course."

"Well, I don't expect to find anything, but I have to reassure myself that at least I looked the rooms over."

"I don't blame you. I needed to do that for the same reason."

"See you in a bit." Roxie went back to the second floor and checked out the hunters' rooms that were only a few doors down from Dylan's room but across the hall.

Trevor smiled and saluted her, knowing just what she was up to.

When she opened the first door, she smelled the scents of all the law-enforcement guys, her brothers, sister, and brother-in-law, Nate, and the four hunters they'd been tracking.

She peered under the bed and checked between the mattress and box springs. The safe door was unlocked and empty. She looked in all the cabinet drawers but didn't find anything. She pulled a chair into the closet and checked behind the extra blankets folded up on the top shelf but there was nothing there. She searched the cabinet under the bathroom sink, but all she found was the hotel hair dryer, spare rolls of toilet paper, and wastepaper bags.

She hadn't really expected to find anything, though she'd been hopeful. She left the room and saw Trevor raise his brows at her in question. Smiling at him, she shook her head, telling him that she hadn't found anything. She gave the other room the same kind of inspection. In there, she smelled that all four hunters had been there too.

Then she went downstairs to see what she needed to do in a managerial capacity. They had a few functions going on in their ballrooms. Blake was handling a wedding anniversary, Landon a birthday party, and Kayla was working on managerial issues.

That was when Roxie saw a party of two women and two men with beer bottles in hand in the lobby, waving them at one another, spilling their drinks, laughing and looking way too inebriated. Then one of the men started to throw up all over the lobby floor. Roxie called the custodial person and went to lead the man to the restroom, but he told her to get the hell away from him, pulled back his arm and made a fist, then swung at her. She caught his arm in a combat defensive maneuver and knocked him to the floor.

Damn it anyway. She was just trying to move him to where he wouldn't be making such a mess— and in front of kids and parents in the lobby too. Kayla saw the whole situation right away and was immediately on her phone calling for backup.

The other guy hit Roxie in the face with his fist, connecting with her eye, and that hurt like hell!

It didn't take long for Blake and Landon to race from the ballrooms where they'd been working to help her. A couple of wolf ski instructors were on their way in for a break and they rushed to her aid too.

She'd gotten the sick guy down on his belly, his arm pinned up against his back. One of the girls tried to kick Roxie with her ski boot, and that would have hurt! Roxie immediately released the guy she had pinned to the floor and grabbed the girl's raised boot and pulled up hard. The girl landed on her backside hard on the floor and she cursed out loud.

Trevor was hotfooting it down the stairs to arrest the four troublemakers, and Dylan was right behind him. He should have stayed in bed, and Trevor was supposed to be protecting him.

Kayla rushed forward with zip ties for the four drunks. The last woman to join the fight had been punching Blake and Landon for trying to tie up the two men, so all four were going down to the station.

Dylan took hold of Roxie and pulled her into a hug. Which she welcomed since her own family was trying to get the drunks in hand while Kayla had rushed off saying, "I'm bringing an ice pack for you, Roxie!"

Deputy Sheriff CJ Silver arrived to take the four suspects in. The sheriff arrived shortly after that.

Roxie hugged Dylan back, smelling his delightful all-male scent and the complimentary gift soaps he must have used while taking a shower, his hair still damp. When she released him, she realized that he had removed his head bandage. She looked his injury over. It was bruised like her eye would be, but his had a cut that was healing too. "Are you okay with not wearing the head bandage any longer?"

"Yeah. It stopped bleeding. I wish I had been down here quicker," he said.

"You just suffered an injury and are supposed to be resting."

Kayla ran back with an ice pack while the custodian began cleaning up the mess.

Roxie thanked her and put the pack on her injured eye.

"Are you okay?" Kayla rubbed her arm soothingly.

"Yeah. I'll have a shiner for sure though. The ass."

"I'll say. All you were doing was trying to lead

the one man to the men's room. I saw everything," Kayla said.

"Yeah, well, you never know how someone who has had too much to drink might act or react."

"Damn," Blake said. "You should have called on us to handle the guy."

Roxie let her breath out in exasperation. "I hadn't planned on taking him down until he tried to hit me. I couldn't believe his friend threw a punch and socked me when I wasn't prepared."

"I loved the way you gave that woman her come-uppance," Kayla said. "Did you know Roxie was former army? So watch yourself around her, Dylan."

Dylan laughed. Roxie smiled. The difference between her sister and her brothers was profound. Her brothers were overly protective; her sister praised her for her actions. Trevor and CJ took the four offenders out to the sheriff's vehicles while Peter gathered everyone's witness statements.

"I should have been there to help you out. Do you want to sit on one of the lounge chairs in the lobby?" Dylan asked, not leaving her side.

"You need to go home, Roxie," Kayla said, and Roxie agreed with her.

Now *Roxie* needed something for the pain! And she was ready to just lie down for a while.

"I'll take you home," Dylan offered.

She smiled. "Sure, let's go."

Landon and Blake were smiling.

"Do you want me to send one of the deputies to watch the house?" Peter asked.

"We'll be fine. Roxie's got all the right moves," Dylan said.

She chuckled. "We'll be all right. We'll call everyone if we have any trouble at all."

"Okay," Peter said.

"But I'm walking with you," Blake said, "and then I'll return to the lodge."

Roxie knew there was no convincing her brother that they would be okay.

Dylan went to his room to get his parka while Roxie and Blake got their parkas out of the office where they had their own storage room for ski equipment.

"Are you sure you're going to be all right?" Blake asked her, pulling his parka on.

"Yeah, we'll probably both just settle on the couch or recliners and watch a movie. Thanks for coming with us to make sure we're okay, Blake."

Blake scoffed. "You don't want me going with you, but I'll feel better if I make sure that you get home and that no one is gunning for Dylan. Though I'm sure the hunters are long gone by now. If the two of you are feeling okay tonight, you can come over to have dinner with Nicole and me. I'll ask Landon if he and Gabrielle want to join us and if Nate and Kayla do."

"Let me ask Dylan if he wants to go too. I promised him dinner at my house otherwise."

"Okay. Just let us know one way or another," Blake said.

"Of course."

Dylan joined them, and they headed outside. Roxie still had the ice pack, and she began to apply it to her eye again. "Blake wants to know if we would like to go to his home and have a meal with the gang or not. It's totally up to you, Dylan, since I said I'd fix a meal for us otherwise."

"Yeah, I'd like to have a meal with the family, particularly since your eye is swelling already. We'll take the night off from cooking," Dylan said.

She smiled. "All right. That sounds good."

Blake said, "Great." He got on his phone, and Roxie knew he was texting the siblings to let them know they were having dinner at his and Nicole's place. Once they reached Roxie's home, he said, "It's all confirmed. Everyone's coming."

"Good." Roxie was glad. She loved to cook, especially when she and Kayla made meals together, but the way her eye was feeling… Yeah, she liked the idea of taking off the night from meal preparation.

When they reached her house, she unlocked the door and let Dylan in. He shook Blake's hand and then she hugged Blake and he took off.

"So this is my home. Would you like something to drink?" She closed and locked the door.

"Your place is lovely, homey. I'd like some water but let me get us some."

"You don't need to baby me."

"Yeah, I do." He gave her a quirky smile. Then, as if he had lived here for years, he started looking through cabinets to find the glasses while she turned on the TV.

"Sorry, they're in the cabinet above the counter, next to the fridge. I guess Blake will take Rosco out for his walk."

"We can take him tonight if you want to walk him then."

"Yeah, sure. Maybe we can all take him for a walk tonight if you'd like."

"Sure."

She suspected Dylan wanted to go with her alone. "I was thinking we could run as wolves tonight afterward, if you'd like to. I think a lot of our people will be running as wolves tonight if they don't find the teen before then and keep searching for him some more."

"And the hunters?" He brought the glasses of water into the living room, and they sat down on the sofa together to watch a movie.

"They won't have the advantage like we do because we can see at night. And we'll have the sheer numbers."

He sighed. "I sure didn't expect to be having this much downtime on the job."

"Yeah, but you need it. They have an APB out on Eddie's SUV so if Jim and the others end up returning to Denver, someone will pick them up. Also, they'll be watching for them to return home as persons of interest in the shooting death of their friend. I guess Peter is going to send word up to Denver about Eddie's death and they'll have someone notify the family, since you positively identified him."

"Right. I don't envy them the task."

She and Dylan snuggled on the couch, and she really liked this. She had dated a lot of the guys in Silver Town, but nothing had ever clicked. She certainly had never cuddled with one of her dates on the couch to watch a movie.

For the first time since her sister moved out, her brothers having moved in with their mates before that, she didn't feel so alone. But this would be for such a fleeting moment. Dylan would be off on another adventure and return to his home base in Denver within days, if not sooner.

They watched part of the movie, but they both ended up falling asleep in each other's arms. It wasn't until much later that she woke up and realized it was nearly time for dinner.

"Hey, are you ready to go to dinner?" she asked, surprised she'd fallen asleep with him.

"Yeah. Is there any dress code?"

She chuckled. "No. It's always come as you are. We're family after all."

"Okay, well, I'm ready when you are," Dylan said and put on his parka, then helped her into hers.

And then they headed out into the snow to the house next door. She hoped her family wouldn't overwhelm Dylan with questions because he was the newcomer in their midst.

Chapter 6

DYLAN THOUGHT IT WAS NICE THAT THEY WERE having the whole family over for dinner and they had invited him. He wondered if they wanted to meet him in a social setting because Roxie seemed to be interested in him and he was showing interest right back.

All bundled up, Dylan and Roxie headed over to Blake's house next door. He thought it was great that the family lived so close to each other so they could help one another out.

Rosco immediately greeted them and so did a tabby cat. She wound her body around Roxie's legs, then Dylan's, as if she knew he was part of the family already.

"That's Princess Buttercup," Roxie said. "We take turns taking care of the two pets, though most nights they stay with me now."

Everyone welcomed Dylan, introducing him to Gabrielle, since she was the only one who hadn't met him yet. Nicole gave Dylan a hug and told everyone about a couple of other cases she'd helped him with.

"These two three-month-old babies are Gabrielle's and my twins," Landon said, "Evan and Trish."

"And Blake and my twins are here, and they're the same age, named Tucker and Ann," Nicole said.

"That's great. As they grow up, they'll be best friends," Dylan said.

"They already like being with each other," Gabrielle said, "so I agree."

"Does everyone want a drink?" Blake asked.

"Yeah, sure," Dylan said.

Everyone else did too.

Blake made vanilla-cranberry mimosas with champagne for everyone, minus the champagne for Gabrielle and Nicole, and Dylan assumed they were still breastfeeding their babies.

Then Roxie and Nicole began serving up the pot roast, potatoes, carrots, and gravy.

"So what have you heard about the hunters or Eddie's SUV? Anything about the teen wolf?" Dylan finally asked.

"The police in Denver told Peter that they checked with the hunters' parents to see if they knew of their whereabouts, but they all said they weren't due home for a couple of weeks," Landon said.

"Did the parents tell the police their sons were out hunting?" Dylan asked.

Landon shook his head. "No. They said the guys just get together every year at this time. They had no idea what they did when they went on their trips."

Dylan let out his breath. "And their sons just

happened to be carrying hunting rifles on their trip for no reason."

"Yeah, I suspect their families know more than they're telling." Landon showed Dylan his phone. A news reporter was talking about the dead hunter found in the woods near Silver Town.

"So Eddie's family knows. What about the families of the three remaining men? How did they react to the news?" Dylan asked. "I mean, if the hunters hadn't called their parents to tell them what had happened to their friend who died while with them…"

They all took their seats at the dining room table.

"I'm sure there's going to be some falling-out between the parents if they had been friends prior to this. Maybe Eddie's parents will tell the police what was going on—reference the illegal hunting and all, not wanting to protect these men if one of them killed their son," Roxie said.

"But then they'd have to admit that they knew Eddie was taking part in the illegal hunting. They might not want to ruin his good name," Dylan said.

"True, but it will come out anyway," Nicole said.

Landon cut off several slices of roast so everyone could serve up what they wanted. "Exactly. So Jim or one of their cohorts might have called Eddie's parents and told them what had happened to Eddie before the police arrived at their homes for questioning—to prep them, so they don't say things they might not want the police to know."

"If the hunters haven't gone home, where might they have gone?" Gabrielle asked.

"Jim's grandfather has a cabin near San Isabel National Forest," Dylan said. "I found them illegally hunting there once before."

Blake smiled. "You sound like a stalker."

Dylan dished some slices of roast beef onto his plate. "Yeah, for those who defy hunting laws or anything else having to do with illegal wildlife activities. I'm their worst nightmare."

"Someone needs to be," Roxie said.

Everyone was dishing potatoes and carrots out of the bowls and pot roast off the serving platter. Then they began eating.

"We wanted to run tonight as wolves," Dylan said, pouring gravy on his roast beef and potatoes.

"To search for the teen?" Nicole asked.

"Yeah," Roxie said. "But we need to walk Rosco first."

"I'll walk Rosco," Landon offered. "I'll just put the babies in the twin carry pack."

"I'll do the same," Blake said. "Then Nicole and Gabrielle can run as wolves."

"Um, if we run as wolves, the babies turn into wolves," Nicole reminded her mate. "But you can take the double puppy-carrier backpacks. They're too little to run in this deep snow."

"Yes! I knew that," Blake said.

The ladies laughed.

"The babies are still waking us up all night long. I'm surprised any of us can function at all," Gabrielle said.

"That's for certain," Landon said. "I thought for sure by now they'd sleep through the night."

"Yeah, you and me both," Blake said.

Dylan chuckled. Roxie smiled and wondered when Kayla and Nate would have kids too. Roxie loved sitting for the babies. Heck, everyone in the pack loved acting as nannies to the new wolves in the pack.

"This is delicious," Dylan said, getting seconds of everything.

They all smiled.

"Family meals are the best," Landon agreed. "We try to get the whole family together for lunch or dinner at least once a week."

Roxie topped slices of homemade pecan pie with whipped cream for dessert for everyone and served them up. After they finished eating, those running as wolves got ready to strip, shift, and run.

Roxie told herself she was not going to look at Dylan when he stripped out of his clothes. But she swore doing so was a wolf condition or just a wolf's curiosity. In the wild, wolves did consider the attributes of a prospective mate—not that she was considering mating him, but they did check each other out as a matter of course. Wild wolves didn't have two physiques to consider—just a wolf's. But she was just as curious about how Dylan would look as a wolf as she was about seeing him as a human.

She was rewarded with one hot, sexy male. His muscles were just exquisite, and she couldn't help thinking how nice it would be to feel his arms wrapped around her in a wondrous hug again. He didn't have an ounce of fat. All those muscles must have been what made him feel so heavy when she had pulled him out of the swimming pool.

She tugged off her last sock and saw him sneak a peek at her and smile, since she had been checking him over too and both got caught at it. Then they shifted into their wolves, and he was just as beautiful in his wolf coat.

He had the most amazing golden eyes and white fur framing them. Then a band of gray surrounded that, and lighter fur extended around his muzzle. His throat was covered with long, white fur. Black guard hairs and gray undercoat mixed together on his saddle. His belly and legs were lighter, and he really had beautiful, distinctive markings. So yeah, his wolf totally appealed to her too.

Roxie was so ready to do this. Her eye was still swollen and bruised, and it hurt, but she wasn't letting that stop her from helping to look for the teen. She did wonder if Dylan was going to search for the hunters at Jim's grandfather's cabin though.

They took off through the wolf door, and she knew Landon and Blake would enjoy walking with Rosco while carrying the wolf pups. Everyone was going to have a good time. Nicole and Gabrielle looked for every opportunity to get some exercise in, though Gabrielle had started back to work at the vet clinic full-time and Nicole was doing some contract work looking into fraudulent claims for insurance companies again.

As they were running as wolves, the chilly wind cooled Roxie's injured eye. It was like putting an ice pack on it for a while, so this worked out great. She and Dylan stuck close together. Kayla and Nate were nearby and Gabrielle and Nicole were in between the two "couples" until they ran into others beginning the hunt.

The wolves in the pack normally didn't all go to run at night at the same time, though some moms or dads were staying home with little ones. Someone else had to man the sheriff's department while they had the four drunks in the jail cell. Of course they always had medical staff on hand at the clinic too.

For three hours, they searched in the dark, a full moon lighting their way, and that made Roxie wonder if Dylan was a royal wolf with few human roots and could shift at will even during the full moon or new moon. She and her brothers and sisters weren't, so they couldn't shift during the new moon at all. They still needed to shift when the full moon was out. She suspected he was a royal so that he could work at the FWS. At the lodge, they always had enough royal wolves to fill in when Roxie and her siblings were having issues with shifting into wolves during the full moon. Though they'd gotten a lot more control over it over the years.

They continued to run until Dylan stopped dead in his tracks, smelled the air, and listened. Roxie stopped beside him, smelling the air and trying to learn what he'd sensed. And then she smelled it too. The teen's scent from the tent they'd found. Gabrielle and Nicole joined them.

Nate and Kayla had run ahead, but when they realized Dylan, Roxie, and the others had stopped, they turned around and came back for them. They did the same as them—sniffed the air and listened, their ears twisting back and forth, trying to hear anything that they could. Then to Roxie's surprise, Dylan shifted and called out, "We're just like you, Luke. We know about the human hunters and their dead friend. We're looking to arrest the men, and we're trying to find you and bring you in for your own safety. Any of the wolf shifters in Silver Town—which is all wolf-run—will take you in."

Then Dylan shifted back into his beautiful wolf. She thought she saw movement then. All of them turned to look that way. A smallish wolf came out of the woods. Dylan woofed at him. Then Nate howled to let the other wolves know they'd found the teen.

Dylan shifted again. "Come with us. We'll get you some clothes, a hearty meal, a hot shower, and a warm bed." Then he shifted again, and he and Roxie turned and headed for Blake's house.

She figured they were going to Blake and Nicole's house because they had leftovers from the pot roast dinner.

She glanced over her shoulder to see if the teen was following them. He was still behind them, wary, not running to catch up to them. If he'd witnessed the murder, even though the hunters had been human and he had to suspect he was safe with her and the other wolf shifters, he had probably been traumatized. But she wondered if there was more going on with the kid. First off, why was he alone? Had he been in trouble himself? Was he a runaway?

They finally ended up at Blake and Nicole's house, and Nicole ran inside first. Blake and Landon were rocking the wolf pups in padded rocking chairs. They had two rocking chairs just for when Landon and Gabrielle came over with their twins and needed to rock them to sleep. Though the daddies could have put them on their wolf beds to sleep.

Rosco belatedly came to greet them as they

all entered the house. Blake and Landon's jaws dropped to see the last wolf to enter the room. "Luke?" Blake asked, then smelled his scent and nodded.

Everyone began shifting except for the teen, and then they were getting dressed. The wolf pups were now babies, still sleeping soundly in their daddies' arms.

Nicole took her son from Blake and then Blake got up from the rocking chair, cradling their daughter in his arms. "I'll get you some clothes to wear, Luke," Blake said quietly so as not to wake the babies, and then he and Nicole headed upstairs to their kids' room to leave them in their cribs.

When they returned, Blake had some clothes for Luke. "You can change in the guest room over there." Blake and Nicole had liked Roxie's home's layout so well—with a separate guest room on the first floor while the family had their bedrooms on the second floor—that they built their home in a similar configuration. Blake carried the clothes into the guest room, and Luke followed him in there.

Blake returned to the living room as they heard the guest room door close, and he smiled at the rest of them. "At least you found the boy, if that's the one we were looking for."

"He is. And yeah, I'm so thankful for that. I'm sure you don't find teens on their own like this that you don't recognize very often," Dylan said. "I guess he'll take care of the rest of your leftovers."

Everyone smiled at the comment.

Landon was still rocking his babies.

"It's time for us to get the twins to bed," Gabrielle said, and she and Nicole began getting Landon and Gabrielle's baby stuff together to pack up in the van.

Then Landon stood up from the rocker, cradling the two babies. Everyone said good night to them. Roxie knew Landon and Gabrielle would want to learn what was going on with Luke, but they needed to get their babies to bed, and she suspected they felt that having fewer people there would be easier on Luke. At least Roxie felt that it would be.

Kayla and Nicole went out to help Landon and Gabrielle with the babies' diaper bags, baby carrier backpacks, and pet carrier backpacks while the parents strapped the babies into their car seats.

In the meantime, Roxie was on the phone, calling the sheriff while she watched out the window as the others packed up the van. "Hey, Peter, Luke is here. We howled to let everyone know we found him, but we needed to get him to Blake's house to feed him and clothe him. He's getting dressed in some of Blake's clothes, and then he's going to have dinner here."

"I'll be over as soon as I take care of an issue with the drunk skiers at the jail."

Roxie was wondering what that was all about as

she heard shouting and cursing in the background on the phone. Then they ended their call. "The sheriff's coming to see Luke as soon as he can get here. He said he was having some issues with the drunks he incarcerated."

Nicole and Kayla had returned to the house after seeing Landon and Gabrielle off. Nicole started heating up the leftovers for the teen.

"I'm not surprised," Dylan said. "They need to sleep it off."

Blake said, "While Luke is getting dressed, does anybody want another cocktail like the ones I fixed earlier?"

"Yeah, I could have one," Dylan said.

"Me too," Roxie said.

"Not me. I'll have a glass of milk." Nicole started bringing the leftover food out of the fridge.

Blake mixed them up some drinks, and then Luke came out of the guest room and joined them in the dining room. Introductions were made all around.

"Come, sit here," Nicole said. "Pot roast? Mashed potatoes? Gravy? Carrots?"

"Yeah, all of that would be great, thanks." Luke ran his hands through his long, curly blond hair and then took a seat at the dining room table.

Nicole began serving the warmed-up food for Luke. "Do you want water, milk, a soda?"

"Water and milk, thanks."

Blake got Nicole and Luke some milk. Everyone

joined Luke at the table while Nicole brought him a glass of water. "How...how did you know my name?" Luke asked.

"We found your ID in your tent," Dylan said. "I had been searching for the hunters earlier and discovered they'd illegally killed an elk. I'm a special agent with the U.S. Fish & Wildlife Service. So anyone who does illegal stuff like that, I arrest them for it."

"They did more than that," Luke said, scarfing down another forkful of gravy-covered mashed potatoes.

"We found the hunter's body. Did one of the men with him shoot him?" Dylan asked.

"Yeah. I was tenting not that far away. I heard them shoot something farther away than that, and I didn't know what to do. Remain in my human form and hope they didn't shoot me accidentally, thinking I was prey? Wear my wolf coat and get out of their sight? But then I heard them arguing with each other, and I went to check it out as a human. Wolf's curiosity. I heard one of the men accusing the other of seeing his girlfriend behind his back. Then the one guy said, 'Don't do it, Jim.' Then Jim shot the other guy, and I ran away so I didn't see what happened after that. I was so afraid they'd hear me running through the snow. You know with our enhanced hearing, it sounds so much louder. They might not have heard me at all.

"When I reached my tent, I was afraid I couldn't

pack it up fast enough to get away from there. But for a moment, I just stared at it, not knowing what to do. Everything I had was in the tent, and I didn't want to lose it. But I figured they'd catch me too easily, shoot me if they thought I'd seen the murder of the other hunter, if I tried to run off as a human. I got inside my tent to strip off my clothes since I was also scared they'd see me shift. I stripped off my clothes as fast as I could. I shifted, tore out of my tent, hating to leave it behind, and ran off as a wolf."

"Did you hear us calling for you earlier? We were searching for you, trying to locate you and put you in protective custody," Dylan said.

"Sure. I heard men shouting my name way off in the distance. The thing of it was I didn't know if it was the guys who killed the other man and they found my ID in my tent. They could have been calling my name, acting as though they wanted to help me. I mean, I had no idea anyone had found the dead man and was searching for me." Luke cut off another slice of roast. He was eating like he hadn't eaten in years. Poor kid.

"Okay, that's totally understandable. I would have worried about the same thing if I'd been in your shoes." Dylan sipped from his drink. "What made you take a chance with us?"

"I smelled your scent from before. I knew you were a shifter. So I figured you would be one of the good guys. The hunters were all human."

Roxie cleared her throat. "Why were you out there on your own? You're from Denver, your instruction permit said."

"Uh..." Luke didn't say anything. He drank some of his milk.

"Your parents. Aren't they worried about you?" Dylan asked.

Tears filled Luke's eyes and he shook his head.

"Okay, look, I lost my parents when I was sixteen," Dylan said. "If something like that has happened to you—"

Luke's eyes widened.

Dylan explained, "Yeah, so I didn't want to end up in human foster care. I didn't have any other family to take me in."

"Oh."

"So I lived as a mountain man until I was old enough to claim my inheritance."

Luke smiled, appearing to like the idea. But it hadn't been safe or fun—all the time—to live that kind of existence.

"Anyway, if that's the situation with you, it doesn't have to be. I'm sure lots of wolf families here would love to take you in," Dylan said.

"We sure would. You can stay with us tonight," Kayla said. "Or you could stay here with Blake and Nicole, but you would probably hear the babies waking my brother and sister-in-law up all night."

Luke smiled again.

"You could stay with me," Roxie said. "I live in the house next door in that direction. We're all family."

Her family didn't look happy that she was offering for the teen to stay with her by herself.

"I could stay with you both," Dylan said. "With Roxie and you."

Blake raised his brows.

"I'm a special agent with a license to carry. I can protect them both," Dylan said, defending his offer.

"Jim tried to kill you," Blake reminded him. "You're as much of a target as the boy could be."

"The hunter tried to kill you?" Luke asked, his eyes huge.

Dylan couldn't argue with Roxie's brother about that. "Yeah, Luke, but I'm hard to kill."

Roxie rolled her eyes.

Chapter 7

DYLAN REALIZED AS SOON AS HE SAID HE'D STAY with the boy and Roxie that he was in for a negative reaction. Roxie looked surprised he'd say he'd stay with her when she hadn't invited him, and it was true he was a target, should Jim still be out to silence him. Or maybe even one of Jim's friends would make the attempt this time.

"That's true, Blake. Sorry, I should haven't invited myself to stay at Roxie's house anyway without her invitation," Dylan said.

"You're welcome to stay with me," Roxie quickly said, throwing him a lifeline when he felt he was quickly sinking in quicksand. "I can also take care of trouble if we should have any at the house, since I was in the army."

Dylan figured she'd mentioned it for Luke's benefit, and he guessed that was how she was able to take down one of the big men in the lodge's lobby who'd had too much to drink.

"The army, cool." Luke asked for seconds of everything but looked at Roxie's blackened eye.

"I received that in the line of duty, but the woman

and guy who started it are sitting in jail right now."
Roxie smiled at the teen.

"I…I'll stay with Roxie and Dylan, if it's okay
with you," Luke said, addressing Blake as if he was
the authority here.

Dylan would rather stay on Blake's good side.
When he worked around wolves, he preferred to
work with them, certainly not against them.

"Or you could stay with us," Kayla said, offering
her and Nate's house for lodging again.

"I'd like to stay with Dylan and Roxie if it's all
right with everyone," Luke said.

Blake let out his breath. "Yeah, sure, if Roxie's
fine with it. If you have any trouble at all—"

"We'll call you and everyone else in Silver Town,
guaranteed," Roxie said.

At least here, the wolves would all help each
other out as a pack. In Denver, Dylan had to rely on
the police for assistance. After Luke finished eating
supper, Nicole served him double portions of pie
topped with whipped cream. He scarfed up both
pieces in record time too.

"How long have you been living in the woods?"
Roxie asked.

"For a week."

Dylan assumed Luke hadn't been getting enough
to eat and running off whatever he managed to eat,
as thin as he looked.

It was getting to be midnight, and they needed

to get to bed. Everyone said good night, and then Roxie, Dylan, and Luke put on their parkas and headed out into the snow to walk over to her place.

"You don't have your bag at my place," Roxie reminded Dylan.

"Uh, yeah. I can run over and get it in the morning."

"I don't have my stuff," Luke said.

"Oh, the sheriff had it all packed up and took it in for safekeeping." Roxie got on her phone and called the sheriff. "Luke's staying with me. Can someone drop off his clothes at my place, Peter?" She pulled out her keys and unlocked her front door.

They all headed inside.

Dylan locked the door after them. He was surprised the sheriff hadn't already come to talk to Luke.

"Uh, yeah." She glanced at Dylan. "Dylan's staying with me too. All right. Thanks." She ended the call. "Sheriff Peter Jorgenson will bring your things to the house, Luke."

"Oh, great. So you said that you were a mountain man?" Luke asked Dylan, sounding really interested in his story.

Dylan was amused. Maybe that was why Luke wanted to stay with him for the night. "It was a way for me to have some freedom as a wolf and not have human foster parents take me in who wouldn't understand a wolf shifter's needs."

"Yeah, that's what I was afraid of. So where did you live?" Luke asked.

"I lived in a tent but turned into my wolf when it was too cold. As a wolf, I could eat what I caught, which meant I did lots of fishing and could drink water wherever I could, unlike humans who would have to filter it or boil it. I ran in the San Isabel National Forest near here so that I couldn't be hunted—legally, anyway. I hid my tent and backpack in a cave and moved it sometimes, just so I wouldn't lose my belongings to somebody who might run across them. You know how much of a disaster that could be. Sometimes, I'd bury my things.

"Living like that wasn't all that it's cracked up to be. I had to keep out of sight of hunters. I ran into a sow and her cubs once, and she chased me off before I ended up getting killed over it. I ran into a pack of wild wolves another time, and they weren't really receptive to my being in their territory. I never ran into wolf shifters. No one who could help me like the people of Silver Town can assist you. By the time I was eighteen and could live on my own in Denver again, I had grown a lot. My clothes were a little too small for me."

Luke laughed. "I think that is so cool. Can you take me in?" Luke sounded hopeful.

"Uh, I'm from Denver. After this job, I'll be taking on another assignment, so I'm not sure where I'll be exactly."

Then there was a knock on the door and Roxie went to answer it. "Peter is here." She opened the door for him, and he came in, carrying Luke's tent and all his gear.

"Hey, good to see you," Peter said to Luke. "I got held up on a case, or I would have been here earlier. Okay, can you tell me what you saw exactly, Luke?"

Then they all sat in the living room so they could talk.

Luke told the sheriff all the details he had given Dylan and the others at Blake and Nicole's house. Then he described the men as much as he could to the sheriff.

"Jim was the shooter then," Dylan said, listening carefully to Luke's description. Tall, dark-haired, with a beard. Luke hadn't seen his eyes, but he was wearing the gray knit hat that he always did. Fennel was dark-haired and bearded like Jim. Xander was red-bearded and red-haired. And Eddie was the blond-haired, bearded man—the one in the shallow grave.

Luke explained how he had left home after learning his parents had died in a car crash and he hadn't wanted to be taken into foster care. So he might be listed as a missing teen out of Denver.

"We'll take care of that. We have ways of updating records and, guess what, you found relatives that you didn't know about until then and they're taking you in. We'll have you adopted so you're legit, but we can let you live with different families until you find one that you truly enjoy being with," Peter said.

"Dylan. That's who I want to be with. He's like me. He has the same background as me. He knows what I'm going through," Luke said.

"He's not from here," Peter said, casting a look in Dylan's direction as if he was assuring himself that Dylan hadn't decided to stay here and he didn't know about it.

Dylan said, "He's right."

"But you could move here, couldn't you? And live with her?" Luke motioned to Roxie. "I could live with the two of you then." He looked so hopeful that Dylan would agree.

Roxie chuckled. "Hey, it's late. Peter, if you don't have any other questions for Luke at this point, he needs to get to bed. So do Dylan and I. Dylan, you can sleep in any of my siblings' bedrooms. It's your choice. Luke, you can sleep in the guest room in there." She motioned to the room on the first floor.

"Thanks, Roxie." Luke sounded a little unsettled as if he had hoped they'd go along with his idea that they would adopt him right away and things weren't working out as he'd planned.

"Okay, I'll see you all later. Oh, if you could, I need your phone number so I can call you if something happens or I need any more information from you," Peter said to Luke. "You too, Dylan."

They both shared their phone numbers with Peter and then he frowned at Roxie. "The guy who punched you is up on assault and battery charges. The same with the girl who tried to kick you and the other man who tried to hit you. The other woman also, for striking your brothers for trying to get her drunken friends under control until law enforcement arrived."

"Good. So they're getting some jail time?" Dylan asked.

"Yep. That's the thing with our justice system here—defense attorneys, the prosecutor, the judge, they're all wolves. Humans who create issues in our town don't stand a chance. These four are also banned from the lodge. Their stuff has been cleared out and they'll be escorted out of town in three days," Peter said.

"Oh, I love it here already," Luke said.

"Yeah, we'll link you up with some other teens so you'll have some friends here too," Peter said.

"That would be great. Maybe someone can go skiing with me? If someone can pay my ski pass and for the ski rentals," Luke said, suddenly sounding really cheered about being here.

"Maybe Roxie can help. She's part owner of a ski lodge." Dylan was glad Luke wasn't thinking the life of a mountain man would be even better than staying with a family here in Silver Town. He needed a stable environment, family to take care of him, friends to socialize with, not like Dylan who had missed out on all that when he was on his own for two years.

"Be talking with you." Peter left.

"I'm really tired. I'm going to bed. Thanks for letting me stay here." Luke picked up his bags.

"You're welcome," Roxie said.

Luke went into the guest room with his bags. They soon heard him showering while Roxie led Dylan upstairs.

"My room is the master bedroom at the end of the hall. If you need anything, feel free to help yourself. If you start to feel poorly—the doctor said head injuries could cause trouble days after the injury occurred even—let me know and I'll get you to the clinic."

"Thanks, and, uh, sorry about inviting myself over to your place."

She chuckled. "I know you did it because you wanted Luke to feel comfortable and he wanted to stay with you. And you wanted to stay with me, you know, because I can keep an eye on you if you have any medical issues and because I saved your life before."

Dylan smiled.

Before he could entertain the thought of kissing her good night, he got a call and glanced at it. "Work."

"Night." She smiled.

He sighed, then answered the phone and headed down the hall to the bedroom closest to hers. "Yeah, I'm still on the case," she heard him tell someone.

Here Dylan thought he was going to finally get to kiss Roxie, but then his boss had to call him this late at night and ruin the moment.

"I learned you were hospitalized—that one of the hunters nearly killed you."

"Uh, yeah." Dylan hadn't been about to call that in. Not when he knew his boss might take him off the case because it was damned personal now. "But I'm fine."

"I have another case for you. Some trapper is setting illegal leg traps out for wildlife near the San Isabel National Forest. Since you're out in that area, see if you can catch anyone setting the traps. In the meantime, grab those traps."

"Yeah, sure, I will. I want to check out the cabin where Jim stays sometimes."

"The police are on this. It's no longer a FWS mission."

"Yeah, it is. They killed an elk." Dylan knew his boss would be shaking his head. Murder and attempted murder of human beings trumped the illegal killing of wildlife any day. "And he tried to kill me, and I'm a special agent for the FWS."

"Exactly, which is why I want you on the trapper case. Since you're one of our special agents who is closest to the location, I want you on it. But only if you're really all right. Otherwise, you're off this case and on medical leave."

"Who told you that I had been injured?"

"*You* should have! I had to learn it from the sheriff of Silver Town."

Hell.

"He called me to verify who you were, since you had your badge on you when you nearly drowned in Timberline Ski Lodge's swimming pool! Not to mention you work for me, and the sheriff wanted me to know that you'd been injured, and I might not hear from you for a bit. He needed to know if you'd been down there on a job to learn if it had anything to do with you being attacked. Also, if you had any family he could get in touch with. You know the drill. You get injured on the job, you go on medical leave until the doctor confirms you can return to work. I don't want you driving back here to get the paperwork done. You can find the necessary forms online. Get the doctor who has already seen you to fill out the paperwork."

"Right. Thanks."

"Where are you staying now?"

"At one of the lodge owners' homes, along with the boy who witnessed the shooting."

"Okay, well, keep me posted on what's happening—medical-wise—and with your case. Otherwise, take it easy. You don't know how peeved I get when we have to fill out all the paperwork if one of our agents dies on the job."

Dylan smiled. "Right." He knew his boss was more worried about keeping his agents alive.

They said good night and Dylan took a shower, but he didn't have a change of clothes here. He usually slept naked, so he just wrapped a towel around his waist and grabbed his dirty clothes, then carried them to the bedroom he was using.

He set his dirty clothes on one chair and the damp towel on the back of another. Then he slipped under the covers, not closing the door so he could protect Luke and Roxie better if someone tried breaking into the house.

He stretched out on the bed, hands locked behind his head. He hadn't caught the hunters, but some good had come of the whole matter. They had found Luke, and he would have a good home to live in. He would have a family that would raise him. Any number of Silver Town pack members would drive him to Denver to be a witness to the murder at a trial—when they caught Jim and could put him on trial. But at least Luke wouldn't be on his own or worried that a judge would put him in foster care.

Dylan sighed. He needed to get with the doctor as soon as possible and fill out that paperwork to take medical leave. He was looking forward to spending more time here with Roxie, but he still planned to check out Jim's grandfather's cabin as soon as he could.

The next morning, Roxie was so annoyed with herself for waking up as a wolf. Usually once she had run as a wolf at night, she wouldn't have issues with shifting right away. But it was the height of the full moon, and that was when she had the least control over it.

She heard Luke talking with Dylan downstairs in the kitchen, and she was glad that the two of them were getting along so well. They were laughing and talking about their adventures in the woods, while she was frustrated and stuck in her bedroom. Normally, she left her bedroom door ajar, but with Luke and Dylan staying here with her, she had shut it for more privacy.

She paced, not wanting them to know she was having trouble with the shifting issue. But she didn't want them to think she was sleeping in all day. She smelled bacon and eggs. She raised her brows, but she had told Dylan he could get anything he wanted. Since she couldn't leave her bedroom, he was welcome to fix himself and Luke breakfast.

She wondered what his boss had said about the case. Had he taken Dylan off it? Was Dylan leaving soon?

She knew he would. Yet she hoped he wouldn't.

Aww, damn it. She couldn't stay in her bedroom until she shifted back. She woofed.

Luke and Dylan quit talking. She hesitated to woof again, but she figured they were waiting to see if she would woof to let them know she was stuck in her bedroom and wasn't a royal wolf. That was one way to tell Dylan and the boy that she had shifting issues. She woofed again.

Then she heard Dylan running up the stairs. She knew it wasn't Luke, whose footfalls would be lighter.

She waited, then sat on her rump. The doorknob twisted and the door opened. Dylan smiled at her. "You're beautiful, you know."

She growled.

He smiled. "Come on down and you can sit with us while we make breakfast."

She growled again but followed him down the hall.

Then they went down the stairs to the kitchen. She was surprised to see Luke turning the bacon in the frying pan.

"Dylan was showing me how to do this. You're not a royal?" Luke asked.

Wasn't it obvious? She growled and sat down on the floor in the dining room and waited, trying to make herself shift. Then she realized if she did, she didn't have any clothes down here!

Someone called her phone, but it was upstairs.

"I'll get it." Dylan raced off, running up the stairs and down the hall to her bedroom.

"I'm a royal, but my mom had recently told me about wolf shifters who had more human genetics,"

Luke said. "We were both really surprised when we heard a woof coming from your bedroom." Luke served up the bacon and eggs on a couple of plates. "Do you want me to serve yours up on a plate and I can put it on the floor for you?"

She growled and shook her head. Normally only her family might be around when she had trouble shifting or when they had the same trouble with it. So she wasn't happy about having virtual strangers in the house who probably wouldn't understand what it was like to have to cope with this.

She heard Dylan on the phone as he hurried to descend the stairs.

"Yeah, Roxie's a wolf. Okay, I'll tell her." He set the phone down on the dining room table. "That was Gabrielle. She said Landon shifted too and Kayla and Blake are staying home in case they shift. Gabrielle told me Nate, Nicole, and she are all royals. She was headed to the vet clinic, and she said if you need anything, Nicole or Nate would take care of it."

Roxie loved her in-laws. They had all been so understanding about the siblings having shifting issues from time to time. She lay down on the floor next to the fire crackling in the fireplace, trying to chill. She was not going to eat off a plate on the floor. This never lasted that long anyway, and she'd shift back and eat then. Dylan or Luke had turned on the fireplace mantel lights, which lifted her spirits a bit.

"I called the doctor this morning," Dylan said. "I was going to run over to the lodge to get my bag for a change of clothes, but Nate did it so I could watch over Luke."

"And you too," Luke said, waving a slice of crispy bacon in Roxie's direction, then crunching on it.

The bacon smelled so good, and she was starving.

"Anyway," Dylan said, "my boss told me I was on medical leave until the doctor says I am able to return to duty."

Roxie lifted her head and looked at him.

"The sheriff told my boss I had almost drowned in the lodge's pool. I don't know if he told him I'd suffered a mild concussion, but I didn't want to mention it. But you know how we are. We heal up faster than humans. Still, if the doc says so, I'm thinking I'll need the whole week to recuperate. I'll be able to go to the Valentine's Day party then. If you don't have a date, I would love to take you," Dylan said.

"Yes," Luke said, sounding as though he thought this might mean he could stay with them if things worked out between Dylan and Roxie. "I want to go too. Can I go?"

She grunted and nodded.

"I can stay at the lodge if you'd prefer me to. Or I can stay here and help you out while you're having shifting issues this week," Dylan said.

"Me too," Luke said.

She appreciated both of them saying so, though she was still feeling growly about it because she couldn't shift back.

"I've got another job to do here, near the national forest. I need to discover who's setting leg traps for animals. The boss doesn't really want me to go after Jim because it's a murder case now and because Jim attempted to murder me, so my boss feels it will be more personal. But I can do both while I'm searching for the trapper," Dylan said. "And it's *not* personal."

Roxie shook her head. She knew Dylan wasn't going to give up searching for Jim so she was glad his boss gave him another job. She couldn't believe someone would be setting up illegal wildlife traps. She hoped Peter and the other law-enforcement guys would help Dylan with both cases.

Luke and Dylan finished breakfast and both of them cleaned up the dishes. Then they moved into the living room to join her. Dylan carried in a cup of coffee, while Luke had made himself a cup of hot cocoa.

They were just watching the flames flicker in the fireplace when she finally felt the urge to shift, her muscles warming and stretching. Yes! Thrilled, she jumped up from the floor and tore up the stairs to her bedroom. *Now* she was ready to eat breakfast if the guys hadn't eaten all the bacon!

She was glad Dylan's boss was putting him on leave until the doctor approved him going back to work. She did like the idea that Dylan could stay here with her to help her out. At least he was able to answer Gabrielle's phone call. Luke was cute about it too, but she felt he should stay with a family who had some teens around his age so he could make some more friends, though he seemed to be really attached to Dylan. She knew how important that was too.

Then again, Dylan wouldn't be here for that long before he returned to work. So why did she want to make sure he stayed here in Silver Town with the rest of the pack?

Chapter 8

As soon as Roxie ran up the stairs, Dylan and Luke went into the kitchen and began making breakfast for her. "Do you think she's going to let us stay here?" Luke asked, his voice low.

"I'm not sure." Dylan suspected Roxie might be okay with *him* staying with her, but as far as Luke went, he thought she might feel he should stay with a family. That was what he would suggest. Though the kid had been through a lot already with losing his parents and then witnessing a murder. Luke seemed happy to be with them, and that was a good thing. But Dylan thought he would feel just as good if he was able to settle in with a family that was permanently living here and could give him all the nurturing he needed.

Then they heard Roxie coming down the stairs. "Boy, I hope you left some bacon for me," she said, sounding cheerful now that she was back to her human self.

He'd been amused that she'd been so growly as a wolf. He felt sympathetic for her but was glad he didn't have issues like that. He was relieved that Luke didn't have trouble with that either.

"I made sure Luke didn't cook them all up the first time." Dylan smiled at her. "Would you like a cheese omelet?"

"Yes, that sounds great. With bell peppers, mushrooms, and onions," she said.

"Coming right up."

"So what do you think about us staying with you?" Luke asked.

"Let's see if a family will take you in," Roxie said. "Dylan won't be here for long and—"

"Oh, gotcha." Luke poured her a glass of orange juice. "You two need to be alone."

Dylan glanced at her to see her reaction. She blushed.

"I think you need to have a family to look after you," she repeated. Then she got a call, and she answered it. "Hello, Peter. I'll put you on speaker."

"Oh, good. I was going to call Dylan next if you were unable to answer the phone. Luke's phone isn't working. I suspect the phone company closed out the account when his parents died. Anyway, we have a family who'd love to take him in. Our pack leaders, Darien and Lelandi, have three fourteen-year-olds, two boys and a girl, and they want Luke to stay with them. If he doesn't like the arrangement, he can stay with another family. We want him to feel comfortable with whomever he stays with," Peter said.

Luke sighed resignedly. "Sure, I'm fine with that."

"Good. I'll be picking you up in a bit," Peter said.

"All right. I'll go pack my bags." Luke sounded less than enthused and headed to the guest room.

But Dylan figured he couldn't stay with Roxie when she was on her own, and maybe Luke wouldn't want to after Dylan left. "Hey, Peter, I have another case to work on too."

"Yeah?" Peter said.

Dylan explained the situation to him.

Peter didn't hesitate to offer assistance. "We'll help you with that too."

Dylan had never figured he would have regular law enforcement helping him with his job, but finding the trapper and his traps benefited all their kind who could step into one of those traps.

Dylan didn't say anything to Roxie about it, assuming they would talk after Luke left. Dylan dished up the hash browns, a cheese omelet, and bacon for Roxie.

"Wow," she said. "Thanks so much."

"Thank you for allowing us to stay here."

It didn't take long for Peter to arrive at Roxie's house just as she finished eating her breakfast. She gave Luke a hug. "We'll have you over for a meal again. You're still part of my family and of the pack as a whole."

Luke gave her a hug back. "Thanks, Roxie."

Dylan shook Luke's hand. "I'll be sure to see you before I leave."

Luke nodded and swallowed a lump in his throat, then headed out to the sheriff's car. "He'll be in good hands," Peter assured them.

"Right," Roxie said.

But Dylan was thinking Luke might not like being with a family that had younger teens, even if being with the pack leaders' family elevated his position. Dylan figured Darien wanted to take him in to make sure the teen was protected in case the hunters showed up in Silver Town.

When they left, Roxie said to Dylan, "I felt a little badly that he had to go. I think he did too."

"Lelandi came and spoke with me about how I was feeling when I was at the clinic. She told me she is a psychologist. If Luke needs one to talk to, she will be perfect for the job—being a wolf and all," Dylan said.

"Oh, good. That's so true. Thanks for breakfast. It was first class."

"You're welcome. I don't want to put you out, but if you'd like me to stay here and help you while you're dealing with shifting issues…"

"Yeah, sure, and thanks. I didn't want to say anything until Luke was going to a family's home because then he might have felt left out. But that would be fine with me. So what are you going to do? Sit still and stay here?"

Despite doctor's orders or his boss saying he needed to take time off, he didn't want to sit around Roxie's house.

"You mentioned the hunter's grandfather's cabin," Roxie said.

"Yeah." He had to check it out. Though he figured other law enforcement officials would too. But they wouldn't be wolves. They wouldn't know if Jim's, Fennel's, or Xander's scents were there or if they were recent, like the wolves would.

———

"You can't go alone." Roxie was serious about it. She realized he was used to working on his own, but it was too dangerous for him after being injured and considering the danger these men represented since one tried to kill him. "You said it was near the national forest. Darien's cousin Eric Silver is a forest ranger there. He can meet you there. And others of the pack would go with you. They'll be eager to arrest the hunter setting traps too. But you can go only if you have the doctor's permission."

He smiled at her. "Sure thing."

"I know how you guys are. My brothers are the same way. They have a mission to accomplish, and they do it even if they're sick or injured."

"Yeah, I guess we're all kind of like that. What about the Valentine's Day party?"

Roxie smiled as they cleaned up the kitchen. "Yes, you can 'take' me though I'll already be there because we're throwing the party for the pack at our ski lodge."

"I'll escort you from your house then."

She glanced at him. "It's a deal. It is a black-tie affair, by the way."

"You don't think I own a tux?"

She laughed. "You very well might. But while you've been running out here? Chasing down bad guys? I doubt you have it packed in your bag, just in case you had the chance to take a she-wolf to a black-tie Valentine's Day party."

He chuckled as he finished scrubbing the frying pan he had used for the omelets. "Okay, in truth I don't own one. Do they have a store in town that sells them?"

"You're in luck. We have all kinds of celebrations here—Victorian Days, even. A couple of shops carry whatever we need for whatever event is going on."

"I'll have to check them out. You're really okay with me staying here? I didn't even ask if you might be seeing some guy. He wouldn't like that a bachelor male wolf was staying here with you."

"Oh, I'm sure there will be some bachelor males in the pack who are a bit envious. No one I've ever dated—not that I'm saying I'm dating you, mind you—has ever stayed with me overnight. And here you come along—"

"I nearly drowned in your pool, for starters…"

She smiled and dried the pan he'd just washed. "Yeah, you know never has a guy gone to such drastic measures to meet me."

"Well, it worked, didn't it?"

She put the pan away and she pulled him in for a kiss. "Yeah, and I'm damn thankful you were okay, after the fact."

He wrapped his arms around her and began to kiss her like he wanted to keep her. She liked that feeling. Warm, glowing, the heat growing. Her heart was beating faster, and so was his. His hand moved to the nape of her neck and caressed her. She felt tingly all over.

She tasted his mouth, felt the tenderness in his touch, and soaked it in. Ohmigod, she loved kissing him and him kissing her. She wanted to take him to the Valentine's Day party and keep him even after that.

But she had to get him dressed for the occasion and that meant taking him shopping. She placed a playful kiss on his nose. "Come on. If you're up for it, let's go and get you that tux before you change your mind," Roxie said.

He laughed. "No way would I change my mind about taking you to the Valentine's Day party."

"Good. I'm glad to hear it."

Then they headed into town in her car. As soon as she reached the town, she parked at the shop, Faye's Formal Wear, and smiled. She could just imagine what everyone would be saying if they saw her visit the shop with Dylan.

———————

Dylan had never shopped for anything as dressy as a tux. As a special agent for the FWS, he worked mostly undercover, and dressy had never been his style. He was glad Roxie would be there to help him figure this all out.

She introduced him to Faye Blackstone, a pretty redhead with shining green eyes. "She's the owner and manager of the store," Roxie said. "We need to find Dylan a tux for the Valentine's Day party."

Faye was still staring at him, and she finally said, "You're the man who almost drowned in the pool."

Roxie laughed. "He's a special agent for the Fish & Wildlife Service, but everyone will remember him as the man who almost drowned in the pool."

Dylan smiled. "Yeah, that's me."

"I'm so glad you can take the ribbing so good-naturedly," Roxie said.

He got a kick out of the wolves of Silver Town. He really was having a good time here.

Faye offered them pieces of homemade fudge and cups of hot cocoa. He thought that was a cool way to entice customers to buy even more. The chocolate fudge chock-full of pecans was out of this world. Dylan took a sip of the cocoa. Roxie ate some of the mocha-and-chocolate-swirl fudge. Faye encouraged them to try out the different varieties. After they had their cocoa and fudge, they washed their hands and then Dylan began to look through a rack of tuxes. This wasn't going to be easy.

Roxie was pulling out white dress shirts and holding them up to eyeball them and him to calculate whether they'd work on him or not. "Any of these would work so that you can wear it to the more formal functions but also for more informal wear. You never know when you might need one."

He wasn't planning on telling her he didn't ever wear fancy white collared shirts to anything and ruin whatever image she might have of him. "Right."

"Do you have black socks?" She ran her hand over the socks.

He smiled. "Nope. Not with me." The ones he did have back home *weren't* dress socks.

She set a pair on the counter. "What about a bow tie or a tie?"

"James Bond always wore a bow tie." He smiled. The ladies laughed.

"James Bond it is." Roxie picked out a bow tie for him.

Dylan was still undecided about a tuxedo as he poked through the ones hanging on the rack.

Roxie started pulling dress pants off a rack and handed them to him. "You can try these on." Then she began checking out each of the tuxes. She was pulling them off the rack, looking them over, and handing each of them to him that she liked. She didn't seem to be in a hurry to rush through the experience. It was more like she worried he would get exasperated if they took too long at this. Sure, shopping wasn't normally his idea of a good time, but he'd never experienced having anyone interested enough in him to do this for him, and he had to admit, he really liked it.

Faye was taking a phone call and telling a customer what she had available in the line of tuxes. So Dylan wasn't the only one who needed one at the last minute. He was glad for that.

This was a lot easier than he thought it would be while Roxie was the one picking them out.

She found three waistcoats she liked and was about to hand them to Dylan, but Faye ended her call, took them from Roxie, and gathered up the dress shirts too. "I'll put these in a dressing room for Dylan."

Before Faye could return for the pants and tuxes, Dylan and Roxie heard the doorbell jingle and they turned to see Lelandi bringing Luke in to get him a tux.

"Hey, I didn't expect to see you here," Luke said, eyeing the handfuls of pants and tuxes on hangers that Dylan was holding on to.

"Yeah, you should never put off things until the last minute," Dylan said.

"That's what Lelandi said!"

Lelandi smiled. "I sure did. Why don't you look at this rack, Luke? The clothes are more your size."

Roxie handed Dylan one more tuxedo. "That's it. Why don't you try them on and see which you like the best?"

"Are you going to wait for me so I can model them for you?" Dylan had no idea which he would like the best. Besides, getting a second opinion worked for him.

Roxie nodded. "Of course."

Lelandi helped Luke pick out some clothes. Then he rushed with the clothes into the dressing room next to Dylan's to try them on.

Dylan came out of his dressing room to model the first set of clothes and said to Roxie, Lelandi, and Faye, "What do you think?"

The three ladies looked him over. "Love it," Roxie said. "With black dress shoes, socks, and the bow tie, it will be perfect. Oh, and cuff links too."

"Yeah, that looks great," Lelandi said, Faye agreeing.

"Okay, great. So that's it then," Dylan said, glad that was over with.

"Nope," Roxie said. "This is an investment. I want to see them all on you."

This was going to take forever. Here he thought he'd be out of here in no time. Before Dylan could return to his dressing room, Luke hurried out, still buttoning his white shirt.

"What do you think?" Luke asked Dylan.

Dylan smiled. "You look like James Bond Jr."

Luke smiled and turned to Roxie and Lelandi. "Do you think this is all right?"

"Yes," Lelandi said. "You look great."

"I agree. Very handsome," Roxie said.

"I don't have to try anything more on?" Luke glanced at Roxie as if she knew better than anyone about these things.

"Nope," Roxie said. "That looks perfect on you."

"Oh, wow, thanks. Be right back. Save me some fudge." Luke rushed back into his dressing room.

Dylan cocked a brow at Roxie, hoping he'd get a reprieve, but she waved him into the room. "They resell kids' formal wear because they grow out of their things so quickly. What he picked out is perfect for him. He looks great in it. You will be keeping yours for other events so you need to make sure it's the one you like the best," she said.

Smiling, Dylan shook his head and returned to the dressing room. He really liked the fit and style of the shirt and trousers, so he would just try on the other tuxedos and waistcoats. By the time he left the room to model the second tux, Luke was setting his new clothes on the checkout counter and asking Faye if he could have some fudge.

Lelandi paid for his clothes and sampled some of the fudge too.

Everyone watched as Dylan came out in his boot

socks and the tux ensemble each time, but they all agreed that they liked the first one he had modeled best. Luke was grinning at him, as if he knew he had gotten out of having to do all that extra work for nothing.

"You had to try all of them," Roxie said, justifying her actions. "It's so costly, you need to be sure it's the right one."

"Yeah, I know. And you will too, Luke, when you're fully grown and will keep the formal attire for longer." As if Dylan thought he'd ever wear it again unless he was invited to another formal event down here.

He still had to buy dress shoes and cuff links. Faye had the cuff links in her store so he picked out stainless-steel ones he wanted. He would have to go to the shoe shop for the dress shoes.

Once he had made his purchases, he was glad everyone had helped him decide. He would have just picked out the first set of clothes he pulled off the racks. Though in retrospect, those were the ones everyone had liked best.

Faye gave both Luke and Dylan a box of her fudge to go home with them. They thanked her for the fudge, and she thanked them for coming to the store and buying their tuxes for Valentine's Day.

"A trip to the shoe store is next, right?" Dylan asked.

"Yeah!" Luke said, sounding eager to do this, which surprised Dylan.

When Dylan was that age, well, if he hadn't been running around in the wilderness when he was sixteen, he wouldn't have been interested in shopping for dress clothes.

They placed their packages in their vehicles and walked down to the shoe store a short distance from the formal-wear shop. Inside, they found shoes for men on one side, shoes for women on the other, and kids' shoes in between.

Luke and Dylan were soon trying on shoes, the women checking out the shoes in the women's department.

"So how are things going with you and the Silver family?" Dylan asked Luke.

"It's been great. The triplets were disappointed that I get to go to the Valentine's Day party, but Lelandi said that was only for teens sixteen and up and they'd get their time when they are that age."

"Are you…" Dylan hesitated to say anything further while he was pulling on another shoe, thinking it might hurt Luke's feelings if he was going solo.

Luke looked up expectantly, waiting for him to finish what he had to ask.

Well, hell, Dylan had started the conversation. He might as well finish it. He stood and looked in the mirror at the shoes. "Are you taking anyone to the party?"

Luke smiled. "Yes! Everleigh Boatman. Her parents own the new movie theater, Silver Town

Theater, and she is my age. She and her brother, Benjamin, are going to the party, but I get to escort her." Luke beamed.

Dylan slapped him on the back. "Good. Do you know how to dance?"

"Lelandi is giving me a quick dance lesson. What about you?"

Dylan smiled. "She might need to give me one too."

"You better hurry and do it. Valentine's Day will be here before we know it." Luke walked around in a pair of new shoes, made a face, and sat down to try on another pair. "Those pinched my toes. I like sneakers better."

"Yeah, I agree with you there. Or hiking boots."

Then they both picked out a pair of shoes and found the women had picked out some too.

"Dylan said he needs dancing lessons too," Luke joked to Lelandi.

Everyone laughed. Dylan should have known Luke might bring it up.

"I can teach you what you need to know," Roxie said, "unless you want Lelandi to show you."

"Yeah," Dylan said, not wanting to admit he knew how to dance in front of Luke. "You can show me, Roxie."

Lelandi just smiled at him as if she knew what that had all been about.

When they left the store with their purchases,

Luke was talking away about the Valentine's Day party, about skiing with the Silver triplets, about skiing with Everleigh when she wasn't working at the movie theater selling popcorn. "I'm going to start working there too."

"That's wonderful," Roxie said.

"Yeah, and Lelandi and Darien are teaching me to drive. They're getting me a used pickup truck to drive to work and to the ski lodge once I have my driver's license," Luke said.

It sounded like Luke was happy to be with the Silvers, and Dylan was glad about it. It was better that he wasn't living with or adopted by the Boatmans, whose kids were his age, because it seemed Luke had really taken a liking to Everleigh.

At their cars, they put their purchases inside and said goodbye to Lelandi and Luke, then headed home. Dylan was glad to get this done.

"So you need dance lessons?" Roxie asked.

"Lelandi is giving them to Luke, and I said she might need to give me some."

"To make Luke feel better about it?"

Dylan laughed. "Yeah, and it sort of backfired when Luke brought it up."

"Well, if you need any, just let me know."

They finally arrived at her place and hauled their purchases into the house. "What did you buy?" he asked Roxie.

"A pair of dress shoes to go with my dress so I can spend the night dancing with my date."

He smiled. He loved a challenge.

Chapter 9

THAT EVENING AS ROXIE AND DYLAN WERE PRE-paring dinner, someone knocked on her door, and when she answered it, she was surprised to see Luke standing on her front doorstep, smiling at her and looking a little sheepish. "Uh, sorry, I left one of my bags on the other side of the bed. I thought I had gathered everything up earlier."

She swore he wasn't telling the truth and suspected he wanted a reason to come back and see them. What if they'd been in the middle of something private?

He smelled the aroma of beef stew cooking in the kitchen and said, "That smells good."

"I'd invite you to stay for dinner but I'm sure the Silvers already have plans to feed you there," Roxie said.

"Oh, they said I can eat over here if it's all right with you."

"Are you sure? We have plenty of extra food for all of us, but I don't want to upset the Silvers if they plan to have you eat with them. I'll just give them a call." Roxie wasn't sure if Luke was telling the truth. He appeared to be anxious about things, and given the way he'd shown up here, she suspected he felt more comfortable with them, or with Dylan, in any event. Then she frowned. "Did they just drop you off here?"

"Yeah, they said it was all right if I ate here," Luke said.

But he hadn't made sure it was all right with Roxie! She got on her phone and called Lelandi. "Hey, it's Roxie. I guess one of you dropped Luke off here to get his other bag."

"Yes, and he said you invited him for dinner."

Roxie sighed. "Okay, well, he's certainly welcome to join us anytime, and once Dylan leaves, he can still come over to see me at any time he wants." She wanted to remind Luke that Dylan wasn't hanging around. But then she wondered if that was why he wanted to be here. To hang around here to get to know Dylan more because he was leaving soon.

"I think he wants to see more of Dylan," Lelandi said.

"That's what I was thinking."

"Maybe, if it's all right with you, he can visit sometimes during the week. The kids want Luke to go skiing with them tonight, and he said he wants to. After dinner, he can head over to the lodge and ski with them," Lelandi said.

"Yeah, that certainly works." Roxie thought Lelandi was a wonderful and caring pack leader. Luke couldn't be in better hands.

"Then Darien will pick them up from the lodge tonight."

"Okay. I'll let him know. Thanks, Lelandi." Then Roxie set her phone on the dining room table. "Serve up three bowls of stew, Dylan. Luke's staying for dinner and then going skiing with the Silver triplets. But you know, Luke, you should really ask me if it's all right first to come and have dinner with us."

"I was afraid you would have said no."

"I wouldn't have. But we might have been going out for dinner or not made enough food for three. And you need to be honest with the Silvers and with us."

Luke took in a deep breath and exhaled it. "Okay. About the skiing…" Luke said, hurrying to set the table as if he wanted to show how helpful he could be since he got a reprieve from eating dinner with Darien's family. "I wondered if Dylan could go too."

"No," Roxie said, frowning at Luke.

Dylan chuckled and Luke laughed. "Ohmigod, you two sound like you're mated already. There's hope yet," Luke said.

"He can't go, even if he'd love to, because of his head injury. If he banged it again in a bad spill, it could have dire consequences," Roxie said, pouring everyone a glass of ice water.

"Yeah, she's right, as much as I hate to admit it, or I'd take you right up on it. Roxie could even go skiing with us."

"Exactly." Roxie sat down to eat with them.

"But you might turn into a wolf?" Luke asked her before he began eating his stew like he hadn't been fed in forever.

"No. I should be good now since I was a wolf already this morning. But I'm staying at home for Dylan." Roxie saw Dylan open his mouth to speak and she suspected he might tell her to go ahead and ski, but she gave him a look that said not to, and he quickly concentrated on spooning up some of his stew instead. Luke needed to be with the Silver triplets to have some fun if he was going to get to know them.

Then Dylan said, "Yeah, just in case I feel worse."

She was worried about asking Luke how it was going with the Silvers in case he said he hated it over there, but she had to know if the reason he was here was that he was really unhappy being with them. "So how are things going with Darien and Lelandi and the triplets?"

"Oh, they've been great. They gave me a room of my own. Lelandi said that it had been Jake's room, but he was now living with his mate, Alicia, in their own home, so he didn't need it any longer. I played computer games with Benjamin. On some of them, he's way better than I am. They said they'd get me my own computer so I could use it for homeschooling and playing games. Jake took his computer with him, but he left his desk behind. Everyone's super nice. Darien is very much the alpha in charge of everything. Lelandi is more laid-back, but she's just as alpha, and it's funny seeing how much control she has over him. The triplets love it. But they're only fourteen, you know."

"You'll meet some other teens who are older," Roxie assured him.

Then they finished dinner, and they heard a knocking on the door. Roxie went to answer it. Darien and Lelandi's triplets were there, smiling. She was surprised to see them here, but maybe they wanted to make sure Luke went with them skiing. "Is Luke ready to hit the slopes?"

"Yeah, coming!" Luke called out, hurrying to take his empty bowl into the kitchen. "Thanks for dinner."

"You're welcome. Have fun skiing," Roxie said.

"We will," the kids all shouted and headed off to the ski lodge.

Dylan joined her at the door and smiled. "He seems to be happy enough. It's all going to be an adjustment. Even if he'd stayed here, it would have been."

"You know, he must have been an only child. So that makes a difference too—to be suddenly living with not only foster parents but a few kids he doesn't know when he was used to being an only child," Dylan said.

"At least Lelandi will know how to cope with it.

Sorry for speaking for you when Luke asked if you wanted to ski with him." She began clearing away the rest of the dishes.

Dylan put the leftover beef stew in a container and set it in the fridge. "You were only looking out for me."

"I was afraid you would say yes, and I would have to contradict you." Roxie put the dishes in the dishwasher.

He began scrubbing the pot they'd cooked the stew in. "No way would I have told him I was going skiing. I would love to, in truth, since you have such a lovely ski resort here and the powder looks great. But I could see injuring myself in some mishap, even just breaking a leg, and then how would I explain that to my boss? I can't return to work because the doctor put me on medical leave for a head injury, but I can go skiing? Yeah, it wouldn't look good at all."

She laughed. "Yeah, I could see you having to look for a new job then."

"In Silver Town? Maybe that wouldn't be such a bad thing after all."

She smiled. "I'm sure you enjoy your job."

"I do."

"Hey, like Luke said, we have a new movie theater in Silver Town. Would you like to go and see something? They even have those recliner seats and two of the theaters are 4D." She checked her phone.

"4D?"

"Yeah." She found a thriller she wanted to watch. "What about this one?"

He raised his brows as he read the description. "Yeah, I'm all for it."

"We can buy our tickets online and pick our reclining loungers."

He looked at her phone. "Yeah, these seats would be good. Not too close to the screen and in the middle so we can really see the whole screen."

They headed out to the theater in her car since his truck was still parked at the lodge. "Why don't we pick up your truck on the way back, and you can park in the garage since you'll be here for the rest of the week. That way if we have hail, your truck will be protected."

"Yeah, sure. Thanks. I guess you don't have much trouble with car theft, vandalism, or break-ins at the resort."

"Not usually, but we have had some incidents with not-so-nice guests, just like Jim and his hunter friends staying in two of the rooms. We did also have hail this summer that caused a lot of damage."

"Okay, thanks."

"Which reminds me," she said and called the front desk at the lodge. "Hey, Eliza, can you cancel the reservation for Dylan's room?"

"Sure thing," Eliza said.

"Thanks!"

When Roxie and Dylan arrived at the Silver Town Theater, she said, "A lot of work went into this to make sure it still fit in with the quaint feel of an old, western silver town in Colorado but at the same time with lots of lighting and to make it feel modern and unique."

"It looks great." They went inside, and even though they'd just had dinner, he bought buttered popcorn and bottled water for them.

This was so much fun. The theater was so new, she hadn't even gone to it with a date yet. Just with her family once. Roxie and Dylan found their seats and sat down to watch the movie. They finished their popcorn, and he reached over and took hold of her hand. He was so sweet.

She snuggled next to him. The theater was cold, but mainly she enjoyed getting warm with him. The thriller was great, a real edge-of-the-seat twister. The American family was trying to get out of a country in the middle of a coup.

What made it even more exciting was that the seats moved, throwing Roxie and Dylan and the rest of the movie patrons forward as the family in the movie jumped across the top of one building to a much lower one down below. Everyone in the theater shouted "Whoa!" or "Oh!"

Rain poured down on the family, and a spray of water hit Roxie and Dylan. They laughed. Then the family got onto a scooter, the two adults and two kids all squished together, trying to reach the embassy for protection. They took a hard right to avoid the rebels, and the theater seats rocked that way, and then the family took a hard left down another street and the theater seats moved that way. Then the scooter was going down a steep set of stairs, bumping all the way as the theater seats bounced and tilted forward.

Everyone in the theater was laughing.

The family reached the embassy, but it had been destroyed, and they had to find another way out. They managed to get into a rowboat and made it across a river to the neighboring country and got asylum, the rain pouring down, while a mist of water squirted out at Dylan and Roxie.

She just loved this theater. Dylan was laughing as they left the room. "Now that is 4D. I loved it," he said. "I've never been in one like this. I noticed an ice cream parlor near here. Would you like to have an ice cream treat?"

"Yeah," she said. "That would be great." She drove them to Silver Town's Sweet Dreams, a new ice cream shop. It was decorated as a 1950s ice cream parlor, and everyone loved the new addition to the town.

"A root beer float for me," Roxie ordered.

"I'll get a toffee and chocolate-chip hot fudge sundae." Dylan brought out his credit card.

"You know we'll have to run as wolves after this,"

she said. "We've eaten so much, and I'd love to stretch my legs—running as a wolf this time. But do you think you'll be okay if we do it?"

"Yeah, I was fine last night, and like you, I wouldn't mind working off some of the extra calories we're having," he said, paying for their ice cream. Then they sat down at one of the tables and began eating their delightful desserts. "You can shift again, right?"

"I sure can. I'm good now."

"Good. Then that's just what we'll do." He offered her a bite of his toffee and chocolate-chip ice cream topped with hot fudge and whipped cream.

She smiled, thinking how cute he was to share his treat with her, and ate it. "Ohmigosh, that is really good." She'd never thought of combining toffee ice cream with chocolate. Then she held out her root beer float. "Want a sip?"

He chuckled. "Yeah." He took a swig. "Now that is really good."

"Yeah, everything they make here is."

They caught a few wolf-pack members' eyes, and they smiled. The word would spread through the pack for sure.

As soon as they finished their treats, they returned to Roxie's house. "Why don't you move your truck into my garage and then we can run as wolves. Do you want to run with the family or just the two of us this time?"

"I'd like to run with just you this time, if that's all right with you."

"Yeah, it sure is." She always ran with some members of her family, so this was different for her. But she was going to enjoy this time with him. Once he was gone, she would be just running with the family again. She had to admit she liked that they could just strip and shift, then run. They didn't have to wait to get the kids ready as wolves.

"I'll be right back." Dylan took off to get his truck, and it wasn't much longer until he was parking in her garage and joining her in the house.

Then she saw Luke's bag by the dining room chair where he'd been seated for dinner.

Dylan glanced in the direction she was looking and laughed. "Looks like Luke will be back."

"Do you think he left it on purpose?" Roxie pulled off her jacket.

"Maybe, or the triplets distracted him and he forgot about it."

"He'll have to come for it tomorrow. We're not waiting around for him tonight to return for it," she said.

"Yeah, right. I wish he had a working phone and we could text him."

"I'll text Lelandi and let her know we're going running as wolves and he forgot his bag again."

"All right." Dylan continued to strip off his clothes.

She texted Lelandi and got a text back from her: I'll tell him. We're getting him a new phone tomorrow.

Roxie texted: Great! He needs one. We're off to run as wolves.

Lelandi: Enjoy!

Then she put her phone on the table and hurried to finish stripping really quickly while Dylan shifted and headed to the door. She soon joined him, and the two of them took off on their wolf run.

She really wanted to check out the area where Luke's tent had been, but she thought that Dylan should have another night of rest first. If he was feeling better in the morning, they could run as wolves before dawn and check it out.

For now? She was just having a fun run with the hot wolf. Running with him as a couple was glorious.

Chapter 10

EARLY THE NEXT MORNING, ROXIE RUSHED TO dress and make breakfast so she and Dylan could go on a wolf run and check out the area around the crime scene again.

Finally waking, Dylan came down the stairs to have breakfast with her. "Good morning. You should have woken me up."

"Good morning, Dylan. I figured you needed the sleep. How are you feeling?" She quickly served up breakfast burritos of fried potatoes, ham, eggs, bell peppers, and onions wrapped in a tortilla.

"I'm feeling great. Are you needed at the lodge really early this morning?" Dylan asked, frowning.

"No. We're going for a wolf run. I want to do it when it's still dark out. But only if you're okay."

"I am." He hurried to make cups of coffee for them.

"We're going to check out the crime scene."

He looked at her, surprised.

"Yep. We're going to run there as wolves."

He smiled, looking as eager to run as a wolf to check things out as she was.

They sat down to eat, and he licked his lips. "Man, these are really good. When did you get up?"

"Probably about half an hour before you did. I just had to get us going so we could get on our way if we're going to run as wolves."

They finished breakfast and set the plates in the dishwasher. "We'll just let the frying pans soak while we run, and I'll clean them when we get back."

"I'll do them."

She loved how he was always in there cleaning the kitchen when they had meals.

Then they began stripping out of their clothes in the living room and she felt the heat fill her blood and her muscles until the shift occurred. As wolves, they raced outside. She loved to run and have fun, but she really wanted to check out where the murder had taken place again and where Luke's tent was located, just in case there was anything there that they had missed. When she steered Dylan that way, he was right with her, and she knew he wanted to do this too.

———

Dylan wasn't entirely surprised that Roxie wanted to check out the crime scene again since she really hadn't looked it over that well the last time. He was glad she wanted to because he definitely wanted to. Her wolf's curiosity and also the need to stop those from doing harm to fellow pack members most likely had all to do with it.

They finally reached the crime scene where Eddie had been buried. They sniffed around the area, looking for any other evidence as to what had happened. They dug at the snow but didn't see anything. Then they took off to check the area where Luke's tent had been, and when they reached the location, they could smell food. Both of them looked up, and sure enough, a bag was hanging way up between two trees to keep the food away from cougars, raccoons, or bears, if any had been woken from their long winter nap. Because of the concern about finding the teen and the hunters at the time, no one must have noticed it.

They looked at each other. They'd have to come back some other time when they were in their human form. There wasn't any rush to get the food, but Luke would probably like to have his food bag back. They saw another bag tied up in another tree, but Dylan wasn't sure what that was for. They'd have to come back for that too.

He was kind of surprised the hunters hadn't taken Luke's ID from his tent before the wolves found it. If the hunters had planned to get rid of a witness to the killing of their friend, they would have done better getting rid of his ID. Dylan suspected they'd been in too much of a hurry to catch up to Luke, not knowing that he was running as a wolf.

Dylan nudged Roxie to let her know he was

ready to continue their search, and they started to move, trying to find the men's scents again. Though tracking footsteps was no longer possible because of all the snow, they could still smell the scents of all the people who had been out here looking for the hunters, the hunters themselves, and Luke.

They smelled where Luke had run to a cave at some point, but the hunters had never found it. But Dylan did smell the scent of the trapper too. He must have visited the cave. Hopefully he didn't put any traps down nearby. Dylan shifted. "Watch for traps. I smell the scent of the trapper here."

She woofed in agreement and then he shifted back.

Roxie and Dylan didn't find anything in the cave that indicated Luke had lived there for any time. Just his scent.

They discovered where Xander and Fennel had split off from Jim, but then a couple of miles after that, Fennel and Xander became separated. The question was—was it on purpose or accidentally? By then it could have been snowing heavily. They followed Xander's scent until they reached a frozen stream… Well, at least it was frozen on top. They could see water flowing under small sections of broken ice. It appeared someone had stepped on the snow on top of the frozen stream and his large boots had gone through the ice.

Dylan smelled Xander's scent there. He woofed

at Roxie, asking if she wanted to go farther, and she nodded. They headed across the stream. The wolves were light enough, and their weight spread out more so they didn't break through the ice and continued on their way. They walked for about three miles and kept smelling whiffs of Xander's scent on the chilly breeze. Had Jim not come back for Xander? Had he left him here to fend for himself? Had he picked up Fennel? Maybe Jim hadn't been able to find the other two men.

Dylan didn't smell any sign of Jim or Fennel in this direction. Dylan and Roxie continued to follow Xander's scent and ended up going in a wide circle. Dylan looked at Roxie. She woofed, telling Dylan that was what she'd smelled too.

They went in a wider circle to locate Xander's scent again, figuring he'd gotten lost and circled around and ended up back here where he had started. If Xander was unfamiliar with his surroundings, it would be easy for him to get lost, unless he had a compass to keep him on track.

Xander had hiked deeper into the woods, not headed toward any roads, small or otherwise. When Dylan and Roxie came to a river, they lost track of Xander's scent completely. They stared at the river, still flowing except for the ice on its banks, and they could hear the water flowing underneath that. They looked at the bank on the other side. They couldn't tell if Xander had crossed the river and ended up on the other side. Too much snow had fallen and hid any tracks. Because of the direction the wind was blowing, they'd have to be over there to actually smell his scent. But Dylan wasn't sure about taking Roxie over there. The river was so cold and moving so swiftly, he wasn't sure Xander could have made it himself. An experienced team of searchers would have to check it out via another path, and he'd want to be with them when they did.

He nudged at Roxie to indicate he wanted to leave, and she licked his face. But ignoring his plan to leave the river behind, she stepped into the water at the edge of the river. He assumed then that she wanted to continue the search. In a way he did too. But he worried about her swimming across the river. If he'd been on his own and hadn't been injured so recently, he wouldn't have hesitated to continue looking for the hunter. He did worry about Xander, despite hating what he did while he was hunting. What if the hunter was injured, suffering from hypothermia, lost, dying, or dead?

Roxie glanced back at Dylan, but before he could tell her again that they should return, she ran into the river until she was deep enough to swim and began paddling. Dylan tore into the water and hurried to catch up to her. He liked a woman who could quickly make up her mind and stick to the plan even if he had reservations about it.

Pulled by the strong current, they were being

carried downriver. They continued to make their way across the cold river, their wolf coats keeping them warm enough. If they were in the water way too long, they could get hypothermic.

Then they were finally making progress to the shore, reached it, and climbed out. They shook off the excess water clinging to their fur and began searching for any sign of Xander's scent in the breeze again.

Now that they were on the opposite bank, safe from the hazards of swimming across the river, he hoped they didn't run into Xander holding a rifle with them in his sights. They kept moving until they finally picked up his scent. They ran for about a half hour, Dylan thought, when they found the scent had stopped. They searched the area and discovered a small cave and Xander's scent on the outside. Dylan needed to venture inside to learn if Xander was in there. He nipped at Roxie, wanting her to stay outside the cave in case Xander was in there and ready to shoot anything that moved into the cave entrance.

She growled back and he knew she wanted to go with him. But he didn't want her to get shot. Dylan and Roxie were in their wolf forms, and he wouldn't blame Xander if, in this instance, he saw them and thought he had to defend himself and shot at them.

Roxie looked ready for action, tense, her tail held still, her ears perked and listening to any sounds she might hear of anyone or anything in there. That was the other thing. Dylan didn't want to disturb a bear if one should be hibernating or a cougar if one should be staying in there. He didn't smell anything else, so he moved slowly into the cave. It was bigger than it appeared from the outside. Deeper in the recesses of the cave, he smelled Xander's scent. And a bear's. But the bear's scent smelled like it was last season's. Xander's was recent. Then Dylan saw a body in a sleeping bag. Not stirring.

Dylan moved closer and heard Xander's slowed heartbeat and knew then the man was alive. Dylan also knew blood vessels and arteries would narrow in colder weather, reducing blood flow to the heart, which could mean Xander could suffer a heart attack. If he was hypothermic, he could be in serious trouble. Dylan was also worried about the hunter's rifle and any other guns Xander might be armed with if he disturbed him to see if he was okay.

Dylan found Xander's rifle and picked it up in his teeth. Then he carried it out of the cave, dropped it in the snow, and shifted. "He's in there," Dylan whispered to Roxie. "He might be hypothermic, but I was afraid to get too close to check on him when his rifle was with him in the cave. He might have other weapons too." He shifted back into his wolf coat to stay warm.

She shifted. "Then we howl and if he comes out

or stirs in there and makes any noise, we'll know he's all right. We'll tear out of here and keep running until we're far enough away and howl for help." Then she shifted back into her wolf.

Dylan woofed at her in agreement. He hoped Xander didn't have any other guns packed away in the cave. He and she howled. He thought maybe someone might hear them. Some of their own kind would come to investigate, but it could take way too long, and he didn't believe Xander had the time to wait it out.

They watched the cave entrance but didn't hear anyone rustling around inside. Either Xander was sleeping like the dead, or he was close to being dead.

Dylan went back inside and discovered Xander hadn't moved. That wasn't a good sign. He wasn't playing possum, Dylan didn't think. He shifted and rushed over to check on Xander, hoping he didn't have a gun tucked in his sleeping bag with him.

A shadow moved in behind Dylan and he turned to see Roxie filling the entryway of the cave in her wolf form. He sighed deeply and hurried over to the man and turned him over. He found he was practically dead. Ah, hell. Dylan wanted him in jail or fined, not dead.

Dylan said, "He's barely alive."

Roxie shifted. "Okay, so we start a fire for him and one of us can lie with him and warm him." Then she shifted back into her wolf. She moved into the cave to lie next to Xander like Rosco had done with Dylan after she'd pulled him from the swimming pool and he had been hypothermic.

Dylan went through some of Xander's bags and found some clothes, two handguns, an ax, a lighter, a canteen, and other camping items. As much as he didn't want to wear Xander's clothes that smelled of him, Dylan had to put them on if he was going to get a fire started and save the hunter's life. After pulling on Xander's spare camo pants and a sweatshirt, socks, and boots, Dylan slipped on Xander's parka and was about to push his foot into one of the boots but felt something move inside it. Not an animal, but something else. He poured it out and found it was Xander's cell phone. "Hot damn. I'll call this in, then I'll get some firewood." He finished putting on Xander's boots, then he left the cave to get a signal and called Peter, the phone nearly dead. "Hey, we found Xander. I'm calling from his cell phone." He explained that he was in bad shape, suffering from severe hyperthermia. He gave Peter the coordinates for their location. "We'll do the best we can to warm him up, but he needs medical attention right away."

"We're on our way," Peter said.

The phone died. At least Peter knew the situation and where they were so he and others could come to help as soon as they could.

As remote as it was out here, Dylan was glad the wolves knew the territory, unlike he did. He was certain Roxie would also be familiar with the area. Though she hadn't been from here originally, so maybe not.

"I'll be right back with some firewood," Dylan said to Roxie. He grabbed the hunting ax and hurried out of the cave to return to a fallen tree they'd passed in the woods nearby. The dead branches would be perfect for making a fire. He chopped away at it, glad Xander had an ax in his camping gear so Dylan could make short work of this.

After Dylan had gathered what he thought would be a good start, he carried the armload of firewood to the cave. "I'm going to build the fire next to the entrance of the cave so we can ventilate the smoke," he told Roxie. He used the lighter to start the fire, and it caught hold. He headed back into the cave so he could check on both Roxie and Xander.

Xander appeared to be warming up some, thanks to Roxie's wolf body heat. Dylan dug around in Xander's things again and found a Beretta 92 pistol. "I'm going to chop up some more wood for the fire and put this somewhere for safekeeping. I'll be right back."

Roxie nodded. Then he hurried off to get this done. He didn't want Xander coming to and having a heart attack because a wolf was resting next to him. As Dylan headed outside and put the gun on a ledge next to the entrance of the cave, his next thought was about Fennel. What if Fennel had been caught out in these freezing temperatures, hadn't found a cave like Xander had, and hadn't survived? What if Jim had stranded the two men on purpose for just that reason? If his friends died, there would be no witnesses to testify against him to say he had killed Eddie. But Luke would still be a loose end. Well, and Dylan because Jim had tried to kill him, most likely because Jim thought *he* had also witnessed the murder. Maybe Jim thought that was why Dylan was tracking him in the first place. To arrest him for the murder, not for killing the elk.

Dylan trudged through the snow again and finally reached the fallen tree and chopped away at it until he had some large chunks of wood to keep the fire going for a while.

Then he returned to the cave and put the wood on the fire. He hoped Peter and the others wouldn't take too long to get there.

"I'm going to move Xander closer to the fire and pile everything he has got on top of him. It appears when he got hypothermia, he began peeling off some of his clothes." Dylan dragged Xander in his sleeping bag over to the fire. Then Dylan pulled out every bit of clothing from Xander's backpack and layered them on top of him. While Xander's face and front of his body were facing the fire, Roxie instinctively stretched out to lie against his back to warm his backside as a wolf.

Dylan warmed up some water from Xander's canteen and tried to get Xander to drink some of it as he began to revive. "Who...hell," Xander croaked out between parched lips when he saw it was Dylan.

"Yeah, it's me," Dylan said, smiling a little. "I found the elk you and your friends killed. And your buddy Eddie."

Xander's eyes widened.

"I guess you thought you'd be gone well before his body was discovered. You almost joined him in death, by the way."

Xander must have felt the warmth at his back and tried to look over his shoulder to see what it was from.

"That's Roxie, my new search-and-rescue wolf dog. She has worked with police before and knows how to take suspects down. You're lucky she was with me, or we wouldn't have located you until it was too late. You were on death's door," Dylan said. He still could be. Dylan read him his rights, just in case Xander started to confess to what had happened.

Xander drank some more of the water from the metal cup, then lay back down and closed his eyes. "What now?" He stuttered the raspy words because he was so cold and weary.

"The sheriff, his men, and the EMTs are on their way, but it's a bit of a trek out here. When we were tracking you, it looked like you got yourself turned around a few times." Dylan was glad Xander hadn't seemed to notice he was wearing some of his spare clothes. At least if Xander did, he didn't say anything about it. How would Dylan have explained that?

Xander grunted.

"I don't blame you really. You're not from around here. If I hadn't had an excellent scenting dog with me following the circles you made, I would never have found you." Dylan also had the excellent scenting capabilities, but it truly was because of Roxie that he'd kept going with the search. "So what happened exactly when Eddie was shot?"

Xander didn't say a word. Not that Dylan expected him to confess. He had always lawyered up before, and this was an even more serious offense.

An hour later, which seemed like forever, some of the men from the sheriff's department and the EMTs arrived on snowmobiles. The EMTs checked Xander over and told him that Dylan and Roxie had saved his life. Then they put Xander on a sled and drove off. CJ Silver and Trevor Osgood followed the EMTs on snowmobiles as deputy sheriffs in charge of security.

Dylan left the cave and returned with Xander's

rifle and pistol while Peter and Jake searched through Xander's belongings. "We're taking all his things with us as evidence," Peter said.

"I'm wearing some of his clothes," Dylan said.

"We gathered that you wouldn't have been here as a human while Roxie was a wolf since you had been using Xander's cell phone, not your own. Not to mention we smell his scent on the clothes and they look too small on you," Jake said. "Roxie, we called your family to tell them that you and Dylan had been searching for one of the hunters and to let them know you and Dylan were both safe. Do you want to ride back with us?"

"Yeah, we do." Dylan wanted to search for Fennel's scent, but he and Roxie had spent hours out here already, and his head was hurting again. He knew they both needed to get warm and take a break.

Peter put out the fire and helped Jake gather the rest of the evidence, while Dylan pulled off Xander's clothes and shifted. Jake took those clothes and put them on the sled.

Together, Roxie and Dylan jumped on the sled tied to Jake's snowmobile, and they headed back to the lodge. They took a logging road that led them to a bridge that crossed over the river, so no getting wet this time. Dylan curled up with Roxie and nuzzled her face. Two bad guys found—though the one was now a victim—one teen rescued, and two more bad guys to go. Well, three because they had to find the trapper too. Not too bad on this mission so far.

When Jake parked the snowmobile at Roxie's home, he cut the engine and said to them, "Our forensics specialists will be looking for blood on all of Xander's clothes."

This worried Dylan because what if they discovered Eddie's blood on the clothes Dylan had borrowed and found Dylan's DNA on the clothes too? The hunters could make up a story that Dylan had stolen Xander's clothes, pretending to be him, so angry that these men continued to break laws and get away with it that he killed Eddie in a fit of rage.

Roxie leapt from the sled before anyone else could make a move and raced through the wolf door, opened the door, and peeked out. "Come inside. We all need to talk." She closed the door, and they gave her a moment, figuring she was busy dressing.

Then she opened the door and Dylan and Jake joined her inside and locked the door. She walked into the kitchen. "Hot cocoa for everyone?"

"Yeah, thanks," they both said while Dylan dressed in the living room.

"So what do we do about this, Jake?" she asked as she made them mugs of double chocolate cocoa.

Dylan noticed Roxie's bra, panties, and socks near the coffee table and figured she'd dressed in a hurry to let them in. He tucked her undergarments under a couch cushion, hoping he wouldn't forget he'd hidden them there.

"Hopefully, there's no blood spatter on the clothes Dylan was wearing, because if there was and Dylan's DNA is now on his clothes, we couldn't turn it over for evidence. In any event, you didn't have a choice if you were to save Xander's life. Once Xander is stabilized at the clinic, Peter will question him. You're welcome to join him, Dylan, since technically this was your case in the beginning. Were you able to ask him anything at all?"

"No, I just told him I found the elk they killed and then we found Eddie's body. He looked surprised to hear it," Dylan said. "And I read him his rights."

Roxie brought mugs of hot cocoa into the living room and then she turned on the mantel lights.

Dylan started a fire in the fireplace, thinking how nice it was with Roxie like this after finding Xander alive and keeping him that way. Normally, Dylan would have gone home to an empty house, no decorations at all. Sure, he'd start a fire, but other than that, it was just...empty. He'd thought he liked it that way until he met Roxie. "I was afraid Xander was going to have a heart attack upon hearing the news. In retrospect, I shouldn't have mentioned it, but I had hoped he would tell us what happened. At least his version, made-up or otherwise."

They took a seat on the couches.

"A part of me wanted to see if we could find out where Fennel had gone and if we could learn anything about Jim or Eddie. Maybe because of his hypothermic condition, Xander wasn't talking." Dylan took a sip of the cocoa. "Wow, this is good."

"Everything's better with double the chocolate," Roxie said.

"Boy, that's for sure." Then Dylan started talking about Xander again. "I suspect Xander will lawyer up once he has recovered more. They always do. Since this time Fennel and he are accessories to murder, the incentive to get off scot-free will be even greater. But yeah, as soon as Xander has recovered enough, I want to go with Peter while he speaks with him."

"Too bad he didn't say if he knew where Fennel was. Well, I'll let the two of you get washed and warmed up. Peter will let you know when he's going to the clinic," Jake said, then finished his cup. "Thanks for the cocoa."

"You're welcome. Is anyone going to guard Xander's room?" Roxie asked.

"Yeah, we're all pulling shifts for a couple of hours to make sure he doesn't try to leave and no one tries to get to him," Jake said. "Oh, and Doc said that when he put you on medical leave, that didn't mean you were supposed to be taking long wolf runs in search of lawbreakers, Dylan."

"Uh, yeah, about that. Roxie and I were just going to stretch our legs as wolves, and we smelled Xander's scent and had to follow it." He figured that might come back to bite him.

"Uh-huh, that was what I told Doc. He didn't believe it for a minute. But by now he's getting used to working with wolves. Dr. Summerfield and his pediatrician wife, Adelaide, had worked with humans before. So as wolf shifters, they're thrilled to be here, but it's been a new experience for them."

"Because of our enhanced healing abilities," Dylan guessed.

"Exactly. And our stubbornness to keep working when we should be resting."

"Well, I'll try not to let it happen again," Dylan said, though he really wanted to continue searching for Fennel, if he was still out in this weather.

"I know what you're thinking, but we've got more search parties out looking for Fennel."

"That's good. I guess that means no helping out to guard Xander's room then," Dylan said, just throwing the notion out there.

"Right. If someone attacked you and knocked you out, no telling what could happen to you the next time," Jake said.

Dylan reluctantly agreed.

"Oh, we nearly forgot. We need to have someone pick up Luke's stuff hanging in the trees where his tent was located before he decides to go back for them, worried someone might take them. One was a food bag and not sure what the other bag was for. He shouldn't be out on his own until we catch these men," Roxie said.

"I agree. I'll take care of it. Does Luke know they're still out there?" Jake asked.

"I don't know... We'll call him and tell him that you're having someone pick the bags up so if he remembers them, he doesn't try to go out by himself or with the other kids," Roxie said.

"Good idea. Darien texted everyone in the pack with Luke's new phone number as a way for him and them to reach out to each other. I'm going to get on this then."

"All right, thanks," Roxie said.

Roxie and Dylan walked Jake to the door and said goodbye. Once they shut the door, she said to Dylan, "Do you want to call Luke now and tell him that Jake's taking care of his camping bags?"

"Yeah, I'll get right on it." Dylan called him then and explained everything while Roxie put their cocoa mugs in the dishwasher.

Then she started to scrub the pans from breakfast.

"Okay, good show. Jake's on it," Dylan said to Luke, and then they ended the call. He took over cleaning the pans, and she got a call from her brother Landon.

She put the call on speakerphone. "Hey, Landon.

I'm sorry I didn't call you. We'd just planned a short wolf run, and then I would have been in to work, but we got sidetracked."

"It's not about work. We were worried about you. You were gone for five hours out there. We couldn't get hold of you, so Kayla dropped by your house—but you and Dylan had left your phones and your clothes behind so we knew you went for a wolf run. Since we expected you at work, naturally we were concerned when you didn't show up. Peter sent some of his men with Blake, and they searched your scents for a couple of hours, reached the river, and lost your scents. They thought you had back-tracked and gone home. But when you called Peter with the dying phone, he let us know where you were and that you were safe."

"I should have called you. But everyone was asleep still when we went out running. I'm so sorry," Roxie said.

Landon sighed. "Hell, we learned you swam across the river."

"Yes, and we saved Xander's life."

"Right. But wake us and tell us if you're going out like that."

"You'd still send a search party out on us."

"Yeah, of course. What are big brothers for?"

She smiled. "Okay, I'll wake one of you to tell you whenever I'm going to run with Dylan on my own."

"Is he a bad influence?"

"No, he's not a bad influence. It was my idea."

Landon laughed. "Why am I not surprised."

Dylan smiled at Roxie.

"I'll be in after lunch."

"All right."

Then they said goodbye. "I can't believe we were out there for a whole five hours. Everyone was upset with us for taking off and not letting them know where we'd be."

"You told him you were the bad influence, not me." He put the pans he'd cleaned on the drying pad. "If it wasn't for me getting involved with these guys, you wouldn't have done this."

She shrugged. "I didn't want you to take all the credit for finding Xander."

Dylan chuckled.

"Let's get cleaned up and then we can have some lunch. I agree with Jake. You shouldn't be pulling guard duty. What were you thinking?"

Dylan just smiled at her. He hadn't had anyone really care about his welfare in years, and he really liked that everyone did here in Silver Town.

"I'm not looking forward to going in to work," she said, heading up the stairs.

"Your siblings are all going to give you grief for worrying them."

"Yep. Every last one of them."

Chapter 11

ROXIE COULDN'T BELIEVE THEY'D MANAGED TO locate Xander and was so relieved they had. Just like when they'd found Luke and he was okay. If they could have found Fennel too, that would have been even better. But she was sorry she'd worried her family so. When she looked at her phone, she realized everyone had called and texted her, looking for her and Dylan.

She and Dylan headed up the stairs, but he suddenly turned and went back to the living room. She wondered what was up and watched him. Then she saw him pull something out from under a couch cushion. He hurried to rejoin her on the stairs and handed her underwear to her.

She laughed and took them from him and continued upstairs.

"I put them away so they weren't lying on the floor in full view for everyone to see," he said.

"Thank you. I'd forgotten about them. I was trying to rush to put on my pants and sweater so I could make sure Jake stayed to tell us what was going to happen. I'm grateful you tucked them away."

"I didn't relish shifting in the snow to talk anymore so I was happy you told Jake to come inside to talk," Dylan said.

"What was in Luke's other bag? Did he tell you?" she asked, taking hold of Dylan's hand and walking him to her bedroom.

"Yeah, his deodorant, toothpaste, toothbrush, and shaving kit, just in case any wild animal got wind of it and wanted to tear into the bag. He said he lost his toiletry kit on a camping trip one time because he'd left it in his tent when he went hiking with his parents. He wasn't about to make that mistake again. He said the bear had bitten into his tube of toothpaste and chewed on his toothbrush."

"Eww."

"Yeah, that's what I thought. Hey, I'm sorry I got you in trouble with your family. This is my case, and I take full responsibility. I should have thought about them worrying about you when you didn't show up for work. I'm so used to doing these jobs on my own that I didn't think of that."

"No way. I insisted we cross the river to find Xander. Let's get a shower."

———

Shower together? If that was what Roxie had in mind, things were really looking up between them, and Dylan was all for it.

"The first time we were in water together, the water was warm, but you weren't dressed right for it." She began pulling off her sweater in the bathroom.

"The swimming pool?" He slipped his sweater over his head. "Yeah, a parka and boots were a little much for the pool. I'll have to go swimming with you when I'm not wearing so much." He pulled off his shirt and dropped it on their sweaters.

"I'll hold you to it. Do you have a bathing suit?" She pulled off her pants.

He chuckled. "No. That's something I didn't think to bring with me on this mission."

"There's a shop that has everything you might need for a vacation in Silver Town." She tackled his belt. "The second time we were in the water together—"

"It was cold, and we were both wolves." He ditched the rest of his clothes.

"This time," she said, climbing naked into the shower and pulling him in with her, "is perfect. No clothes, hot water...yeah."

She had a nice big walk-in shower, and they had lots of room to clean up without running into each other. She even had an overhead sprayer and a separate sprayer, but she pulled him into her arms and began to kiss him under the spray of hot water, telling him in no uncertain terms that this was what she wanted, that she needed the closeness between them. Now this was really nice as he began to kiss her back. He pushed a wet straggle of hair off her cheek, and her eyes heated with passion, their gazes colliding in that moment. She gave him a mischievous smile that confirmed what he believed. She wanted to take this a little further.

As wolves, they couldn't have consummated sex or they would be mated wolves—for life. Normally, he would have been more cautious about going even this far with any she-wolf he had just met that he wasn't asking to mate. But Roxie compelled him to delve into this more. To kiss her and caress her. To see her naked in his arms, soft, sumptuous, curvy, beautiful. To taste her sweet lips, her tongue, her skin. To listen to her heart and his thumping wildly and hear her soft sigh. To breathe in her excited and sexy scent, telling him she was eager to take this all the way, if they had been ready for it. To feel the wolf touching him in return, her fingers gliding over his biceps, whisper-soft, her tongue teasing his, her breasts pressing against his chest.

She felt wondrous against his body, like she was meant to be there with him, holding each other close, tongues gliding over each other's. Her gaze softened, her eyes closing as she appeared as lost in the kiss as he was. He had no control over his burgeoning erection that pressed against her, eager to fill her to the brink, throbbing with need. He was trying to let her set the pace, to see how far she wanted to take this—just get sudsy and rinse off, kiss and caress and hug, or more.

That was when she swept her hands down to his hips, pressed him hard against her, and rubbed a little, making his arousal jump. If she rubbed him any more, he was going to come.

He figured he'd go for the gold, but if she indicated in any way that she didn't have that in mind, he'd stop. As soon as he slid his hand over one of her breasts and kissed the other, she seemed just as willing to keep going. He moved his hand lower, caressing her hip, and then worked his way to her mons. She spread her legs a little. Yeah, she was all for it, and he was glad he hadn't misread what she wanted to do. He wrapped his arm around her back to give her support and began to stroke her clit as she melted to his caresses.

She began to cling to him, her soft sighs morphing into breathy moans. He was so wrapped up in kissing her luscious lips that he didn't feel her tensing at first. Then she tightened her hold on him and clued him in that she was about to come. He pressed his finger between her feminine folds to moisten it, and she came with a cry that was guttural and filled with passion.

For a moment, she held on to him as if she couldn't stand without his support. And then she took a deep breath and let it out, the hot water sluicing down their skin in a waterfall of warmth.

Her eyes met his and she smiled. She slid her hand down to his erection, her mouth curving up even more. Then in sync, she began to stroke his arousal, and he was kissing her mouth, his hands cupping her face.

But the end was near, just from smelling her musky scent and her pheromones, hearing her come, feeling her body against his as if it were meant to be. All he could think of was wanting to enter her in the worst way, when he knew he shouldn't even be thinking of that! Not this early in the game. Especially when he didn't even work in the Silver Town area. And yet thoughts kept flashing through his mind of how—if he were to find a mate—she would be just like Roxie.

He groaned as she stroked him, her tongue pressing into his mouth with exuberance, and he met her tongue with his with just as much enthusiasm.

She continued stroking him. He felt the sweet pain of needed release and the pleasure of knowing he was just on the verge of…coming. He cried out, swearing that he had to have more time with her, to feel this again with her, to keep on going.

Then the water started to chill a bit, and they laughed and hurried to wash off the rest of the way, turn off the shower, and hop out to dry off.

After they dressed, they went to the kitchen, and Roxie began frying chicken wings, boiling noodles, adding a garlic herb sauce, and boiling some spinach, loving how willing Dylan was to take her up on sexy ventures.

"Do you still want to go to see Xander with Peter when he's able to be seen? I saw you take your medicine for the headache." Roxie served up their chicken wings on a platter while Dylan ladled out the noodles. She brought glasses of water to the table, and they sat down to eat.

"Why not? Oh, because Doc might read me the riot act?" He smiled.

"Exactly." Roxie took a bite of her chicken wing.

"Yeah. I'm just having a slight headache is all."

"Right. You way overexerted yourself today. I don't think your boss would approve. What if Doc puts you on bed rest?" She arched a brow.

Dylan laughed.

She smiled. "You laugh, but Dr. Summerfield takes the care of his patients to heart and doesn't want them to end up back at the clinic because of overdoing things."

Dylan chuckled. "I really like him. Lunch is delicious, by the way."

"Thanks. Chicken wings are one of our favorite family meals so I thought you might enjoy them after our harrowing experience."

"Yeah, it really hits the spot. You know"—he

paused and took a sip of his water—"I was worried about us crossing the river."

"Oh, I'm so sorry about that. I thought you were concerned I couldn't do it, but you must have been worried that you might have trouble because of your recent head injury."

"Right."

But she knew he had been more concerned about her, and she appreciated it, really. She'd been worried about the hunter's health and welfare and didn't want to go so far out of their way to reach the logging road and bridge to cross it and then have to backtrack all along the river until they found Xander's scent again. She also had the notion that Dylan worried she couldn't make it across the river, and she had to prove to him she could if the situation called for it—which she felt it did. She did feel bad that she hadn't considered Dylan's recent injury before she had gone into the river. She knew he would have swum after her no matter what to make sure she stayed safe. But she also felt bad that she had worried her family needlessly.

They finished their meal and then Dylan got a call. "Yeah, Peter." He glanced at Roxie. "Sure. I'm on my way." He ended the call with Peter. "Peter said Xander is awake."

"Okay, I'll clean up here, and I'm going to run over to the lodge and see what I can do to help."

"I'll meet you over there in a little while."

"All right."

Their eyes met and they shared small smiles. Then they kissed sweetly at first, softly, but the kiss morphed slowly into something much more passionate. She realized just how much she loved kissing him, and he seemed to love kissing her back. He parted his lips for her, and she took advantage of the opening and stroked his tongue, prolonging the pleasure.

Then they took a deep breath and pressed their heads together. She smiled. "I'll see you soon."

"Absolutely."

"Good luck with the interrogation."

"Good luck with the lodge activities."

Dylan drove over to the clinic in his truck, looking eager to finally learn something about the case. She didn't blame him. She wanted to know too. Everyone in Silver Town did.

Roxie hurried to clean up their dishes and started corned beef, potatoes, cabbage, and carrots in the slow cooker for dinner tonight and then headed over to the lodge. Once she was in the lobby, she saw a couple of drunks yelling at Minx in the bar and grill. Roxie immediately called CJ, since she knew Peter was busy with Xander, and hurried into the restaurant to deal with the unruly customers.

As soon as Dylan arrived at the clinic, Carmela, the office manager, waved him back to the room.

He stalked off and found Trevor guarding the door. "Peter's in there waiting for you."

"Thanks." Dylan walked in, hoping that he was going to get some answers too.

Peter was standing over Xander's bed, showing he was the alpha and wanted the truth. Dylan took a seat nearby, showing he was a bystander and not in charge of the investigation unless Peter handed the questioning over to him.

Peter read Xander his rights, then said, "So tell us what happened."

"I was hiking, and I got lost."

Convenient lie, Dylan thought, but he didn't say anything as Peter wrote some notes on a small pad of paper.

"What about Jim and Fennel? They left you on your own to die of hypothermia in the snow?" Peter asked.

Xander looked at his bandaged hands clasped together on top of his stomach covered in a white blanket.

"Okay, so the four of you went hunting, killed an elk, and then what happened?" Peter asked.

Xander looked over at Dylan. He focused his gaze back on Peter and shrugged.

Peter let his breath out in a huff. "You know, Jim drove off in Eddie's SUV. He left you and Fennel behind. Did he do it because you were a witness to Eddie's murder? Did he wager on Fennel and you never making it home alive—thereby eliminating a couple of witnesses who knew what he'd done?"

Xander looked at his hands again.

"I take it you didn't agree with what he'd done," Peter said, but Xander didn't answer him. "We haven't found Fennel yet. Is there anything you can tell us to help us locate him and, if he's in bad shape, that we can use to save his life?"

Xander didn't say anything.

"Okay, so you're indicating Fennel's not that great of a friend," Peter said.

"Use your wolf dog to locate him," Xander said, glancing at Dylan, challenging him to the task.

Peter smiled a little, but then his demeanor turned serious again. "We have search dogs with us, and we have search parties going in shifts to try and locate Fennel. But Fennel might not be lucky enough to find a cave and hunker down like you did before we can locate him. If he is out there, he might have already succumbed to the cold."

"I don't have a clue. We fought and we went our separate ways, and then we were caught up in the snowstorm. I was trying to find a place to get out of the snow and ended up blindly walking into the river. The currents took me downstream, and I had to reach the opposite bank. That's why I was so cold. If I hadn't had to swim in the river, I wouldn't have been so bad off. I stumbled upon the cave and was grateful there wasn't anything sleeping in there during the storm. I changed out of my wet clothes and put dry ones on and then got into my sleeping bag and tried to get warm. But I was freezing and I couldn't warm up. I needed a fire, but I couldn't leave the cave or chance losing my way back to it."

So the clothes Dylan had borrowed could have been worn by Xander when Jim killed Eddie and then any evidence washed off in the river. Peter glanced at Dylan as if saying he thought the same thing. He nodded.

"Okay, so what was the fight about between you and Fennel?" Peter asked.

"I don't remember."

"Convenient," Dylan said. "Was Fennel upset about Jim killing Eddie, and you told him to suck it up?" So much for leaving this up to Peter to ask all the questions. Dylan couldn't help himself when it came to wanting to know all the answers. Besides, Peter didn't seem to mind and had asked him to be there during the questioning, probably so he could bring up things that Peter didn't think of since Dylan knew so much more about the men than the sheriff did.

Xander frowned at him. "I don't know anything about Eddie's death. I didn't know he was dead until you told me."

"Ahh, okay. So why did you split up from Jim? Did

he tell you to look for the boy who had seen you, Fennel, and Jim at the crime scene?" Dylan asked.

"I didn't know about Eddie's death," Xander said again.

"All right, but you were in the boy's tent. You and Jim and Fennel. Then you were hotfooting it after the kid because you wanted to silence him—until Jim got the idea to split off from the two of you to get Eddie's SUV and the bags all of you had left in the ski lodge's rooms," Dylan said.

"Your wolf dog told you that?" Xander raised a brow.

Yeah, that was hard to explain.

"Who shot the elk?" Peter asked.

"I don't know. Not me. Not the guys. We just came across it and someone else had shot it."

Peter said, "You and your friends were illegally hunting with suspended hunting licenses. Who do you think will be found guilty of the charges?"

Xander waited a long time before he said anything. "I don't know anything except I was out hiking—"

"With a rifle that might have been used to kill an elk and a handgun you were carrying too. Since the gun's serial number had been removed, we've also got you on those charges. Accessory to murder? That too."

"Anyone could have shot Eddie. Another hunter even."

"Another hunter illegally hunting like the four of you?" Peter asked. "You didn't know if the boy had seen you all at the crime scene or not. But he did. We found him. He's in safe custody and he'll testify against all of you."

"I want to talk to my lawyer." Xander folded his arms on top of his chest and looked mutinous.

"Sure. One last time, I want to ask if you have any idea where Fennel might be? If you care about him surviving this," Peter said.

"I don't know. When we split up, he went the way he thought the road would be. I went the other way. We...we didn't agree about which way to go. Maybe he made it to the road when I sure as hell hadn't. Maybe Jim picked him up already, or maybe someone else did. I really don't know."

"All right," Peter said, sounding satisfied. He looked at Dylan. "Do you have anything more you want to ask or say?"

"No. I'm just glad we found you," Dylan said.

"Yeah, I agree," Peter said.

Then they left the room. Peter said to Trevor, "If he gives you any trouble, let me know."

"Sure thing, boss," Trevor said.

"I told Jake I'd help take some guard shifts while I'm here, but Peter said no to that," Dylan told Trevor.

Trevor smiled as he watched the doctor coming down the hall to speak with someone. "I bet."

"Guard duty?" Doc asked Peter, glancing at Dylan.

"Hey, Jake said no and so would I." Peter smiled.

"Good." Dr. Summerfield eyed Dylan for a moment and then said, "Come with me to an exam room."

"I'll meet you in the lobby," Peter said.

Which surprised Dylan. He figured Peter didn't really have any more to say to him about Xander. Maybe he wanted to know if the doc put him on more restrictions.

"Yeah, Doc," Dylan said, walking into the exam room. He was about to take a seat on a chair, but Dr. Summerfield motioned for him to sit on the exam table.

The doc listened to his breathing, shined a light in his eyes, listened to his heartbeat. "Okay, I know you feel the need to find these guys, and I totally understand that. But we have a lot of people here who are looking for them, and I don't want you injuring yourself to the extent that you could be permanently disabled."

"I agree."

"Okay, well, I have to say I admire you and Roxie for finding Xander. He wouldn't have survived much longer, and he's suffering from frostbite on his toes and fingers. It looks like I'll be amputating some, so he didn't get out of his situation completely unscathed."

"Hell."

"Yeah. I'll let you go talk to Peter. I hope we get this situation wrapped up soon," Doc said.

"Me too, and thanks, Doc." Dylan headed off to speak to Peter in the lobby.

"Did Doc give you hell?" Peter asked.

Dylan laughed. "Sorry that I started to talk to Xander while you were questioning him."

"No problem. You had been there from the beginning. You knew these men. I figured if I missed asking a question that might shed a light on something, you would think of it. We made a good team. So I was going to say that if you ever need a job here, I could hire you as one of my full-time deputies."

Dylan couldn't believe it. He had no idea the sheriff would be interested in hiring him to work for him.

"Yeah, after all that you've done and with your extensive criminal investigative background— don't think I didn't look into it already—we could use you here. If you ever decide you want to come down here and join the pack, you've got a job." Peter shook his hand and then headed out.

Dylan smiled at Peter. He really liked him. He was on the ball, already trying to steal him from the FWS to work for him.

At the receptionist desk, Carmela smiled. "You didn't expect that, did you?"

"Nope. I love it here."

"Yeah, it's a great place to live and to have a family."

"I can see that. Have a great day."

"You too," she said.

Dylan went outside and got into his truck feeling like he was walking on air. It wasn't often—make that never—that someone out of the blue offered him a job that could be right up his alley. He loved the business of going after people dealing in wild-life issues. But he also loved the idea of living with other wolves, socializing with them, helping them, like they'd been aiding him. And of course there was Roxie. He didn't think a long-distance relationship with her would work out. After this afternoon, hell yeah, he wanted to really get to know her better.

He drove to the lodge at the ski resort, telling himself he needed to think this over a bit more before he made a decision of that magnitude. But he was thinking that this could be just what he needed in his life.

Chapter 12

BLAKE AND LANDON WERE OFF TAKING CARE OF banquet room parties and didn't hear the commotion in the restaurant as Roxie tried to defuse the situation with the men. Four local wolves eating an early dinner nearby, all retired military and fit to take out any combatant, immediately rose from their table and headed toward Roxie and Minx to help them out.

"This is slop. I told you we shouldn't eat here. Gouging prices and meals not fit to consume," the one man said to his friend, loud enough for everyone in the whole restaurant to hear.

Which infuriated Roxie when she saw the two men had eaten everything but a couple of crumbs from their blue cheese triple-meat burgers. All the french fries on their plates were gone too. She knew a con when she saw one. "You ate the meals in their entirety. You didn't leave a scrap of food. Which tells me the burgers and fries were pretty good." Roxie looked over their dinner bill again. "Not only that, but you drank three beers apiece and they're part of your bill." They were just trying to get out of paying their dining bill.

She said to Minx, "Minx, you can go." She wanted the young waitress out of the way in case this got physical. Roxie was trained in hand-to-hand combat. Minx wasn't.

"Hey, guys, just pay the bill. They don't need any scam artists in here. The food's excellent and everyone knows it. Hell, people come out of their way to eat here for special occasions even," Michael Hoffman said. He was relatively new to town, a retired army Special Forces officer. He had been eating dinner with his brother, Daniel Hoffman, his brother-in-law, Bryan Wildhaven, and his wife, Carmela, who were all also retired military.

Roxie wouldn't have to lift a finger this time. She had plenty of muscle to help her out.

"Butt out," the one man said to Michael.

Roxie suspected the two men had drunk more than just the three beers at the restaurant. Most likely, as inebriated as they were, they'd been drinking on ski breaks. Drinking too much and civility didn't go hand in hand.

"We're not paying for this crap," the other man said, shoving Roxie out of the way, only because the three men and Carmela that had come to her rescue looked like a wall of muscled power and he was trying to make a hasty getaway in the opposite direction through the weakest link, which he figured was her.

As soon as he shoved Roxie, she went to take

him down with one of her maneuvers, like she'd done with the drunk guy in the lobby earlier, but Daniel took hold of the man and slammed him on the floor before she could. And he did it with a lot more force than she could!

Everyone in the restaurant—wolves and humans who didn't know they were watching wolves—cheered.

The other guy raised his hands to show he wasn't intending to leave, but he wasn't bringing out a credit card to pay for the bill.

CJ soon ran into the building and caught Landon's attention where he was just leaving one of the ballroom functions he was managing.

The two of them raced to the restaurant and then Roxie explained everything. Daniel told them about the man on the floor needing to be charged with battery for shoving Roxie.

"It looks like you licked your plates clean. You need to pay up," CJ said to the men.

She guessed the guys had thought they could bluff their way through this. But the wolves stuck together.

"Let me up, man," the one on the floor said.

Michael helped him up and CJ cuffed him.

"What's that for?"

"For battery and attempted theft of goods," CJ said.

"I'll pay the damn bill," the other man said. He got his credit card out and Roxie ran it.

She got a stolen-card notice. She handed it to CJ. "Stolen credit card."

CJ handcuffed him too. "We'll sort this out down at the station."

Peter arrived then and helped CJ haul the men out of the restaurant.

———————

Dylan was just coming into the lobby when he saw the sheriff and deputy taking two men out of the restaurant in handcuffs. Peter said to him, "I told you I'd hire you on the spot if you want to switch jobs. As you can see, we do have a need for another full-time deputy."

"I might just have to take you up on it." Dylan glanced back at Roxie and Landon talking to Minx, and he wondered what had happened this time.

Before he could ask, Peter said, "The men wouldn't pay their bill and then one offered a stolen credit card for payment, not to mention that the other shoved Roxie."

Dylan couldn't believe it. He wanted to take care of the guy who shoved her.

"Both Roxie and Minx are okay. Talk to you later," Peter said.

Dylan shook his head and hurried off to the restaurant. Peter and CJ took the men outside to their vehicles. Hell, Roxie's eye was just healing up where the one guy had hit her, the bruise green and yellow now. She didn't need another. He had smelled the beers on the men's breath. They were intoxicated like the other men had been.

Roxie glanced over to see him and still looked angry, but then her face brightened and she hurried to meet up with him.

He pulled her into his arms and gave her a hug. "Hey, you need a protector."

She laughed. "So do you."

"I agree. Are you all right?"

"Yeah. It just got ugly when they tried to say our food wasn't good, but they'd devoured every bite and then refused to pay for it." Roxie introduced Dylan to the two men he hadn't met yet that had helped her out, and they all greeted him.

Landon was talking to Minx, asking her if she was okay. Then Michael and his kin sat down to eat the rest of their meal.

"We've had a few cases of dine and dash where the patrons tried to slip out without paying for a meal, and we've always caught them and criminally charged them. This was different because they thought they could say the food was bad and not pay for the meal," Roxie said.

"Well, having eaten here already and seen all the reviews of your restaurant, I know that's not the case," Dylan said.

"Yeah. What did Xander have to say?" Roxie asked.

"Nothing much. He didn't know where Fennel got off to. He wouldn't tell us anything about the case. But with Luke's testimony, at least everyone will know the truth."

"That's for sure and that's why he needs to be kept safe at all times." Roxie led Dylan into the lobby.

"I agree. Do you need my help with anything?"

"No, just relax in the lobby. I'm going to work, but you can just take it easy."

"You are sure you don't need me to do anything else?"

———

Roxie could tell Dylan didn't like the idea of just relaxing. He was probably always on the go.

"Have something to drink on the house."

He laughed. "All right."

She got him a beer out of the kitchen and handed the bottle to him. "Now go sit down and people watch."

He thanked her, then took his beer into the lobby and sat on a chair near Rosco's bed. Rosco immediately got up to greet him, and he started petting the dog. Roxie smiled. She liked a man who knew how to relax as well as get a job done.

Roxie ended up helping Blake with a large anniversary party. When they finally finished with it that evening, she glanced out the ballroom door to see what Dylan was doing. He was gone. She wasn't surprised. She just hoped he wasn't out running around looking for Fennel.

"Hey, we're done here," Blake told her. "Why don't you go home and watch over Dylan? But no more running off without telling us where you're going from now on."

"Right. Landon has lectured me. Kayla has given me her two cents' worth. Even Gabrielle said never to worry about Landon and her getting enough sleep because of the babies. She knew that was one reason I hadn't called them. Nate even called to say how upset Kayla was."

"Okay, good. I hope that you got the message," Blake said.

She knew her family only wished the best for her and wanted to keep her safe. "I did. Thank you. But thanks for the congrats for saving Xander's life too." She looked around at the lobby. "Dylan left." Then she noticed Rosco wasn't in the lobby, and she saw Kayla was at the front desk. Landon finished up with the venue he was taking care of and joined them. "Where's Rosco?" Roxie asked.

"I don't know. I've been with you for the last couple of hours," Blake said.

Landon shook his head. "I've been busy too."

Roxie and her brothers headed to the counter to speak to Kayla. "I thought Rosco was just lying on his bed," Kayla said.

Then Dylan came into the lobby walking Rosco. Everyone sighed with relief. "What? Everyone was busy, and Rosco was dying to go out," Dylan said.

They laughed. "Thanks so much for doing that," Roxie said. "Let's go home and have dinner."

She was glad she had started a meal of corned beef, cabbage, potatoes, and carrots. It would be ready to eat as soon as they arrived home.

"Boy, this smells so good," Dylan said once they'd ditched their outer winter gear, and he began pouring their glasses of Chablis.

"Yeah. I love making pot roast, corned beef, or brisket in the slow cooker so the meal is done when I get home. I have lots of leftovers and sometimes I'll freeze some of it for another day. Sometimes I make it for some of my family members or all of them. Other times, they're busy and it's all just for me."

He chuckled. "Well, this is going to be delicious."

He set the table and she brought over glasses of water. Then he began to dish up the food.

She placed a tub of butter on the table.

"I rarely eat at the dining table back home," Dylan said.

"Don't tell me. You're at your desk searching for clues about the guys you're after." She carved up some of the corned beef that was cooked to perfection and served it on his plate while he was dishing up potatoes, cabbage, and carrots.

"Yeah. This is so much nicer. Having your

company, eating your great cooking, learning about your day."

"I'm usually sitting in the living room watching TV and eating. So this is a nice change for me too. More like the old days when I ate with my family at the table."

"Well, this is really nice for me for sure." He mashed his potatoes with his fork, and then he buttered them.

They were enjoying their meal when Roxie got a call from Nicole. She figured Nicole needed her to do babysitting duty. "What's up?"

"Hey, we're having that rewilding meeting tonight at seven. I was supposed to be there, but I wondered if you could take my place. The babies are so needy right now."

"Yeah, sure, Nicole."

"What about Dylan?" Nicole asked.

"He can come with me or chill out here."

Dylan glanced at her and smiled.

"Okay, I'll be there. No worries." Then Roxie ended the call with her sister-in-law. "I have a meeting to go to at seven at the lodge. Do you want to go with me? It's about rewilding some of the area around the coal mines that have been closed for a decade to return the land to nature."

"Yeah, that's right up my alley. Anything to do with returning habitat to the wild animals works for me."

"Good. We are just in the planning phase. We

won't actually begin planting until the snow has melted, but we want to be ready for that. All the businesses in town will be represented and individuals involved in it will be at the meeting. You don't have to go if you don't want."

"No, I'd love to go."

After they ate dinner, they watched a thriller and then it was time to go to the meeting. Roxy was glad Dylan wanted to go with her. They arrived at the lodge and went into one of the banquet rooms. Everyone took their seats. Michael and Carmela Hoffman, who were in charge of the project, got up to talk.

Carmela spoke first. "While serving in various areas of the world as an army officer, I always dreamed of how wonderful it would be to reclaim dry, desert regions and turn them into forests, a place for biodiversity for wildlife habitats for our kind and for the wild animals that share our world. When I saw the old coal mine, I wanted to turn the lands into a wildlife nature reserve, and everyone in the pack was in agreement. We have several steps we need to take to accomplish this here where the old coal mines were closed down. First, we'll need a rooting medium for the forestation to work. We'll need to have a good four feet of soil and weathered brown sandstone mixed together for deeply rooted trees. We plan to get started on this as soon as the snow has melted, and we can grade the land and then add the mixture."

Michael continued. "After that phase is done, we'll be lightly grading the soil medium, loosely compacting it so the tree roots can grow. We'll do this when we have dry conditions. With a good soil medium that's only lightly compacted, the trees will grow much faster. Then we'll plant a variety of native-crop trees for diversity. A fifth of the seedlings should be trees that can exist in an open environment until the other trees fill in. They'll be mixed with the rest of the varieties like they are found in a natural setting. They'll help to improve the soil and make a home for wildlife."

"So the last thing to know is we need to take care of the seeds and seedlings. Proper handling is key. Seeds can't be in direct sunlight or freeze; seedlings shouldn't be allowed to dry out," Carmela said. "We have also talked to Lelandi and Darien about growing some crop trees, creating a Christmas tree farm and an almond tree grove. We have so much land to reforest that it will be perfect. At some point, we'll be able to pick out our own Christmas trees and even have almonds for—"

"Candied almonds!" someone shouted from the floor.

"Yes, after only three years," Carmela said, smiling.

Everyone laughed. That sounded delicious to Roxie. She glanced at Dylan to see how bored he was. He was taking notes. Where did he get a note-pad and pen? He really was a fascinating character. She just knew he would be wishing he was some-where else during this whole talk. Maybe he was taking notes about what he had to do next concern-ing capturing Jim.

"We need to sign up on different teams to accomplish each of the steps to make this work," Michael said.

"I'll take care of ordering the seeds and seedlings and ground cover," Dylan said.

Everyone turned to look at him and smile. Roxie was staring at him in disbelief.

"As a Fish & Wildlife Service special agent, I know all about habitats for wildlife. I'm up for getting all the plants we'll need. I'll just need to know how much coverage we need it for." Dylan winked at Roxie.

She blushed. She rarely blushed.

"Okay," Carmela said, still smiling. "We have the money to buy them. You would just need to decide on the best varieties to plant in the area."

"I can certainly do that," Dylan said.

Then everyone signed up for doing the various jobs, Roxie adding her name to plant the seeds and seedlings. She asked Dylan, "Are you coming down from Denver to help me plant the seeds and seed-lings when the weather warms up?"

"I sure am."

"This place kind of grows on you, doesn't it?"

He laughed. "It does. Actually, I might not be 'coming down.'"

"Yeah, you could be working on a job." She was disappointed that this would be the way it would be between them when she really wished she could keep dating him.

"Down here."

She frowned at him, not understanding what he was saying.

"I got a job offer."

He was quitting his job at the FWS? "A job for here? Not at the Fish & Wildlife Service though."

"Nah. Peter offered me a job as one of his deputies."

"Ohmigod! You're going to take the job as a deputy? You're moving here?" She couldn't wrap her mind around it. But she was already getting excited about it. She knew he loved his work, so was he doing it so he could be with her? He was such a dream. And she was all set to date him.

He laughed. "Yeah. I thought I should think about it for a while longer, but I mean, there's really nothing to think about. Working with other wolves, still protecting wildlife, socializing with other wolves, and hell, once I met you, it was just the incentive I needed to make the big change in my life. The offer of a job helped too."

She leaned over and gave him a hug. "Welcome to Silver Town for good. You don't know how glad I am that you're staying here with us."

He kissed her. "Thanks. I didn't want to give you up, and I knew a long-distance relationship wouldn't work out between us. Not when I have to go to so many places that are so far away from Silver Town. I still need to give my boss two weeks' notice. He's going to be shocked."

"Well, we are going to be thrilled to have you living here. Me especially. You need a job that's less dangerous." And close to her!

He smiled. "I doubt being a deputy sheriff will be a totally safe job."

"Yeah, but you've got a ton of reserve deputy sheriffs to back you up." She was so thrilled.

"Hell, all I'll need is you to watch my back."

She chuckled. "Anytime you need me, just holler."

They realized everyone had signed up for what they wanted to help with on the rewilding project and were listening to Dylan and Roxie, waiting to welcome him to the pack. If he'd had any doubt about joining them, he didn't now. He was all smiles, shaking everyone's hands, getting hugs from the women at the meeting, and looked absolutely thrilled at the welcome.

Then with everyone having signed up for whatever they were doing to participate in the project, Roxie and Dylan headed back to her place.

"Let's watch another movie and then it's time for bed," she said.

"That sounds good."

He made them some hot chocolate, and she started the fire in the fireplace and turned on the mantel lights.

Then they settled down on the couch together, snuggling. Oh, yeah, his taking a job here was just perfect for her. And unless he was against it, she was taking him to bed with her.

When they finished the movie, she took his hand and led him to her bedroom upstairs. "Unless you want to stay in the other bedroom?"

He smiled down at her, telling her in no uncertain terms he wanted to be with her.

Chapter 13

THE NEXT MORNING AFTER A GLORIOUS NIGHT with Roxie, making love to her, sharing her bed with her, Dylan sure was rethinking his priorities. She was utterly amazing, and he'd never felt that way about another she-wolf.

He slipped out of bed with an important mission to accomplish while trying not to wake Roxie. He was still on medical leave, but he went downstairs to call his boss to give him notice. First though, he told his boss about locating Xander and then he gave him the news that he was quitting his job with the FWS. He wasn't leaving Silver Town for anything. Well, except to finish his job with the FWS, but after that, he was settling here with the pack.

"Are you serious?" Mr. Bentley asked, knowing Dylan rarely joked about anything. But his boss also knew Dylan lived for working at this job.

"Yeah. I just love it here."

"Well, there's something to be said about country and small-town living," his boss said, still sounding surprised about the whole business.

"Yeah, since I've been here, everyone's been so

kind and welcoming." Dylan let out his breath. "I've also met a woman…"

Mr. Bentley laughed. "*Now* I know what really made you decide to move there. I was still trying to figure that out."

Dylan chuckled. "Yeah, well, she's super special."

"She has to be. Wait, she's not the one who saved you in the swimming pool, is she?"

"Yeah."

"Then she truly is special. But you'll be working for us for a couple more weeks, correct?" his boss asked.

"Yeah. I want to catch Jim and Fennel, and if I have time, I'd really like to catch that trapper. I hope I can get it all done in the two weeks I have left."

"You've got it. And I'm glad you'll do it. You're one of the best special agents I have. I've never had anyone work for me who can track people down like you can."

"Thanks. I can't wait to do it."

"All right. Congratulations on locating Xander. He's damn lucky you found him. About the other assignment—good luck on locating the trapper."

"I'll be looking for him and the traps too. I really appreciate all you've done for me."

"Well, if you ever decide to return to work for me, you'll be more than welcome back."

"Thanks."

They finally ended the call, and though it was

hard to give notice, Dylan knew it had been the right thing to do. He was so glad he was staying here. Even if Roxie and he didn't mate, he decided he wanted to be with the pack, enjoying all the social functions, but he sure hoped it would work out between him and Roxie. He thought the world of her, and he loved her family too.

Even Luke was hoping Dylan would stay.

Roxie came downstairs and smiled at him. "Did you call your boss?"

"Yeah. I hated to tell him because he's been such a great boss to work for, but I love that I'm staying here. Though I do have to work for him for another two weeks."

"Okay, good." She pulled Dylan into her arms and hugged him. "I guess that means we're officially dating."

"Hell yeah. I knew if I left here to return to Denver, any number of bachelor wolves would be knocking your door down to date you."

She laughed. "Truthfully, I've dated a lot of them. But you're the only one I want to continue to see more of."

"I'm sure glad for that. At first, I was a little afraid it was because you felt sorry for me being injured on your lodge property."

"Nope. I mean, sure I did feel bad that we didn't prevent it from happening in the first place, but I was glad you were here where I could discover you.

And our pool water is heated, unlike if you'd fallen in an icy river. I'd say this calls for a celebration— you giving notice and going to work for the sheriff's department."

"And dating you. Let's go to the Silver Town Tavern for dinner. I haven't taken you there yet, and I've heard the food and atmosphere are really good."

"They are. Sam and Silva own it. Make reservations for tonight, and we can celebrate."

"All right. I'll do that and then tell Peter I'm taking the job." Dylan got on the phone and made the reservations, and then he called Peter next. "Hey, I just gave notice at my job and will be ready to start work two weeks from today."

"Good show. I'll set you up for training and then schedule you for shifts and duties."

"Thanks for the opportunity."

"You're welcome. I figured you needed to get to know a particular she-wolf better, and the only way to do that was if you were living in Silver Town."

Dylan laughed. He hadn't figured his new boss would be into matchmaking. "Hey, what's going on with the men who wouldn't pay for lunch at the ski lodge and had a stolen credit card?"

"They were charged with a Class 1 misdemeanor and will get a hundred days in jail in Green Valley. We have an arrangement with them that we don't keep prisoners here long-term. The mayor is a gray wolf, and he understands the situation we have with being completely wolf-run here. Anyway, they also received a thousand-dollar fine each. They could have gotten a year in jail, though they'll probably serve less time than that with good behavior. They'll probably think twice about using a stolen credit card, trying to scam a restaurant out of paying for a meal, and battery."

"Good. I'll let Roxie know. Talk to you later." When he finished the call with Peter, Dylan said to Roxie, "It's done."

She gave him a hug. "I'm so glad you'll be staying here with us."

"I am too because I get to keep dating you. I can check on renting an apartment. We're dating exclusively, but I don't want you to feel like I'm rushing our relationship too much."

Roxie smiled. "You want to check out my competition?"

"Hell, no."

"Then it seems foolish to rent an apartment. You can stay here with me, and if things don't work out, you can get an apartment," she said.

"Are you sure?"

"Absolutely. If we can't live together, we can't be mated wolves anyway."

"True." He was glad she was willing to take him in.

"And so far everything's worked out between us. We're both low-maintenance."

"I agree."

"So we can do it on a trial basis," she said.

"Thanks. That really works for me."

"Me too. I am thrilled to have you stay here and keep me company."

"Yeah, me too. I haven't ever lived with anyone other than my parents when I was younger, but I'm really enjoying it," he said.

"That's good. I always forget you're an only child."

Then Dylan told her all about the business with the two men who wouldn't pay for their meal.

"Yes! Brett Silver, our local reporter and cousin to Darien, will report on it and then if anyone else—who is not a wolf—thinks to pull that at our businesses in town, they'll know what they'll be faced with."

———

That night, Roxie was excited about going with Dylan out to dinner. It was tantamount to proving she and Dylan were a couple now.

"Are you ready to go?" She was wearing a sweater dress that she'd worn at work, which felt a little dressy, but it was nice for wearing to the tavern tonight.

He glanced at his attire.

She grabbed his hand, knowing just what he was

thinking. "You look great. Anything works for the wolf-run tavern."

"Good. I don't have anything really dressy with me, other than the tux and all."

"I love your sweater and cargo pants. You look like a hero to me."

He smiled.

Then he drove them to the tavern in town. The windows were decorated with little white fairy lights, and two big, hand-carved grizzly bears guarded the entrance. Dylan opened the door for Roxie. The place had been a hum of conversation, music playing in the background, until they stepped into the tavern. Everyone looked to see who the newcomers were.

Smiles appeared on the patrons' faces, and glasses of beer or other drinks were raised to them as if Roxie and Dylan had announced they were mating. But she knew the word had to have already spread that Dylan had taken the job as a deputy sheriff and was joining the pack while helping them to find traps, a trapper, and hunters on the lam, so he was one of the good guys. They were welcoming him into the wolf pack, and Roxie was so glad about that.

Silva hurried over in her high-heeled boots—the first thing Roxie always noticed—a pretty sweater top with sparkles around the neckline, and faux leather pants, with her brown hair piled up high on her head. She always looked like a million bucks, Roxie thought.

Roxie introduced Silva to Dylan, but Silva said, "Oh, sugar, we all know just who he is," and led them to their reserved seats.

Roxie hoped she wouldn't mention the business with Dylan being in the pool.

"I can't wait for the Valentine's Day party. I bet you'll kind of be glad when it's all over, Roxie, since you've been working so hard on it," Silva said.

"Oh, I can't wait to enjoy it. I'll be working on setting up the Mardi Gras party after that."

"Count Sam and me in for that too." Silva looked at Dylan as if she wanted to know if Roxie and he were a couple.

Roxie also knew that as well intentioned as Silva was, if anyone shared anything with her, she would share that news with all the pack in a heartbeat. She truly had a heart of gold and was definitely a matchmaker.

"Dylan's taking me to the Valentine's Day party depending on his workload. If he can catch the guys he's trying to hunt down, he'll have to do that instead."

"Oh, sure. Well, I'll be hoping he won't be off in the woods during the party. What would you all like to have to eat?"

They ordered slices of the standing prime-rib roast, potatoes, and carrots for dinner and wine.

"Good choice." Silva went to get their wine and glasses of water and returned with them. She also brought them a loaf of fresh bread. "Enjoy."

"We will," Roxie said.

Then Darien and Lelandi came into the tavern with Jake, Darien's triplet brother; Alicia, Jake's mate; Tom, Darien's youngest triplet brother; and Elizabeth, Tom's mate, and stopped by their table first. "Welcome to the pack," they all said, the guys giving Dylan hearty slaps on the back and the ladies all giving him hugs. Since Jake and Tom were the subleaders of the pack, it was important for Dylan to meet them and their mates.

Dylan was smiling. He looked like he was enjoying the camaraderie.

Roxie was so glad he was part of the pack now.

A couple of wolves who were ski instructors, Kemp and Radcliff Grey, came into the tavern just then, talking about a wolf they'd seen they hadn't recognized. "I thought he was acting strangely."

His twin brother agreed. "Hey, Darien, do you know of any wolves that are mostly black with blond legs and torso and a black collar of fur? His face was mostly white, but the top of his head and around his eyes were black."

"No. Where was he when you saw him?" Darien asked.

"Near the ski resort, but when we went to check him out—" Radcliff said.

"He ran off. He shouldn't have been wearing his wolf coat during the daylight hours," Kemp said.

"Well, it was almost dusk," Radcliff said.

"But still, it was light out," Kemp said.

"We figured he had to be one of our kind," Radcliff said. "Or he wouldn't have gotten that close to the resort."

"Or a rabid wild wolf," Kemp said.

"Did you catch his scent?" Darien asked.

"Yeah, but it wasn't anyone we knew by scent," Kemp said.

"Keep a watch out for him. If he returns, let us know. We'll get some men out to chase him down and find out if he's one of our kind or not," Darien said.

"Will do," Radcliff said, and he and his brother found seats at the bar.

Then a group of four men entered the tavern, and Sam, though he was the owner of the tavern, hurried to throw them out as if he were the bouncer. "I'm sorry, gentlemen, this is a private club only."

They were human. Roxie had never seen Sam in action when he had to toss anyone out of the place. He was like a big grizzly bear.

To Roxie's amazement, Dylan immediately joined him to help him out. But several other diners rose from their seats to offer their assistance too.

Silva came over to Roxie and Dylan's table and smiled. "Dessert is on us." Then she said to Darien and his party, "Do you want your usual?"

Everyone in the Silver party, except Jake and Tom, took their seats at a table reserved for the pack leaders and their family. The pack subleaders stood by Roxie's table in case Sam and Dylan needed their help.

Sam and Dylan got the men out of the tavern without getting physical, but there was quite a discussion going on between them. Finally, they walked off and Sam shut the door, thanked Dylan for the assistance, and returned to the bar.

Dylan rejoined Roxie at their table while Jake and Tom smiled at him.

"You got free dessert for saving Sam. They never give us free dessert when we help him out," Jake said. "You must have done something right." Then they joined their family at the Silver table.

Dylan smiled at Roxie and raised his brows in question.

"Silva likes you."

Dylan chuckled. "As long as you like me, I'm happy."

"You're a dream come true. But just for your information, every male wolf in here would have come to Sam's aid if he needed them too. You just beat everyone to it. Believe me, everyone will know about your heroics by morning."

"I love being with a pack. As long as I'm doing things right, of course," Dylan said.

"Yeah." She laughed. "That's the key."

Chapter 14

THE NEXT DAY, AFTER ANOTHER NIGHT OF WON-derful intimacy with Roxie, Dylan was feeling great. He woke before she did, slipped out of bed without waking her, grabbed his clothes, and left the bedroom. Downstairs, he dressed, then called the clinic and made a doctor's appointment to get off medical leave. Once he was done, glad to get an appointment this morning, he went into the kitchen to make breakfast—a tortilla breakfast wrap with ham, cheese, and spinach. He coated and cooked the egg in the tortilla to make the egg part of the wrap. Then he flipped the scrambled egg layer and cooked it on the other side. He was just adding the ham, cheese, and spinach when he heard Roxie coming down the stairs.

"You're up early this morning. That means you're up to something." Roxie was wearing a pretty blue sweater, pants, and boots, looking beautiful and ready to handle the winter wedding she was working on at the lodge today.

"You're going to be at work all day and—"

"You can't relax." She made coffee for both of them.

"I feel great, and I have a job to do." Dylan had

never had a case he hadn't solved. He wasn't about to let Fennel die in the cold or allow Jim to get away with murder and attempted murder if he could help it.

"Wow, these look really delicious." She sat down at the dining room table and took a bite of her wrap. "It *is* delicious."

"Thanks. I figured it would be nice and quick to make—ten minutes and it's done—but also it would be nutritious and stay with us until lunchtime."

"It will. Okay"—she took a sip of her coffee and set her mug on the table—"are you going to get the doc's approval first?"

"Yes, ma'am. I have an appointment with the doc in half an hour."

"Good. And then?"

"If he signs the paperwork taking me off medical leave, I'll call my boss and tell him I'm back on the job. I'll ask the sheriff if I can borrow one of the snowmobiles, and I'll head out to Jim's grandfather's cabin."

"With some more men," she said, not asking a question.

"Yeah. I'll see who all can go with me for sure. I'm still trying to track down the two men, not just one, and because it's a case of murder, not just illegal hunting, I should have backup. I'll have a first aid pack, a rifle, and a gun, and I won't be on foot.

With deputy sheriffs to support me, I'll be ready for the hunters."

"Okay, good. Will you be back in time for the Valentine's Day party?" She sounded as if she believed he wouldn't be.

"Of course. I wouldn't miss it for the world."

"Unless you're about to catch up to Fennel or Jim."

"Yeah, but this will probably be just a scouting mission." He didn't want to miss taking her to the party, and he certainly didn't want to screw up anyone else's plans for Valentine's Day.

"Well, I know how important this is to you. So you just do what you need to accomplish and don't worry about the party. You have a really important job to do, and everyone is counting on you to finish it."

He knew that wasn't true. Everyone was trying to find the two men themselves to take them in. They hadn't been waiting on Dylan to get better, not as important as it was to locate both of the hunters.

They quickly finished up their breakfast wraps and then she put the plates in the dishwasher while he cleaned up the rest of the kitchen. He glanced at the clock. "I've got to run."

She kissed him. "Let me know how things are going."

"I sure will. I hope everything works out well with the wedding."

"Oh, you and me both! We can never tell with

these things." Then she put on her snow boots and parka, and he walked her outside.

He gave her a tight hug and kissed her again. "I'll keep in touch."

"I sure hope you can." She kissed him back and headed off to the lodge. He returned to the house, threw on his parka, got into his truck, and drove to the clinic.

As soon as he arrived, he saw Gabrielle trying to calm two fussy babies. He hurried over to take one of them and walk him while she walked the other, looking so appreciative. "Ear infections," she told him.

"Oh no." He comforted the one he was holding and realized how easy it was to do. He'd never held a baby in his arms, and he wasn't sure he could do it properly.

"They should be fine once they are on antibiotics."

"That's good."

Then a nurse came back to get her so she could see Dr. Adelaide Summerfield, the pediatrician, while Nurse Charlotte took the baby from Dylan and smiled at him.

Carmela told Nurse Matthew that Dylan had arrived to see Dr. Kurt Summerfield, the family physician.

The nurse came to get Dylan and took him to an exam room, then checked his vitals. "Doc thought you weren't going to come. That you'd changed your mind and wanted to be on medical leave for a little while longer."

Dylan smiled because he didn't think Doc could be serious.

"He'll be right in to see you." Matthew left the exam room.

Dr. Summerfield came into the exam room a couple of minutes later and shook his head at Dylan. "So you want to go back to work, eh?"

"Yes, sir. I've got a job to do and—"

"Nobody else can do it. You do know that the sheriff has had search parties out every day looking for the last two hunters you're after, right?"

Dylan opened his mouth to plead his case, but the doc continued, "If you can run as a wolf for a half a day, swim in a raging river, and save the life of one of the three men, I'd say you're ready to go back to work. *Only* if you haven't had any more headaches, no blurring vision, feeling nauseous or dizzy."

"Nope, no headaches for a few days. I'm fine. I really feel ready to do this. I know I had been pushing it before."

"All right. If you're going with Peter's men, I want to let him know that if there's any change in your condition at all, you have to be returned to the clinic at once."

"Yeah, that sounds good."

"No matter what is going on. I'm serious about this."

"Right. Gotcha."

Doc filled out some paperwork for Dylan and said, "Here you go. Don't make me regret taking you off medical leave."

"Thanks, Doc." Then Dylan hurried out of the exam room with his papers in hand before the doctor changed his mind.

Carmela smiled at him. "You're going back to work, I take it."

"Yeah. I want to get this job done before the Valentine's Day party."

"Good luck with that," she said.

"Thanks!" He headed outside into the cold snowy day and felt such a relief. He got on his cell phone and called Peter first. "Hey, can I borrow someone's snowmobile, and is there anyone who can come with me to search for Fennel and Jim? I want to travel to Jim's grandfather's place."

"Yeah, I'll get a fresh group of men together. I think you met them at the restaurant yesterday. Michael Hoffman and his brother, Daniel, and Michael's brother-in-law, Bryan. They're all reserve deputies, and CJ will go with you too. I'll give them a call and they'll meet you at the lodge," Peter said.

"Okay, I'm on my way there now. Thanks, Peter."

"Doc sent me a text concerning your medical condition."

"Yeah, he said he would tell you that I was fine unless—"

"You aren't. The team will be briefed on your condition in case anyone sees you having trouble and you don't realize it yourself," Peter said.

Or Dylan was being too stubborn about wanting to push on. "Thanks, Peter."

"You're welcome. Keep me in the loop."

"Will do." Dylan drove to the lodge and called his boss. "Sir, I just got the doctor to take me off medical leave so I'm back on duty. I'm working with some local deputies to look for Fennel and Jim."

"I'm glad you're feeling better. Take care and good luck!"

"Thanks." Dylan parked his truck in Roxie's garage and gathered his gear for the trip. He carried everything with him inside the lodge. He saw Roxie directing the delivery of wedding flowers, but as soon as she observed him, she came over to see him.

"What did Doc say?"

"I'm good to go. I'm going with CJ Silver and the men you introduced me to yesterday at the restaurant. We're riding snowmobiles. And don't worry. Everyone has been alerted to my medical condition, though the doc said I was fine, but if I have any trouble, they'll make sure I return to the clinic."

"Good. That's what I love about living here. Everyone's so helpful." Then more flowers arrived for the wedding. She gave Dylan a kiss. "I'll try to see you before you leave." Then she hurried off.

Dylan was sitting in the lobby with his gear and petting Rosco when CJ showed up.

"Everyone's on their way. I've called my oldest brother, Eric, the forest ranger, and he'll meet us on the way to the cabin," CJ said.

"Good."

The other men arrived as a group. They looked ready to handle this and they were eager to head out, but Dylan said, "Uh, can you wait a second?" He hurried into the ballroom to say goodbye to Roxie before he took off.

She was in the middle of setting up the seating when he joined her. "The guys are all here and I'm on my way."

"Okay. Good luck and stay safe. I won't be there to save you this time if Jim gets the best of you."

He smiled. "He won't this time."

They warmly embraced each other and the two of them kissed. When he kissed her, Dylan forgot about anything else but the softness of her lips pressed against his, warming him, their hearts beating faster. She was not conducive to wanting to go out and do his job!

"You've got to go." Roxie caressed his face. "Just be safe."

"I will be."

"You'd better be."

He kissed her lips again and smiled. "Or you'll give me grief. I'll call you when I can."

"I'll be glad to get any news from you."

He headed out with the guys, so hoping that they would be able to find their quarry soon.

Chapter 15

THAT NIGHT, AFTER ROXIE SUCCESSFULLY MAN-aged a wedding in two of the ballrooms, she got a call from Dylan. She was so glad to hear from him and know that he was safe wherever he was while he and the others were trying to locate Fennel and Jim. At least she sure hoped so.

"Hey, we're still chasing Fennel's scent so he seems to be alive. We just haven't caught up to him yet," Dylan said, sounding excited to be on the hunt and trying to resolve this case. She didn't blame him. If she were him, she'd want the same thing.

"So you'll be camping the night with the guys out in the woods?" She figured there would be no way that they'd be back in Silver Town tonight. Not unless they had just found the two men quickly before they had even reached Jim's grandfather's cabin and returned home.

"Yeah. I'm so sorry. I should have anticipated it would take longer than just a day."

"No, don't be. You're just doing your job. What about the other guys who are with you?"

"Yeah, they're all in on this. They're a great bunch of guys."

She knew they were, and she was so glad they were there backing him. "Okay, good. How are *you* doing?" She was still worried Dylan might be having headaches or even other health issues that might be related to the injuries that he'd suffered.

"Fine. No problems at all. I feel great."

"All right." She was glad to hear it and hoped he truly was and that he wasn't just trying to tough it out.

"How did the wedding you were handling go?"

"Oh, it was fantastic." She swore it was the best one she'd ever managed. "The bride and everyone in the wedding party were so nice. They were just so happy at the wedding. We had no major glitches and I'm just going home now. Since you've kept Michael out in the wilderness, I'll ask Carmela to come join me for dinner."

"I'm glad the two of you can do that. I'm sorry I kept Michael out here."

"She's used to it since she was in the army too," Michael said in the background, undoubtedly over-hearing their conversation.

"Of course. Carmela and I were actually stationed at the same post one time, and she and I met each other. So we're friends," Roxie told Dylan. While in the army, Carmela had won numerous awards for her archery skills. She was fun to be around. Roxie and Carmela didn't often have a chance to have dinner together because Carmela and her husband were always together. That was the problem with Roxie being a single she-wolf.

"Good. Well, we're setting up camp and then making dinner, so I'll let you go," Dylan said.

She could hear the guys all talking and laughing, telling each other they could get their tents up faster than the others. They sounded like they were having fun, and she couldn't help but be amused. "Stay safe."

"We will."

Then they ended the call, and Roxie got in touch with Carmela, hoping she would like to join her for dinner. "Hey, you might have already heard from Michael, but if not, Dylan called me and said the guys are camping out for the night."

"Yeah, I figured they would be. Michael showed me how far it was to Jim's grandfather's cabin before he left, but if they were sidetracked, it would take longer than a day. Plus, they still have to return home. He already called to let me know."

"Oh good. Do you want to get together with me for dinner and drinks? We could have classic lasagna with cheese and meat sauce and whiskey sours." Roxie was sure hoping Carmela could. Roxie really missed being with Dylan after work.

"Oh, yeah, I'd love it. I'll make the drinks. What time do you want me to come over?"

Yes! "Would six be okay?"

"I'll be there. Thanks! See you soon."

Then Roxie got a call from Kayla. "Hey, Nate's on an overnight stakeout investigating a case of worker's comp insurance fraud in another town. I wasn't sure if Dylan had come home yet. If not, do you want to have some dinner with me?"

"Oh, absolutely. Dylan's gone and Carmela's husband is with him, so I asked her over. I didn't know you were also going to be all by yourself. We'll make it a threesome. Does lasagna sound good?" Roxie was just thrilled. She had figured Kayla and Nate would be together tonight or she would have called her too.

"That sounds great. I'll be right over and help you make it."

"Terrific!"

Kayla really liked Carmela too, so Roxie knew the three ladies would have a ball. Roxie told her the time that Carmela was coming over and then they ended the call. Roxie was so glad that Carmela and Kayla were having dinner with her. She hurried to get the place straightened up. Kayla came over a few minutes after that to help her make the lasagna.

When Carmela arrived at six, Roxie invited her inside. "Kayla's mate is also on an overnight job out of town, so it's ladies' night out, or in, I should say."

"Oh, sweet. They're the best. So what do you think about Dylan?" Carmela stepped into the kitchen to make them whiskey sours.

Roxie was surprised that Carmela would bring up her relationship with Dylan right away. She thought Carmela should at least wait until they were sipping their whiskey sours.

Kayla was setting the table and glanced at Roxie to see what she'd say. "Short and direct. I like that."

Roxie laughed. She hadn't really talked to Kayla much about Dylan because they'd both been so busy at work. When they weren't at work, Dylan had been with her for most of the time since he was released from the clinic. She hadn't wanted to talk to her sister about him when he could overhear their conversation.

Roxie pulled the lasagna out of the oven. "Well, Dylan's really great. Not once did he have any issue with me when I had trouble with shifting. That's aways a concern. Now that he's going to move into the area, it won't be a case of us seeing each other long distance. That wouldn't have been sustainable, I don't think."

"I agree. I couldn't imagine dating a wolf who lived in Denver when I lived here." Carmela set their drinks on the dining room table while Roxie served up the lasagna.

They sat down at the table and began to eat. "So what is he going to do about living accommodations?" Kayla took a sip of her drink. "Ooh, this is super good. When we all get together from now on, you're making the drinks, Carmela."

"I agree about the cocktails," Roxie said after taking a drink of hers.

Carmela laughed. "That's what Michael always says to me when he grills for us."

"Well, they're great," Kayla said.

"So is the lasagna. I'll have to get your recipe."

"As to the living arrangements with Dylan, he thought of going to an apartment, but he's already been staying with me for about a week and we enjoy each other's company. I miss having my family here with me, so I'm happy with the arrangement. If we agree we're perfectly right for each other, we'll mate. If not, he can get an apartment and start seeing some other she-wolves."

"What do you think's going to happen?" Carmela asked.

Roxie smiled. "I saved him. He's mine."

Carmela laughed. "That's what I figured. You wouldn't just let some wolf live with you unless you already really felt something for him."

"Oh no, you're right. She wouldn't. You've seen how she dates a wolf. They do some things together, but she would never invite them to stay overnight." Kayla cut into her lasagna again. "And then she's inviting Dylan to stay long-term? The lasagna is delicious, by the way."

"Thanks. We made it just right." Roxie loved making meals with her sister, and she missed that they didn't get to do that very often any longer.

"Yeah, he's really special. I don't believe I could find anyone who is as great as he is for me."

"I felt the same way with Michael," Carmela said.

"When I rescued Dylan from the pool and brought him back to life, I never thought he'd be someone I'd end up dating." Roxie sipped her drink.

"Yeah, but as soon as you could, you were at the clinic, and you were seeing him. I knew then there was more to it than just wanting to know if he had survived his injuries," Carmela said.

"Heck, I didn't even know if he was a bachelor yet." Roxie shook her head.

Carmela laughed. "There was that. So you lucked out."

"Only because he and I get along so well."

"We have a lot of bets riding on this right now," Kayla said.

"Oh?" Roxie should have known that would happen. It often did when a couple of wolves looked like they might be interested in a mating. "Is that why you're asking me how it is going between us? So you can get the inside story and know which way to bet?"

The ladies laughed, but Roxie figured that was some of the reason, not only that they were curious which way this was going. As far as Kayla was concerned, Roxie's mate choice would impact on the family too since they were so close-knit.

"Which way are you gambling on?" Roxie asked.

"Ha, this is the first time you're letting a guy stay at your place. I'm betting you're going to mate him," Kayla said.

"Yeah, I agree with Kayla. Unless something big turns up that changes the way you both feel about each other, I'd say yeah, you're going to do it," Carmela said.

Roxie smiled. "We'll see." But she was definitely leaning that way.

"The guys you dated before said no way would you mate the outsider, not when there are so many of them who would love to be the lucky guy," Kayla said. "By the way, Landon is on the fence about your relationship."

"Landon is?" Roxie was surprised to hear it. She figured the whole family would believe she was stuck on Dylan for good.

"Yep. He says you're so picky." Kayla smiled.

Roxie laughed. "Well, he's right. Blake thinks we will mate?"

"Yeah. Blake said you saved Dylan, and you would be claiming him for your own."

"I had another thought too. What about Luke? If you and Dylan end up being together, Luke will want to move in with the two of you, I bet," Carmela said.

Roxie laughed. "Well, I think he's in the perfect place with Darien and Lelandi and their kids as long as he's happy with the arrangement."

Carmela finished another bite of the lasagna. "Yeah, I think so too. But it doesn't mean Luke won't want to suggest moving in with the two of you."

"I agree with you there." If Roxie and Dylan were living together, getting to know each other, they didn't need a teen to take care of too. He needed a stable family.

Chapter 16

DYLAN WAS GLAD MICHAEL, HIS BROTHER, brother-in-law, and Deputy Sheriff CJ Silver were with him. They made a great group for teamwork and camaraderie. That night, they had set up camp, and the next morning, they made breakfast over a campfire like they had been working together for years. Then they packed up and headed out toward the cabin in search of Fennel and Jim. They hadn't run into any sign of tracks or scents since early yesterday.

They were still trying to reach Jim's granddad's cabin. It was only a couple of hours away now, and Dylan figured even if neither of the men were there, they might be able to learn if the men had visited. Maybe Dylan and his team members would get a clue at the cabin as to where the hunters had gone. The law enforcement agencies in Denver had been watching to see if either of the men had gone back to the city. But the hunters hadn't returned as far as the police had witnessed. The hunters hadn't checked in with their families. Or not that any family member was admitting to.

"What's happening with Xander?" Dylan asked CJ, figuring if anyone was in the know, he would be.

"Doc cut off the tips of four of his fingers and removed two of his toes. The guy got off lucky. Doc says he figured the reason it was so bad was that he had fallen into the river, then swam across and trekked a long time in snowdrifts without getting into dry clothes and warming up. He wouldn't have made it if he hadn't found the cave to hole up in and then you and Roxie located him," CJ said.

"Yeah, well, I don't think thanking me is on his agenda."

"I know. Once he recovers, he'll be jailed unless he can get bonded out. Right now, all they have on him is that he witnessed the murder and tried to hide the body so he's an accessory to murder. Luke said he and Fennel helped Jim to hide the body, and then they all took off."

"They ought to get some time in jail for that," Dylan said.

"Exactly."

Then they packed up their camp and headed off to the cabin. A mile from there, they ran into Eric Silver. He hugged CJ, his youngest quadruplet brother, and shook everyone else's hands. "I ended up reaching the cabin first to do some scouting. Someone is at the cabin. I don't know the men's scents, but smoke is coming out of the chimney. Someone else could be staying there. I wanted to warn you and figure if you're going to catch Fennel or Jim, we need to approach it in stealth mode."

"Let's do this," CJ said.

"Hell, let's go then." Dylan was so hopeful they would catch at least one of the men. As soon as he got close enough to the woods surrounding the cabin, he said, "I smell Fennel's scent."

They parked their snowmobiles a thousand feet from the cabin. Humans wouldn't be able to hear a snowmobile beyond 750 feet.

Dylan might not have been in the military like some of the men with him, but he was ready for the hunt and just as capable of taking down criminals after years of martial arts and weapons training. Plus, with a wolf's enhanced senses, he had the advantage over his human prey.

CJ divided the men up to approach the cabin from different directions, each of them taking a window or the front door to ensure Fennel didn't slip away if he was in there.

Michael was at one end of the cabin while Dylan was at the other end watching the windows from the woods. Eric and Daniel were watching the front door and windows out front. CJ and Bryan were out back watching the two windows that way. They were ready to move in closer as soon as CJ gave them the signal. All of them had their guns out.

But then Dylan heard movement to his right. It sounded like someone was trudging through the snow nearby. Fennel? Maybe he wasn't even in the cabin right now.

Dylan slowly moved in that direction and saw Fennel gathering more wood for the fire from a stack of firewood piled high. Fennel's back was to Dylan, and he wasn't carrying a rifle. He could have a gun on him though. As soon as Fennel had an armload of wood, Dylan said, "Fennel, this is Special Agent Dylan Powers. Turn around slowly. Drop the firewood and get on your knees. Put your hands behind your head."

Dylan didn't shout the words, afraid Jim could be inside the cabin and start shooting at everyone. Fennel seemed frozen with indecision and didn't move a muscle to comply, still carrying the load of firewood, still with his back to Dylan.

"Xander has been picked up and is in jail." Dylan hoped talking to Fennel about what had happened to another of his friends would defuse the situation. "We know about Eddie's murder. This isn't just about the four of you killing an elk." Even though technically only one man had actually shot the elk. He paused to let that sink in. "We have a witness who saw exactly what happened."

Fennel's shoulders dropped. He'd been standing so stiffly until Dylan told him the news about the witness. He appeared resigned. He had to know it would come to this.

"You're not going to get yourself out of this one as easily as you have done with your previous charges," Dylan said.

Still holding the firewood, Fennel slowly turned around, and Dylan saw he was carrying a holstered gun.

Dylan had the safety on his gun, but he was holding it in case Fennel thought to shoot it out with him. "If you're even thinking about going for your gun, don't. I have several Silver Town deputy sheriffs with me. Drop the firewood, then very slowly pull your gun from its holster and throw it into the snow," Dylan said, not liking the way Fennel appeared to be still weighing his options and not complying. Dylan suspected Fennel figured he was alone because Dylan always was when he had arrested these men in the past. But a lot more was at stake this time.

The cabin door opened, creaking slightly, but Dylan didn't believe Fennel could hear it. Hopefully, one of the other men with Dylan was checking it out, or if it was Jim, the other guys would grab him, which was the best-case scenario.

"Is Jim here with you?" Dylan asked.

"No. He said if we got separated and didn't find each other again, we'd meet up here. In the woods, Xander and I parted company because he thought he knew how to get here, and I thought I knew which way to go. I knew he was wrong, but once Xander got something in his head, he's damned stubborn."

"Fennel, I know you didn't kill Eddie. You need to

cooperate with us and drop the firewood, hand over your gun, and allow yourself to be taken in. You have a choice. Do the right thing. Remember your family." Dylan continued to keep his gun at the ready.

Suddenly, Eric and CJ approached Fennel from behind. Dylan was glad they were coming to back him up in case this got out of hand.

"This is Fennel Keaton. He has a gun, but he won't drop the firewood or his gun," Dylan told them.

"I'm Deputy Sheriff Silver. Drop the firewood and your gun," CJ said, his gun aimed at Fennel.

"The cabin is clear," Eric said. "The only person who has been here recently is this man."

Dylan knew Eric meant that he couldn't smell anyone else's recent scent. Dylan was glad that Fennel hadn't lied to him about being alone.

Finally, Fennel released the load of wood in the snow and carefully removed his gun from its holster and dropped it into the snow. He raised his hands above his head. Thank God.

CJ and Eric rushed forward to get his gun and grab Fennel. Once CJ secured the weapon, Eric put zip ties on Fennel's wrists.

"Fennel said Jim and Xander were to rendezvous with him here," Dylan said.

"Your friend Xander nearly died," CJ said, hauling Fennel into the warm cabin. "You have Dylan to thank for saving his life."

Everyone went inside the cabin to get warmed up. Michael, Bryan, and Daniel watched out the windows in case Jim unexpectedly showed up.

"Xander was being a stubborn idiot. I knew the fastest way here. He thought he knew best but he didn't," Fennel said, eyeing Dylan. "He should have stuck with me like I told him to. I'm not surprised that he nearly died."

They made Fennel sit down at the kitchen table.

CJ read him his rights. "I'm going to record this interview. Are you okay with that?"

Fennel nodded.

Dylan wasn't surprised that CJ would get whatever he could out of the hunter before they took him to Silver Town. Maybe they'd learn something more about where Jim was. And, of course, what had really happened.

"We have a witness who states you were there when Jim killed Eddie and you did nothing to stop it. Not only that, but you helped cover up the body," CJ said.

For a long time, Fennel studied Dylan. Dylan wondered what was up with that.

"It's his word against ours." Fennel tried to appear unshaken, but they could smell his fear. Sweat bubbled up on his forehead. He wiped it away with the sleeve of his sweatshirt, but the sweat beaded right up again.

"We have forensic evidence that proves you were

there and helped conceal Eddie's body. Xander told us everything so he'd get a lesser jail sentence," CJ said.

"Hell." Fennel glowered at Dylan as if it was all his fault.

Dylan thought it was smart of CJ to make it sound like Xander was spilling his guts. At least Fennel wasn't asking for a lawyer yet. "You know I don't think Jim planned to return to the cabin to pick the two of you up. I believe he thought you'd never make it. He took off for the ski lodge, packed your stuff and everyone else's in Eddie's SUV, and tore off. Well, after he attempted to murder me."

Fennel took a deep breath and let it out, his eyes widening. It took him several minutes before he began to tell them what had happened as if weighing his options first. "Hey, I didn't bargain on any of this."

"So when Jim fought with Eddie and shot him, you didn't try to talk Jim out of it?" Dylan asked.

"Jim was furious that Eddie had been seeing a girl that he had dated a few times. Jim had never said he was dating her exclusively. But Jim was enraged when..." Fennel stopped talking.

"When what, Fennel?" CJ prompted.

Fennel let out his breath. "Okay, look. We'd had a few beers and I hate to admit it, but Jim was telling us all about his conquests, as if he's this big lady's man. He does it all the time, acting like he has the market on women. Frankly, I was sick of it. The girl in question liked being with Eddie a whole lot better than she did Jim. I figured Eddie and Jana might even have what it took to tie the knot. Eddie was keeping the whole thing hush-hush, but I'd seen them together a few times, so I knew they really cared about each other. Hell, I don't know what came over me to say anything about it, but I said something offhand like, 'Yeah, but can you keep one happy like Eddie can?' Hell, as soon as I said the words, Eddie gave me a wide-eyed look like I was treading on dangerous ground. It was too late. I couldn't take back the words."

"What's Jana's last name?"

"I never knew it. Anyway, Xander appeared puzzled because no matter what was going on, he always seemed to be out of the loop when it came to who was seeing whom. Jim noticed the anxious expression on Eddie's face and figured out just what was going on. Maybe he had suspected it all along, except I had to go and shoot my mouth off and confirm it." Fennel shrugged. "As soon as Jim raised his rifle and threatened to shoot Eddie, I knew this wasn't good. Eddie was begging him not to shoot him. Jim was shouting at him, asking him how long he'd been dating Jana.

"Xander and I just froze. I mean, I realized at once I would be considered the messenger, and I didn't want Jim to shoot me, so I kept out of it. I'd already said way too much. I knew Jim would be furious that I knew all about it and hadn't told him sooner. Xander was trying to 'hide' in the background so Jim wouldn't even remember he existed. Eddie said, 'All Jana was to you was a one-night conquest.' But I knew Eddie wasn't right. Jim had dated her a few times, not just one night. Still, as far as I know, Jana wasn't seeing Jim any longer when she started dating Eddie. Then Jim shot Eddie."

"Jim sent you and Xander in search of the hiker who had witnessed the murder, right?" Dylan asked.

"We were all looking for the hiker to see what he knew," Fennel said. "But yeah, it was Jim's idea. He said we were all implicated in the whole sordid affair because we did nothing to stop him. We buried Eddie. We would all go down if anyone had seen what had happened."

"So if you'd caught up with the hiker, then what? You were supposed to rough him up and make sure he didn't talk?" Dylan asked.

Fennel didn't say anything.

"Jim would already be wanted for murder. Do you think if he had caught up to the witness, he would have just warned him not to talk?" Dylan asked.

Fennel squirmed in his seat. "We didn't plan to kill the kid. We heard someone moving through the woods within hearing and seeing distance of where we were. We didn't see him, but we found his tracks and they led us straight to his tent. There was no sign of him. No sign of his tracks anymore. Just an animal's tracks. A wolf's, it appeared to me. We found his ID, saw he was a teen from Denver. We figured if we didn't find him in the woods, we could stop in on him in Denver when we all returned."

"And?" CJ asked.

"It was Jim's call. Jim split up from us so we could cover more area. I told him I thought it was a grave mistake. It was beginning to snow hard, and I thought we should all stay together. He didn't agree. He never told us he was going to return to the lodge and grab Eddie's car and all our stuff. He was supposed to be looking for the kid like the rest of us."

"So you knew the kid had overheard the whole thing, including the murder of your friend Eddie," Dylan said. Something had to have happened that made them more than suspect Luke had heard everything that had gone on, and that was why they had gone and searched for him.

"When Jim told us to split up to search a broader area for the kid, we didn't do it." Fennel didn't explain why they were so sure Luke had heard or seen anything. "Jim took off in another direction, but not toward the lodge. Xander and I stayed together because it would be safer. But then Xander and I got in an argument about which way to go," Fennel said.

"I'd been tracking the four of you."

Fennel's eyes grew big again. "You were?"

Dylan swore his reaction was not only exaggerated but that he and the others had suspected he was following them. Then again, maybe not. Maybe only Jim had realized Dylan was tracking him and that was why he attempted to kill him. "I pursued Jim back to the lodge. I suspect he thought I'd seen what he had done to Eddie and was going to arrest him for that. And that's why he tried to kill me."

Fennel sighed. "Yeah, it seems like that's the case."

"What about the rest of you?" Dylan asked.

"Nope. We had no idea you were following us. I'm sure Eddie would have been alive if we'd known that."

"Yeah, but in the heat of the moment? Do you think Jim would have gotten control of his emotions?" Dylan asked.

Fennel shrugged. "Maybe. I can't believe Jim left us to fend for ourselves."

"Some friend, right?" Dylan said. "We know he was the driving force behind all this."

"Yeah. Like always." Fennel frowned. "So you really think he didn't plan to come here to meet up with us at all?"

"He's your friend. What do you think? If it were me, I'd suspect he thought the two of you would never survive in the snowstorm. That someday someone would find both Xander's and your bodies when the snow melted. Well, and Eddie's. If the teen had succumbed to the cold too, there wouldn't have been any witnesses to tell the true story," Dylan said.

"Hell." Fennel didn't look happy about the prospect, but he didn't look entirely surprised.

"He took your bags and Eddie's SUV from the lodge so it would appear the four of you had just checked out of both your rooms. He could even come up with his own version of the story if the two of you had died. He could have said one of you shot Eddie instead," Dylan said. "He might still claim that."

"Have you found Eddie's SUV yet?" Fennel asked.

Dylan shook his head.

Fennel sat up taller, looking a little smug. "All right. Well, I'll testify against Jim, but I need to know what kind of a deal I can get."

"We'll have to talk to the DA about that," CJ said. "Let's get going. We can make it back to Silver Town by nightfall if we go now."

They put out the fire in the fireplace and packed up Fennel's things, then loaded his gun and rifle on Dylan's snowmobile. CJ called in the situation to Peter. Fennel was riding with Michael, and Eric told them he was returning to the national forest where he worked.

They said goodbye to Eric, CJ thanking his

brother for coming to help them with this. Then Eric headed back to the national forest reserve and the rest of them drove back to Silver Town.

Dylan was looking forward to being home with Roxie. He realized how much he needed her in his life. He knew Michael and CJ would also be glad to be home with their mates. Fennel would be sitting in jail next to Xander once they got his written testimony and until he could get bail.

Halfway home, they took a break to have lunch. Dylan called Roxie but she sounded frazzled. "Yeah?" she said.

"We got Fennel. He's alive and well."

"Wonderful."

"We're headed home with him now. I'll be in tonight. I'm not sure how late it will be, but we'll be in."

"That's great. I've got to go." Then Roxie hung up on him.

CJ had been laughing with his mate. Michael was smiling as he talked to his wife. The other guys smiled at Dylan. Yeah, his call to Roxie hadn't gone well. He wished he could rescue her from whatever ordeal she was dealing with. He hoped it had nothing to do with him.

"She's thrilled we'll be home tonight," Dylan said, hoping everything was okay between them and that she was only dealing with issues at the lodge today that had taken her full attention.

"Yeah." Daniel was still a bachelor like Bryan, and he was nodding too, but neither looked like they believed him. Maybe because Dylan hadn't even said goodbye to her before she hung up on him.

Dylan figured the guys thought he was in trouble with Roxie, which might give them a chance to date her. Then he wondered if either of them *had* dated her already! They were still eating, and he couldn't stop thinking about Roxie. He made a quick call to Kayla. "Hey, is everything all right with Roxie? I called her and she seemed completely overwhelmed. I was worried about her."

Kayla said, "Oh, Dylan. Yeah, we're dealing with a major disaster. I've got to go." She hung up on him.

Hell. What had happened? Dylan pocketed his phone, but he was frowning.

"What's wrong?" CJ asked. He'd finished his call with his wife and had overheard Dylan's call to Kayla.

"I'm not sure. They're dealing with a major disaster, Kayla said."

"Okay, well, let's get going so we can get there sooner."

Dylan appreciated that CJ felt his concern and wanted to get this show on the road. If Dylan could, he'd help with resolving whatever disaster they needed assistance with at the lodge.

Roxie couldn't believe they had pipes freeze and break not only in the lobby bathroom but also in the fire sprinkler on the roof. The one on the roof could have been even more of a major disaster if she hadn't caught it in time, though shutting down the water for the whole lodge had been a necessity and had caused a lot of problems for the guests. Thank God for the wolf pack. They were over in force to fix things—to repair the pipes, clean up the water, get the electricity back on, get their lodge activities going—but it still took several hours to get it all done, and poor Dylan had to call her right when she was trying to get everything coordinated to fix things. By the time she had a moment to call him back, he must have been riding on the snowmobile or in the middle of trouble and he couldn't answer the phone.

She hoped he was all right. She texted him several more times whenever she had a moment, but she still couldn't get ahold of him.

"Hey, we almost have everything under control," Blake said. "It's so good that you caught the one on the roof before it was a total disaster."

"Oh, I agree. I was just on the second floor and thought I heard something like water shooting out on top of the roof, so I went up to check it out," Roxie said.

"Well, it's a damn good thing you did," Landon said, joining them.

They were sopping wet and looked a mess. They had to get cleaned up and change after dealing with all that cleanup. They smiled at each other and took a break to go to their homes, Landon going with Blake so they could shower and dress in clean clothes.

Then they were back to work, ready for the next adventure. Though Roxie was sure hoping that was the worst one they'd have to deal with today.

Chapter 17

WHEN DYLAN AND THE OTHERS FINALLY ARRIVED at the lodge, he hurried to grab his camping gear off the snowmobile, shook everyone's hands—except Fennel's, of course—and strode into the lodge. CJ was taking Fennel to the sheriff's office, and Peter was waiting for him there. But Dylan only had thoughts about seeing Roxie and offering his help if she needed it. He couldn't wait to see her and just hug and kiss her.

Rosco rushed to greet him, which always delighted Dylan. The Saint Bernard treated him like he was one of the family. Dylan petted Rosco and put his camping gear on the floor by the dog's bed so no one would trip over it in the lobby.

Then Blake joined him, carrying Buttercup cradled in his arms. "I'm late for dinner with Nicole so I can't talk, but I'm glad to see you back. I'll see you later. I want to hear everything about your trip and finding Fennel when we have time to talk."

"Yeah, sure," Dylan said. "Uh—" Before he could ask about the trouble they'd had, Blake was out the door with Rosco and Buttercup. Dylan headed to the registration desk to speak to Kayla. He didn't see any problems at the lodge, but it had been hours since he'd called Roxie, so in that time, they probably had already dealt with it.

Kayla looked frazzled, her hair damp and in straggles around her face. She smiled at him. "Crisis averted. We had frozen pipes burst in one of the lobby restrooms. We had water everywhere. Then Roxie discovered a fire sprinkler on the roof had broken. That was really serious business. I was in the middle of a wedding gig, and Blake and Landon were busy with other issues. Roxie was trying to get the plumber out pronto, the water stopped, and the place cleaned up when you called. Everyone had to stop whatever they were doing and race to help her deal with all the issues. It was a real mess."

"Damn. I wish I could have been here to help you out." Though capturing Fennel had been really important, not to mention Dylan was glad Fennel was alive and hadn't died of hypothermia or from any other cause.

"How did things go with you, Dylan?" Kayla asked.

"We caught Fennel, and luckily he was healthy and is willing to testify against Jim." Dylan couldn't have asked for more from him.

Kayla's jaw dropped. "Wow. That's really great."

"It is. We got lucky. They could have all held their tongues and then it would have been their word against Luke's. We have other evidence, but it really helps for Fennel and maybe Xander to turn on Jim. So where's—"

"Roxie? I'm right here," Roxie said, heading toward him, and he wheeled around to give her a hug. "Whoa."

He smiled. "I so missed you." Her hair was just as damp as Kayla's and she looked just as tired, but she was beautiful. "What are you and Kayla still doing here? I was going to go to the house, but it was dark there so I figured you were here."

"It was a really long day. But I'm through. I'm so ready to go home." Roxie hugged him tightly and shivered. "You are so cold. Let's get you to the house and warmed up, and you can tell me all about it."

"You can tell me about your disaster today too."

"Ha! I figured Kayla had filled you in." She smiled at Kayla. "Night, Sis!"

"Night, Roxie!"

Then Nate arrived at the lodge. "Hey, guys. I finally made it back from my stakeout and thought you'd be at home by now, Kayla. I heard you had some trouble."

Kayla laughed. "Yeah, let's go." She and Nate followed Roxie and Dylan out of the lodge, then waved goodbye as Roxie and Dylan made it to Roxie's home and Kayla and Nate walked past Blake and Nicole's home to their own.

Roxie unlocked the door. "Blake took Rosco and Buttercup to their place for the night because you were returning home and they wanted to give me a break."

"I saw him doing that, but I wondered if that had been the plan all along."

"I had them last night while you were gone. When you said you were returning, I told Blake and he said he'd take them. I'm so sorry that I couldn't talk to you when you called. I texted and called you later, but you had to have been on your way home by then."

"No problem, though I have to admit I was damned worried about you."

She smiled. "I was really overwhelmed at the time. Did you eat any dinner?" She almost sounded hopeful he hadn't.

"No, we had lunch on the trail, but we wanted to get home before it was too late. I can just make a tuna-fish sandwich or something." But he really wanted to have dinner with her—fix it for her—after her hard day if she hadn't eaten already. He checked his phone and saw all her text messages and he smiled.

"No way. You need a nice hot meal. Besides, I'm starving. I had lunch too, but with the mess we had at the lodge, I never ate dinner and figured I'd just have it with you when you got in." Roxie ran her hand over his arm.

He smiled and kissed her mouth. "Okay, good. So what do you want me to make?"

"We can have spaghetti if that works for you. I defrosted hamburger for the meat sauce, and I have all the rest of the ingredients we'll need. Tomatoes, tomato sauce, mushrooms, onions, garlic cloves, bell peppers. How does that sound to you?"

"I love everything you fix. I can make it, and you can put your feet up and tell me what happened at the lodge today."

"We both had a wild and adventurous day. We'll make it together."

"Okay. Do you want me to cut up all the veggies?" he asked.

"Yeah, sure." She pulled the container of mushrooms, an onion, garlic, and bell peppers out of the fridge. "I'll start the hamburger." She brought out a pan and began cooking the meat. "I was thinking we could go out to dinner tomorrow night if you aren't busy trying to capture Jim."

"Tomorrow night works for me. We didn't find any sign of Jim at the cabin, so we're kind of stuck on where to go next unless I stake out his place. But I suspect he's not returning there. He might have even thought if the other guys arrived, they'd get arrested. Though I had considered he might have believed they'd never make it there alive. A warrant is out now for his arrest at least." He told Roxie about how they captured Fennel. "It was anticlimactic. I expected him to go down fighting, but I don't think he would kill another man just to get him out of the bind he's now in. He's just too beta. The same with Xander. Jim had to have orchestrated the whole thing, and I believe what Fennel told us."

"Okay, good. Then you'll have the bastard. You just need to catch him. Or the police do."

They mixed the ingredients together and cooked them some more, adding tomato sauce and spices. She tossed a spinach salad with tomatoes, black olives, and mushrooms while he made garlic toast.

Roxie told him all the details of the frozen pipes in the lobby restroom and the sprinkler on the roof of the lodge and what a mess that had been. "We all went home to clean up and change clothes, but Kayla and I didn't have time enough to fully dry our hair."

"Well, I still wish I'd been there for you."

"Thanks. Would you like some wine?" She brought out a couple of wineglasses. "Merlot?"

"Yeah. We deserve it."

"We do. We had a rough day." They finally served up the spaghetti, salad, and garlic toast and sat down to eat, clinking their glasses together.

"So you don't have any ideas about where Jim could be?" Roxie took a drink of her wine.

"No. But tomorrow, I want to speak with Fennel and Xander again and learn if there's anywhere else Jim might have gone if he hasn't already fled the country."

"Oh, that would not be good."

"I know. Damn, this spaghetti is good," Dylan said, getting ready to take another bite.

"Yeah, and it's great for leftovers too. I love your garlic toast."

"Thanks."

"By the way, Carmela asked where you were staying, and I told her here. I had dinner with her and Kayla last night, so the word will likely get back to my brothers," Roxie said.

Dylan reached over and squeezed her hand, worried she was changing her mind about having him stay there with her. He would do whatever she needed him to for her peace of mind. "Will it be a problem?"

She laughed. "No, or I wouldn't have said you could stay. But if you're going to be at my house, you might as well...stay. Permanently."

"I don't want to be presumptuous, but you don't mean you want to mate me, do you?" God, he hoped so.

She smiled. "You may be presumptuous all you want. Yeah, I sure do want to mate you. I love you."

Absolutely thrilled, he rose from his chair and pulled her from hers and wrapped his arms around her, kissing her, tasting the wine on her lips. "You have made me the luckiest wolf alive, and I love you right back."

"You don't mind that you'll gain a whole family,

parents even, since Nicole and Nate's parents will adopt you too?" She sounded worried that he would be.

"I would be thrilled. I've been alone for way too long. I thought I was fine with it until I met you. I could never go back to living on my own and be happy like I've been with you—no social life, no one to enjoy meals and movies and share such an intimate connection with."

"I've been lonely now that my sister and brothers have found mates and moved out. I knew they were important in my life, but I didn't realize how hard it would be for me when everyone was mated, some of them having kids, and for me being the odd man out. But that's not why I want to mate you. I absolutely adore you. When I couldn't shift back and you let me out of my bedroom, raced up the stairs to get my phone, and acted like none of it was any big deal? That meant the world to me. We have been having a great time living together. I thought of waiting until after you finished working for the FSW, but I'm not going to change my mind. What about you?"

"Not me. I sure don't want to wait." He couldn't be happier that she didn't want to wait.

"Do you want to finish dinner and then—"

"Yeah. Let's do it." He kissed her again, and then they sat down and started eating the rest of their salads, then ate more of their spaghetti. "When I saw you in that haze after you revived me on the pool deck, I thought you had the most beautiful brown eyes. I swore you were an angel."

"You needed one."

He chuckled. "I sure did. I was surprised to learn you were a wolf. I should have known you were the perfect one just for me."

"I was glad to learn you were a wolf too. I knew you would heal up faster because of it. I liked that you were working for the Fish & Wildlife Service, searching for bad guys who were harming wildlife and arresting them when you could."

"Yeah, it was a great job, long days, but because I didn't have a family, it worked out fine for me. *At the time.* I will be glad to be here in a deputy sheriff role, close to home and loving on you."

"That's what I want to hear. Now I know I'll have a date for the Valentine's Day celebration."

"A mate. For every special couple occasion and otherwise."

"Even better."

———

Roxie and Dylan finally finished the rest of their food and wine, cleaned up, put the remaining spaghetti in the fridge, and raced each other up the stairs to the bedroom. She was laughing as he was so close to her, teasing her, but unlike her

sister who would try to pass her, he was a gentle-
man and just having fun with her. She loved playing with him.

She figured her brothers might have told her
to wait and date Dylan longer, for *them* to even
get to know him better—as in drilling him about
his whole life—but they hadn't waited when they
met their mates. Wolves often didn't. So she wasn't
delaying this. Kayla and Nate had waited way too
long—to Roxie's way of thinking—but Roxie
wasn't anything like her sister. Roxie knew in her
heart what was right. And that meant being with
Dylan as his wolf mate in perpetuity.

As soon as they reached the bedroom, she sat
on the bed to pull off her boots, but he crouched
before her and pulled them off for her. She loved
his tenderness and helpfulness. He yanked off his
boots next. She stood up from the bed and began
stripping off her clothes, her sweater going first, his
after that.

Then he wrapped his arms around her in a wondrous, loving embrace. "You saved me not only
from death in the swimming pool but a lonely existence that I hadn't even realized I'd had," he said,
looking down into her eyes with his beautiful blue-
eyed gaze.

She smiled up at him, hugging him back. "Being
with you has been the best thing ever for me. I was
just as lonely, only I wasn't fully aware of it because

I'd had my family around me so much of the time. All my life, actually. But I needed to find my own mate."

"I'm glad you chose me to be the one." He cupped her face and kissed her. "I couldn't be luckier than that."

She kissed him back, their tongues teasing, tangling, tasting each other's, their hearts already beating harder, the heat filling her blood. She knew it wasn't that she had to shift, though for a moment she had worried about it. But no, it was all due to Dylan, the wolf and man who could make her heart sing with a whispered word, a sigh, a smoldering smile, a lingering gaze.

"I haven't been into hugging people much," he said quite honestly, as if that was a shortcoming of his.

But she'd found him totally huggable, and he'd sincerely returned the affection when her family or others in the pack had embraced him. She realized it was probably because he hadn't been around other wolves that much, no family, friends who were wolves. It was understandable that he hadn't been hugged all that much or felt the need to hug anyone else. Not until he arrived in the wolf pack of Silver Town, all well meaning and welcoming.

"Does it bother you?" she asked, determined to let him know just how much his hugs meant to her.

He smiled. "No. Truly, it's been amazing. But I love hugging you the most. I just wanted to tell you it's something I haven't experienced in a long time. Since my parents died actually."

She hated that he hadn't had them in his life, and she was all for making it up to him. "Well, as long as you're all right with it, you'll have a ton of wolves who will give you hugs. Me most of all."

"I'm counting on it."

"Good." She was glad he liked the affection because she was certainly the one to show it. Then she began kissing him again while she tried to unbuckle his belt. She unzipped his zipper, and he removed his pants and worked on her skirt button.

But then, as if he changed his mind, he moved her to the bed and laid her down, lifted her skirt up, and pulled off her tights. He removed her panties and tackled her bra, slipping it off her and tossing it aside.

Then he hurried to tug off his boxer briefs, but she was still wearing her skirt! He slid his hand up her naked thigh, teasing her. She wanted his fingers stroking her in the center between her legs now. But she had to admit this was erotic, and she felt a hint of naughtiness while not being able to see where his fingers were traveling as his mouth latched onto a nipple and sucked.

She loved when he did that. It made her nether

region tingle with need even more than it had been. But his fingers were moving too slowly for her, and she wanted to guide them just where she wanted them to work their magic.

But then he was caressing her short, curly hairs, searching for the right spot, and she was barely breathing in anticipation. He moved his mouth to her other breast, and she was concentrating on the sensory nerves in her nipple that were jumping with excitement at his touch when he began to stroke her between the legs. Oh, she was in heaven.

He was totally a keeper. She had no doubt in her mind about that. She arched against his fingers, wanting faster strokes, harder, yes, there, perfect. She clutched at his arms, not realizing she was doing it until he moved his mouth to kiss hers and his movement clued her in. She moved her hands over his back, sweeping down his muscles, realizing just where they were taking this. It wasn't just making love to another person. This time, they were taking it all the way. This time, they would be one for life.

But his strokes were stealing her thoughts and all she could feel was the core of her rising up to respond to his intimate touch, their pheromones swirling around each other in a mating dance of their own, the overwhelming love that enveloped her until she cried out with orgasmic delight. She truly was glad she was alone with him in the house now!

Then his heated, passionate, ravishing kiss gentled. He pulled his mouth away from hers, her hands gently grasping his neck, wanting to pull him close for another kiss, but she waited to hear what he had to say. To see if he was going to kill her with the announcement that they should wait a bit longer.

"You're—" he started to say.

"Ready, yes, go, do it."

"Before you change your mind?" he asked, arching a brow.

She gave him a slow, predatory smile. "Before you change yours."

He laughed and the sound of his fun-loving laughter tickled her.

"All right." He pulled off her skirt and centered himself on top of her and pushed in gently at first until he filled her all the way to the hilt. He held himself there. "All good?"

"Keep going." It was done. He had penetrated her with his sex, and they were mated wolves. But he had to find his pleasure in her too.

He began to thrust, his beautiful body working over her, his muscles bunching up and fascinating her, the smell of their muskiness filling her with fresh need.

Her own body was thrumming with her recent

climax, and he was so hard and huge that she loved the way he filled her up. She rocked against him, but then he paused again. Was he coming too soon? But then he moved beside her so that he could come in from behind, drawing her leg over his, and he began thrusting again, only now he could reach her clit and he began to stroke her again. She didn't think she could come again so soon. But he was so hard and this was so erotic, especially with the way he nibbled her ear, licking her neck and kissing her shoulder, stroking her to encourage her to come, that she felt the climax rising in her again.

She placed her hand over his, moving his fingers faster, harder, slower, slower, hard, but slow, and then she was crying out again, not believing he could make her come in such a position. Then he was groaning out her name, sounding satisfied as his warm seed spilled inside her.

For a moment, they lay there joined, perspiring, happy, tired, feeling great. He kissed her, then smiled. "Shower time?"

She smiled. "Anytime."

Without another moment's hesitation, he scooped her up and carried her into the shower. She couldn't believe it when he began to wash her that he was hardening up at the same time. "That's what you do to me."

She smiled, wrapped her arms around his neck,

rubbed her body against him, and felt his erection brush up against her. "I knew you were the only one for me."

She realized now her house would be his house. He would be part owner of the lodge too. Their family was expanding by one. Kids would probably follow. They would have a pack within the pack of their very own.

Chapter 18

After Dylan and Roxie finished eating blueberry waffles covered with blueberry syrup that morning, he pulled her onto his lap at the dining table. "Waking up to you is the grandest thing ever." He gave her a leisurely kiss on the mouth, licking the blueberry syrup clinging to her lips.

"I love my new routine." She licked his lips and smiled. "You taste so sweet."

"*You* are sweet."

"Only when I'm not riled." She smiled sweetly with a hint of mischief. "So I have an anniversary party to manage today. You're going in to the jailhouse to talk to Xander and Fennel, right?"

"Yeah. I'm afraid they're going to be released, then return to Denver. I need to talk to them before they go," Dylan said.

"Good luck on learning what you can from them, especially concerning where Jim might have run off to."

"Thanks." He had mixed feelings about learning where Jim might be. If Dylan had more places to look, he was afraid he'd be gone for some time and miss being with Roxie. With her in it, his life had changed so much for the better. "I hope your party goes perfectly right."

"It will, I'm certain."

They cleaned up after breakfast and called her family on a conference call to give them the news that she and Dylan were mated.

"Hey, we won that bet hands down," Landon said.

Blake agreed.

"I thought you weren't sure about me mating Dylan, Landon," Roxie said.

"I always knew it would happen," Landon said.

Kayla laughed.

Then everyone congratulated them, including Gabrielle before she went to the vet clinic and Nate, who was getting ready to check on a client's case of potential employee fraud. Nate and Nicole's mother, Nelda, said, "You realize we're adopting you like the rest of the kids, right, Dylan?"

As if Dylan and the Wolff siblings were kids, but Roxie loved how Nicole and Nate's parents treated them all like their own kids.

"Yeah, I couldn't be more delighted," Dylan said.

"Well, we knew it was a sure thing," Nelda said. "We bet on the two of you both mating too."

Gary, Nate and Nicole's father, agreed.

Roxie laughed. She had never expected Nate and Nicole's parents to bet on them too.

"This is cause for a family celebration. A night at

Sam and Silva's tavern for a dinner out or a family dinner at home?" Kayla asked.

"I opt for a night out," Gabrielle said, Nicole agreeing.

"All right. As soon as we can schedule it, that's what we'll do." Roxie was thrilled everyone was so welcoming to Dylan.

Then everyone said goodbye, though she'd see her siblings in a few minutes. She kissed and hugged Dylan. "They love you like I love you."

"I'm glad for that. As much as Jim is a menace to society, I do have him to thank for helping bring us together."

Smiling, Roxie shook her head. "I would have loved if it had been in a different way. Like running into you in the pool while you were wearing swim trunks—the right attire."

"Yeah, that would have worked for sure." Except he would never have been swimming in their pool for recreational fun. Not when he had a job to do.

When Roxie walked inside the lodge, Dylan drove into town, eager to learn anything more about Jim's whereabouts from Fennel and Xander. Dylan arrived at the jailhouse, and Peter and CJ greeted him, both holding on to mugs of coffee.

"We just fed them," Peter said.

Dylan took a deep breath of the aroma at the lounge of the sheriff's office. "It smells like some-one had ham and cheese omelets."

"Yep. We treat our prisoners right." Peter took a swig of his coffee.

"Did you get anything more out of them?" Dylan asked.

"No. We've been monitoring everything they've been saying to each other, though we have them separated so they can't see each other. They were talking about the weather, seeing their families, wishing things had turned out differently, but no specifics." Peter motioned with his coffee mug in the direction of the cells. "Who do you want to talk to first? We'll move him into the interrogation room."

"Xander." Dylan hoped he had changed his mind about keeping mum about the whole thing. Dylan wasn't sure Fennel knew anything more, but he was going to question him too.

CJ walked into the cell block. "You have a visitor."

When Xander saw it was Dylan, his whole posture sagged as if he thought he had a friend coming to see him and was feeling more upbeat until he realized Dylan was about to interrogate him.

"Come in here and take a seat, Xander. Do you want some more coffee? What about you, Dylan?" CJ asked.

"Yeah, that would be good. A teaspoon of sugar, lots of milk or cream for me. Thanks, CJ," Dylan said.

"Me too," Xander said.

After CJ brought them their coffees, Dylan took

a seat across from Xander. Dylan knew CJ and Peter would be watching and listening in on the conversation through a one-way mirror, unless they had to leave for something that required their immediate attention.

"All right, so you know that Jim took off with all your luggage and Eddie's car and left the two of you stranded," Dylan said.

"You know, you and the others have been all over me about all this," Xander said.

"Right. But what we need to know is where Jim might have gone to. If he figured his grandfather's cabin was too hot and we'd be looking for him there, where else could he have gone?"

Xander huffed. "So Jim must have figured that and told us to rendezvous with him there anyway." He was holding on to his cup of coffee with his good hand, the other bandaged. He was looking into it as if he could find the courage to tell them the truth or maybe a way to get himself out of the mess he was in. "Okay, if I tell you some other locations where he might have gone, what if he tries to kill me? Or Fennel even, thinking either one of us or both of us had told on him?"

"If we can locate him, we're taking him into custody."

Xander let go of his cup and ran his hand through his hair. "The sheriff told us the DA said we'd get a deal if we testified against Jim."

"Yeah, but we need to locate him and take him into custody."

"All right." Xander cupped his coffee cup again. "There are four other places we used to go for hunting that you might not know about. They're not that far from Jim's grandfather's cabin. About fifteen to twenty miles."

"He owns several?" Dylan was kind of surprised because when he'd checked property records for Jim, he hadn't seen anything other than Jim's palatial home in Denver. And he already knew about his grandfather's cabin.

Xander shook his head. "Two are cabins owned by lawyer friends of his. They rent them out when they're not using them. They have families and I know at least one of them is in Cancún right now." He told Dylan the names of the lawyers and an idea of where the cabins were located. "Another is an abandoned structure, but it has a fireplace, roof, walls, and windows. The inside is pretty sparse. Just about anybody uses it. We've met up with other hunters there, hikers even, looking to get out of the cold for the night and warm up by the fireplace."

Dylan suspected CJ or Peter was looking for the locations of the cabins right now as Xander told him about them. "And the fourth place?"

"A condo at Breckinridge Ski Resort. The place is booked solid for the ski season, so I mentioned it last. Unless Jim moves in on someone who has leased it, I doubt he'd go there." Xander gave him the address. "I mean, the only other places he would go would be to see his parents, grandparents, and a sister in Denver. But I'm sure you already know about all that, and most likely someone's been watching them."

"Right." They needed out-of-the-way locations where Jim could be hiding out. It would be too easy to catch him at a family's residence. The police in Denver and a couple of the FWS guys there were watching the family's homes. "Is he pretty well equipped to stay out in this weather for days on end, do you think?"

"He's pretty handy at wilderness survival, but I don't believe he'll be able to manage weeks of living in the snow without finding a place to hole up."

"All right. Can you think of anything else that might help us in locating him?" Dylan asked.

Xander's eyes teared up. "Eddie was our friend. He didn't deserve to die. I blame Fennel for revealing the affair Eddie was having with Jim's supposed girlfriend and not letting sleeping dogs lie."

"Did you know about the affair?" Dylan asked.

"Yeah, of course. I knew about it. The guys think I'm clueless about what's going on sometimes, but I don't get into the squabbles. I just ignore them, trying to pretend none of it exists. I was mortified when Jim raised his rifle to shoot Eddie. I thought he was just threatening him. I didn't think he was actually going to shoot him. When he fired his rifle, I was numb. I watched Eddie stare at him for a moment, his jaw dropped, then the firearm went off. Eddie clutched his chest, and then he went down. There was a hell of a lot of blood.

"For what seemed like forever, none of us moved. Jim had lowered his rifle, but I–I just wanted to blend in with the snowy woods and pretend I wasn't there, that I hadn't seen what Jim had done. I was just in shock. So was Fennel. I knew—since he'd been the one to let the cat out of the bag—that he felt Jim would turn his rifle on him. If Jim had killed Fennel, he would have killed me too, since I would have been the last eyewitness. At least that's what we thought."

Xander drank the rest of his coffee. "Then we heard the kid in the woods, and we all realized he probably witnessed the whole rotten mess. That's when Jim told us to help him bury Eddie fast. There was all that blood on top of the snow." Xander gave a little shudder. "It took forever to cover it all up. And Eddie too. Then Jim told us to go after the kid. We'd taken too long to bury everything so by the time we found the tent, the teen—we discovered at that point—was gone and we couldn't locate him. Jim was frustrated and furious. That's when he said we had to split forces and search a broader area for the kid. Of course, I worried that there'd be more of them. I couldn't imagine a sixteen-year-old on his own out in the snowstorm that was brewing. I tell you, I wouldn't have done anything to him if I'd found him. Just told him to get as far away from us as he could."

Dylan wasn't sure he believed him.

Xander scoffed. "Hell, the one who was in danger ended up being me." He raised his bandaged hand.

Dylan shook his head. "Fennel said it was up to Jim as to what you did to the boy."

"Hell, no. I was like Fennel, wanting to stick together, but when Jim left us, I told Fennel we needed to rendezvous at Jim's cabin like he told us to do and forget the kid. The boy wasn't going to survive out there, and we couldn't find him anyway. We couldn't get any cell phone reception at that point, so we couldn't check in with Jim. We trudged through the snow for what seemed like hours. Then Fennel and I argued about the quickest way to the cabin. That was my stupid mistake. I was sure he was leading us in the wrong direction. I tend to get turned around in the woods, but I couldn't admit it to either Fennel or myself."

"If you'd made it back to Denver, what would you have done?" Dylan asked. "With regards to the boy?"

"Nothing. That was all on Jim."

"Fennel said that you would find the boy in Denver and talk with him." Dylan was just curious as to what Xander would say in response. Since it had never come to that while they had Luke in safe-keeping, it would all just be Xander's word.

"Fennel might have said so, but I didn't plan to have anything to do with it. Or with Jim any longer. If he could turn on a lifelong friend like that, none of us were safe around him. Besides, Jim has a history of flying off the handle."

"Oh?"

"Jim's juvenile records were sealed, but yeah. His dad, who was a lawyer at the time, got him off on all charges."

"What had Jim done?" The news wasn't surprising to Dylan. Oftentimes someone who was involved in illegal activities had started out at a younger age.

"We were all out hunting with a friend named Holson. We were sixteen at the time, and Holson was riding Jim about dating some girl in high school. Holson was asking if he couldn't do any better than that, and Jim was getting madder about it by the second. I don't know why Holson would rile him like that. It was really stupid. We were all carrying rifles. Holson knew Jim had a temper, but he just kept at it, and Jim shot him dead."

"Hell. How did he get off? Besides that his father is a lawyer."

"The finding was an accidental shooting while hunting. The rest of us, Eddie, me, Fennel, all knew better. But we all agreed to say that it was an accident. I wonder if Eddie would have said something differently way back then if he had known how it would have ended for him on this hunting trip," Xander said.

"No kidding. Okay, so who tried to stop Jim from shooting Eddie?" Dylan asked.

"What?"

Dylan would have thought that despite the heat of the moment, everyone would have remembered the part where someone shouted to Jim not to do it, according to Luke's recollection. "Someone told Jim not to shoot Eddie?"

"Oh, uh, yeah, that was me."

"So you did try to stop Jim from shooting Eddie."

"Uh, yeah, but Jim just went ahead and did it because when he gets that riled up, there's no stopping him."

"What is Jana's last name?" Dylan asked, wanting to get a confirmation from her about the dating situation. Maybe she hadn't stopped dating Jim and was still seeing him while she was dating Eddie also.

"I...don't know her last name. It just never came up in any conversation."

"Do you know how Jim met her?" Dylan asked.

"At a pub in Denver, but I don't know which one."

"Okay, thanks." Dylan took their empty coffee cups. "If you have nothing more to say—"

"Watch Jim get off. He always does. If either

Fennel or I had shot Eddie, Jim would have thrown us under the bus." Xander stood up, and CJ came in to put him back in the cell.

"Thanks for talking to me," Dylan said to Xander.

"You gotta get him or I'm afraid Fennel and I aren't safe," Xander said, then left the interrogation room with CJ.

Then CJ brought Fennel into the room to speak with Dylan and left them alone. "Okay, so where do you think Jim might have gone?" Dylan asked.

Fennel shrugged. "Back to his grandfather's cabin? I don't know."

"If we can get him into custody, the better off you and Xander will be."

Fennel told him about the other places Jim might be. The same ones that Xander had mentioned. Dylan wondered why Fennel would have been hesitant before to tell him where Jim might be holed up for now. If Dylan were Fennel, he'd want Jim caught. Then again, maybe Fennel felt some loyalty to Jim, no matter what had happened between the friends.

"You never said how Jim nearly killed you," Fennel said, fishing for information, looking a bit smug again.

Dylan leaned back in his chair, figuring the way Fennel was acting, he had hoped Jim had killed him. "Is there anything else you can tell us that will help us to apprehend Jim?"

"Nope. That's all I've got. Good luck."

Dylan left the room, and CJ took Fennel back to his cell.

Dylan went to speak with Peter after that. "Okay, so can we get a team together to check out these places?"

"Yep. The same guys are going to back you up, including CJ. We've got to get this done before the Valentine's Day party." Peter smiled.

Dylan knew Peter was only joking. Who knew how long it would take to get this done? "Hey, if it runs longer than that, I want everyone to return to the party. I'll get him on my own," Dylan said.

Peter shook his head. "Are you kidding? Daniel and Bryan are single so they don't have any issue with not returning in time for the celebration. But CJ, Michael, and you? I don't even want to think of what the she-wolves would say about that. If you don't find Jim at one of the locations in a reasonable amount of time, return here before the big event, and you can go out again after Valentine's Day."

"Yeah, that will work." Though Dylan hated to have to tell Roxie he was leaving again. He was certain she would understand, but he just didn't want to leave her. That was a complete turnaround for him from being gone all the time and glad to do it, tracking down perps, to wanting to be around home all the time to see Roxie. "Okay, I've got to get packed, and I'll meet everyone—"

"At the lodge with snowmobiles gassed up and ready to go." Peter slapped him on the back. "CJ, are you ready to go?"

"And get this done? Hell, yeah."

Then Dylan headed back to Roxie's house and called her. "I have some locations where Jim might be hiding out."

"Don't tell me they're in Denver or another state."

"Nope. Only fifteen to twenty miles from Jim's grandfather's place. So the same crew is going with me as before."

"Oh, that's not bad then. You'll locate him in no time at all."

"We hope so, but we plan to come home if we don't find him before Valentine's Day."

"Unless you have a lead. The guy's a murderer. He attempted to kill you too."

"And he killed a friend when they were sixteen and got away with it."

"No way," Roxie said.

"Yeah, so he's gotten away with murder already. If I have anything to say about it, he's not getting away with Eddie's murder."

"I agree. If you can't make it back in time for the Valentine's Day party, you can wear your tux for our wedding. I already reserved all three banquet rooms for June eighth, new moon, no issues with shifting."

He wanted to hug and kiss her. "I can't wait."

"Yeah, my sister and sisters-in-law and Nicole's mother are helping me plan the whole thing."

"If you need me to do anything, just let me know."

"So you're going now?"

"I'm almost to the house. I'm going to pack up and meet everyone at the lodge. Then we're heading out."

"Okay. No matter what I'm doing, just come and say goodbye before you leave," she said.

"Absolutely. I wouldn't leave without saying goodbye, honey."

"Good. I've got to run. See you in a few minutes then."

He was glad she wasn't upset with him about not being there and even being understanding if he couldn't make it back in time for the party. He didn't want to miss it for anything, unless he was about to capture Jim.

He arrived at the house and pulled his camping gear out of the garage. Once he grabbed some clothes and slipped them into his backpack, he packed up food for a few days in case they had to be out for that much time.

Then he walked over to the lodge and found Roxie talking to Kayla at the front desk. He kissed Roxie. "Sorry that I have to run off again."

"No way," Kayla said. "You need to stop this guy from hurting anyone else."

"I so agree." Roxie hugged him. "Hmm, just come back to me in one piece." She kissed him long and with feeling.

God, she felt so good pressed against him, and he wished they had time to make love one more time before he ran off into the snowy woods again.

"I'll be waiting for you. Is Michael going with you again?" Roxie asked.

"Yeah."

"I'll call up Carmela and have dinner with her until you return if she'd like."

"Nate will be home tonight, but if he goes out of town overnight while Dylan and Michael are gone. I'll let you know, and I'll eat with the two of you," Kayla said.

"Absolutely," Roxie said.

Then the guys started showing up.

"Are we ready to go?" CJ asked.

"Yeah, let's go so we can reach that first location pronto," Dylan said. He kissed Roxie again and embraced her soundly. "I'll keep you posted when I can."

"Okay, good."

Then the guys took off with their camping equipment and loaded everything on their snowmobiles. Dylan was so ready to get this done. He just hoped they'd find Jim at one of the cabins. The first one they looked at preferably, so they could get this over with.

"We had to release Xander and Fennel on bond. They're returning to Denver. But at least we have both their testimonies," CJ told Dylan. "I don't think they're going to run unless they're afraid of Jim, should he return to Denver."

"Yeah, I agree."

Then they all mounted their snowmobiles and headed off in the direction of the first of the cabins. Dylan sure hoped they'd find Jim and no one would get hurt.

Chapter 19

"HEY," KAYLA SAID TO ROXIE AS THEY WATCHED Dylan leave the lodge with the other men, and she gave her a hug. "I know you were really excited to have a mate and a date for the Valentine's Day party finally, for the first time in years."

Roxie sighed. "Yeah, but I was being honest when I told Dylan they had to catch this guy. Sure, if they haven't had any luck and want to come home for the party, great. But if they are following his trail, they've got to get him."

"I know. But I also know you'll be disappointed if he doesn't make it home in time for the party."

"I'll take Rosco tonight."

"Okay, and Buttercup?"

"Absolutely. She misses her buddy if they are apart." The two of them were practically inseparable when it came to bedtime.

"I have firsthand knowledge of that," Kayla said.

That night, Roxie had a pepperoni pizza with Carmela at her place and they had wine with their dinner. Even though the ladies wanted to have meals with their guys, they were enjoying dinners with each other until the men were home. When

Roxie returned to her house, she said to Rosco, "Are you ready for a walk?"

He was wagging his whole butt hard, eager to go on his walk.

She attached his leash to his collar. "Okay, buddy, let's go." She loved taking Rosco on walks, even though lately Dylan had distracted her. She loved just smelling the chilly breeze, feeling the soft flakes of snow fluttering around her face, listening to the breeze teasing the branches surrounding them.

But then she saw a wolf she'd never seen before— his face mostly white, the top of his head and saddle nearly black, his torso and legs blond except for a black collar of fur. A *lupus garou*? A wild wolf? She wouldn't think one would come that close to her and her family's homes. If it was a *lupus garou*, she wondered if he was thinking the same thing about her—that she was one of his kind. If so, was he staying at the lodge? But then she remembered the twin brothers' description of the wolf near the lodge when she and Dylan were eating at the tavern. And she wondered who he was, if it was the same wolf.

She couldn't smell his scent, but she really wanted to. She began moving toward the wolf to see if she could get a whiff of his scent. Rosco was quiet because he was used to wolves and being around strangers at the lodge and elsewhere, so he didn't bark at the wolf.

The wolf stood its ground for a few minutes

more and warily watched them, appearing a little unsure how to react. Then he bounded off into the woods. That worked out even better for her. She and Rosco continued to walk toward where the wolf had been standing, and this time, she got his scent. It still wasn't anyone she knew, but she was wary of his actions. Maybe he *was* a *lupus garou* and staying at the lodge but was afraid *she* wasn't one of his kind. But Rosco was so noticeable at the place, she couldn't imagine a fellow wolf staying there who wouldn't recognize him by sight or scent.

She sighed. "Rosco, do your duty. I'm getting cold." She punctuated her comment with a shiver. She looked up at the starry night sky and thought of Dylan out there with the others and wished he had been on the walk with her and Rosco. And once they returned home? They would have warmed each other up right properly.

———

The next morning at work, Kayla said to Roxie, "We saw you walking Rosco back to your house last night. We could have gone with you if you'd let us know when you were going."

"When you and Nate were having a date night? No way. I did see a wolf I didn't know out there though."

Kayla let out her breath in exasperation. "You should have told us."

"I went off to smell his scent in case I saw him at the lodge sometime. Well, smelled him at the lodge, rather. He wasn't menacing. He seemed harmless. So what's on the schedule today?" Roxie just hoped her sister wouldn't tell Blake and Landon about it. They'd both give her grief for not going with someone else if lone wolves they didn't know were hanging about.

"I have a wedding to take care of. And you can start crafting the Valentine's Day decorations if you'd like."

"Oh terrific." Roxie much preferred decorating to handling wedding parties. Except when it came to her own. Kayla took care of the promotions. She needed to make up brochures and would redo their website after the Valentine's Day party for Mardi Gras. That morning, Roxie began creating a banner to turn the lobby into a theme of romance and love, thinking all the while about her very own wolf sweetheart and so glad she'd have him to celebrate with this year.

A group of teens, including Luke, the Silver triplets, Luke's girlfriend, Everleigh Boatman, and her brother, Benjamin, came to the desk and offered to help make more Valentine's decorations.

"Our art teacher wanted us to use our artistic talents to create decorations for Valentine's Day. To make it really special, we wanted to hang them here at the lodge where so many people can see them, if it's all right with you," Luke said.

"Oh, that would be great." Roxie was so pleased Luke was getting to do fun things like that with a bunch of other wolf teens and was happy to do it.

They brought in plastic tubs of art materials and began making a "Happy Valentine's Day" banner. The kids also made string hearts of beiges, reds, pinks, and white to put up in various places as decorations. They worked on green garlands and added red hearts on sticks that Lelandi had purchased for them. Lastly, they created a heart wreath that was covered with red crepe paper and little red hearts to hang on the wall behind the reception counter when it was time. This was the first year the teens had helped with decorations, and everyone was having a blast. Roxie treated them to a free lunch at the restaurant before they returned to do some more schooling.

She couldn't wait to roll out the love carpet in terms of creating decorations for the special occasion. She tended to be that way. Before she was even finished with one event, she was ready for something new and different. After this, they were having their very first Mardi Gras party!

For the rooms that were rented for a Valentine's Day getaway vacation, they would add rose petals, a heart-shaped box of candy, heart gift cards for the various shops in town, candles, a vase of flowers, and heart balloons. With Kayla's promotional moxie, they were having rooms booked way ahead of time just for the Valentine's Day couple retreats! They would also decorate the restaurant in a love theme of red roses and tapered candles on all the tables.

Kayla went back into the office and started creating brochures that they would print out, which meant Roxie had a moment for lunch. She walked inside the restaurant, and as soon as she did, Luke waved to her. "Come join us," he said.

That made her feel great. Roxie joined the kids, and Minx hurried over to get her order. "The tuna salad and a cup of hot tea. Thanks, Minx," Roxie said.

"Be right back with it."

"Thanks so much to all of you for helping to create the decorations for the lobby. They're just beautiful," Roxie said.

"You're welcome," Benjamin said. "It was fun doing it and being able to show it off to everyone coming through here." Then he cleared his throat, looked serious, and said, "So would you ever bite a human?"

Feeling a little panicked at hearing the question, Roxie quickly looked to see if anyone else could hear them. At least all the customers around them were wolves for now. "If I had no other choice, I might have to."

Luke frowned at Benjamin, then took a sip of his soda. "I told them I would bite someone only if I felt I didn't have any choice."

"Sure, it's understandable." Roxie realized this had to be the thing all the kids wondered about. Getting into a situation like that and having to deal with it. They were taught not to bite humans when they were wolves—or otherwise—but in a dire case where a wolf didn't have a choice, she could understand it.

"But you might not bite a human," Cathy, one of the Silver triplets, said. "I mean, even if you thought you didn't have a choice."

"I might be too scared." Roxie figured their parents had talked to them about this, and she hoped she didn't steer the teens wrong if she said something differently from their parents. "We're taught to avoid biting others—except when we're all wolves playing in fun. But if we are faced with a situation like a hunter could shoot us and we couldn't get away, or we are protecting someone else, then I hope I would be brave enough to face my fears and stop the man before he killed me or someone else. Biting a human is not without consequences, of course."

Minx brought Roxie's salad, selection of tea, and a teapot of hot water to their table, smiled, and raised her brows, appearing to be glad she wasn't having to answer these tough questions. "Do any of you need anything else?"

"No, thanks," the kids all said.

Then Minx left the table to wait on some skiers who had just entered the restaurant.

"But if he's a bad guy," Cathy's brother Mark said. "Someone who would kill us, I mean. That's what Dad said. Mom said that everyone has a good side to them, even when they seem to be all bad." Mark folded his arms, looking cross, like he went along with his dad's philosophy.

"Yeah, I agree with Mark," Greg, their other brother, said.

Roxie had to smile about that. Lelandi was always psychoanalyzing a person, but that could be good too. And Lelandi was right about everyone—or at least most everyone—having a good side to them.

"But if he's a bad guy, then you bite him and now he's one of us?" Mark said. "We don't turn bad guys."

Greg shook his head.

"Mom said the bad guy would change his ways. That he would have a new outlook on life," Cathy said.

"Which is probably true," Roxie said. "I can't imagine him being one of us and still wanting to hurt our kind."

Everleigh smiled at Luke. "Well, if someone threatened to kill me, I would hope Luke would be with me. I think he'd be a hero."

Her brother, Benjamin, laughed. "Don't believe her. She would be the one biting the bad guy before Luke had a chance."

Everleigh rolled her eyes at her brother.

Then Luke got a call and answered it. "Uh, yeah, Roxie treated us to lunch. We finished all the decorations." He smiled at Roxie. "Okay. We're on our way as soon as she's finished eating. Thanks. Bye." Luke put his phone in his pocket. "Our teacher, Mr. Tucker, said to take all the time we need and then we're going to do some science lessons."

Not wanting to keep the kids longer than she should, Roxie finished the rest of her lunch and walked them out to the lobby. "How does everyone feel about biting someone now?" She felt they hadn't really finished the conversation and she hoped their parents wouldn't be calling her up and telling her she shouldn't be discussing this with them.

"I'd bite the bad guy if I didn't have a choice," Everleigh said.

"Yeah, I would do the same as my sister," Benjamin said.

"Me too," both of Darien and Lelandi's boys said.

Cathy conceded, "Unless I was too scared."

"I–I wouldn't do it for anything, except to protect myself. I mean, if that happened to me. I, um, might not even be thinking of the consequences at the time. Just that it was either him or me." Luke bit his lip, then changed the subject. "Anyway, Mr. Turner said we're studying snowflakes."

"That sounds like fun," Roxie said.

Then the kids said goodbye and she got a call

from Dylan, and that made everything else that was going on fade away as she glanced around the room at the lobby that was decorated in love, wondering if he would still feel it was a silly thing now that they were together—in love.

Chapter 20

AFTER DYLAN TOOK A BREAK TO TALK TO ROXIE on the phone, he and his team made their way to about a mile from the first of the cabins that was closest to the lodge. They parked their snowmobiles and walked so they wouldn't alert Jim if he was staying there. As soon as they started trudging through the snow to the cabin, Dylan got a whiff of Jim's scent. "I smell that Jim has been here."

"But the scent isn't recent," CJ said, smelling the area.

"Yeah. Unless he has holed himself up in the cabin and hasn't gone anywhere since he left his scent out here, but I smell other recent scents, so someone else might be staying here right now," Dylan said.

"I bet Jim came by to see if he could stay here for a while but realized someone was already here," Bryan said.

CJ and Dylan went to the front door of the cabin while the rest of them circled around the place, observing the windows just to make sure no one climbed out of one of them. CJ knocked on the door, and a blond, bearded guy with the brightest blue eyes came to the door. "Yeah?"

"I'm Deputy Sheriff Silver looking for a Jim Johnson as a person of interest in a case."

The man rubbed his whiskered chin. "What does he look like?"

CJ showed him a picture of Jim.

"What's he wanted for?"

"For questioning in a hunter's death."

The guy's eyes widened. "Yeah, the guy was here. He was looking for a place to stay and had been here before, he said. He was carrying a rifle. I should have figured something was wrong with that picture. It's illegal to hunt with a rifle right now, which is why we're out here with our bows."

"Can I get your name please?" CJ asked.

"Yeah." The man gave him his name, phone number, and address so CJ could make a report of it.

"All right, so what did he say exactly, to the best of your knowledge?" CJ said.

"Jim said he got hit by that snowstorm and he needed to get warmed up and have a good night's rest. The cabin has two bedrooms and there are four of us staying here, so we let him sleep on the couch, gave him dinner that night and then breakfast in the morning. He thanked us and left that morning."

"When was he here?" Dylan asked.

"Two days ago."

Dylan let out his breath. If only he'd known about this before. Xander hadn't been talking earlier though, and Fennel hadn't mentioned it to them when they had first questioned him.

"Did he say or give you any clue as to where he was going next?" CJ asked.

"No. I asked because I wondered where he was going to go. He said he wasn't sure. I asked him if he was out here on his own. He said he was with two other hunter friends, and they'd gotten separated in the snowstorm."

"He was at the Silver Town Ski Resort staying at the ski lodge. He was driving an SUV. When he came here, was he on foot?" CJ asked.

"Uh, yeah. If he was driving a vehicle, he didn't park it at the cabin. He hiked here carrying a back-pack, and he was half-frozen. He really didn't look well, which was why we took a chance and fed him, then let him stay with us."

He must have ditched Eddie's vehicle. It would make sense. He was familiar with this area, so he could really get around. But still, where had the vehicle gone?

"Do you have any idea which direction he went when he left the cabin?" CJ asked.

"No. We said goodbye to him and then we gathered our gear to hunt and left."

"All right. Well, thanks. If he returns here, please call us." CJ gave him his business card.

"Sure thing."

"Where are your friends?" Dylan kept thinking

they'd suddenly come out of a bedroom or something. It seemed odd they wouldn't be here with him. Dylan had been waiting for CJ to ask, but when he didn't, he figured he'd better.

"They went hunting with their bows without me today. I've been feeling under the weather. I think I ate something that didn't agree with me last night. But my friends were fine. There wasn't any reason for them to hang around while I've been in and out of the bathroom most of the night and this morning. When they return, I'll ask if they remember anything else, and they can give you a call."

"Okay, good, thanks," CJ said.

Then CJ and Dylan left, and the others joined them to head out to the snowmobiles and drive in the direction of the next cabin on their way.

The sun was already setting, which meant by the time they reached the cabin, it would really be dark. They still needed to set up camp and have dinner. Then they would let their families know they were safe and where they were. Being able to see well in the dark was one of the great benefits of being wolves.

They parked and CJ told them the game plan again. "Since Jim stayed with the other hunters for one of the nights, I suspect he has tried to do the same at all the places he has stayed before. Keep alert. Same configuration as before. Dylan and I will go to the front door. The rest of you will watch the windows on the back and ends of the cabin."

Then they moved off toward the cabin, saw lights on inside, and heard lots of laughter. Dylan hoped he and CJ didn't ruin their evening, but he did smell that Jim had been here. Recently too. Yesterday or today, much earlier today, possibly.

CJ knocked on the door, and everyone got quiet inside. Dylan wasn't surprised. Whoever was staying here probably wouldn't be expecting company.

"I'm Deputy Sheriff CJ Silver with some of our deputies from Silver Town," CJ said, calling out when they didn't answer the door.

They understood why the people in the cabin were reluctant to open the cabin door to strangers in the night when it was so remote here. Then again, hopefully these people hadn't done anything criminal.

They saw a man peek out a window.

CJ showed him his badge. The man opened the front door. "Yeah?"

"We're looking for a man who has been hiking out here, armed with a rifle and backpack, Jim Johnson. Has he been by here?"

"We were out cross-country skiing all day, and when we returned just before dark, we found someone had broken in and taken some of our food," the guy said.

A woman joined him at the door. "He took all our bread and sandwich meats, the ass."

"Did he actually break in?" CJ asked, noticing there seemed to be no damage to the cabin.

The guy looked at the woman.

"Everyone thought someone else had locked the door. So I guess it wasn't locked and he just walked in while we were off skiing," the woman said, sounding annoyed.

"Yeah, it won't happen again," the guy said.

"He didn't take anything else?" Dylan asked.

"Some of my socks," the guy said. "I figure he needed clean, dry socks. He was gone before we got here."

"This is what he looks like if you see him." CJ showed the couple his picture. Then another couple came out of a bedroom to see what was going on, and they looked at Jim's picture. They shook their heads, indicating they hadn't seen him before.

"So who is he? What's he wanted for? Do we have to be worried?" the first guy asked.

"He's wanted for questioning concerning the shooting of his hunter friend."

"Hunting with rifles? That's illegal at this time of year," the second guy said.

"Shooting a friend is illegal," the girl who was tucked under his arm said.

"If you see him, call us." CJ gave them his business cards. "We're setting up camp about a mile from your cabin. The men with me are all deputized. So if you see him or have any kind of emergency, just call and—"

"Hey, if you're out here looking for this guy and still have to set up camp in the dark, it's going to be too hard for you to make your camp. And if you haven't eaten, why don't you eat with us?" the first guy said.

"Are you sure?" CJ asked.

"Hell, yeah. We're firemen when we're not having fun skiing. We work with you guys, so you're welcome to join us for a meal and some beers. There's plenty for everyone."

"Yeah, we have a huge pot of hot chili on the stove," the one woman said. "Come on in."

This was an unexpected perk. Dylan was glad that they were going to get a hot meal and cold beers, and they didn't have to fix a meal themselves after they set up camp.

"You can even sleep on the floor of the living room, if you want," the other fireman said.

Dylan wondered if they kind of wanted them to be here to protect them in case Jim showed up.

"We can set up camp where we left our snowmobiles," CJ said.

Dylan tried not to show his exasperation with CJ. He was going to be working with him as a deputy sheriff soon. But maybe CJ sensed something wasn't right, and he wanted to discuss it with them privately.

"It's too dark out," the guy insisted. "You're more than welcome to stay here. And really, if this Jim character is a problem and tries coming back here, we'll feel better if we have a bunch of deputies on hand."

That was exactly what Dylan had figured, but CJ was in charge, and he'd leave it up to him as to what they would do.

"Yeah, sure," CJ said. "We can do that and thanks so much. We'll just get our snowmobiles and park them here. We have our backpacks with them."

"All right. We'll serve up the chili as soon as you return," the first woman said.

When Dylan and his team reached the snow-mobiles, they all took a moment to call their families to let them know where they were. CJ explained, "I didn't want to impose on their generosity but then realized they'd feel better with our protection."

"I'm glad you decided we should stay there," Dylan said.

"Hey, I saw you looking a little peeved at me." CJ smiled. "And I've got to work with you, so..."

Dylan smiled. "I was thinking the same thing."

The guys chuckled. Michael said, "I was hoping you'd tell CJ we were staying, Dylan."

Daniel said, "Me too."

Bryan just smiled.

Then the guys all called home.

"Hey, Roxie, how are you doing?" Dylan asked as soon as he got hold of her.

"Oh, Dylan, I'm so glad to hear from you. Everything's fine here. Oh, we had a fight between two skiers. Peter had to come and was going to arrest the one, but his friend said he wasn't going to press charges. They wouldn't say what the argument was about, but they did come to blows in the lobby. I had a time reining in Rosco, who wanted to break them up. Blake and Landon stopped them, and Kayla called the sheriff. So that was my excitement for the day. Where are you at on this business with Jim?"

"We went to the first cabin closest to the resort, and Jim had actually been there, had meals with them, and stayed overnight."

"Oh no. So you just missed him. What about Eddie's SUV?"

"Jim had hiked in, the people said. So now we're at the second cabin on our list, and the people invited us to have dinner and stay with them overnight."

"Oh, wow, that's great. I'm so relieved all of you are safe and going to have lodging and hot food for the night."

"Yeah, we'll get warmed up and sleep in our sleeping bags by a fire. It couldn't have worked out better. They said Jim entered the unlocked cabin and stole some of their food while they were cross-country skiing."

"Why would he stay in this area if he had Eddie's vehicle and could have gone anywhere?" she asked.

"That's what has me bothered. I mean, it's possible he figured the SUV was too hot to drive in, but... Oh, everyone's waiting on me. I just wanted to call and tell you we're good and we're safe."

"Thanks! Call me before you take off in the morning. Where are you going next?"

"To the abandoned cabin. I'll call you in the morning. Love you, Roxie."

"I love you, Dylan."

Everyone was smiling at him, ready for a hot meal.

"Sorry about that," Dylan said to the other men.

"Been there and am still there," Michael said.

"Me too," CJ said.

They all laughed and headed for the cabin, a hot meal, beer, and a good night's sleep, if Dylan could quit thinking about hunting Jim down for a minute or two.

Chapter 21

JUST THAT ONE CALL FROM DYLAN HAD MADE Roxie feel so much better. Carmela had already arrived bearing butterscotch schnapps and crème de cacao to add to milk to make a butterscotch drink for them for fun.

They were making chicken thighs, mashed potatoes, gravy, and green beans, but then both had gotten a call from their mates.

When Carmela and Michael said good night, she began making the drinks. "I'm so glad to hear the guys are staying at a cabin tonight. I know if they'd gotten too cold, they would have shifted into wolves, but I feel better that they're having a hot meal and a cabin to sleep in this evening."

"Oh, me too. I keep thinking about Xander losing some of his fingertips and toes." Roxie shuddered.

"Yeah, that was awful." Carmela handed Roxie one of the butterscotch drinks. "Michael said they were having chili and beers. So not too bad."

Roxie laughed. "Dylan didn't tell me they were drinking beer too." She took a sip of her drink before she served up the food. "Oh, this is delightful."

"Thanks. I love it. Michael isn't that fond of

them so it's fun to make them for us since you like it too."

"Oh, yeah, this is great. Kayla would love this too."

"I bet. So what do you think?" Carmela took her seat across the table from Roxie. "Will they find Jim at the abandoned place?"

"I wouldn't have thought so since he had Eddie's SUV and I really didn't believe he'd hang around here. But since he's been at both the cabins within a long hiking distance of the abandoned one, I'd say it's possible."

"That's just what I was thinking. Okay, now, what about the details of your wedding?"

Roxie smiled. "My favorite color is robin's-egg blue, and so far everyone in the wedding party likes that color to wear. What about you?"

Carmela gave her a thumbs-up. "We're two peas in a pod."

———

That night at the cabin where Dylan and his teammates were staying, the firemen shared stories about fires they had put out. The ladies, who were both real estate agents, talked about their near disasters—a rattlesnake on the back porch of a home one of the women was showing to prospective buyers, the other finding a bunch of kids skateboarding in an empty house that she was trying to sell. Dylan's group contributed tales of Daniel, Michael, and Bryan's army experiences, situations CJ had been involved in while working as a deputy sheriff, and cases Dylan had worked concerning criminal conduct with regard to wildlife.

Then everyone cleaned up after supper, said their good nights, and headed for bed.

"I was thinking about the woman Eddie dated. Neither Fennel nor Xander knew Jana's last name, but maybe Eddie's parents know her full name," Dylan said, his voice low so as not to disturb the people renting the cabin as he settled into his sleeping bag.

"We'll call them first thing in the morning," CJ said, zipping his sleeping bag up to his chest. "It's too late to call them now."

Dylan wished he'd thought of it earlier. Something kept bugging him about the case. Why would Jim ditch Eddie's vehicle and then hike around to these cabins looking for a place to stay? He could have driven off somewhere and been long gone. It didn't make any sense.

Dylan ran his hands through his hair. "I don't understand why Jim would be on foot in this area when he could have left a long time ago."

Bryan chuckled. "You aren't like this with Roxie, are you? I mean, working out the case with her while she's trying to fall asleep?"

"He has other things he's doing with her when they go to bed," Michael said. "Guaranteed."

The guys all laughed.

Daniel sighed. "Dylan's right though. I've been thinking the same thing."

"Maybe Jim returned here because everyone would believe he had taken off and gone for good? And here he is, still in the same area," CJ said.

"That could be. We need to learn all we can from Jana, if we can find out where she is. And we need to see if Eddie's SUV is still in this area. I can't imagine Jim dumped it somewhere miles from here and walked back." Dylan folded his arms across his chest and looked up at the beams on the ceiling.

"Though he could have gotten a lift," Bryan said.

"True." Dylan thought about it some more. "We need to see if we can learn what happened when Jim killed Holson. Even if the records are sealed because he was a juvenile back then, and even though he was found innocent of the charges, there undoubtedly were news articles about it." Dylan didn't want to sleep. Well, it wasn't that he didn't want to, but he wanted to check out the abandoned cabin. If Jim was staying there, he'd be there at night, Dylan suspected. During the day, Jim could be out running around, and they'd have to wait for him to return. He glanced around at his friends. Everyone appeared to have fallen fast asleep.

Dylan got up and walked outside, then shut the

door. He went into the woods and removed his clothes and shifted. There was one way to find out if Jim was there. Run like a wolf. It wouldn't take him that long, and he'd be a silent hunter. If he learned Jim was there, then he'd come back for his teammates, and they'd make an arrest.

Before he could race off, he heard someone walking through the snow, following his path. Dylan whipped around. It was Michael.

"You didn't think you'd go on your own, did you?" Michael gave him a half smile.

Dylan gave him a wolf's smile back. He *thought* they had been sound asleep.

"The guys said if we find Jim, come back for them and they'll join us." Michael quickly stripped off his clothes and shifted, and the two of them took off. Riding on snowmobiles would have been quicker but noisier. Running as wolves was perfect.

They finally reached the abandoned building and saw smoke coming out of the chimney. Both of them approached the cabin from different directions. Then they were standing on their hind legs in the snow, peeking through the dingy windows, looking for any sign that Jim was in there.

Dylan saw a backpack and nearby a body in a sleeping bag, completely covered up. Dylan couldn't tell if it was Jim or not. But he did smell his scent, and it was strong at the front door. There were a couple of other male scents there as well.

Michael came around the cabin and Dylan indicated the window that he could look through that would show an occupant. One of them would have to stay here while the other went to get the rest of the team. If the person in the cabin tried to leave, the wolf staying here would have to keep him there until the rest of the men arrived.

Dylan couldn't let the guy get away. They needed to question him to see if he'd seen Jim, if it wasn't him.

Michael bumped against him and took off for the cabin they'd been staying at. Dylan was glad he didn't have to convince Michael to return while he stayed here, but he suspected it was because Dylan had been after Jim all along.

Dylan sat on the front porch out of the snow to keep warmer, waiting for the gang to get here. He sure hoped this was Jim and not some other hiker who was sleeping in the living room. Dylan did smell two other male's recent scents. It appeared they might have shared the cabin for a bit recently. Dylan hadn't seen anyone in either of the other rooms. There was no furniture inside, just a wooden floor and a fireplace.

He envisioned Michael waking up everyone to get dressed and join Dylan. Even so, Dylan knew they would be eager to capture Jim, if it was Jim, and wouldn't begrudge Michael waking them up. It would mean they could return home and they were eager to do that. Tomorrow was Valentine's Day, and if they could get this done tonight, that would be perfect.

The other men in their party finally arrived at the cabin. Michael had brought Dylan's clothes. They'd parked the snowmobiles away from the cabin so the occupant wouldn't hear them.

Once Dylan shifted and dressed in the woods, he joined them at the cabin. He was glad they had waited for him. Dylan, CJ, and Bryan went inside all at once, the others waiting outside.

Dylan poked the man in the sleeping bag with the toe of his hiking boot a couple of times before he stirred awake, sat up quickly, and looked like he had seen a ghost. The fire gave off enough light so that he could see the three of them looking down at him, weapons drawn. He quickly held up his hands. "I don't have any money."

It wasn't Jim, damn it. CJ introduced them to the man.

"Do you know this man?" Dylan showed him a picture of Jim on his phone.

The guy looked at it, and his gaze shot up to Dylan's. He knew Jim or had met him here. He was sweating, even though the cabin was chilly except for where he was near the fire. But even then, it wasn't hot enough to make him sweat.

Was he in trouble for something he had done himself?

"We know he has been here," Dylan said. "We need to speak with him."

"Arrest him, you mean."

"Where is he?" Dylan asked.

The guy shrugged.

"When was he here last?" CJ asked.

"Two days ago."

"He's wanted for questioning," CJ said. "If you've lied to us, which I know you have, we can charge you with aiding and abetting a man wanted by the police for questioning in a case of murder and attempted murder."

CJ was right. Jim had to have been here more recently, not two days ago as strong as his scent was.

"You need to arrest Fennel. He's the one who shot Eddie," the guy said. "Who did he attempt to murder?"

Everyone in the house just stared at him. Dylan knew it wasn't true. That Jim must have filled this guy's head with lies. Yet it made him rethink everything in a flash. Dylan had smelled Jim's scent when he'd whacked him in the head and nearly killed him.

"Is that what Jim told you?" Dylan asked.

"Yeah, we've been friends forever. And Fennel has a quick temper."

"So does Jim," Dylan said.

"And who told you that? Fennel?" the man asked.

Dylan frowned. "Jim shot a friend while they were hunting when they were teens." Dylan hoped, if Fennel was lying about all this, they'd learn that he was the one who had killed Holson.

"Yeah, but it was accidental."

"Were you there?" CJ asked.

"I was."

So that confirmed that Jim had shot Holson. Was this guy lying about the rest? "Were you supposed to be hunting with these guys this time?" Dylan asked.

"Yeah, but I'm a forest ranger and I was still working so I got here late. Well, actually, I was supposed to go to the ski lodge and meet up with them, but Jim called me and told me all the trouble that had happened. I told him he needed to turn himself in and square what had happened with the police."

"Do you know Eric Silver?" CJ asked.

"Uh, yeah, he and I get along really well. We've swapped out shifts when he needed to do something with his wife. Wait, you're...you're the deputy sheriff in Silver Town. His youngest brother, right?"

Well, that changed things up a bit. So maybe the man was telling the truth.

"Okay, what's your name and let's see some ID." CJ pulled out his phone while the man tugged a wallet out of his pocket. "Hey, sorry to wake you, Eric, but I've got a man here who knows Jim and the other hunters and says he works with you. A"—CJ looked at the ID—"Aaron Tuff?"

CJ looked back down at Aaron. "Okay. Well, if he's out here hunting with a rifle off-season—"

"I'm bowhunting." Aaron motioned to a bow and quiver of arrows across the room. "And I get together with Eric to play racquetball sometimes."

Dylan looked at Aaron's ID, but then took a picture of him and sent it to Eric, just in case he wasn't who he said he was.

"No. We've got it covered. Give Penny a hug for me. We'll talk later, Brother." CJ ended the call. "You know Fennel and the other men's hunting licenses are suspended, don't you?"

"Hell. They said they got off on the last charges. I wasn't with them any of the times they got into trouble over that," Aaron said.

Dylan confirmed that. He'd never seen this man with them or smelled his scent before.

"Okay, look, after Jim shot Holson, I could never touch another rifle for hunting or otherwise. Every time I did after that incident, I'd have flashes of seeing him die. I started hunting with my bow, and sometimes the guys hunt with me during bow season. But they still prefer their rifles. If I had known they weren't going to play by the rules this time, I wouldn't have agreed to get together with them. They know that."

"Did Jim have his bow with him when he saw you?" CJ asked.

Dylan was wondering about that too.

"He said he had left it back at the lodge in his room that he shared with Eddie."

"Why did he run? If he didn't kill Eddie? Why didn't he get hold of the police?" CJ asked.

"After Jim accidentally shot Holson as a teen, he knew everyone would look at him as the shooter. Besides, Fennel told him he would go down for this. Fennel's rifle had jammed when he was going to shoot the elk and he borrowed Jim's. Then Fennel got into a confrontation with Eddie and shot him. It was Jim's rifle, but Fennel did the shooting. So now how was that going to look? Not only that, but Fennel and Xander have always been the best of friends. They stick up for each other. They were angry that Jim accidentally shot Holson, but I understood and was just damn glad I hadn't been the one to accidentally shoot him. Jim came clean about that right away. He didn't try to cover it up. But I knew it had bothered Jim all these years. Eddie stuck up for Jim. So did I. Fennel and Xander resented us for it."

Dylan asked, "What was the confrontation between Fennel and Eddie over?"

"Fennel had been dating a woman named Jana and then he started seeing other women. Jana dated Eddie, and according to Jim, Xander riled Fennel by telling him that Eddie was seeing Jana. Words were exchanged and then Fennel shot Eddie."

Dylan rubbed his whiskered chin in thought.

So the whole story had changed. "What about the reason Jim tried to kill *me*?"

"What?" Aaron was frowning. "How? When? Where?"

"At the ski lodge after Eddie died."

"Jim didn't go back to the lodge. He saw Fennel headed in that direction and he went the opposite way. Then the snowstorm hit. He was afraid that Fennel would try to kill him after setting him up to take the fall for Eddie's death so he couldn't tell the real story. Jim went to his grandfather's place for a day, figuring he would be safe there, but then he left, worried Fennel would catch up to him since they said they'd meet up there."

"Fennel was wearing Jim's clothes then?" Dylan asked. "I recognized his hat." And he smelled like Jim, but Dylan couldn't explain that part.

"I told you, Fennel set Jim up. Fennel conveniently fell in a river they were crossing before they killed the elk. I told Jim when he mentioned it to me that I wasn't hunting with them any longer if he and the others were going to hunt with rifles out of season. I can't afford to jeopardize my job. Anyway, Fennel got his clothes all wet. The ones he was wearing and the ones in his backpack. I mean really convenient, right? Then he has nothing to change into. Of course at the time, Jim only thought it was bizarre since Fennel is the most sure-footed of all of us, but then he just figured accidents happen."

"What about Xander? Didn't he offer any of his clothes to Fennel to wear? What about Eddie?" CJ asked.

"Both men are too short, and they're only slightly built. Their clothes wouldn't fit Fennel. Both Jim and Fennel are muscled and taller. So Jim finally offered to let him wear one of his changes of clothing, though he didn't look happy about it. But Fennel had to change into dry clothes or possibly end up with hypothermia."

"So then those are the clothes Fennel wore to shoot the elk," CJ said.

"Right. And he had to still be wearing them when he killed Eddie. If they had any blood spatter on them from either crime scene, everyone would think it was Jim's fault. Jim's clothes, his rifle."

"Hell," Dylan said. If all this was true, Fennel still had Jim's clothes. But he hadn't been wearing them when they found him at Jim's grandfather's cabin. "What about the boy they were looking for? The one they thought had witnessed the murder?"

"Oh, yeah, Jim mentioned him. He said if the teen had seen the murder, he would be his witness to prove his innocence. He said he looked for him—to safeguard him—but he couldn't find any sign of him. Not even a trail. He said it was really bizarre. All he found were wolf tracks."

"What do you think?" CJ asked Dylan.

"I think we had Fennel right where he should have been, and now he has been released and he's the one we wanted." Damn it to hell. "Where is Jim, Aaron?"

"I'll call him." Aaron got on his phone and tried to get hold of Jim, but there wasn't any answer. "I'll send him a text."

CJ and Dylan read his text: Hey, Fennel told the police you killed Eddie. I told them you didn't. Get your ass here so we can make sure he goes to prison and not you!

There was still no response.

"What do you want me to do? I'll do whatever you need me to so that the right person goes to jail for the crime," Aaron said.

"Everything you say is hearsay since you weren't at the scene of either the shooting of the elk or Eddie. It's Jim's word against Fennel's," Dylan said.

"I don't know if either Eddie's family or Fennel's knew that they were dating Jana, but that would be something you can check into. I don't know her full name or I'd tell you what it was. All I know is Jim never dated her. That puts a hole in Fennel's story right away," Aaron said.

Despite the early morning hour, CJ got on his phone and called Eddie's parents first to see if they knew Jana's last name. "Hi, this is Deputy Sheriff Silver out of Silver Town, and I'm so sorry for your loss. I'm trying to locate a girl that Eddie had been dating. Yeah, I know it's really early. I'm sorry. It's vitally important or I wouldn't have called you until later today. Would you happen to know her name?"

Everyone there was waiting for the response. "Jana. Pink Ink on Instagram? Okay, thanks. You wouldn't happen to know her phone number, would you? Okay… Uh, yeah, we're zeroing in on the suspect. Thanks again." When he got off the phone, CJ said, "They don't know her last name. Whittington, Whiting, Wilcomb, something like that. But the husband and wife were disagreeing about it. Eddie's mother said that Jana went by Pink Ink, and the mother loved all the pink composite artwork Jana did. So she would check it a few times a day. She sent me the link, and I just sent it to all of you. We need to get in touch with Jana and verify that she didn't date Jim, just Fennel and—"

Dylan was already trying to find her on Facebook, and he found her. TikTok too. "Here she is. On Facebook, she mentioned dating Eddie. No mention of either Fennel or Jim."

"She could have deleted her posts once she started seeing Eddie," CJ said.

Michael said, "I've got Eddie's Facebook page up. It shows him with her at a sandwich shop in Denver and at a park earlier this year and a few other date-type pictures. They're all smiles, and he seems to really be into her. It says they are dating. But no last name. Just Pink Ink as her handle on Facebook."

"Wait," CJ said. "Look at her friends. A sister wishes her a happy birthday earlier in the year. And so does a brother—bingo! We have a last name. Whitmore."

Chapter 22

AT THE ABANDONED CABIN, AARON TOLD DYLAN and his teammates, "You guys can stay here for the rest of the night if you'd like to."

Their accommodations had really taken a dive, but Aaron did have a fire going, and it was better than tenting in the snow if they didn't have to do it tonight. Not only that, but it was still only two in the morning.

"Yeah, thanks, we'll stay here," CJ said. To Dylan, he said, "We told the cross-county skiers we were not returning to their cabin, not wanting to disturb them further, though we hadn't been sure what we'd find here."

"Do you have any idea where Jim might have gone?" Dylan had to know what had truly gone down. He felt sick that they could have let the real murderer go. That they had all believed Fennel's story.

"I don't," Aaron said. "I'm sorry. I wish Jim would turn himself in so this could be settled. But I understand he's worried that no one will believe Fennel did this instead because of how carefully he framed Jim for the murder."

Even with their enhanced abilities, Dylan realized how they could have been manipulated. Not that Fennel, if Jim's story turned out to be true, knew they could smell scents, but he'd planned this out well enough that he wanted the blood spatter on Jim's clothes, not his own, when he shot Eddie.

Dylan figured CJ wanted to stay here at the cabin in case Jim showed up. He was glad about it, thinking that would work out well for them.

But when morning came, Jim hadn't shown up, and Dylan wasn't sure where to look next. CJ was on his phone, updating Peter about what they had learned. The sheriff would get in touch with their pack leaders and let the rest of them know what had happened in case any of the men showed their faces in Silver Town or the surrounding area. Damn, it was Valentine's Day, tonight was the party, and Dylan was torn about the whole matter. He wanted to be with Roxie in the worst way, but he wanted to get Jim into custody so they could hear from him firsthand what had happened. At least according to him.

Roxie and her brothers and sister, along with a slew of other pack members, were busy setting up things in the three ballrooms for the Valentine's Day party tonight when she got a call from Dylan. She was always thrilled when she heard from him but also a bit apprehensive when he called. She hoped he'd tell her they'd caught Jim and were coming in, but she had a feeling that hadn't happened. "Yeah, what's going on?"

"A friend of Jim's said Fennel shot Eddie, not Jim."

"The friend witnessed it?"

"No, Jim told him. But I've thought about it all night and it's possible it went down the way he said it had. CJ's calling the girlfriend that he supposedly was seeing at the same time Eddie was. But Jim says Fennel was seeing her."

"Hmm, okay. That's quite a twist. But Luke said he heard one of the men cry out, 'No, Jim.'"

"Right. Another nail in the coffin? Both Fennel and Jim are the same build and coloring, so if Xander had shouted, 'No, Jim,' then anyone witnessing the killing would think Jim was the one holding the rifle. Because Jim's on the run, and there's also the business where I thought he had struck me at your swimming pool—"

"Well, what about that?" Roxie just couldn't wrap her mind around the whole scenario that Fennel had done this and not Jim.

"According to Jim, as his friend told us, Fennel was wearing Jim's clothes."

"Ahh, okay. So you're still looking for Jim."

"Yeah. He has to realize that Fennel might want

to eliminate him so he can't dispute what Fennel and Xander have concocted. If that's the case, we need to give him protection and get his testimony."

"All right." She didn't ask Dylan if they thought they might make it home tonight. She didn't need to tell him how much she wanted him to be here with her. But she knew he felt the same way and there was no reason to make him feel badly about it. "Well, you've got to locate him."

"We do. CJ is on the phone with the girlfriend to see who she really dated."

"Oh, good. I love you, you know. I want you to get the right guy who not only killed Eddie but nearly killed you. I know you'll do it," she said.

"I want to be with you. I wanted to help you get ready for tonight. I hate that I'm not there for you."

"You have a job to do. Everyone is helping set things up for the party so we're good here. And if Fennel is the guilty party, he needs to be re-arrested."

"I agree. I've got to go. CJ has some news. I'll call you later."

"Okay, thanks. I've got to go too. I love you," she said.

"I love you, honey. And I will be there if I can."

"I know you will. Just don't take any chances."

"Right."

They ended the call, and she took a deep breath and saw Kayla coming to join her. "Hey, what's up?" Kayla asked, looking worried.

Roxie told her what had happened.

"Ohmigod, they released Fennel from custody," Kayla said.

"Yeah. Fennel thinks he has gotten away with this if it's all true."

Kayla gave her a hug. "Well, if the guys don't get back in time for the celebration, you know everyone will be dancing with you, Carmela, and Laurel. I know you want to be with your mates, but the guys will make sure you're not all wallflowers."

Roxie laughed. "Thanks. That's great."

"So what's up?" Landon asked, stopping what he was doing. The same with Blake.

Roxie adored her family. They wanted to make sure she was going to be okay if Dylan didn't make it back tonight in time. That made her feel a little better. Her family was the greatest.

When CJ got off the phone with Jana, Aaron had already left the cabin to go bowhunting as a ruse to see if Jim would meet up with him. "Okay, so here's the story. Jana dated Fennel, but he was way too volatile at times and way too controlling. She had dated him for about two weeks when she called it quits and began to see Eddie. She really liked him. She dated him for a month before this all went down. She can't believe that Eddie is dead. She was crying. When I asked her who knew she was seeing Eddie, she said Jim and Xander saw her out with Eddie on a date. She and Eddie were careful not to let Fennel know. Eddie had told her it wouldn't go over well with Fennel if he learned of it, even though Fennel was dating a slew of other women at the time. He just wouldn't want to see her dating one of his buddies and really liking him."

"So she thought Fennel was capable of killing Eddie for it?" Dylan asked.

"Yeah. She said she'd never dated Jim. He was seeing a girl named Trixie. He really liked her, and he wasn't in the least bit interested in Jana," CJ said.

"Okay, so that means that Fennel has lied to us," Dylan said.

"Exactly. So we need to find Jim. I'm thinking we should head out to see if he tries to join up with Aaron," Dylan said.

"Let's go." CJ pulled his backpack onto his shoulders, and everyone did likewise, then they all headed out of the cabin and took off in the direction that Aaron had gone.

An hour later, they finally located him. But he was alone.

Aaron took a deep breath and let it out. "If you all are going to pursue me, Jim's not going to try and meet up with me."

"This is serious business with Jim," CJ reminded him.

"Yeah, I know. And I appreciate you for trying to take care of him. But I haven't seen him, and he hasn't reached out to me. I don't have any idea where he might have gone."

"Okay, thanks, Aaron. We'll get out of your hair," CJ said.

Then they continued to search for any sign of Jim. They just weren't finding his scent anywhere. The snow had fallen during the night, and if he'd left tracks, they were buried. But they should have smelled his scent still.

They smelled someone else though. A man's scent and it was recent. "Hell," Dylan said.

"What's wrong?" CJ asked, glancing at him.

"I smell the trapper's scent. The guy has set traps all over. Poison traps, leg traps, both illegal. I don't know who it is, but it's the same man's scent that I've smelled before when I came across one of his traps in the past."

"That's the same guy that we were supposed to help you locate?" CJ asked.

"Maybe. My boss didn't have any names. But if we can catch any of these guys, the better for all of us. Let's spread out and look for any traps he left behind," Dylan said. They needed to at least confiscate them. Maybe they could lift some DNA off the traps to prove who he was, if he was in the system.

Then they all moved apart and started looking for any traps, using long sticks to poke around at the snow wherever they smelled the man's scent the strongest, wherever he had lingered the longest.

That's when Daniel called out. "Got one here!"

They joined him and dug it out and set it off. Dylan hated men who did crap like this. Anyone could be at risk of stepping into one of them.

They spent hours continuing to search for more of them and found three more when the light was beginning to fade.

"Hey, we haven't found any sign of the trapper or Jim and it's getting late," CJ said. "Let's head on back to Silver Town."

"Yeah, it's getting to be party time," Michael said, sounding eager to get back to his mate.

"Let's go." Dylan pulled out his phone to call Roxie.

CJ said, "Better just surprise them, in case we end up running into either of these guys we're after and don't make it home in time."

"Yeah," Michael said. "They'd be more annoyed or worried if we said we were coming home and then never made it."

Dylan conceded, though he still would have called Roxie if the other guys weren't adamant about going silent.

They returned to their snowmobiles and took off for home. It was going to be late when they got in. He wanted to speed up, but it would be bad if anyone ended up flipping his snowmobile in a race to get home.

Chapter 23

THE NIGHT OF THE VALENTINE'S DAY PARTY, Roxie was so excited, but she was worried about Dylan and the other guys too. She had spent all day getting the ballrooms ready for the whole pack, which helped get her mind off waiting for word from Dylan. She'd had one call from him that said they hadn't located Jim, but they'd found four traps set by the trapper Dylan was trying to locate, so that was good news. But that probably meant they wouldn't make it home in time for the party.

Even Luke and his girlfriend, Everleigh, and her brother, Benjamin, came to assist them. Everything was done in pink, red, and white heart-shaped helium balloons, tables covered in white tablecloths, pink candles surrounded by white roses, elegant and fragrant. It was beautiful and she was so glad it had all turned out so well.

"Let's go home and get dressed," Kayla told her, giving her a hug. "Everything's done to perfection. It looks beautiful. Everyone will just love the whole setup."

Roxie took a deep breath, put on a smile she

wasn't feeling, and hugged her sister back. "Let's get ready then."

Kayla, Nate, Blake, and Nicole headed out with her to their homes to dress for the party. Nanny wolves were babysitting the babies. Landon went home to dress and bring Gabrielle back to the lodge. Roxie just wished she knew what was going on with Dylan and the others.

When they were dressed to the nines, they returned to the ballroom. Everyone was arriving to the party with smiles and hugs. Roxie, Blake, Gabrielle, and Kayla were greeting all the pack members who were attending the party. Landon was making sure the servers were serving all the drinks. Nate was checking on the food. They had an open bar and the food, buffet style, was ready for everyone to eat.

Carmela and CJ's wife, Laurel, also came to stand with Roxie since both their mates were out there with Dylan searching for Jim though Laurel had two mated sisters who were coming soon. Darien and Lelandi and the rest of the Silver families were arriving and meeting with everyone too. Luke was with them, and his date, Everleigh, was just beautiful.

Nelda and Gary arrived all dressed in their finery and looked wonderful. Nelda gave a hug to each of the ladies whose mates were searching for Jim and the trapper. Gary said he'd dance with each of them if their mates didn't arrive at a decent time. Roxie loved them both as if they were her own parents. Then Nelda and Gary went off to get some food.

"I brought CJ's tux with me and texted him to tell him it's here in your office if he makes it here in time," Laurel told Carmela and Roxie.

"Oh, me too," Carmela said. "I brought Bryan's and Daniel's also. If they arrive before midnight, it'll be faster for them to just dress here rather than go home."

"Since we live right next door to the lodge, I just left Dylan's tux at home," Roxie said.

"I don't blame you," Carmela said. "I'm starving. Let's get something to eat."

"And to drink," Laurel said.

The ladies were right. Even though Roxie could barely think of anything other than wanting to wait right at the entryway to the ballroom for Dylan's arrival, she knew he wouldn't want her missing out on the party and worrying about him. Besides, she figured he enjoyed the thrill of the hunt for bad guys more than he was interested in dressing up for a formal ballroom affair.

"That's the spirit," Carmela said as the three ladies clinked their glasses of champagne together. "Besides, you know the guys would rather hunt than dance in tuxes. So there's no reason for us not to enjoy ourselves."

"That's exactly what I was thinking." Roxie set

her glass on the table where they were going to sit, and then she and the other ladies followed suit before they went to the buffet table and started serving themselves dinner. "This is so much fun."

"Oh, you outdid yourself. Everything is just wonderful. The decorations, the food, the music. And everyone looks so elegant," Laurel said.

"Yes," Carmela said. "Everything is so grand."

Then Roxie got a call and answered it, seeing it was Dylan, and she braced for the news.

"We're here," Dylan said.

"Really? Seriously? You're back home? Oh, thank God."

He laughed. "We're at your house. We needed to shower, but the guys' tuxes are at your office."

"Oh, we'll get them right over to you." Roxie got off the phone. "They're here, at my place showering."

"We've got this," Landon said, overhearing her, and he and Blake headed for the office and then carried all the tuxes to Roxie's house.

Roxie, Carmela, and Laurel all hugged each other. They were delighted the men were coming to the party. So were the single she-wolves who were waiting to dance with Daniel and Bryan.

So many things had happened this year, and Roxie was thrilled she actually had a wolf taking her to the Valentine's Day party. Luke had decided that living with Darien and Lelandi and the triplets was great. The pack leaders had adopted him that week.

Then everyone who was attending the party was at the buffet, choosing from specialty drinks and carved roast beef on the sideboard along with another of pork roast and several side dishes including roasted carrots, mashed potatoes, green bean casserole, gravy, and potato rolls. Guests were using the tables around the dance floor to enjoy dinner first while a band was playing music.

When the men had taken their showers, dressed, and arrived at the ballroom, they looked like a bunch of suave, sexy James Bonds ready to right any wrong. The ladies were thrilled.

Roxie threw her arms around her handsome wolf, who looked absolutely dashing. She didn't care if they hadn't found Jim or the trapper, just as long as Dylan was with her tonight. She had kept telling herself that he needed to do what he needed to do, but she couldn't help being glad that he was here with her tonight.

They kissed long and hard. "Do you want to eat something?" Roxie asked, not letting him move from her tight hold.

"I want to dance with you just like this. All night long."

"Hmm, I'm all for that. But I hear your stomach growling. We'll dance to two songs, and then you need to eat. I bet you haven't had dinner yet. The ladies and I were about to eat when you called."

"No. We were too eager to return home in time for the celebration."

"I so agree. Tomorrow, you can go out again." Though she really wanted to spend the day with him.

"No way. I'm home. I'll begin looking for the trapper and Jim again the day after that."

"Okay. That's a deal." Though she knew if he had word that either man was in the vicinity, Dylan would be on the case, and she loved that about him. He didn't shirk from his job, even though he could have probably been on medical leave through today at least. But for now, she was dancing nice and slow with her wolf.

Now this was nice. She'd never expected to be dancing with a mate at the Valentine's Day party. This couldn't have worked out any better for her. She so loved him.

She moved her body against his in such a sensual way that he quickly became aroused.

"Hmm, I wouldn't mind taking you home right now," he said.

She smiled up at him. "I'd love to, but I helped to set this all up."

He sighed and kept her snuggled in his arms, not loosening his grip on her as they danced to the music. When the next song played, they didn't want to release each other and both continued to dance for three more songs.

But then at the end of the last one, she finally pulled away from him and said, "It's time for you to eat. I don't want you to pass out on me, and you'll need all the energy you can get for right after midnight. You don't think you're going to just go home to bed to sleep, do you?"

He laughed. "Nope. But I'm damn glad I'll be waking up to you."

"I bet. I'm sure glad you will be too."

He filled up a plate of pork roast and roast beef, potatoes, carrots, and okra. She grabbed a plate and added roast beef, potatoes, and okra for herself. They got some pink champagne and sat down together at a table with her family while Laurel had joined CJ with the Silver family. Luke and his date and her family sat with the Silvers too. Carmela sat with Michael and their extended family with the Silvers, since she and her brother were Lelandi's cousins.

"Hey, we're sure glad you made it here tonight for the celebration," Landon said.

"We all are," Kayla said. "But the guys were all going to dance with Roxie so she wouldn't have felt left out."

"No need to now. But thanks." Dylan leaned over and kissed Roxie. "I'm glad to be here."

"Are you going out tomorrow to search for these guys?" Blake asked.

"No. I'm staying home with Roxie."

"Good, we have a family dinner planned. We'll play games and then go for a wolf run in the evening. Of course you don't have to join us if you need the time alone together, but we want you there if you would like to be with us," Landon said.

Dylan instantly looked at Roxie to see what she wanted to do. She smiled at him, and right away, Kayla said, "You mated the right wolf."

The guys all laughed. Roxie smiled and squeezed Dylan's hand. "Of course we'll be there," Roxie said.

"Good," Landon said. "We're meeting up at Blake's house for the dinner. We'll decide on who runs as wolves and who carries the babies then."

"The guys always do," Nicole said. "It would be too hard for us to carry the twins by ourselves. And the guys are sweet to let us take the time to run as wolves while they carry the wolf pups. When the babies get older, we can let them run as wolves for shorter distances. Especially when we don't have deep snow like this."

"You see what you're in for?" Gabrielle said to Dylan and Nate.

The guys smiled.

"I guess that means all the guys will be carrying the wolf pups and the ladies will all be running as wolves then," Nate said.

Everyone looked at him with eyes agog, but

Kayla quickly said, "We're not pregnant yet. He means when the time comes."

Everyone laughed.

Then they finished eating and drinking and all headed back to the dance floor.

Roxie was certain everyone wanted to know all about what went on during the men's hunt for the bad guys, but she was glad nobody brought it up. For now, she and the others were snuggling close to their mates.

Chapter 24

DYLAN WAS SO GLAD ROXIE AND HE HAD MATED. This was the best thing that could have ever happened to him. He couldn't believe she was his mate, dancing with him during the Valentine's Day party when before he had met her, he figured he likely would have been searching for Jim and his friends alone. No celebration for him. It would have been just one more year blended into another. He really treasured being with Roxie and her family and friends this Valentine's Day.

He had a little over a week left with the FWS, and he desperately wanted to locate Jim and the trapper before he became a deputy sheriff. Though Dylan would still search for them as a deputy sheriff if he didn't locate him by then because he would have the credentials and he had to do it. He smiled. He liked the whole idea. But most of all, because Dylan could be with Roxie a lot more than if he was working out of Denver with the FWS.

Tonight, all Dylan cared about was holding in his arms his seductive she-wolf in a gown of red, a slit up the side, and a bodice that cupped her breasts beautifully as they danced nice and close all over the ballroom floor. He barely noticed anyone else was there, though the ballroom floor was filled with wolves dancing with their mates or girlfriends or boyfriends. The feel of her soft body against his was enough to make him want to skip being here until after midnight and just head on home with her.

Not that he could, he knew. This was mostly all her doing and she'd done a wonderful job on the decorations, music, food, and drinks. Of course she had a lot of help setting it all up, but she had been the one who had planned the whole operation.

He leaned down and kissed her mouth. "You did an extraordinary job on this party."

"I'm just so glad you were able to make it home all right and be here with me tonight."

"Yeah, I didn't want to miss it for the world." He kissed her cheek. "You are so stunning. I love this gown on you. I thought of trying to sneak you away to our house and finish off the night—"

"In bed?"

He chuckled.

"I know you too well. And no. We're all dressed up to party. Despite how many people are here for the celebration, they would miss us if we left."

But they would understand why since they were so newly mated, Dylan figured.

She wrapped her arms around his neck and continued to move her sexy body against his. "If we get too hot, we'll stop and get something to drink to cool us down."

"I'll suffer." He smiled down at her upturned lips. He didn't want to release her for the rest of the night. When he was on the mission, he had been concentrating on that, using all his enhanced wolf senses to locate the perps. But at night, all he could think of was how much he had missed being with Roxie. This was perfect. Better than perfect.

Despite his declaration to hold her the rest of the night, they did finally get some champagne to cool down and also took a restroom break. He was amused when Nicole, Gabrielle, Kayla, and Roxie went to the restroom together.

"Hey," Landon said, joining Dylan since there was a line of women waiting to go to the restroom and none of them had returned to the ballroom yet. He had a drink in his hand and took a sip of it. "I didn't mean to put you both on the spot about the planned family activities for tomorrow, our monthly family gathering. We always do them, but you and Roxie can just join us for the wolf run later if you prefer it."

"No. I look forward to it. I didn't have any family for a long time, so doing things with family again is a real nice change of pace."

"We're your family now too," Landon said. "But Roxie won't mind one way or another as long as you're happy."

Blake and Nate joined them. "Are we talking about the family evening?" Blake asked.

"Yeah. I don't want Dylan to think he doesn't have a say in anything when it comes to family gatherings," Landon said.

"I'm glad to have the extended family. Roxie and I will have the rest of the night together and all day tomorrow. I suspect by the time night rolls around again, we'll be ready to get out of bed," Dylan said and sipped some of his champagne.

The guys laughed.

"We all still feel the same way as you," Blake said. "If we're away from our mates for an extended period, we want to be with them and no one else."

"Except now we have the babies," Landon said, "and that makes it harder for us to have just our own alone time. We'll go out on dates, everyone wants to babysit the kids, but when we're at home? It's a whole other story."

"Tell me about it," Blake said. "When the kids are older, they can stay with other families who have teens to babysit them or kids their age on sleepovers, but for now?" Blake shook his head.

"Well, Kayla and I can't wait to have our own little ones," Nate said.

Everyone looked at Dylan. He smiled. "We're not protecting ourselves from the eventuality, but it would be nice to be a couple for a while before that happens."

"True," Blake said.

Then the ladies returned to the ballroom in their beautiful gowns. Kayla was wearing a red gown like Roxie was, but Kayla's looked more mermaid-like. At least that was what it looked like to Dylan. Gabrielle and Nicole were wearing pink. All the gowns were long and silky and made the women look like a million bucks.

"Hmm, did we miss anything?" Roxie asked, slipping into Dylan's arms and running her hand up his shirt.

"Nope. We were just waiting for our exquisite mates to return from the long line at the restroom," Dylan said. "You should have made an additional restroom just for women."

"Kayla and I suggested it, but our brothers wouldn't go along with it. They said the guys would be looking for the adjoining men's room and would get frustrated they didn't have one too. Besides, we have other restrooms, but this one was the closest to the ballrooms," Roxie said. "Are you ready for more dancing?"

"I sure am." He took Roxie back to the dance floor, and the others also took their mates to dance.

"So what did you talk about while we were gone?" Roxie asked.

"You're as curious as a cat. Landon wanted me to know that we didn't have to go to the family activities tomorrow night and could just join them for the wolf run later," Dylan said.

"Do you want to do that?" Roxie sounded sincere in doing whatever he wanted to do.

"No. I want to enjoy all of it. It sounds like fun. I told them we'd have the day to ourselves."

"And?"

"There was a discussion about the babies. I'm sure everyone's wondering when we're hoping to have some."

Roxie smiled. "I knew that would come up next. First, the betting on whether we would get together or not."

"What?"

"You didn't know about it?" Roxie sounded surprised.

"No. Everyone kept me in the dark about that." He thought it was funny.

"Well, Carmela and Kayla told me. Next it will be who will have babies first. Kayla or me."

Dylan laughed. "I'm all for being a couple for a while, but if it happens, it happens."

"That's what I say. You didn't talk about the case tonight?"

"Nope. It seems that's a taboo subject for the evening, which is fine with me. No one brought it up at all, and I certainly wasn't going to mention it unless someone asked me about it." Dylan dipped her and then brought her snug against him.

"Wow, I thought you told Luke you might need lessons for dancing, and I totally forgot all about asking you again if you wanted to practice. But you don't need any lessons."

He smiled. "I just said that in front of Luke so he wouldn't feel bad that he didn't know how to dance."

They glanced around the ballroom and saw Luke dancing with his girlfriend. He was doing a good job of it. Dylan was so glad they'd found him in the woods, and he was enjoying being with the Silver family and with his girlfriend.

When it was finally getting close to midnight, the music quit playing and everyone got a glass of champagne or another beverage of their choice for before they departed for the evening.

"Happy Valentine's Day!" everyone shouted.

Hugs and kisses abounded. Then with goodbyes all around, more hugs, and more goodbyes, people started leaving the ballroom and going home. The cleaning crew would be coming in after everyone was gone.

"Tomorrow then," Landon said.

"I can't wait for family night," Gabrielle said, hugging on Landon. She also had no other family and she seemed to love doing everything with them too.

"See you tomorrow," Roxie said. Then she and Dylan, Kayla and Nate, and Blake and Nicole all headed outside to their homes while Landon and Gabrielle walked toward the parking lot to their car.

Before Roxie and Dylan entered their home, Blake, Nicole, Kayla, and Nate said their good nights to them and continued to walk to their homes. As soon as Roxie and Dylan were inside, the door shut and locked, he was pulling off her coat, then his own. They slipped off their shoes next. Then he started to unzip the side zipper on her gown, revealing no bra, just creamy, delectable breasts. He kissed her bare breasts.

She moaned as he sucked on one nipple. Then he was hurrying to free himself of his tux, and she took it and placed it carefully on the back of one of the dining room chairs. He was already tugging off his bow tie, but she helped remove his cuff links.

"You are so handsome all dressed up, though I love your rugged outdoorsman look too."

"I would never have figured out what I should wear if it hadn't been for you."

"Yeah, but *you* make the outfit." She pressed her body against his, and he cupped her face and kissed her mouth.

He relished the taste of the champagne on her lips, reminding him how much he'd enjoyed the closeness of dancing with her and had so looked forward to this moment.

He entrapped her with his arms, delighting in a leisurely kiss on her mouth. Then she began unfastening the buttons on his waistcoat. He realized her gown made her sweet body much more accessible since all he had to do was unzip the side and slip it down her hips. Half of her was already naked to his touch, while he still had to remove his waistcoat and shirt to get to that point.

As soon as she removed his waistcoat, she began unbuttoning his shirt. "Too many buttons," he said, feeling a little desperate to get out of his clothes.

She smiled as he cupped her breasts and stroked her nipples with his thumbs. He moved his mouth to her neck and kissed her around to the other side, whispering in her ear, "I love you, honey."

"I love you too."

He leaned down to finish unzipping her gown and held her hand so she could step out of it, and he carefully laid the satiny red gown on the chair.

She finished unbuttoning his shirt and dragged it off his shoulders, holding him hostage, kissing each shoulder with reverence. "You are so...virile."

"You are so incredibly beautiful," he said, and he meant in every way, inside and out.

She tugged his shirt off the rest of the way and smiled. "Let's turn the mantel lights on to make it extra special."

He hauled her close and just hugged her for a moment. She was what made making love special, but he did like the idea of the charming ambience of the fire in the fireplace and the sparkling lights dancing off them and the walls.

"Music?" he asked, holding on to her still, not wanting to lose this closeness between them.

"If you want some, but I'm just as happy with listening to your heartbeat and ramping up the heat between us," she said, taking his hand and leading him into the living room. Then she released him and turned on the lights while he started a fire in the fireplace.

She tugged a futon mattress out of the spare bedroom, and he hurried to help her carry it and set it up. "I have it for emergencies if we need it for extra guests." Then she brought out sheets and blankets and they made a bed near the fireplace, the mantel lights sparkling, captivating.

She unzipped his pants and moved them down his legs. He climbed out of them and set them on her dress. Afterward, he yanked off his dress socks, then had the honor of removing her pantyhose.

She sat on the soft futon, and he joined her to pull off her panties. She cupped his package still covered in his boxer briefs. His erection pulsed beneath her touch, and he was ready to rip his underwear off, but she slowly began to slide them down, unveiling his thick erection that was eager to fill her.

Once he was free of his boxer briefs, he rested one leg over the top of hers, his knee between her legs, and then he looked into her doe-like, brown-eyed gaze, knowing he was the luckiest wolf alive to have her in his life. He caressed her jaw and just felt overwhelmed with emotion in that instant.

Sensing the way he was feeling, she said, "You are just as beautiful and I need you just as much." She ran her hand over his chest, and then she pushed him back against the futon and cradled one of his legs with her hot body, pressing her breasts against his chest. She captured his mouth with a profoundly touching kiss and he opened to her, their tongues exploring, tasting the champagne they'd had.

But making love to her was the best. He ran his fingers through her silky hair, watching the lights dancing off her face. Then he kissed her deeply, hugging her body to his, his arousal already full to bursting. He moved her onto her back again, his leg wedged between hers so he could pleasure her. He swept his hand down her silky skin, working his way to the vee between her thighs, and found her wet and ready for him. He poked a finger between her feminine lips, and she gave a start and a moan. Their pheromones were shouting to do this already, to make the primal connection, both their hearts hammering in agreement.

Not even the cold walk in the snow from the lodge to the house had chilled the heat that had erupted between them on the dance floor. He was burning up, wanting inside her in the worst way. He stroked her, kissing her luscious, sweet breasts, her throat, her shoulder, her eyes, her mouth, loving every bit of her. She was caught up in the fervor of the ecstasy of the moment and cried out with joy. She was so sweet, sexy, so receptive to him that he didn't wait to enter her, claiming her, angling into her for deeper penetration. Then he was thrusting, wanting to reach the pinnacle of the climax.

When they were together like this, making love, it was like they fed the furnace with a blazing fire. Her hands were holding his hips, her body thrusting against his as if she wanted, needed more. Then she shuddered, her inner muscles caressing his hardness. God, he loved her. She bucked against him until he couldn't hold on any longer and released deep inside her with a satisfied groan.

For a long time, they just held each other close, enjoying the afterglow of the moment. "You make me complete, Roxie." He pulled the covers over them. He wasn't sure if she wanted to stay with him down here or go upstairs to bed, but he loved the enchanting ambience of the lights and the fire in the fireplace, making this a truly special night.

"You do the same for me," she said, her voice dreamy. And then she snuggled against him and closed her eyes.

He had his answer. She truly made everything magical.

The next afternoon, Roxie snuggled against Dylan, loving him and so thrilled that he was here with her for the whole day and night. She kissed his naked chest. "You make me want to stay in bed all day." They'd made love again that morning and had skipped breakfast, going back to sleep instead.

He chuckled and kissed her. "Ditto for me. Do you want to have something to eat?"

"Yeah, let's have tangy collard and cabbage slaw and pork chops. We'll have steaks tonight at Blake's."

"That sounds great."

They took a sexy shower together, unable to get enough loving in. When they finished, they dried off, dressed, and then headed downstairs to the kitchen and began preparing lunch.

"This has been the best Valentine's celebration ever for me," Dylan said.

She knew it had been. With her family, she'd had wonderful celebrations, but having Dylan for her mate was just incredible. "Me too. I love you."

"I love you, honey."

They were going to have such a wonderful life together. She knew it.

They finished making lunch and then served it up with a glass of wine each.

"This is superb," Dylan said.

"Yeah, it is. Delicious. We make a great team."

"We do."

After they ate and cleaned up the dishes, they put the futon away and threw the sheets in the wash.

She said, "I've got to make a dessert for tonight. Do you want to help me make it?"

"Absolutely. What can I do to help?"

"Let's make seven-layer magic cookie bars."

"I love them. I haven't had them since I was a kid when I used to make them with my mom," he said.

"That's okay then, isn't it?" She didn't want him feeling sad about it.

"Yeah, absolutely."

She got out all the ingredients while he found a pan for the bars and preheated the oven. Then he started melting the butter and swirled it around to coat the whole pan. She sprinkled graham cracker crumbs evenly over the melted butter, and he pressed them down. He added the semisweet chocolate chips. Butterscotch chips were next and then drizzled condensed milk over that. She sprinkled shredded coconut on top. They finally added pecans on top. She pressed it all together lightly. After they baked the bars, they set them out to cool, put the sheets in the dryer, decided on a movie to watch, and fell asleep on the couch in each other's arms.

When they woke, they smiled at each other for being so tired and missing some of the movie. Then they dressed and walked out into the snow to have dinner with the family that night. Dylan carried the dessert. Everyone was there already. The guys began grilling steaks off the partially enclosed patio, Nicole was nearly done baking potatoes, and Kayla and Roxie finished making a cheesy cauliflower dish. Nicole and Nate's parents were watching the babies.

Gabrielle and Landon were making pomegranate gin fizzes for everyone, except that Gabrielle's and Nicole's were nonalcoholic.

They began serving up all the food and taking their seats at the dining room table.

"Any sweetheart resolutions?" Landon asked everyone.

"I want to go skiing with Roxie," Dylan said, clinking his drink glass with Roxie's. "I couldn't before because of the head injury, and then I was back to looking for Jim and then the trapper too. But first chance I get, I'm skiing with her."

"Oh, that would be great. All expert slopes, right?" Roxie asked.

"Uh, I think I'll work into it with a green and then the blue slopes."

Everyone laughed.

"I take it you don't go skiing much. You're too busy on the job all the time," Roxie said.

"Yeah. When I was a kid, I skied a lot, but that was a long time ago. That's also my resolution. Enjoying life to the fullest with Roxie and all of you," Dylan said. "Seeing more of the sights out here, visiting with pack members."

"Well, we're glad to be taking in another member of our extended family," Gary said.

They all cheered.

"Thanks for bringing me into the family," Dylan said.

"The pleasure is all ours," Nelda said.

"My resolution is having a ball with Dylan and enjoying all the perks of having a wolf mate," Roxie said.

Everyone laughed. She swore Dylan even blushed a little.

"Oh, mine is losing my baby fat so I can snuggle closer to my sweetheart," Gabrielle said, patting her tummy.

"Me too!" Nicole said.

Roxie thought both of her sisters-in-law looked great for having had twins just three months earlier.

"You girls look great," Nelda said.

"Yeah," Landon said. "I can't imagine how I'd look if I'd had twins. You're both beautiful and just perfect."

"I second that," Blake said.

"These drinks are delightful," Nelda said.

"Yeah, they really are good," Gary said.

"The steaks are divine. I love the seasonings you put on them," Roxie said.

"Nicole got them as a special treat for family night." Blake raised his glass to her.

"We need to take a family trip," Landon said.

"Yes!" Roxie said. Now that she had a mate, she was all for it.

"I'm game," Dylan said, reaching out to grasp her hand.

Everyone loved the idea.

Roxie squeezed his hand back. "That's one of the good things about working here and with the sheriff's department. Peter will give you time off whenever you need it."

"Yeah, I can't wait to begin working here full-time."

She couldn't wait for him to work here.

They served up the seven-layer magic cookie bars and enjoyed them before they started their games.

"These are the greatest," Kayla said.

"Yeah," Blake said. "I'm glad you made them."

"Thanks. It was teamwork," Roxie said.

"It was hard not to eat one before we came over here," Dylan said.

Everyone laughed and then they set up phone app games to play, starting with Psych! While each family member was taking turns creating fake answers to trivia questions, those who guessed the correct answer among the false ones earned points. The person who made up the answers would win points for each player who chose theirs as the correct answer.

Kayla won five games, and they all said she was the best at psyching them out.

They did Clue next, to determine who the murder was from a list of characters. Dylan won most of those. But Gabrielle and Nicole had to give up on the game to shift and feed their hungry babies as wolves. It was easier to feed twins that way!

They also did a mobile trivia app that featured themed rounds of questions like in Trivial Pursuit.

Then the mothers finished feeding their little ones and woofed at everyone.

"Are we ready for a run?" Landon asked.

"Yeah, let's go," Blake said. "We'll take a shorter walk with the pups and then run tonight." He and Landon took the pups outside to an area where the snow had been shoveled off to let them relieve themselves, then returned them to the house and packed them in their pup carriers.

The moms remained in their wolf forms while everyone else stripped out of their clothes and shifted.

Landon took hold of Rosco's leash as he and Blake carried the pups on the walk.

The others ran as wolves for a short trip into the woods, because everyone was a little tired after coming in so late from the Valentine's Day party last night and especially the brothers and sisters-in-law with babies getting them up during the evening. But this was important too. The daddies didn't mind walking as humans instead of running as wolves, to their credit.

They finally returned to their homes and said good night to each other.

"Was it worth it to you to have the family night?" Roxie asked Dylan as they walked inside their home and shut and locked the door.

"Absolutely. And returning home with you after the family gathering when I would have been on my own if it hadn't been for mating you? That means the world to me."

"The same to me."

This time, they headed to bed to finish off the day in style.

Chapter 25

THE NEXT MORNING, THE TEAM WAS READY TO head out on a search for Jim and the trapper. Dylan called to let his boss know that they'd found four of the trapper's lethal devices, but no luck on finding Jim or the trapper yet. His boss wished him the best of luck and to be careful.

After they finished the call, Dylan kissed Roxie goodbye and said, "I don't know when we'll return home this time."

"Don't worry about it. The party is over with and now it's back to work for all of us. We're going to spend the morning setting the ballrooms up for the functions for this afternoon and evening. So we're going to be busy. It will be boring compared to what you have to do."

"I wouldn't mind boring if I could help you with all that."

"Thanks, Dylan."

Then he and the other guys left to try to locate Jim and the trapper. They hoped they'd be successful this time. They also spent the day again checking two of the three cabins that Jim was known to frequent just in case anyone had seen Jim again, but no one had.

"We ought to check out his grandfather's place," CJ said after they visited the first two cabins. It was about twenty miles from the abandoned cabin.

"All right. It's getting late. I say we stay at the abandoned cabin tonight and check out his grand-father's place in the morning," Dylan said.

"Yeah, that sounds like a plan," CJ said.

They headed out to the abandoned cabin, and Dylan wondered if they'd find Aaron still there.

When they finally arrived at the cabin, they smelled smoke and saw it curling out of the chimney, and a low light was on in two different areas of the cabin. They also only smelled Aaron's scent around the cabin, no one else's scent. CJ knocked on the door and called out. "Hey, Aaron, it's CJ and our team."

There was no answer, but when they peered through the window, they saw a couple of battery-operated lanterns were on inside.

CJ cautiously opened the door and peered inside. "He's not here."

They went inside and looked around the cabin. Quite a few of Aaron's things that they recognized from before were there—his backpack, sleeping bag, and camping equipment.

"Does anyone feel that something's off? That something's not right?" Dylan asked.

"Yeah," Daniel said. "He could be bowhunting at night but—"

"His bow and quiver of arrows are over there in the corner," Michael said, pointing them out.

They set their backpacks in the cabin, and Daniel and Bryan added wood to the fire while the others pulled out their food packs to make a hot meal—campfire grilled-cheese sandwiches.

They filled the room with more lanterns and turned them on.

"I think we should look for Aaron before we eat." Dylan drank some of his water. "Someone should stay and watch the fire, but maybe a couple of us can see if we can find him. I was thinking he'd gone into the woods to relieve himself, but it has been a long time."

"Yeah, I'll go," Michael said.

"Me too," CJ said.

"I'll stay and tend to the fire and be here if he returns," Daniel offered.

"I'll stay behind with Daniel, and we'll alert you if we have any trouble," Bryan said.

"Good idea," CJ said.

They all left the cabin. Even Daniel and Bryan went with them initially to get more wood for the fire. "Be careful out there," Daniel said.

"Yeah, we will." CJ brought the first aid kit in case they needed it.

They normally would go in stealth mode, but this time they had to call out if Aaron was close by and had been injured or lost his way back to the cabin. They all were calling out to him, trying to locate him. They could smell that he had gone in this direction, so they knew he had come out here. His scent continued on farther, and Dylan wondered why he would have walked so far away from the cabin at night. Unless it was like he'd thought before. Aaron had gone out to relieve himself and didn't want to do it too close to the cabin.

Then Dylan thought he heard a moan way off in the distance. "Aaron?"

"Have you got something?" CJ asked.

They were all spread out, trying to find Aaron.

Dylan kept getting whiffs of Aaron's scents in this direction. "I thought I heard him over this way. Aaron!"

"Help," Dylan heard Aaron say, his voice strained.

It was Aaron! "Hey, guys, Aaron's over here and I think he's injured." Dylan was trying to rush to his aid. "Aaron, this is Dylan and the rest of our law enforcement team. Keep calling out. We're coming to help you."

"Here," Aaron said, his voice still really not much more than a whisper.

Dylan was worried Aaron was suffering from hypothermia. "Keep talking. I'm getting close." He thought he was. But he wasn't positive because Aaron's voice was so distorted.

"Watch where…you're…walking," Aaron gritted out.

The other guys were getting closer to Dylan, and then Dylan saw Aaron half-buried in the snow, his face covered in a ski mask, which would help to keep him warmer. "Aaron! He's over here," Dylan yelled out.

"We're coming!" CJ hollered.

Dylan reached Aaron and pulled his parka off to cover Aaron with. "What happened?"

"Leg," Aaron croaked out.

"Leg trap? Crap! Hey, CJ, we need that first aid kit!" Dylan called out. "Aaron's leg is caught in a leg trap, I think. We need to shovel out the snow around his legs."

CJ called Bryan and Daniel to come help them.

Michael pulled out the first aid emergency blanket and wrapped it around Aaron and then was immediately on his radio while the others were digging Aaron out. "We're bringing in an injured park ranger with a possible leg fracture after stepping into a—"

"Bear leg trap," Dylan said, locating the dangerous device. "Aaron...also has hypothermia."

"Bear leg trap. He has hypothermia. We'll take him to a nearby abandoned cabin where we have a fire going, stabilize him, and then bring him in. Uh, okay. We'll get him ready for transport then." Michael gave them the GPS coordinates. "See you soon." He ended the call and said, "EMS rescue is sending a team to pick him up."

"Oh, even better," Dylan said. He loved how they had so many people who were capable of dealing with problems in the area. But he wished he could trap the trapper with one of his own devices and leave him out to suffer—see how he liked that.

Bryan and Daniel soon reached them.

Once they had exposed the rest of the bear trap, Dylan and CJ carefully opened the trap and Michael eased Aaron out of it while Bryan and Daniel tried to stabilize Aaron's leg as much as possible. The pain was too much, and Aaron cried out and then lost consciousness.

"Let's hurry, but...carefully," CJ said while he and Dylan released the trap and let it snap back into place. "It's better that he has passed out for moving him to the cabin, but we need him warmed up, his leg stabilized, and then we need him conscious. I've been through this before myself, and I know how bad it can be."

"Hell," Dylan said, figuring CJ might even have PTSD from seeing Aaron experiencing the same trauma.

They splinted Aaron's leg with the materials from the first aid kit. Then they carried him to the cabin. It seemed to take them longer while carrying Aaron and trying not to injure him further.

When they reached the cabin, Daniel immediately ran to open the door and threw it open. Daniel hurried to spread Aaron's sleeping bag out for him.

The men settled Aaron on the bag.

"I'll be right back," Bryan said, but Daniel went with him as he left the cabin and shut the door.

Dylan began heating up some beef broth for Aaron to warm him up. "He's mildly hypothermic."

CJ and Michael removed the splint and swore.

"Compound fracture," CJ said. "This is worse than I had." He pulled out a bandage to wrap around Aaron's leg to stop the bleeding, and then they splinted it again.

Aaron stirred. "God, how bad is it?"

Dylan brought him the beef broth as the others covered him up with their sleeping bags.

After giving Aaron the broth, Dylan helped him to drink it to warm himself up. If Aaron had been a wolf, he would heal twice as fast as a human. So CJ had been lucky in that regard.

"It's a compound fracture," CJ told Aaron.

Hopefully Doc could save his leg.

Aaron closed his eyes.

"Don't fall asleep," Dylan warned.

"Yeah. I've had the drill as a forest ranger, since I've assisted in—" Aaron's face contorted with pain. He smelled of it too.

"Are you all right?" Dylan asked, wanting to do anything he could to help him through this until he could get real medical assistance.

"No. But I've helped on lots of emergency medical cases, so I know what I have to face."

"Okay," Dylan said. "We've got a team coming to pick you up. We need to get you sufficiently warmed up."

Bryan and Daniel returned to the cabin with the bear leg trap.

"Good thinking," Dylan said, though he'd planned to retrieve it once Aaron was picked up.

"Hell, that's it?" Aaron shook his head. "I heard someone out there. I thought it might be Jim—that maybe he was afraid to approach the cabin in case someone else was staying there. I went out to see if it was him and talk to him. I kept hearing the sounds of someone roaming around out there and saw a man's tracks. The snow was deeper there. I didn't even realize it until I stepped off, sank down into the snow, and the trap closed onto my leg. I heard a snap and felt pain a few seconds later. That was a horrible feeling. I tried to dig out around the trap, to see if I could free myself, but I kept passing out from the pain. I called out over and over again, but whoever it had been didn't come to my aid. I knew unless you guys, Jim, or possibly the asshole trapper were about, I wasn't getting out of there. Unless someone else just happened to come along, and I didn't think that was likely."

"We're glad we returned here," Dylan said.

"Me too," Aaron said.

Dylan heated up some more broth for Aaron. "Are you feeling a little warmer?"

"Yeah. Thanks. The fire, all these sleeping bags, and the heated beef broth are helping. I take it if you're here, you haven't found Jim yet," Aaron said.

"Not yet. But we're also looking for the trapper who's setting the illegal traps," Dylan said.

"I sure as hell would be too, but it looks like I'm going to be out of commission for a while," Aaron said.

Dylan had mixed feelings about staying here. He wanted to see that Aaron arrived home fine and came out of surgery without any problem. He wanted to be with Roxie tonight.

They made their grilled cheese sandwiches, ate, and made sure Aaron had enough to drink and fed him some more beef broth.

Two hours later, they heard snowmobiles off in the distance. It appeared Aaron's medical team was nearly here.

CJ went outside with his flashlight and waved at the men coming for Aaron.

They were soon greeting each other and hurrying inside to take care of Aaron. "Hey, we'll get you out of here pronto, on heavy pain medication and into surgery," the one man said.

Then everyone helped settle Aaron on a sled. Dylan and Bryan packed up all of Aaron's gear and secured it on the back of one of the snowmobiles. Then the EMTs took off.

"*That,* I hadn't expected," CJ said. "Let's get something hot to drink and then get some sleep."

Everyone was kind of just standing there, and then Dylan began making hot cocoa.

"I suspect everyone was kind of hoping we could return home for the night," CJ said.

"Yeah, I was sure thinking of that. I would want to know that Aaron came out of the surgery just fine," Dylan said.

"And stay with our mates," Michael said.

CJ got on his phone. "Hey, Eric, your friend Aaron caught his leg in a bear leg trap. We're still searching for Jim and the trapper, but I know you'd want to go see him in the morning. Is he married? Single, okay. His boss and his family should be notified… Okay, thanks." He ended the call. "Eric's going to notify their boss about Aaron."

"Okay, good," Dylan said. "I want to catch this trapper."

"Yeah, me too," Bryan said.

The other men all agreed. Then they got on their phones to let their families know where they were and what they were doing.

"Hey, Roxie, I thought we might be coming home with an injured bowhunter."

"Oh, I wish you could be here."

"Yeah, the EMT rescue team came and took him to the clinic. He had a compound fractured leg so we could have done more damage than good if we had tried to transport him with what we have."

"I don't blame you for letting them take care of

it. Is…is the bowhunter a friend of Jim's?" Roxie asked, sounding dreamy, like maybe he'd woken her, and he wished they'd been together tonight even more now, just thinking of snuggling with her, making love, and enjoying each other's company.

"He is." They talked for a while longer, then finally ended the call so everyone could go to sleep.

Then the guys started unrolling their sleeping bags and setting them up to sleep on. Dylan couldn't stop thinking about Aaron and how he could have died if they hadn't found him.

"I smelled the trapper in the area." Dylan climbed into his sleeping bag and zipped it up. "Maybe a week to a week and a half old."

"Yeah, I did too," CJ said. "If the bastard was in the vicinity, just farther away and had heard Aaron's cries and didn't help him, I'll charge him with even more, beginning with attempted manslaughter."

"I would too," Bryan said.

The next morning at daybreak, they made campfire skillet peppers, onions, potatoes, cooked ham, and eggs for breakfast over the fire in the fireplace. Dylan called Doc to learn how Aaron was doing and put it on speakerphone so everyone would know what was going on with him.

"He's on so much pain medication, I don't think

he's feeling any pain. He's had lots of swelling in the injured area. He wanted Peter to set him on a snow-mobile and he'd come and join you on your hunt for the trapper."

Dylan smiled. Aaron would make a good wolf. "Is his leg going to be all right?"

"It's difficult to say at this point. I wasn't about to allow him to join you. I pumped him full of anti-biotics to ward off infection. I was able to set the bones so that he should be able to walk again. But he has had some tears in muscle and tendons, so I had to repair those too. They take longer to heal than bones. Time will tell as to his recovery."

"Okay, Doc, thanks," Dylan said.

"Yeah, well, don't any of you get caught up in those blasted things. They do a lot of damage."

"We don't intend to. Tell Aaron we're all rooting for him," Dylan said.

"I will. Eric's coming in to see him shortly. And Aaron's parents are arriving this evening to be with him. Roxie's made a room reservation for them at the lodge until they can take him home."

"That's good. Tell him we'll let him know when we catch the trapper, even if it takes a while," Dylan said.

"All right. We'll talk later."

"Thanks, Doc." Then Dylan ended the call and they all cleaned up and packed their gear onto their snowmobiles. "Let's find some perps."

Before they started their snowmobiles, CJ got a call. "Okay, thanks, Peter. I'll let the others know. We're on our way there." He ended the call and said, "A couple of our wolves out cross-country skiing found Eddie's vehicle. We're closest to where it was abandoned, so we're to go there and investigate it."

Which meant smelling scents around the vehicle to see who had been in it last. Fennel? Or Jim?

"I've got the coordinates," CJ said. "Let's go."

Though Dylan and his teammates would be more assured Jim was telling the truth and Fennel had lied if they found Fennel's scent was the strongest one left behind, they still couldn't use it as evidence in a court of law.

They drove to an old logging road that was closed during the winter and found the SUV half-buried in snow. Which made sense because whoever took it had left before the snowstorm got really bad.

They parked their snowmobiles and peered in through the windows. Several bags were sitting in the SUV. Dylan was surprised the driver hadn't dumped them somewhere else. He opened the driver's side door. It wasn't locked. And the keys? In the ignition. Dylan wondered if Fennel had hoped someone would locate the vehicle and steal it and everything in it. But then the snowstorm hit, and it was half-buried instead. He smelled Fennel's scent more than any other scent, and his scent was much more recent.

What's more, Dylan saw Jim's clothes, and when he checked them over, he could smell Fennel's scent on them too. "These are the clothes Fennel wore when he killed the elk and Eddie," Dylan said. "I see blood spatter on them."

CJ said, "Bag them." He looked at the bags in the back. "This is Eddie's bag. It's got his name on it, but it also smells like him."

"This is Jim's," Michael said, looking through it.

"Xander's bag is over here," Bryan said.

"Fennel's bag isn't here," Daniel said.

Dylan said, "It appears he truly was the one who took the vehicle, dated Jana, and killed Eddie over it. Had to have been."

"Yeah, I agree," CJ said.

"He should have left his bag with the others," Dylan said. "But if he thought someone might steal the SUV, he probably didn't want them to take his stuff. There's a bow and quiver of arrows back here. Smells like both Jim and Fennel. So maybe someone had thought to hunt legally."

"Or wanted to give that appearance if anyone caught them out here hunting. It's about a five-mile hike from here to Jim's grandfather's cabin," Michael said. "He could have taken his bag with him there, since that's where he was caught."

"When we took him into custody, we confiscated his backpack. We searched for anything that would lead us to Jim," CJ said. "I don't remember finding a bag there like the other guys had."

"Should we investigate Jim's grandfather's cabin again?" Dylan asked.

"Yeah. As soon as we get someone here to pull the SUV out of the snow, we can do that. They'll take it into town and check it for fingerprints or any other evidence that could link Fennel to the crime," CJ said. "I'll call a plow."

This was the part of the job Dylan didn't like. When he had to sit and wait on something. He knew he would have times like that with the sheriff's department too, but he still didn't like the waiting part of it.

Chapter 26

FINALLY, A SNOWPLOW ARRIVED TO CLEAR THE road so that Eddie's SUV could be picked up by the tow truck and hauled to Silver Town. "We'll go over it with a fine-tooth comb when we get to the station," CJ said. "Let's go to Jim's grandfather's cabin now."

Dylan and the others loaded up on their snowmobiles and drove over there. When they arrived, the place looked quiet. No smoke was coming out of the chimney. No lights on in the place. Though if Jim was staying there, he'd probably try to keep a low profile.

They did what they had on previous occasions with some of them watching the windows and Dylan and CJ going to the front door. CJ knocked. "Jim, if you're in there, we need to see you. This is Deputy Sheriff CJ Silver of Silver Town. Your friend Aaron said you didn't kill Eddie. We believe him. He has got a compound fractured leg and—"

A man approached them from the woods, his hands up in the air. *Jim Johnson.* Finally.

"Get on your knees and put your hands behind your head," Dylan said before CJ could. It was true that they believed Fennel had killed Eddie now, but they still needed to be sure Jim wasn't going to become hostile. "Where's your hunting rifle?"

"Inside the cabin. I didn't do it. I didn't do any of it," Jim said, sounding resigned and somewhat relieved it was over.

"That's what Aaron said before he was injured," Dylan told him. "But we need your statement."

"How did Aaron get injured?" Jim asked, his brows raised, appearing surprised.

"Bear trap. We've also been looking for the trapper who did this to him," Dylan said.

"I guess you can't let me help you look for the bastard," Jim said.

"I'm afraid not." CJ read Jim his rights, and then they took him inside.

"You've been keeping out of sight," Dylan said.

"Yeah. I knew this would be the first place you'd look for me. I figured by now, no one would think I'd return here," Jim said.

Dylan motioned to the couch for Jim to take a seat. "Fennel told us where to look for you."

"I figured that might have been the case." Jim proceeded to tell them what had happened. Which was the same thing that Aaron had told them. Jim hadn't faltered from his version in the least. Often, when perps were lying, they'd forget the story they had already told and alter it or decide that another story suited their purpose better.

"I'll be right back," Michael said. "I'm going to see if I can find Fennel's bag in the house."

"What?" Jim asked.

"We found Eddie's vehicle abandoned on a logging road. All your bags—yours, Eddie's, and Xander's—were in the SUV," CJ said. "All except for Fennel's. That's why we came here to see if we could find it. Also, the clothes he was wearing when he shot Eddie were in Eddie's SUV. We arrested Fennel here."

"He's in custody." Jim took a relieved breath.

"Sorry, no. He told a convincing story, and I'm afraid we released him. There's a witness to Eddie's murder, and we'll have him verify that you aren't the shooter." At least Dylan thought Luke would. What if he still believed Jim was the shooter?

"Hell, that's great," Jim said.

"But when Xander yelled out, 'No, Jim, don't,' Luke immediately thought that the person who committed the murder was you, Jim," Dylan said.

"Aw, hell. I didn't know why Xander called out my name. It just didn't make any sense to me."

"Why didn't you try and stop Fennel from shooting Eddie?" Dylan asked.

"Fennel had my rifle! And I didn't really think he was going to do it. Then Fennel shot Eddie, and it was too late to do anything about it." Jim rubbed his forehead.

"Why did you help cover up the body?"

"Like I told you, Fennel had my rifle. He didn't give it back to me until later, and he told us since we all had done nothing to stop him from shooting Eddie and we helped to bury his body, we were all accessories to the murder. I knew my law practice was doomed. I–I just wasn't thinking. And I sure as hell didn't believe Fennel would set me up to take the fall."

"Yeah, great friend, eh?" CJ said.

"Did you know there was a trapper who also might have witnessed the murder?" Dylan asked.

Jim's eyes grew big. "A red-haired and bearded man?"

Now Dylan was the one who was surprised. "You've seen him?"

"Yeah, he shared coffee and breakfast tacos with us one morning. He looked like a mountain man and smelled of body odor, like he hadn't bathed in a while. He was wearing animal skins over his clothes, a hat made of beaver, but under that, he was wearing a white parka and snow pants. He was friendly enough. We figured he was a trapper. But I hadn't seen any sign of him when the shooting occurred."

"Did he offer you a name?" Dylan asked. "If he witnessed the murder, we can try and get his testimony and that would help your case."

"As if anyone like that would agree to go to Denver to testify in a court of law," Jim said.

"What if he's the one who injured your friend

Aaron?" Dylan couldn't tell Jim that the scent on the traps was the same as the scent of the man who might very well have witnessed the murder. But if Jim and his friends knew who the man was, that might help them in locating him and charging him with crimes of his own. Of course, if he had witnessed the murder, they'd also want to know his version of the story.

Jim stared at Dylan for a moment and then frowned. "He said his name was McInerny. That he went by Rusty because of his red hair, but some people called him Mac. He offered us whiskey to add to our coffee, but we declined because we didn't know where he'd gotten it from. But he poured quite a bit into the coffee we made for him, and he was really talkative. We hadn't expected him to be. He asked why we were carrying rifles during bowhunting season."

"This was before the elk was shot?" Dylan asked.

"Yeah, like the day before. Eddie said that we were just hiking, but if a cougar tried to get us, we had to be able to protect ourselves. There wasn't any way of getting anything past Rusty. He said he knew we were illegally hunting out of season and probably didn't even have licenses to hunt. He was a wary old cuss, but he seemed to like us. Fennel was getting really bothered by the talk of doing illegal stuff. But I suspected Rusty was hiding from the law or something himself."

"Did he tell you he was illegally trapping?" Dylan asked.

"No, but he said that this is God's land and that no one had the right to tell him or anyone else what they could do on it. So we took that to mean he didn't see anything wrong in what we were doing—or whatever it was that he was doing."

Bryan had joined Michael to look for Fennel's bag and then Bryan said, "I got Fennel's bag!"

"Where was it?" Dylan asked when Bryan rolled the bag into the living room.

"Stuck up in the attic. We had to find a ladder to reach it."

CJ pulled out a pair of gloves and opened the bag. He started to move the clothes around, and then he found a plane ticket to Bolivia and Fennel's passport. "It looks like Fennel was planning to take a trip. He had to have planned this all along. Okay, so we have Fennel's bag, Eddie's car, and Jim. Let's return to Silver Town. Luke can see Jim and verify he's not the one who shot Eddie," CJ said. "If you didn't know, since Fennel was wearing some of your clothes, when he tried to kill Dylan—"

"What?" Jim's gaze shot to Dylan.

"Yeah. I'd know your gray knit hat from anywhere. The last four times I arrested you for violating hunting regulations, you were wearing it. Fennel was wearing your clothes when he smashed me in the head with his rifle butt, knocking me out cold, and I ended up floating facedown in the ski lodge's pool. Well, then sinking to the bottom. If someone hadn't rescued me from the pool and resuscitated me, I would have been dead," Dylan said.

"Hell. I didn't do it. I wouldn't have done it. Why would I have?" Jim stroked his beard. "The reason Fennel was wearing my clothes was that we were crossing a stream, using a fallen log to reach the other side, and everyone was doing fine. But then Fennel was ahead of me, and he suddenly lost his balance. Don't ask me how. He looked fine and then, to me, it appeared he just…fell. I can't believe the bastard went to such lengths to pretend he was me. Why would he try to murder you?" Jim snapped his fingers. "He thought you were following us and saw *him* shoot Eddie."

"I was following you. I just hadn't met up with you in time to catch sight of everything that had happened. But I suspect that's just what he thought," Dylan said.

Jim ran his hands through his hair. "Hey, man, I'm sorry about the illegal hunting. You won't catch me at it again."

Dylan was surprised to hear him say it. Jim hadn't ever been sorry for any of it. He would just weasel himself out of getting charges for it—almost always. "Whose bow was in the SUV?"

"Mine. I planned to hunt with Aaron, and he wouldn't have approved of me hunting with a rifle.

After what happened between my friends and me on this trip…" Jim shook his head. "What about the trapper?" Jim asked, sounding like capturing him was just as important as getting Fennel behind bars.

Dylan could see that Jim's friend was important to him. "We're still trying to catch the trapper and we'll charge him with attempted manslaughter. But we also need to get his witness testimony if he saw what occurred since he knew you by name, right? You wouldn't happen to know where Rusty was living or staying, would you?"

Jim shook his head. "We all had introduced ourselves. He just said he lived off the land, but he never said where he lived exactly."

"We can take you over to the clinic to see Aaron after you give us your statement," CJ said.

Jim took a deep breath and let it out. "Good. And thanks."

Then they packed up Jim's things while CJ called Peter with the news that they had Jim and Fennel's bag and were returning home. "Yeah, boss. We'll be there in a few hours."

Before dinner, Dylan was thinking, and he was so glad. Tonight, he would be with Roxie. Tomorrow, he would be back to searching for the trapper. He wasn't certain if the other men would be too or if they had other business to take care of. But he was finding that guy.

They drove to the lodge to pick up their vehicles, and Dylan managed to get in a quick trip to see Roxie. She was in the middle of a wedding setup, but as soon as she saw him, she hurried to join him.

"I'm so glad you've found Jim and Eddie's car." She was hugging Dylan to pieces, and he loved it.

He kissed her with enthusiasm and didn't want to let her go. "I've got to get down to the sheriff's office. Darien's bringing Luke there to have him identify Jim as one of the hunters at the scene of the murder but not the man who did the shooting."

"Oh, good. But we're on for dinner, right?"

He smiled and lifted her against him and swung her around. "And all night too. Absolutely."

"I'm so glad." She kissed him again and then she noticed someone was waiting to ask her about something and she smiled at Dylan. "I so love you."

"I love you too. I'll see to this business and then shower up and start dinner if I'm home before you."

"Okay. I'll see you soon."

Then they parted ways and he gave her a backward glance, saw her watching him, and both of them smiled at each other. She was the light of his life.

He went to the house and got his truck, and when he finally arrived at the jailhouse in Silver Town, Darien was bringing Luke to the station to see Jim. If they'd thought Fennel was the murderer initially, they would have had Luke identify him as the shooter. So they'd messed up big time by letting Fennel off.

Dylan wanted to be there for Luke when he saw Jim through the one-way mirror. The other men went home. "I'll bring Luke home after this, Darien."

Darien looked at Luke to see how he felt about it.

"Yeah, sure," Luke said. "That's fine with me."

"Okay, I'll see you in a bit," Darien said.

Darien left and CJ and Peter went in to speak with Jim.

"Show us where you were standing in relation to the others when Eddie was fatally shot," Peter said to Jim.

"Yeah, sure. I was here, northwest of Eddie. Fennel was over there holding my rifle, directly west of Eddie." Jim pointed toward the door. "Eddie was standing diagonally northeast from Xander."

Dylan was envisioning exactly the setup, the angle of the bullet that had been discharged, and he knew that bullet had to have come from Fennel's direction. He glanced at Luke, who was watching everything Jim said and had tears in his eyes.

Dylan patted his shoulder. "You don't have to see or hear any more of this." He reminded himself that Luke was just a boy, though he seemed older than his age, and he'd witnessed a horrific murder.

"It's just as he says it was. The other guy? Xander? He called out, 'No, Jim, don't!' But he was looking straight at Fennel. Not at this guy—Jim," Luke said, pointing at Jim. He looked up at Dylan. "Both those guys set Jim up. How could they do that to him?"

"I know, right? It was an awful thing to do." Dylan frowned, thinking of something else. "We believe a trapper by the name of Rusty McInerny also witnessed the murder. He's a redhead with a red beard wearing mostly white. A fur hat and furs were worn over his other clothes. Did you ever see him while you were in the woods?"

"Uh…" Suddenly, Luke was perspiring a little, his gaze going to the floor. He ran his hands through his hair, and he cleared his throat. "I…uh, was running as a wolf, and I saw a man like you described, and I saw him setting a trap. I wanted to set it off but couldn't while he was in the area. Later, when I had shifted and was dressed, I returned and triggered the trap with a stick, then yanked it out of the ground and buried it in another area so he wouldn't find it."

"I wouldn't want you putting your life at risk like that, but that's exactly what I did when I was your age with traps that a trapper had set. I wreaked real havoc with him. Good job," Dylan said.

Luke shoved his hands in his pockets, looking dejected, not like he was pleased with Dylan's praise of him.

"You did a good thing." But Dylan suspected there was more to the story then.

"I–I started following him, tripping his traps

before he could hurt anyone with them. I was really careful not to be seen, and I got rid of ten that way. I knew I was doing something right by the animals and anyone else who might come across the traps but…" Luke let out his breath in exasperation.

"Okay?" Dylan was getting a bad feeling about this, though he wasn't sure what could be wrong with this scenario. Then he got it. "He saw you shifting."

"Worse." Luke looked up at Dylan, tears filling his eyes.

"You had to kill him?" Dylan was surprised. It was something they had to do sometimes, but Dylan could understand how distraught Luke could be over it.

Luke shook his head and wiped his nose with his sleeve. "He…he chased me with murder in his eyes. I knew he was going to kill me. I went to the cave I often used when I needed to get out of the bad weather. And…and he followed me in there. But it was dark inside and he couldn't see like I could. Then he turned on a flashlight and I knew he'd shoot me as soon as he saw me. He had a rifle on him. I was as deep in the cave as I could go. I hurried to strip off my clothes and turned into my wolf. It was the only thing I could think of that would give me a fighting chance."

"You bit him."

"I feel terrible about it. Everyone's been so

welcoming. Everyone's treated me like part of the wolf pack, like a friend, part of the family. I should have told you right away."

Dylan gave him a hug. "Hey, these things happen sometimes. He had you between a rock and a hard place. You did the only thing you could do to protect yourself. Everyone will understand."

Luke sobbed.

Dylan felt awful for him. "Hey, you're not in trouble."

"My parents drummed it into me that I"—Luke choked on tears—"was never supposed to bite any human as a wolf, ever. That if I did, I was supposed to kill the person. I–I couldn't. I–I just couldn't do it."

"It's okay. Really. We'll find the trapper and take him into the pack. If he can't adjust to being a wolf in a pack where someone looks out for him all the time, then Darien will make a decision on how to handle it."

CJ joined them, but Dylan saw that he'd been listening in on some of the conversation.

Dylan said, "Do you have the traps that we located, including the one that injured Aaron, CJ?"

"Yeah, I sure do. Why?" CJ asked.

"Luke needs to smell them to see if the man he saw was the same one who set other traps that he had located," Dylan said.

CJ took Luke to the evidence room and Luke

smelled the scent. "Yeah, that's the redheaded guy's scent that I smelled on the traps. The one who came after me and I–I bit."

"Okay, we'll take care of it. We don't want you to feel like you can't talk to any of us about things like this. Or any other issues, really," Dylan said.

"Yeah, I agree with Dylan on this. Darien's my cousin. You won't be in trouble for it," CJ said.

Then Peter came out of the interrogation room. "So who killed Eddie, Luke?"

"Fennel did." Luke swallowed hard, still appearing upset about what he'd done to Rusty. Luke appeared to be on the fence about whether Darien would think it was all right that he'd bitten a human. "Jim wasn't holding a rifle. Fennel was and he aimed it at Eddie and shot him. Xander was holding a rifle too. I swear if Jim had intervened, Xander might have shot him. I can't believe Xander was in on the whole thing. They must have known I was there watching. Why else would they have pretended Fennel was Jim so that I would overhear it?"

"I agree," Peter said, glancing at Dylan as if wanting to ask why Luke was so upset.

"I'll be happy to testify against them," Luke said, wiping his eyes again.

"Me too," Dylan said. "Luke also identified Rusty McInerny as the man who had set several traps that Luke triggered and hid. But Rusty caught him at it at the very last, and the only way Luke could defend himself was to bite him."

Peter nodded. "I'm sure Rusty won't want to be setting traps any longer. Good job, Luke. We'll bring him into the pack. I'll tell Jim that you identified Fennel as the shooter. Why don't you take Luke home? I'm sure Roxie can't wait to see you, Dylan."

"Thanks. I'll do that." Dylan slapped Luke on the back. "Now we just have to get Fennel back into custody. He was planning a trip south of the border. Hopefully, he didn't manage to slip away down there already."

"You don't think he'd come after me, do you?" Luke asked, sounding worried as they got into Dylan's truck.

"He'd be foolish if he did. And of course, we need to catch Rusty and teach him all about what we are."

"I want to do it. I'm responsible."

"I'm sure Darien will be amenable to that. Though others in the pack will keep an eye on him too," Dylan said.

"This is going to be like how it was for Roxie, isn't it? Growly when she shifts when she doesn't want to," Luke said with regret.

"Well, everyone's different. He might not be bothered by it at all. We just never know."

"Have you ever turned anyone?" Luke asked,

looking hopeful that since Dylan had been in the same situation as him, he might have done something similar.

"No. I got lucky. How are things going with you and the Silvers?" Dylan drove out into the countryside where Darien and Lelandi lived.

"Great. Though Lelandi said she wanted to talk to me about what I had to go through at the jailhouse. Her kids say she's always like that." Luke took a deep breath and let it out. "She's going to want to talk to me about turning Rusty too."

Dylan nodded. "It can be a good thing having a psychologist in the family."

"I'm glad you're mated to Roxie." Luke brightened. "I knew you would be. I saw you dancing with her at the Valentine's Day party. You looked like you didn't need any dance lessons."

Dylan almost laughed. "It just came naturally when we began to dance together. You're right about us being together."

"Do you have to talk to Lelandi?" Luke asked.

"About what?"

"About what you went through? I mean, I witnessed a murder, but you were almost murdered."

"She talked to me about it when I was at the clinic. Lelandi's smart and knows her profession, but she's also tenderhearted and intuitive. She really wants us to feel okay about what we went through." Dylan finally reached the Silvers' country estate and parked on the circular drive out front. "It'll get better. Just know it isn't your mistake." Dylan gave him a hug.

"Thanks, Dylan." Then Luke smiled. "Um, I'm invited to the wedding, aren't I? Yours and Roxie's?"

"How would you like to be one of my best men?"

"Really? You mean it?"

"Yeah, and thank you for straightening all of us out about who murdered Eddie. We might not have gotten the right man if it wasn't for you witnessing the whole affair."

Luke straightened in his seat. "I'm so glad I didn't become a mountain man like you had to be when you were my age. Maybe I could be a deputy sheriff when I get older."

"I know you're working at the movie theater for now, but I'm sure Peter, or even Nate and Nicole, who have their PI business, could give you some apprenticeship work. It would give you a step up if you decided to go into law enforcement. Especially after you were trying to stop a trapper from injuring or killing animals."

"Will you recommend me? I don't know if everyone's going to be all right with me turning Rusty."

"Hell, yeah, I'll recommend you, but you don't need my recommendation. Everyone's behind you on this or anything else you set your heart on doing. We're here for you." Dylan thought about it and wondered if Luke was afraid to tell Darien about turning the trapper. "Do you want me to talk to Darien about you biting the trapper?"

"No…I'll do it."

"All right." Then Dylan hugged Luke again and Luke finally got out of the truck, waved at him, and hurried off to the house.

Dylan waved goodbye before Luke opened the front door and disappeared inside, shutting the door behind him. He knew Luke was going to feel bad about the business with Rusty until they located the trapper, and hopefully the man would forgive him.

Dylan drove off for home, a hot shower, dinner, and lots of loving Roxie. He finally reached the house, parked in the garage, grabbed his gear, and carried it inside. "Honey, I'm home."

The house was quiet and dark, so he assumed she hadn't made it home yet. After he cleaned up his gear, then put it away, he grabbed a glass of water before he took a shower and dressed. He'd call her to see if she needed his help with anything after he showered, though he was going to make dinner.

They also needed to find Rusty pronto so that they could tell him what he was experiencing was normal for one of their kind. Dylan figured he would be out on more manhunts, only this time he would also be looking for a wolf.

He needed to return to Denver, pick up his stuff, and return here. Maybe this weekend. The rental was furnished, so he didn't have to take anything with him but his clothes and other personal effects, not to mention his groceries.

Dylan went up the stairs to the master bedroom and shed his dirty clothes in the bathroom. As soon as he was in the shower, he rinsed off and then lathered up, wanting to stay in there forever. He closed his eyes as he washed his face, then heard the shower stall door open and opened his eyes to see a naked Roxie joining him. He gave her a big smile. Things couldn't get better than being home with her like this.

"Hmm, I like seeing all these soap bubbles on you, fun to pop," she said running her hands over his soapy skin.

He wrapped her in his arms. "I'll just have to cover you in my soapy bubbles so I can pop yours too."

She laughed and they began kissing, the shower spray hitting his back and the top of his head. He turned around so she could have the warm water on her back and then he kissed her again, his hands on her breasts, massaging them.

But then he was pouring out some soap and slathering it all over her, rubbing his body against hers, getting himself—and her—worked up. Forget dinner for the moment. They were making love in bed first. But they didn't make it out of the shower in time for that.

Chapter 27

"Hmm, are you going to run off again tomorrow?" Roxie asked, snuggling against Dylan that night. She really felt for Luke—for having bitten the trapper and turning him, and for the trapper, who wouldn't know what kind of a mess he'd gotten himself into. She wondered then if that was why the teens at the lodge had brought up the idea of biting a human and whether they should do it or not. Had Luke wanted to tell them about his own situation, or had he told them already because he'd been so bothered by it? No matter what, the silver lining would be the trapper most likely wouldn't be setting traps any longer.

"To search for Rusty, yes. Of course if Fennel makes the mistake of returning here, we'll arrest him too. But if that doesn't happen, the police will take care of Fennel wherever he ends up. Even as a deputy sheriff, when I have that job, I can only go as far as our jurisdiction covers."

"That's true. Who all is going with you after the trapper?" Roxie asked.

"I'll check with Peter in the morning. He wants this taken care of just as quickly as I do because

Rusty could shift in front of hikers, skiers, all who are human and cause real trouble for us. And we sure as hell don't want him biting someone."

"You're right. I just don't want you out there on your own."

Dylan smiled at her and kissed her nose. "With a wolf pack, I've got backing."

"Good." Tonight, she just wanted to fall asleep with her wolf, enjoying the fresh scent of him and feeling his gloriously warm body next to hers. She loved how nice it was to have a wolf of her own.

The next day, Roxie and Dylan finally got out of bed, dressed, and made breakfast together. When they finished eating, Dylan called Peter to see how he wanted to do this. He figured the team he normally had would be switched out with some other reserve deputy sheriffs so that the other men could take care of their own business. "So, Peter, I'm going back out to look for that trapper." Dylan realized it was hard for him to actually ask for help.

"Yeah, CJ and the rest of the guys were just waiting for the word from you."

"Oh, great. As soon as they're ready to go, I'll be ready. I'll just wait for them at the lodge again, like usual." Dylan was so glad Peter was backing him all the way. Then he reached over and clasped Roxie's hand. "They're meeting me at the lodge."

"Okay, good. I wasn't letting you go until I knew for sure others were going with you."

He smiled and kissed her. He never imagined having a mate who would always look out for him on his jobs, when in the past, he thought nothing of handling cases on his own.

When Dylan and Roxie arrived at the lodge, he hadn't expected Luke to come with the other men. Luke was eager to help find Rusty, and Dylan couldn't have been prouder of him.

"Hey," Luke said, smiling at him when they met up at the lodge. "When I told Darien and Lelandi I wanted to help you locate Rusty, they were all for it. They said that it would be good to have some closure."

Dylan had some reservations about it. He didn't want Rusty to lash out at Luke for what he had done to him, though they would all protect Luke.

For the rest of the week, Dylan and the others, including Luke, went in search of the trapper during the day, making a few night excursions, but were home for the rest of the night to be with their families. It was finally Friday night, and Dylan planned to take off the weekend to clean out his apartment. He'd already given notice at his apartment the day he had decided to stay with Roxie and take the deputy sheriff job.

"Everyone's fine with you taking off the week-end to move, you know. And everyone will help you with it," Roxie told him as he and she walked home from the lodge.

"I don't have that much stuff. Pretty much all that I have there is clothes and food." Though he hated to give up on searching for Rusty, Dylan had to move his stuff out and clean the place up.

"All right, well, don't worry about someone else catching Rusty."

He smiled at her and kissed her. That was what was really bothering him about the whole situation. He looked forward to the downtime with Roxie, but he wished he had accomplished finding the trapper first.

"How about we go up to Denver tonight instead of tomorrow morning? We can stay the weekend to pack, clean, and see the sights?" Dylan asked.

"Yeah, that would be great. Should we have dinner up there?" She went to the master bedroom to pack a bag for the weekend. "I've got a couple of ice chests in the garage we can take. We can get ice in Denver."

"Yeah, I want to take you to some restaurants I really like that you don't have in this area and to some other places that I haven't been to since I was a kid. That's great on the ice chests." He packed his bag too.

"Let's go then." She called Kayla and told her

they were leaving tonight to stay in Denver. Nate and Kayla were already taking care of Rosco and Buttercup because Dylan and Roxie were going to be gone for the weekend. "No, we've got this. Dylan said he doesn't have too much to pack up. Yeah, we're going to see the sights. I'll let you know when we return. Thanks. Love you." She got off the phone and said to Dylan, "Kayla will let the rest of the family know we're taking off tonight instead of tomorrow."

"I already told my boss I was taking the weekend off. He wasn't surprised now that I have you in my life. Before that, I worked all the time," Dylan said, carrying their bags down the stairs.

"That's not good for you." She climbed into Dylan's truck in the garage.

"You are what's good for me all the way around." He loaded their bags into the back seat along with a couple of ice chests she had for the food in the fridge and freezer at his apartment.

"The same for me."

Then they were on their way to Denver, and he couldn't wait to show her some of the places he loved and see the sights he hadn't been to since he was a kid and his parents had been alive. He hadn't been interested in any of that since then, not until he had Roxie in his life and was eager to share it with her. He'd even made reservations at one of the nicest hotels, which she totally approved of.

Roxie was so glad to get this done—and so was Dylan. He'd bought a few clothes in Silver Town, but now he would have all his clothes and he wouldn't feel so much like he was living out of his suitcase. No longer was he a bachelor male living alone on his own but a mated wolf living with her. She was curious to see what his place looked like, to smell him there, to learn more about him. This had been his domain, his kingdom, as much as her place had been hers. But now he was every bit a part of her home.

When they finally arrived at the apartment complex, he parked, but he kissed her and said, "I think I straightened it up before I left the apartment, but I'm not sure."

She laughed. "You are great at our house, so I don't care what your place looks like. That was when you were a bachelor and you weren't expecting company anyway."

"Okay, I wanted to warn you just in case."

They pulled the packing boxes out of his truck and carried them to the outer doorway of the apartment complex.

"I hope no food spoiled since you've been away for so long," she said.

"No. I only defrost what I'm going to eat right away. Everything is frozen otherwise. I used up the last of the eggs and milk before I left. I wasn't sure when I would be back, though I really thought I would have caught these guys before I returned home. Then again, I didn't think I'd be looking for a murderer."

"I agree."

They went down the hall to the front door of his apartment, and he unlocked it. They were both burdened down by boxes, so when they stepped into the room and came face-to-face with Fennel holding a rifle on them, they both just froze.

They hadn't smelled his scent at the front door. Why not? Roxie wondered if Fennel had broken in through a back window or... She saw the back door to a patio. Dylan's apartment was on the ground floor. It would have been easy for Fennel to gain access to the apartment.

Dylan didn't have his gun with him. He hadn't planned on hunting anyone down.

"What do you want with us?" Roxie began to put the boxes down on the floor.

"Shut the door," Fennel said.

Dylan threw his boxes at Fennel, knocking his rifle out of his hands. Then Dylan dove for Roxie, pushing her out of the apartment. "Run."

She wasn't leaving her mate alone with Fennel for anything. She knew Dylan was trying to protect her. And she knew he wasn't letting Fennel get away with this. Roxie couldn't either because Dylan would be chasing him forever.

But she did stay outside the apartment for the moment while Dylan tackled Fennel before he recovered his rifle. That was when Roxie raced into the apartment, looked for something that she could use to disable Fennel, and saw a lamp on a table next to the couch. She grabbed it and pulled. It was plugged in. *Naturally*.

She ran over, yanked the cord out of the outlet, and raced across the room with the lamp in hand. Dylan and Fennel were matched in height, but Fennel was heavier than Dylan by maybe thirty pounds. The two were fighting with each other, Fennel trying to reach his rifle, Dylan wrestling to keep him from getting hold of it.

Roxie waited for the perfect moment, then swung the lamp just as Fennel was on top of Dylan and struck Fennel hard in the head, knocking him out.

"Call 911." Dylan shoved Fennel off him and checked him for a pulse, then headed into the kitchen. He pulled open a drawer and grabbed some duct tape. After he taped Fennel's wrists behind his back as he lay on the floor unconscious, Dylan checked the man's pulse again.

"He's not dead, is he?" Roxie already had her phone out and had called 911. "A man who's wanted for murder and attempted murder, Fennel Keaton of Denver, needs medical attention at my boyfriend's apartment." She wanted to call Dylan her husband, because as mated wolves they were mated for life, but she wasn't technically married to him by human standards with an official marriage certificate, and she didn't want to complicate things.

"No. He has a steady pulse. That was good thinking. And fast," Dylan said to Roxie.

"I was in the army," she reminded him.

He smiled. "Good thing for me."

"I'm Roxie Wolff and we're at Dylan Powers's apartment." She gave the 911 operator Dylan's address while Dylan wrapped Fennel's head with a bandage to stop the bleeding. She should have felt bad when she had injured the man like that. But if he had gotten hold of the rifle, she didn't doubt Fennel would have shot them both.

"We're sending an ambulance and the police to your location. Is he conscious?" the operator asked.

"No, but he has a pulse." Roxie could hear his heart thumping hard.

They heard sirens off in the distance and she was hoping they were coming for Fennel. She saw Dylan's bloodied nose and bruised cheek. She hurried into the kitchen to get some paper towels and stop the nosebleed. After the police saw and documented what had happened, she would wash the blood from his face.

"I love you." She glanced around the apartment. It was a mess.

"This is *not* my doing. Fennel must have been staying here since we let him go and then had the police issue a warrant for his arrest again," Dylan said. "He would have figured no one would ever suspect he'd be hiding out here—least of all me."

"I agree."

Then Fennel started to come to. They heard the sirens right outside the apartment building. Good. Finally. It hadn't taken them long, but every second seemed like hours, and she wanted Fennel treated for his injury and then taken into custody before he could hurt anyone else.

The door to the apartment was still wide open. They heard footfalls racing down the hall. "Police!" one of the men said before entering the apartment.

"We've got everything under control," Dylan said. "I'm a special agent with the FWS. My girlfriend is here with me. Fennel Keaton is the one you're after."

The officers began coming into the apartment. Dylan showed them his badge and ID. Once the police were assured Fennel wasn't going to shoot anyone, the paramedics were called in and they took care of Fennel and transported him to the waiting ambulance.

Dylan filled in the local detective, Detective Price, on exactly what had happened and how it had ended here.

"All right. Here's my business card if you think of

anything else," Detective Price said. "He'll also be charged with breaking and entering."

"Good. Here's my card if you need me for anything else," Dylan said to the detective.

Then the police left, one of them taking Fennel's rifle, and Dylan and Roxie looked at the mess Fennel had made of Dylan's apartment.

"Believe me, I did not leave my apartment looking like this," Dylan said, noticing the piled-up dirty dishes in the sink, food wrappers everywhere.

"Once the warrant was issued for his arrest, he must have realized you knew he had lied about everything." Roxie began putting the dirty dishes in the dishwasher. "He could have just washed the dishes."

"Yeah, I agree, but I don't believe he had my best interests in mind." Dylan started to throw away the trash and then cleaned the pots and pans. "Here I thought I'd left the place nice and clean at least as far as the kitchen went, ready to just pack up my belongings and move out, and that would be it."

"We'll take care of it. I'm just so thrilled we caught him without anyone dying. There would have been a million more questions asked if I'd killed Fennel. Your place would have been taped off as a crime scene." She wrapped her arms around Dylan and kissed him. "And then we wouldn't have been able to clean out your apartment and take your clothes with us." She kissed him again. "I would have had to take you shopping again."

He laughed and kissed her. "I'm glad you didn't kill him. He needs to go to prison for what he's done, and you didn't need to have this on your conscience."

"Well, this totally calls for a celebration."

"I agree. I'm going to quickly call my boss and let him know Fennel has been caught before he sees it on the news."

Roxie smiled, then gently cleaned the blood off Dylan's face. "Yes, you should do that. When your boss learns you caught him in *your* apartment, he might really be upset with you if he didn't learn it from you first."

"Exactly." Dylan got on his phone while Roxie started the dishwasher, then headed into the bedroom.

Chapter 28

AFTER PACKING AND CLEANING, DYLAN AND Roxie left the apartment, climbed into his pickup, and drove to the restaurant. When they arrived and walked inside, it smelled delightful.

"The bread is homemade, and they make their own beer." The place was a lively eatery and Dylan really liked it.

"That sounds good. I love the lighting and music in here."

They were seated in a cozy booth, the lighting low for ambience, and the food was delicious. Dylan had come here on a date once, on one of the rare occasions he'd taken a wolf out on a date, but he wasn't about to mention that to Roxie. He just figured Roxie would really love this place. It was one of the best restaurants in Denver.

After looking at the menu, Roxie ordered butter-poached lobster, brussels sprouts, olive-oil-fried potatoes, and wine. Dylan got the seafood paella, but when the server brought their meals to the table, they both shared part of their dinners with each other. They didn't actually portion the food onto each other's plates. They fed each other from their plates. It was a lot of fun. He was so glad she was here in his stomping grounds and seeing something beautiful, not just thinking about cleaning out his apartment and dealing with Fennel. He hoped the police would keep him in jail and wouldn't let him out on bond.

They finished their dinner and left the restaurant to go to a club for dancing. It was vibrant, lots of dazzling lights, and the music was geared to encourage lovers to dance. They got a table and put their coats over the backs of their chairs and then ordered a couple of Hot Cocoa Dreams—hot cocoa with green Chartreuse liqueur, topped with whipped cream and a piece of praline brittle.

After taking a sip of their drinks and kissing each other to seal the chocolate dream—hmm-hmm— Dylan took her hand and escorted her to the dance floor.

It didn't matter how fast the pace of the music was, they held each other close, working the magic. He loved the closeness, the kisses, their bodies sliding against each other. They might not be dressed to the nines like they were at the Valentine's Day party, but he felt like a million bucks while he held his beautiful mate in his arms, moving to the music, feeling in sync with the rhythm and his wolf at the same time. She was a gem no matter what she was wearing.

They danced to four songs and then they sat down to enjoy the rest of their drinks.

"This is great here. I'm so glad we decided to stay in Denver tonight and didn't wait until tomorrow morning so that we'd have the rest of the weekend to be here," Roxie said.

"I figured this was the perfect opportunity to see some sights you don't get to see while you and your siblings are running the lodge."

"Yeah, this is like a honeymoon retreat until we take a longer one. With no problem with shifting issues, it's the perfect time to do it too." She leaned over and licked his lips. "I love your chocolate and whipped cream."

He licked her mouth. "I love yours too."

Then they were back to dancing, kissing, and practically forgetting about the music or where they were. Afterward, they decided it was time to go to a hotel rather than stay at Dylan's apartment. They might skip the cocktails and just go to their room to make love. It was up to Roxie.

As soon as they parked at the hotel, they took their bags with them, went into the lobby to get their key card, and then she was pulling him to the elevator. "I'm ready to go with you up to the room. It would have been fun to have a cocktail, but I feel like I've had enough to drink and I just want to get you in my arms in bed."

He smiled. "Just my thought too."

They rode the elevator up to their floor, then raced each other down the hall to their room.

When they got there, she swiped her key card and opened the door. He placed their bags on the floor, then swept her up in his arms. He shut the door, carried her to the king-size bed in the bedroom, and dumped her on the mattress.

She laughed at him. Smiling, he pulled her shoes off and heeled off his own.

The suite was a honeymoon one with a living room and kitchen. It was beautiful, though they wouldn't really need the kitchen. Unless they wanted to eat breakfast in their room in the morning.

He lowered himself on top of her and she wrapped her arms around his neck. They began to kiss. This was what he had wanted. To make love to his mate after she'd made him so hot and aroused while dancing. He figured it would always be a condition of their closeness, which he was glad for. He never thought he'd find a mate on a FWS mission away from his home in Denver. Making love to her here brought it all home for him in the best possible way.

———————

Roxie kissed Dylan back, loving that they were together like this in Denver, she and her wolf. No other she-wolf could make any claims to him. No other wolves in his past mattered.

She devoured his lips and he growled, responding in kind. He ran his hand under her sweater, caressing her belly. He swept her away with his touch and she wanted nothing more than to open up to him, to pull him in, joining with him in sexual pleasure.

She tasted the Hot Cocoa Dream, the Chartreuse liqueur of herbs, lime, and citrus spice and whipped cream on his lips and tongue, continuing the enjoyment of the cocktail in her thoughts, but the melding with his warm lips added to the pleasure. His kisses were just as deep and passionate.

Then he was pulling her sweater over her head and running his hand over her lacy bra, cupping a breast, squeezing, making her nipple taut with need. He opened the fastener at the front of her bra with deftness and lifted the lacy fabric away to expose her breasts to the cool air. He laved a nipple with his tongue, licking, kissing. He took the nipple between his lips, pulling on it slightly, tormenting her with need. She moved under him, wanting them both to be naked and him inside her now.

She tugged at his shirt, and he hurried to yank it off over his head. She smiled, running her hands over his chest and tweaking his nipples. She loved the silky feel of his hot body beneath her fingertips.

But then he was kissing and licking her other nipple and she tensed with the pleasure of his tongue and lips. He paused in the exquisite torture of her, placed his hands on her jeans and unfastened them, then pulled them down her hips. Oh yeah, she was so ready to get to the next stage.

He kissed her panty-clad mons before pulling off her socks, and then she pushed him onto his back. She began unbuckling his belt. Then she was unzipping his zipper and easing his jeans off his hips. Once she pulled off his pants, she kissed his boxer-brief-covered arousal, which immediately jumped at her touch.

She smiled and ran her hand over his arousal. He flipped her over on her back and began sliding off her panties. Then she tugged his boxer briefs down and he was free of the rest of his clothes, perfectly naked to her just like she was to him.

Their hearts were beating rapidly as he kissed her tummy and then began stroking her clit. She was so hot and ready for this, so sensitive to his touch that she could barely deal with the all-consuming, pain-pleasure of his strokes. He dipped a finger inside her, and she nearly came apart. He pushed his finger as far as he could, stroked her inside, and she groaned out loud.

But then he began stroking her with his thumb, his other finger still inside her. She couldn't last. She was so near to heaven, and then she came in a wondrous explosion of pleasure. "Ohmigod."

He smiled and buried himself in her, and this felt just right, just where he belonged.

Dylan loved how Roxie responded to his touching her so intimately. He thrust into her, and she moved with him, working it. He kissed her passionately, deeply, wanting to consume her. He ran his hand over her breast, slowing down his thrusts, wanting this to last as long as he could hold on. But the way she was kissing him, her hands sweeping over his hips, she wasn't making it easy for him to hold off.

He loved being inside her to the hilt, the feeling of them joined, her wetness surrounding him. And then he was coming, his name slipping from her lips in a half moan, half appeal. He followed her in bliss, releasing, cherishing the woman who had become his mate.

Once they had seen the sights in Denver and packed up Dylan's things in the truck, they headed back to Silver Town. Dylan was so glad he had all his clothes and could unpack them at their house and truly be living with Roxie and not feel like he was living in two different places at once.

When they arrived at the house, they moved all his clothes into the closet and dresser drawers. "I feel like I'm really home now." He paused and took her hand and pulled her close, cupped her face and kissed her.

She kissed him and pushed him onto the bed. "You *are* really home and all mine."

"And you are mine."

After making love, they had dinner and then climbed into bed for the night. He was glad that he was all settled in with her. They snuggled together, but then they made love to each other again.

In the morning, it was back to searching for the trapper and working at the lodge for Roxie.

Before his trip, Dylan had spent several days on the FWS job still searching for the trapper. Every night, he'd returned home empty-handed.

"You got the other guys," his boss said on his last night with the FWS. "I know you'll get the trapper. Good luck with your deputy sheriff job. If you ever want to return to work for me, just let me know."

"I sure will. Thank you, sir, for everything." Dylan had been thought of as a bit of a rogue while he was investigating crimes, but that was because he was a wolf and could find things other special agents couldn't. He was glad he would be working with others like him who understood what it was like to be able to see at night and locate the scents of wrongdoers.

Chapter 29

AFTER THEY RETURNED HOME, ROXIE AND DYLAN stayed up so late that night that they slept in the next morning. She knew she had to start putting up the decorations for Mardi Gras next, but she and Dylan just couldn't seem to get up that morning. Finally, they did, dressed, had a quick bite to eat, and she was off to the lodge while he was off with his regular team of deputized sheriffs to look for the trapper.

That night, Dylan arrived home before Roxie got there and pulled cheese-filled ravioli, tomato sauce, herbs, shredded mozzarella cheese, and Parmesan cheese out of the freezer to prepare one of his favorite easy dishes from when he had lived in Denver. He thought Roxie might like it when she got home. He finished baking it and was just pulling it out of the oven when he heard Roxie at the door.

"We have the dog and cat tonight," she said, bringing them into the house and setting Buttercup on the floor. "Ooh, what are we having for... Ravioli? Oh, yum."

He smiled. "I should have asked you if it appealed to you for tonight."

"Oh yeah. Are you excited about your new job as a deputy sheriff?"

"I am." Dylan wrapped his arms around Roxie and kissed her soundly as Rosco and Buttercup tried to get him to pay attention to them. "Oh, all right," he said and leaned down to pet them. "Peter wants me to start off with training, rules, that sort of thing, tomorrow morning."

"But you'll be off looking for the trapper."

"Nope, not tomorrow. It's a training day. I'm sure if someone spies our trapper, I'll be on the mission, but he said not for now. Are you ready to eat?"

"I'm starving. I didn't think you'd get home before I did today. This smells delightful. Thanks for fixing dinner. An added perk to being mated to you for sure."

"I'm glad I could do it."

They sat down to eat dinner and talked about their days, cleaned up after dinner, and then they got bundled up to take Rosco for his walk that night. As usual, the dog was super eager to head out.

They walked the same path where Dylan and Roxie always took Rosco. The snow was trampled down here more, making it easier to walk. A light flutter of snowflakes was falling. The moon was waning. A few stars were sprinkled across the partially cloudy sky.

"We're supposed to get a snowstorm tonight, so

I'm glad you came home and didn't stay out with the guys. Not to mention that you made it in time to fix a delicious dinner."

"Yeah, we all agreed it was time to stay home for a couple of days until the weather straightened out. And I really wanted to show you I could cook a meal on my own too."

"Well, you did that. It was delightful."

They had walked a couple of miles when Roxie stopped. Dylan saw the wolf then too. He was mostly black except for his underbelly and legs that were mostly white. "Do you know him?" Dylan asked. "Wait, doesn't he look like the wolf that Kemp and Radcliff described to Darien at the Silver Town Tavern when we celebrated my taking the deputy sheriff's job?"

"I don't know him. But I saw him before when I was walking Rosco. He wasn't menacing or anything, but he seems to be hanging around the area. I agree with you about the description of the wolf Kemp and Radcliff saw."

Dylan handed her the leash. There was one way to determine if the wolf was a shifter and that was to shift. He started to pull off his clothes. Roxie watched the wolf, not saying a word to Dylan. He was glad because he didn't want her to ask him what he was going to do. If it was a *lupus garou*, he'd know just what Dylan had in mind. He had to get closer, to be downwind of him so he could smell his scent, to see if he recognized it from anywhere. But Dylan was afraid if he just tried to walk toward the wolf in his human form, the mystery wolf would run off. As a wolf, Dylan could chase him down.

Or at least try to.

Dylan pulled off the remainder of his clothes, shifted, and then walked slowly toward the wolf while Roxie and Rosco stayed where they were. He was trying not to spook him, but he had to know what the wolf's intentions were and he suspected he was a *lupus garou*. Truth be told, Dylan was hoping it was the newly turned trapper that they needed to take in for questioning. It could be that the wolf was unsure how to make the connection with others of their kind, but he was drawn to them, wanting to know what he had become, what they were.

As soon as Dylan got close enough, the wolf turned and raced off. Dylan wasn't letting him get away, and even Roxie howled in her human-produced wolf howl. If Blake and Nate heard her, the two of them would be out here to help him. Dylan was running too fast to stop to howl.

He outmaneuvered the wolf, smelling that he was indeed Rusty McInerny, thanked the heavens for that, and pounced on him, taking him down into the snow. Dylan heard other wolves howling— Blake and Nate, Kayla even. They were coming from their homes. Nicole would be watching the babies so he knew she couldn't come to help.

Dylan had the wolf by the throat, not hurting him but letting him know he was pinned down and not going anywhere, applying pressure every time Rusty tried to move. They had to bring him into the fold, make him part of the pack, and learn everything he knew about the murder.

Then Rosco was barking, Blake and Nate running full out to reach Dylan and Rusty. Kayla wasn't with them, but he heard her howl near where Rosco was barking and Roxie was still standing. So he assumed Kayla was protecting them in case she needed to.

It sure was great having family close by like this.

Blake and Nate reached Dylan, and Blake shifted. "That's Rusty, isn't it?" Blake asked.

Dylan released Rusty and the wolf just lay in the snow panting, looking like he was afraid Dylan would go for his throat again if he moved a muscle. Dylan shifted into his human form while Blake returned to his wolf. "Yeah. Rusty, we're not going to hurt you. You were a witness to one hunter killing another and we need your testimony." He wasn't going to mention the part about his traps and injuring Aaron so badly right now. They just had to get Rusty back to one of their homes and then have the sheriff pick him up for questioning as a witness to the murder.

"If you run, we can kill you. If you come with us, you can be part of the pack. Cooperate and you'll find a family of wolves here to watch your back and to welcome you." Dylan shifted back into his wolf. He wasn't planning on killing Rusty. He just had to let him know he could.

If they couldn't get him to return with them willingly, they'd call it in to the sheriff—well, Roxie most likely had already—and then he could take the wolf back in a crate.

The wolf hesitated, then got up. Blake, Nate, and Dylan surrounded him, Nate at the back ready to nip Rusty in the butt, Blake to the right of Rusty, making sure he didn't run off, and Dylan on the left side of the wolf with the same intention.

When the wolves finally reached Roxie, Kayla, and Rosco, Roxie was holding on to Dylan's clothes and said, "The sheriff's meeting up with us at our house."

Dylan woofed at her.

They would have to loan Rusty some clothes, and Dylan assumed the guys would stay with Dylan, Roxie, and Rusty until the sheriff arrived.

Once they were at the house, Blake and Nate stayed in their wolf forms, acting as guards. Roxie set Dylan's clothes on the couch, and he shifted and began to get dressed. Once he was finished, he headed upstairs to get Rusty some clothes. After a few minutes, he brought down some sweats and socks, then put them in the guest room for Rusty. "If you can shift back, you can take a shower, dress, and come out and join us. The sheriff will be here soon."

Dylan joined the others in the living room and started a fire since it appeared they'd be up for a while longer. Catching the trapper was a good thing.

Kayla left the house and returned with Nate's and Blake's clothes. Then they dressed and Roxie and Kayla made everyone hot cocoa.

Rusty finally joined them as Peter and CJ arrived. Introductions were made all around.

They all sat down in the living room, Rusty taking a seat on one of the recliners. Peter—and CJ—could be intimidating when they wanted to be, but they sat down on a sofa, not standing and towering over Rusty as if they were his inquisitors.

But it was Dylan who asked what Rusty had seen firsthand when the hunters were having the disagreement.

Rusty drank all his cocoa, then set the mug down on the coffee table. "It all started a few days before I saw the fight. I mean, I saw the boy before." Rusty took a deep breath and let it out. "I was setting traps, hunting."

"Illegally," Dylan said. "You weren't just trapping animals. You were using poison and illegal leg traps."

"Yeah."

"Okay, go on," Dylan said.

"The boy had been watching me, unbeknownst to me. But when I returned to check on my traps, I discovered they were missing. I finally watched to see who was stealing them. I thought for certain it was a fellow trapper. Someone who had a grudge against me for trapping in his territory, though I didn't know who it was. That's when I saw the boy."

"Luke," Dylan said.

Rusty shrugged. "I didn't know his name."

Roxie got the trapper some water, and then she and Kayla ended up getting everyone else some.

"I chased after him, wanting to question him about my traps, to make him tell me where he'd hidden them or even set them up. To scare him so he wouldn't mess with my traps anymore. Hell, here I was the trapper, but what if he had set them up somewhere else and—"

"You stepped in one," Dylan said, wanting to tack on that it would have served him right.

"I chased after the boy and cornered him in a cave. At first, I was reluctant to go in there. What if he had set the traps in the cave? What if he had a hunting rifle? What was he even doing out there on his own? Anyway, I turned on my flashlight and went inside. Everything happened so fast after that. I saw a wolf, not the boy. The thought flashed across my mind that the wolf had killed the boy, but before I could shoot it, the wolf bit my hand. I dropped my rifle and raced out of the cave. I ran from there, trying to get away from the wolf."

"Did he follow you?"

"For a while, yeah, then he turned and ran off. His wickedly sharp teeth had torn through my glove and had cut the skin on my hand and some of the tendons, but I figured I'd got off lucky because he could have torn my whole hand off, crushed the bones even. I had to go back for my rifle, and after wrapping some cloth around my injured hand, I returned to the cave, scared shitless. I had never been scared before of anything in my life. Well, maybe once when I ran into a grizzly up north in Montana.

"I went back for my rifle, and it was gone. I cautiously walked into the cave where I'd dropped my flashlight and searched the place. There was no sign of my traps, no rifle, no sign of the boy's body or of the wolf. That night, I returned to my campsite, and I began feeling strange. I was afraid I'd contracted rabies. I was burning up with fever, and I stripped off my clothes and then... Well, hell, I didn't know what happened to me."

"You were one of us," Peter said.

"A werewolf? I don't believe in such a thing. Or at least I didn't. I was able to smell scents like I could never before. Heard things that kept me on edge. But when I was at my camp, I heard a shot fired off in the distance. I'd served in the army in

Afghanistan. I have PTSD. When I heard gunfire, I hit the ground and couldn't move from there for what seemed like forever. Then I heard some men fighting with each other. I finally got up the nerve to check it out. I recognized the men's voices: Fennel, Jim, Xander, and Eddie. I'd had breakfast with them two mornings before I'd been bitten. I saw the boy who stole my traps hiding in the trees, watching the hunters fighting. I circled around out of sight of the boy and the hunters to get a better look for myself, to see what was going on. When Fennel shot Eddie, I was shell-shocked. When I ate with them before, I'd felt some tension between Fennel and Eddie, but they'd all seemed cordial enough."

"But you're sure Fennel was the one who shot Eddie?" Peter asked.

"Yeah. Unless they'd given me false names, which I doubt. But the one guy was Fennel. I know the one named Xander called out to Jim not to do it, but it didn't make any sense. Xander was looking right at Fennel when he said the words. I switched my attention to Jim to see what he was going to do. I thought maybe Jim planned to jump in front of Eddie to protect him. But he just looked at Xander like he didn't know why he said that.

"Then Fennel shot Eddie and the sound of that gunfire hit me like a sonic blast. I was on the ground, my paws over my nose, hiding from the enemy. Fennel was yelling at the others, telling them they were accessories to murder and to help him hide the body. That's when the boy began to leave, afraid they'd learn he'd witnessed the whole thing. He tripped and fell over a branch, snapping it. The men all paused in what they were doing, and I knew they were going to go after him."

"You did nothing to try and help him?"

Rusty rubbed his forehead. "I was going to. And then all of a sudden, bam! I was feeling hot and turning into my human form in the snow, no clothes, no rifle. What could I have done? I ran back through the snow to my camp and got dressed. They had taken off after the boy. I waited until they were well out of sight. Then I took off north of where Fennel killed Eddie."

"One of your traps caught a forest ranger named Aaron," Dylan said. "If we hadn't found him, he would have died."

"Hell, man, I'm sorry. You probably don't believe me, but I went to every location where I'd set traps before that the boy hadn't found and triggered them, then buried them deep where no one will ever find them. Being one of you has changed my way of thinking. I'm sorry about Aaron and I'm willing to do whatever it takes to make amends to him," Rusty said. "I heard him cry out, but I was a wolf, and I couldn't help him. I knew if I had approached him, he would have thought I'd come to eat him. When I finally was able to return to free him, he was gone."

"And Luke? The boy who was stealing your traps to protect wildlife and our kind?" Peter asked.

Rusty sat back in the chair.

"He believed you were going to kill him," Dylan said.

"I was going to get him to tell me where he put the traps. I wasn't going to kill him. But I didn't find him in the cave. I found a wolf. I thought the wolf was going to kill me!"

"He didn't have any other way of defending himself. Normally, we don't bite anyone as a wolf," Dylan said. "As you can see, there are consequences for doing so. You'll have urges to shift during the full moon and sometimes during other moon phases. You won't be able to shift during the new moon no matter what."

"Wait. The boy is a wolf? The one that bit me?"

"Yep. We'll show you the ropes," CJ said.

"Why were you out here?" Roxie asked. "On our land?"

"I smelled the boy's scent in this area, that he had come to this house even. I wanted to catch him, to ask him about the wolf, then Dylan goes shifting in front of me. I knew I was in trouble and ran."

Then they heard a knock at the door and Blake answered it. "Darien, Lelandi, Luke, come in."

Now their pack leaders would talk to their newest pack member. And Luke had come for closure.

Luke looked apprehensive, like he thought Rusty would want to kill him for what he had done to him. Rusty rubbed his red beard and stood up from the chair. Dylan thought when Rusty was standing, he looked more like a big grizzly bear.

Rusty sighed. "Hey, thanks for stopping me from trapping animals like I had done. I don't think anything would have changed my mind like your method of reforming me."

"I–I didn't mean to. We're not supposed to," Luke said.

"Yeah, that's what they said. I–I didn't know you and the wolf were one and the same. No hard feelings." Rusty shook Luke's hand and slapped him on the back.

"We're the pack leaders of the Silver Town wolf pack," Darien said. "Darien and Lelandi Silver. Since Luke is a gray wolf shifter, that's what you are. Lelandi is a red wolf. I'm a gray. We've adopted Luke, and we want you to stay with us until we find you another solution to your living situation."

"I'm not going to be a prisoner?" Rusty sounded surprised.

Darien smiled, albeit a little evilly. "You have a job to do. Testify along with Luke against Fennel who killed Eddie. Fennel also attempted to murder Dylan. So the hunter needs to be sent to prison. I'm sure Luke will feel better about having bitten you if he can get to know you. We'll also find you work to do in the pack that will help you to feel like you're one of us."

Though Darien didn't mention it, Lelandi was sure to be important as their psychologist in helping Rusty to deal with everything he'd gone through since being bitten. And even help him to cope with his PTSD.

Roxie and Dylan gave Luke hugs. He looked so relieved that Rusty had forgiven him. The pack leaders and their new charges left. Peter smiled at Dylan. "Forget training tomorrow morning. You're ready for work. With the snowstorm coming in, I'm sure we'll be in rescue mode."

Dylan nodded and wrapped his arm around Roxie's shoulders.

"See you at work tomorrow," CJ said, and he and Peter left the house.

Kayla, Blake, and Nate gave Roxie and Dylan hugs. Kayla said, "Do you want us to take Rosco and Buttercup for the rest of the night?"

"Nah," Dylan said. "If it wasn't for taking Rosco for his nighttime walk, who knows how long it would have taken us to catch Rusty."

"Oh, we'll have dinner tomorrow night at seven at the Silver Town Tavern—the whole family," Kayla said.

Roxie smiled. "We'll be there."

Then they all said their good nights and Rosco and Buttercup settled down in his bed. Dylan put out the fire and raced Roxie up to their bedroom.

"You got closure tonight," Roxie said, pulling off Dylan's plaid flannel shirt.

"So did Luke." Dylan helped her out of her sweater.

"Yeah, he looked really relieved. Wait. Before the snowstorm hits, we need to go to the pool," she said, hurrying to remove her pants and opening a drawer. "You have your swimsuit now too."

"Are you sure that's what you want to do right this minute?"

———————

Roxie knew Dylan wanted to make love to her, but she really thought this was important. For both of them. "It's just like the night we first met. I haven't been swimming since I found you sinking in our pool. Don't you want to experience your dip in the pool in a good way?"

"Sure." He finished stripping off his clothes and grabbed his swimsuit out of a drawer. Then he pulled it on and dressed in sweats like she was doing. "Just for a little while."

"We'll have a good time." She hurried to get beach towels for them, her beach bag, bottled waters, and then they bundled up.

Rosco looked up at them from his bed as they headed for the door.

"You stay here tonight," Roxie said. Then she and Dylan left the house and walked the short distance to the lodge. It was snowing, but not real hard yet.

Inside, they both said hi to the night manager, Eliza, and went inside the pool room. After stripping off their outer clothes, they both dove into the pool.

"Now this is more like it," Dylan said, pulling Roxie into his arms.

"Yeah. I came over here that night because I was lonely. Then I met you and all that changed for me."

They kissed each other, then finally swam to the pool divider to the outside of the pool. She hesitated and had a flashback of seeing Dylan sinking in the water, fully clothed, facedown. Then he took her hand, and they swam under the divider.

When they surfaced, they saw Rusty running as a wolf, headed straight for the pool, Luke and the Silver triplets chasing after him in their wolf coats.

He wasn't going to be able to stop in time. She just knew it. Rusty tried to stop, but he wasn't used to running as a wolf and being able to turn on a dime. Unable to keep his footing, he fell right into the pool. The teens slipped on the wet patio and ended up falling in too.

Roxie and Dylan just treaded water, staring at the five wolves swimming in the pool. Darien and Lelandi would have a fit when they learned of it.

The wolves swam under the divider and made their way up the stairs. When Dylan and Roxie reached the indoor pool, the wolves were headed for the registration desk. Thank God the lobby was empty at this time of night.

Eliza called out to Dylan and Roxie, phone in hand, "I've got this!" She let the wolves into the office and shut the door. Then she said, "Um, Lelandi, this is Eliza at the Timberline Lodge…"

Dylan smiled at Roxie. She smiled at him.

"I think I've had enough swimming for the night. What about you?" Roxie asked him, climbing out of the pool.

Dylan joined her and started to dry her off. "I'm all for what comes next."

They might not have had a long swimming session, just like the night she'd found Dylan in the pool, but now she knew she could swim to the outdoor pool without feeling too much stress— especially when he was with her. By the time they were dressed, the snow was really coming down.

"Is Darien coming to pick them up?" Roxie asked Eliza at the front desk.

"Yeah. The kids were running with Rusty, playing tag, showing him how much fun it could be running and playing as wolves. They didn't expect him to fall into the pool, nor for them to follow him. Luke wanted to know if they could stay with you tonight." Eliza winked.

"Another time," Roxie said. Tonight was her and Dylan's night. The kids—and Rusty—would have to deal with Darien and Lelandi on their own. "Night, Eliza."

"I don't blame you two. Night, Roxie, Dylan," Eliza said.

"I was afraid you would say yes to allowing Luke, Rusty, and the triplets to stay with us," Dylan said to Roxie as they headed out into the snow.

"Nope. If we get snowed in, I want it to be with just you, well and Rosco and Buttercup. I love you with all my heart, Dylan."

He smiled. "Just the way I want it. I love you to the moon and back, Roxie."

Epilogue

IT WASN'T LONG BEFORE ROXIE AND DYLAN WERE decorating the lodge for the upcoming Mardi Gras party. And they decided that a St. Patrick's Day–themed party would have to be next.

"Thanks for being my sweetheart at the Valentine's Day party," Roxie said to Dylan.

"Once you were my sweetheart, I was all in."

Luke and his friends arrived at the lodge to help with making decorations for the Mardi Gras party, and Dylan had been a great role model for him by giving him tips as a deputy sheriff. Even Rusty wanted to help with the decorations. She swore he had become a kid again.

They'd learned he was thirty, had lost his family in a flood, and had been living mostly in the woods from then on, though he had an inheritance and sometimes would go into Loveland and buy new clothes. They'd even all gone skiing together— the teens, Roxie and Dylan, and Rusty. It was as if the kids had to keep him out of trouble since he was a newly turned wolf, but he had it in mind he was keeping them out of trouble since he was the adult among them. Rusty had totally turned his life around and everyone was glad for that. As far as Dylan's former boss knew, the trapper was gone, vanished, never to set traps again.

When they stopped for lunch, Roxie and Dylan each had a roast beef sandwich, grapes, and celery sticks at the restaurant. She loved how he could relax now that he was working as a deputy sheriff—get the job done, willing to work any hours, take care of problems, and help others out, but when he had time off and he was with her, he was the perfect mate. Her family adored him just as much.

Kayla and Nate joined Roxie and Dylan. "Well, when are the two of you going to have kids?" Kayla asked.

"Don't tell me. You're pregnant," Roxie said.

"Yes!" Kayla said.

"Woo-hoo!" Roxie gave her sister a hug and kiss.

"So you're up next," Kayla said. "We're excited about your June wedding too."

Roxie would love to have kids, but she was enjoying the time as a newly mated wolf with Dylan. "You know it seems strange to be putting on our own weddings in our ballrooms. I never thought when we started to run this lodge that we would end up marrying there."

"I know, right? And everyone in Silver Town is attending."

Roxie hugged her again. "Well, eat up. We've got to get back to work."

Dylan congratulated both of them and then they went back to decorating.

Nate looked just as thrilled, and Roxie was glad for both of them.

"You know, the pressure is on," Dylan said.

"Right." Roxie smiled. "But we are not in a rush. I know we'll be great parents, but I enjoy being a couple too. Are you in a rush?"

He laughed. "With making love to you? I'm always ready for that. But I'm fine with whenever we have the kiddos."

"Do you ever wish you were working for the FWS? I know you loved the kind of work you did there."

"No. Never." Dylan drank some of his water. "But until you came into my life, I would never have considered working at anything else. You made the change worth it. I love working with the wolves here and all the celebrations!"

"Hmm." She paused to give him a hug and kiss. "After St. Patrick's Day, we'll have the May Day celebration. You know, rebirth, spring, flowers…"

"Dancing around the poles because they represent fertility."

She laughed.

———

Dylan was looking forward to the rest of the year, Thanksgiving, and Christmas with Roxie's whole family, his now too. He never would have guessed his near-death experience could turn into a whole new way of life with family, friends, a wolf pack to belong to, a new job, and a mate he couldn't live without.

Luke, Rusty, and Dylan were still waiting to be witnesses at Fennel, Jim, and Xander's trial. The wheels of justice moved way too slowly, but at least the perps were behind bars.

Everyone finally finished decorating the lodge, and then it was time for Roxie and Dylan to run as wolves. Afterward, they were heading back to the house, showering and making love, just like two newly mated wolves would do.

Love reading Roxie's love story?
See how her sister Kayla made her match in

WOLF ON THE WILD SIDE

USA TODAY BESTSELLING AUTHOR

TERRY SPEAR

"Crackles with
mystery, adventure,
and passion."
—Library Journal
for Seduced By the Wolf

WOLF
ON THE
WILD SIDE

Chapter 1

EARLY THAT SUMMER MORNING BEFORE HEAD-ing into work, Kayla Wolff and her quadruplet sister, Roxie, were running as gray wolves on their wooded acreage, not expecting any trouble. Except for a cougar they had to chase off once and a black bear another time, they usually didn't have any wildlife difficulties. They'd had to sic Sheriff Peter Jorgenson on hunters last fall though.

Kayla was excited about getting together for dinner tonight with Nate Grayson, the only wolf she'd dated since moving to Silver Town, Colorado, a wolf-run town. Nate's sister, Nicole, had actually mated their brother Blake.

Kayla loved it here, and she was planning to mate Nate on the Fourth of July in a little over two weeks if he didn't ask her beforehand.

Along with their two brothers, she and Roxie owned and managed the Timberline Ski Lodge nearby. She had been busy serving as the catering manager for a wedding yesterday, so she was glad to get back to working on promotional stuff today.

As wolves, she and Roxie had been playing with each other when they heard the sound of two men speaking on their property. Other wolves in the pack were welcome to run here anytime, but the others usually ran in the pack territory. And their brother Landon had property with his mate, Gabrielle, around her veterinary clinic, so they often ran as wolves there rather than at the lodge.

Kayla didn't recognize the men's voices. She and Roxie drew nearer, circling around and keeping low so the men wouldn't see them, trying to get a whiff of the men's scents before they alerted the sheriff that they had human trespassers. They could be just wolf guests from somewhere else, and Kayla and Roxie certainly didn't want to alienate wolf visitors to the area. Unless they were causing trouble.

The hot summer breeze kept shifting, and they had to keep circling when they normally would avoid humans at all costs. Though Kayla did have the notion of just chasing them off as wolves. That was definitely her wilder wolf side coming to play.

She listened to the men's conversation in the meantime, and finally, a black-haired man with a curly beard and reddish sideburns came into view. He was a stocky figure wearing a T-shirt that stretched tautly over muscled arms and chest, jeans tight on bulky thighs, a black cap shadowing his features, mirrored glasses, and hiking boots. It was early morning and there was no need to wear sunglasses at this time. The woods were shaded and dark and the sun still just dawning. The other man was tall, not as muscled, with short blond hair; he looked about the same age as the bulky guy—mid-to-late twenties—and was wearing a blue-jean ball cap, a gray T-shirt, jeans, sneakers, and polarized aviator sunglasses.

"I told you. With your experience, it's a piece of cake. He'll pay us good money to do it," the blond guy said. "His uncle is good for his word."

"You're sure you can trust the others?" The muscled guy sounded dubious.

"Hell, yeah. We grew up together. We're all friends. They're eager to do it and to follow your lead since you're experienced at this kind of thing. It's copacetic."

"It better be. You know what happened the last time."

"Yeah, and you didn't know those guys. This time it'll be different."

"I'll talk it over with his nephew first."

The blond guy didn't say anything more, but he looked annoyed, his mouth pursed, as if he expected the bulky guy to go along with the program based on his words. "Yeah, sounds like a good idea," he finally said, as if he had no choice in the matter.

Roxie was on the move again, trying to get closer. Kayla wanted to woof at her sister to stay with her. She didn't want them to move any closer to the men, afraid that if the two of them did, the men might spy them more easily. Sure, she and

Roxie hadn't been able to smell them to see if they were human, but she was all for circling them further. If they were wolves, no problem, unless they were up to mischief. But humans? They could be unpredictable.

"All right, but it better work out." The muscled guy turned around and saw Roxie.

For a moment, everyone froze. Kayla ran at the men to give Roxie time to move, then turned quickly and bolted out of there, hoping her sister was gaining on her and the men were running in the opposite direction and not planning to shoot them if they were armed with guns. Kayla heard movement in the woods behind her and glanced over her shoulder to see Roxie catching up to her, her eyes filled with excitement.

Relieved it was just her sister and there was no sign of the men, Kayla thought she could use less excitement in her life. When she had to serve as a wedding caterer and deal with a bridezilla like she'd had to a couple of weeks ago, that was enough of a "thrill" for her. She and Roxie both managed the brides, but Roxie could get growly with an unreasonable one, so Kayla often just took care of them to avoid problems.

Roxie nipped at her in fun. Kayla nipped back at her, glad everything had turned out fine. Though she was going to lecture her when they returned to their home next to the lodge. She was glad their sister-in-law Nicole hadn't been with them because she was pregnant. She and their brother Blake would run with Roxie and Kayla most mornings, but Nicole had been under the weather with morning sickness of late.

After Kayla and Roxie reached the house and ran in through the wolf door, squeezing in at the same time—their usual routine—they raced up the stairs to their respective bedrooms to shift and dress for work.

Once Kayla had shifted, she called out to her sister, "You shouldn't have gotten so close to the men!"

"You shouldn't have tried to grab their attention so I could get away."

"What if they'd been armed?" Kayla pulled on her panties.

"They weren't. They didn't have anywhere to hide a gun, holster, nothing."

Kayla sighed, glad to learn that. She had really worried about it. She fastened her bra. "All right, but you shouldn't have gotten so close. I was going to circle around them further to catch the breeze headed in a different direction. So did you smell their scents?"

"Human. But since they seemed to be there having a private meeting and then saw a couple of wolves, I figure they won't be hanging around, so no sense in calling Peter to try to locate them and fine them for trespassing."

"Okay." Kayla buttoned up her blouse.

"Hey, you've got to admit that was an interesting aside to our normal morning jaunt through the woods."

"Yeah." Kayla laughed. "It was memorable, all right. But don't tell our brothers. If we do, they'll leave their pregnant wives home to run with us to ensure we stay safe. Even if the guys wanted to stay home with them to make sure they were fine, Nicole and Gabrielle would make them go with us." She finished dressing.

"Absolutely. Mum's the word."

Kayla wondered how long that would last! Within a pack and with them working so closely with their brothers at the lodge, she suspected the word would get out one way or another.

Acknowledgments

Thanks so much to my beta readers, Donna Fournier, Darla Taylor, and Lor Melvin, who help me with the final touches before I turn the manuscript in. Also, thanks to Deb Werksman who gave me the chance to share my world of wolves with all my readers. And to the cover artists, your work always wows me and helps to get my wolves noticed!

About the Author

USA Today bestselling author Terry Spear has written over a hundred paranormal and medieval Highland romances. One of her bestselling titles, *Heart of the Wolf*, was named a *Publishers Weekly* Best Book of the Year. She is an award-winning author with two Paranormal Excellence Awards for Romantic Literature. A retired officer of the U.S. Army Reserves, Terry also creates award-winning teddy bears that have found homes all over the world, helps out with her grandchildren, and enjoys her two Havanese dogs. She lives in Spring, Texas.